STERNER STUFF

The Novels of Stanley Middleton

STERNER STUFF

Stanley
Middleton

HUTCHINSON
London

First published by Hutchinson in 2005

1 3 5 7 9 10 8 6 4 2

Copyright © Stanley Middleton 2005

Stanley Middleton has asserted his right under the Copyright, Designs and
Patents Act, 1988 to be identified as the author of this work

Hutchinson
The Random House Group Limited
20 Vauxhall Bridge Road, London SW1V 2SA

Random House Australia (Pty) Limited
20 Alfred Street, Milsons Point, Sydney
New South Wales 2061, Australia

Random House New Zealand Limited
18 Poland Road, Glenfield
Auckland 10, New Zealand

Random House (Pty) Limited
Endulini, 5a Jubilee Road
Parktown 2193, South Africa

The Random House Group Limited Reg. No. 954009

www.randomhouse.co.uk

A CIP catalogue record for this book is available
from the British Library

Papers used by Random House are natural, recyclable products made from
wood grown in sustainable forests. The manufacturing processes conform to
the environmental regulations of the country of origin

Typeset in Times by Palimpsest Book Production Limited,
Polmont, Stirlingshire
Printed and bound in Great Britain by
William Clowes Ltd, Beccles, Suffolk

ISBN 0 09 179729 2

For Myra Plant

Ambition should be made of sterner stuff.
Shakespeare: *Julius Caesar*

We live by admiration, hope and love.
Wordsworth: 'The Excursion'

I

Sun flashed as he swivelled his legs out of bed.

He had slept with the windows open and the curtains undrawn. Now at the beginning of September he knew that it must be after 6 a.m., the best time of the morning according to his father. He picked up his wristwatch from the bedside table. Ten minutes after the hour and not a sound from the rest of the hotel. People would be up and about, for breakfast began at seven thirty, but they made no noise. He decided against a shower and shave, there'd be plenty of time for that, pulled on a pair of trousers and a short-sleeved shirt, then carried his shoes so that he'd wake nobody, slipped into an anorak and crept out to the corridor, which stood empty in its darkness. Tiptoeing downstairs he emerged into the foyer, sat to pull on his shoes, stood again to look over the long shadows on the bright lawn, tried the main door.

Not surprisingly it was locked. He pulled the bolts back and fiddled with the lock.

'Up in good time, sir?' The voice behind startled him. He had heard no one approach.

'Yes. It's beautiful at this time of the morning.' He looked his companion over. He'd be, he decided, the owner of the hotel.

'Mr Montgomery, isn't it?'

'That's right. Francis Montgomery.'

'Room eighteen.' He gave the impression that he had committed to memory all the details of the visitor's life: home address, car number, the newspaper he had ordered. 'Let me let you out.' The hotelier moved forward, rounded him, played with the door, had it open in no time. 'There we are, sir.'

'Thanks,' Montgomery said. 'I'll have twenty minutes' walk. Is the sea close?'

'I'm afraid you'll not manage that both ways in twenty minutes.'

He spoke cheerfully, as if there was a distinct advantage keeping the sea at a respectable distance. 'The nearest village is two miles that way' – he pointed right – 'and seven that.'

'Thanks, thanks. I'll stick to the roads, I think. No brushing dew from lawn for me, as yet.'

'That's poetry, isn't it?' the man asked, standing subserviently to usher the guest into the open air.

'Gray's "Elegy".'

The man bowed his head. Frank Montgomery went out, rapidly managed the half-circle of six steps and on to the gravel, raising a hand in farewell. He'd turn left; there seemed nothing to choose between the two roads. He began to sing to himself, quietly, as he stepped out.

> 'Dear thoughts are in my mind,
> And my soul soars enchanted.'

A touch of wind rustled the long grasses on the verge. The tall hedge to his right blocked the view behind it, though he could see the hills mistily in the distance, one crowned by a television aerial. 'The lark in the clear air.' To his left stood trees in the copse that hid the hotel from the sight of people on the road.

He stopped again, this time in a patch of sunshine. The sun had surprising power for the time of day and the season. He screwed up his eyes and continued to hum. He plucked a length of grass stalk and put it between his teeth, chewed the end and examined it before he set off again, this time at a fair pace.

This was the beginning of a long weekend's holiday, its main objective to sit and sketch, pencil and watercolour. He ought to have his book with him now, but he had not yet unfastened his painting bag. That piece of hawthorn hedge, allowed to grow almost to the size of a tree, would be worth noting. He looked at it, closed his eyes and tried to recall it so that he could fix it in his mind and reproduce it with his pencil in some other place. His exercise was, as he expected, only partly successful. He repeated the process. A lorry rattled down the road, empty as far as he could see. The driver had made no gesture of greeting, had perhaps not even noticed him as he stood on the grass verge. He waited, in no hurry, until the vehicle clanked out of earshot, when he glanced at his watch and decided to turn about for the hotel.

Breathing deeply, as he invariably did before he started on a picture, he set out on the slightly uphill gradient towards the hotel. A bird darted across the road, too quickly for identification. Frank Montgomery whistled after the creature. It did not return.

This was real enjoyment to him, to be alone, with plans in his head but without harassment, nobody pressing him. His wife had driven off yesterday to visit her mother in Beechnall; she'd be there for at least a week. His mother-in-law had just come out of hospital after a stroke and Gillian had gone to give her divorced sister a hand. Her condition would be discussed by the two but it seemed almost certain that their mother was so badly disabled that she would be consigned to a nursing home, with the consequent ruthless spending of her savings, even the selling off of her house. Mrs Housley was barely in her sixties, and until her recent, unexpected illness a lively, argumentative leader of women. Now, according to report, she was hardly able to talk and incapable of crossing a room without the aid of a Zimmer frame. Both Gillian and her sister had jobs, both were solicitors, but more often than not disagreed over family decisions. They had done so since they were small, so that Frank guessed the time the two spent together with their ailing mother would be, to say the least, uncomfortable. Gillian had gone down to Beechnall expecting the worst. He had offered to accompany her but she saw, she said, no advantage in that for herself, or him, or anyone else.

He turned into the hotel drive between trees and strongly growing shrubs. He had almost reached the front steps when a young woman emerged from the front door.

'Lovely morning,' he said.

'Yes,' she answered, 'if it keeps like this.'

'Won't it do that?'

'Not according to the television. But they get it wrong as often as right in this corner of the globe.'

She slipped into a small waiting van, backed at speed and drove off. Inside, the hotelier, manager, whatever, was sorting a pile of newspapers, consulting a card. 'Your *Guardian*, Mr Montgomery.' He handed the paper, papers, over.

'That's here in good time.'

'We don't dawdle about in this part of Wales. That was the newsagent's girl you'd see outside.'

'It's not seven o'clock yet.'

'I know, I know. But our guests like their papers early. Want to read them at breakfast.'

'You don't approve of that?'

'I never did it; I was never allowed to and I didn't leave home until I was twenty-seven.'

'I see.'

'There's nothing worse than a crumpled newspaper with splodges of marmalade all over it.'

'No.' He shot towards the stairs. 'I'll go and make myself fit to be seen in public.'

In his bedroom he glanced at the headlines, showered, shaved carefully before changing into slightly more respectable clothes. He looked out of the window, combing his wet hair flat. He stared into the mirror to adjust his parting, then considered wearing a spotted silk neckerchief, but decided against it. This was a casual holiday. He rummaged in his painting bag, making sure he had packed it properly. The sketchbooks he'd use that morning were at the top. Very satisfactory. No mistakes so far. He wondered when he'd make his first. He knew where his initial outing would lead him. There'd be more than a day's sketching there, especially if he walked both ways.

Downstairs he was alone in the dining room and he enjoyed himself with his full English breakfast. He never ate that quantity at home nor drank three cups of coffee, so that he now sat replete at the table, wondering if he had packed indigestion tablets. No other guests appeared until he rose to leave the room; an elderly couple who remarked on the clemency of the weather and said that this was their last meal here. He wished them a good journey, but the man said, 'We live only twenty miles away.' He smiled, patting wavy white hair. 'But it might be a thousand.'

Montgomery tried to guess the man's occupation, but was uncertain. Upstairs he cleaned his teeth again, dropped sketchbooks, paintbox, drawing board into his capacious haversack and set out, mobile phone in his pocket so that Gillian could get at him if necessary. He did not take an easel; had he done so he would have travelled by car, but this was a day to reconnoitre, to dash at the paper so that tomorrow he could sketch properly, prepare big pictures. Frank did not altogether approve of this line of action; he'd do better, he believed, to take out a full box of painting equipment so that if he found, as he might, something worth working on, he could start with, at least, an idea of the finished picture.

He set off over the fields, then left footpaths to cross the main road leading down to the sea and the castle, and then after cutting through a copse he stopped alongside a river, widish here, sparkling in the sun. Hesitating for only a minute or two he trudged upstream, found what he was searching for: a series of black rocks forming a rough bridge for those with steady nerves. He hitched up his rucksack and crossed by these stones, which this morning stood by some inches clear of the water. He'd been over here in winter when the tops of the rocks were below the surface and difficult to recognise and negotiate. Now, less than a hundred yards away, crouched the priory walls, his objective for the morning. The path was well trodden and had obviously been cleared at the beginning of the summer, but now it was deserted, its emptiness emphasised by the screwed-up white bags, cling film or silver paper from chocolate bars left behind by visitors.

He sat down on a rock outcrop and began to sketch. He drew for over an hour and a half, thoroughly immersed, before he rang his wife. She sounded moderately cheerful, having been left in charge of the preparation for lunch by her sister who had gone out to do shopping. Their mother was in bed, not well at all, and waiting for the arrival of the nurse, delayed for some reason this morning, who usually washed and dressed her. It seemed likely that she'd stay where she was today since she seemed almost without any power in her body or her will. Yesterday the nurse said that her mother should go back into hospital and had promised to ring the doctor on that account. Gillian expected the doctor about noon.

Montgomery described his morning's occupation.

'Are you warm sitting about?' his wife asked.

'Yes. This rock's getting harder by the minute, so I shall move soon.'

'All going well?'

'Yes. I've one or two ideas already. I've spent the last half-hour doing a piece of hedgerow.'

'That shouldn't have taken you long.'

'I had several tries.' He counted them over two pages of his sketchbook. 'Fifteen.'

'Good Lord. Were they so difficult?'

'Not so much difficult as interesting.' He heard a doorbell clearly over the phone line.

'Ah, here's the nurse. Back to duty. I'll ring you if there's any change up here.'

''Bye. I love you.'

'You.'

She switched off. He hadn't heard anything, but he guessed that the last sentence was delivered peripatetically as she moved to answer the nurse's summons. He stood to stretch his legs, walked a few yards this way and that. A gleam of sunshine touched the priory's stones. He reached down for his sketchbook and with his pencil swiftly mastered the ruins, the trees, the river. He stared at the sunshine on a short pillar of stone, sketched it with care; before he had completed it the sun had disappeared behind clouds.

'Hello.'

A female voice startled him. He turned.

A young girl was squinting over his last sketches. 'They're very good,' she said, with an air of confidence.

'Are you an expert, then?'

'No. Not yet. I did history of art at A level.'

'And passed?'

'I got an A, let me tell you.'

He was surprised. She was thin, with dusty fair hair, a dress of faded yellow, sandals and no stockings. Her breasts were small, but protruded through the thin material. He had guessed she was, at most, fourteen. Her last answer she delivered with confidence. She continued her scrutiny of his book.

'You must be older than I thought.'

'I'm nineteen. How old are you?'

'Forty-seven.' Her question he deemed impertinent. She regarded herself as his equal. He stared across at a low ruined corner of the priory church, but did not draw.

'Are you a professional?' she asked.

'In the sense that I sometimes sell my pictures, yes. But no, if you mean do I live entirely on my painting.'

6

'You're very good,' she said.

She jumped down from the knoll above him, her frock ends flying up to her waist. Without embarrassment she squatted down to his right. She was smiling now. 'Am I being a nuisance?' she asked.

'Well.' He didn't know the answer. He'd worked hard enough that morning and could do with a break.

'I'm going to do history of art at university. Cardiff. And so I like to talk to people who do a lot of painting.'

'Do you meet many of them hereabouts?'

'Quite a few. This is fine country for painting and would be even better if it didn't rain so much.'

'Do you do any yourself?' he asked.

'No. I'm not very good. I'd love to be able to, but I'm not much use.'

'Will you be able to use your degree?'

'I expect so. They tell me if you join somewhere like Sotheby's they have to teach you all over again. I suppose it's because they think in commercial terms.'

He moved off to inspect the priory from different angles, as though the girl weren't there. Quite unabashed, she followed him round.

'Tell me', he said over his shoulder, 'when you see something that will make a decent picture.'

'You need to go no further,' she said, surprising him again. 'From here, looking obliquely.' She indicated the direction with all the authority of a traffic policeman.

'I agree,' he said. 'It would. You've chosen well.' He slapped his pockets. 'I've left all my sketchbooks back there. You wait here and I'll fetch them. He strode away and was back in no time, carrying a thermos flask as well as the books. The girl stood, legs apart as if she thought movement from her might obliterate the picture.

'Take this,' he said, handing over the flask. 'Unscrew the top. We'll both have to drink from the same cup if you don't mind.'

'What is it?' she asked.

'Coffee with sugar and milk.'

'Good.' She followed instructions as he began to draw two

lightning-quick outlines, postcard size. Sipping the coffee, she watched him.

He put his head to one side, then the other, muttering to himself. He then knocked off a slightly larger version. 'Better,' he said.

'Do you always start like that? With these outline sketches?'

'No,' he answered. 'In my case I find that if I draw, I look, and look harder. That's the advantage. Some people would knock off their largest sketch immediately.'

'They would have done their looking?' she asked.

'There's no telling. If you do enough of it and are any good you'll find your own way round it.'

At the end of the morning she left him. She had revealed that her name was Fiona Heatherington and that her father kept a hotel just off the main road. She asked if he'd be there the next day and he said he had not made up his mind. If it were fine he'd come back and start a large picture. That would mean coming in the car, bringing his easel along and all the rest of it.

Fiona stood for a few minutes, then turned to go. As she did so, she asked, 'Would you mind if I came here again tomorrow to watch you?'

'No.'

'I'm not a nuisance to you?'

'No. I don't mind talking as I paint. If I began to get into trouble, then I'd want to be quiet. But you'll notice. I shall be red in the face, and muttering and swearing to myself.'

She thanked him and walked swiftly away.

In a corner of a notebook he made a swift sketch of her retreating back.

II

Next morning Frank Montgomery was not quite so early at breakfast, but drove his car down to the priory ruins so that he could
take all his painting gear, two easels, table and canvas seat. The
weather was even finer and he lost no time in setting about a
large watercolour. He'd spent some minutes on yesterday's
sketches and then had begun before ten o'clock to paint. There
was no sign of Fiona Heatherington. He had looked forward to
talking again to the girl, though he guessed once she arrived she'd
delay him with her modest questions.

Thoroughly immersed he painted hard, breaking off for ten
minutes to sip a cup of coffee he did not really want and walk
about. He had rung his wife last evening and they had talked for
a quarter of an hour, an unusual length.

Gill's mother, Mrs Housley, was no better, it appeared, either
physically or mentally. The prospect of being snatched from her
home seemed to trouble her greatly. Though she was unable to
talk coherently, she could demonstrate her distress if the subject
was raised. Moreover, she showed little sign of physical improvement. A nurse called in every morning and evening to wash her
and dress her, or change her nightclothes if they decided against
getting her up; the professional was a model of common sense
who advanced her suggestions in a modest way, which made
Gillian and her sister feel part of the process of consultation.
Rosemary and the younger Gillian worked for once in harmony.
Rosie had little sympathy with her mother, for she had some
experience of caring for an older person. Her ex-husband's mother,
Mrs James, had lived near her daughter-in-law's house for the
last year of her life, suffering from Alzheimer's disease, and since
her daughter-in-law spent three days a week in the office at
Goodman and Chivers, and worked the rest at home in her study,
they had employed a laconic middle-aged woman to look after

9

the mother in her dumb unhappiness, her double incontinence and invariably low spirits. On her free days and at weekends Rosie was kept at home caring for the old lady.

'I don't know how much Joe's mother understands,' Rosemary used to complain to her sister, 'but she knows how to stir me up. In the end, I had to harden my heart against her.'

'Doesn't Joe help?'

'Not a hand's turn. Leaves it all to Mrs Seagrave and the night nurse and me. He won't put her into a nursing home. Says it's not fair, but he'll not take any share of the responsibility of looking after his mother at home.'

This experience had scarred Rosemary.

'She seems unable to think or talk properly, but, by God, she knows how to play you up.'

'Is it deliberate?' Gillian would ask. 'Isn't it that we expect them to act like co-operative, mature adults, and when they don't that makes for disappointment?'

'I don't know the ins and outs of it,' Rosemary answered. 'We were at loggerheads on the days I was supposed to be looking after her. I suppose it wasn't deliberate, but she couldn't have been more awkward if she'd tried.'

When Rosie and Gillian talked it over now, as they did often, they confessed that they found Mrs Housley difficult, but in Rosemary's view less awkward than Mrs James.

'Mother looks ill, physically so. Ma James was strong; she could shove me away without any difficulty.'

Frank turned these reported conversations over in his mind as he painted. They did not interfere with his fluency or his imagination. They troubled him very slightly as he paused and then, as he resumed work, drove him harder into a doubly rewarded concentration. This morning the picture grew satisfyingly from its very beginning, so that by one o'clock it was done and he was able justifiably to put it to one side. He knew that the next time he looked at it he'd want to make slight alterations here and there, changes which he was sure now would not improve it.

He ate his lunch quickly, sandwiches he'd had made up in the hotel, finished his coffee, carefully looked over his now completed morning effort and decided he'd sketch the river. He wandered down to the edge, stopped, dashed at his paper for a few minutes, then either tried again or moved a step or two. This was real enjoyment to him. He put one foot on a black stone in the stream, and it turned malevolently over so that he soaked his sock and shoe. He did not mind; he had both a towel and clean socks in his car.

'Hello,' a voice called from above. Fiona.

Frank dragged himself up the bank. She stood by his painting.

'What are you doing down there?' she asked.

'Getting my feet wet.'

She stood now in front of the picture of the priory. 'That's very good,' she said. 'Superb.'

'Steady,' he answered. 'You shall explain its excellences to me in your best academic manner. But let me deal with my feet first.'

He dragged off his shoe and sopping sock, reached in for a towel. He sat in the car to dry himself, found a pair of socks, replaced one, showed them to the girl.

'Odd socks,' she shouted, laughing.

'Now, madam, explain this to me.'

'The thing I like best about it is that it looks like what it's supposed to be. I know you'll say if I want that then I should take a photograph, but if you can do it and at the same time make a thoroughly satisfactory painting, then that's better. It shows you're good.'

'Not many artists would agree with you,' Frank said. 'Even great painters. If somebody comes to look at a picture and all they can think of is "that wall's too high" then they're not bothering about the aesthetic experience. It's quite likely they won't know what the original place is like.'

'I'm telling you what I want.'

'And why, young lady, do you insist on that?'

'Works of art consist of successfully surmounting self-imposed obstacles.'

'I agree.' He did not wish to argue further.

'How long did that take you?' Fiona asked.

'Two to three hours, or thereabouts. This and one sketch.'

'You're a fast worker. I'd never get all that detail in. Or colour variation. Not in that short time.'

'I'm only suggesting it. That's partly trickery on my part, and a sympathetic attitude on the part of the viewer.' He jerked upright and asked, 'Shall I sketch you?'

11

Fiona looked surprised, blushed suddenly. 'You wouldn't want to,' she said.

'Let me decide that.'

He turned over the page of his large sketchbook, told the girl to stand comfortably with her back to a silver birch, moved a step or two this way and that, and began rapidly to draw.

'Resting time,' he called out after a few minutes. 'You can move about.'

'May I have a look?' she asked.

He passed the book over. He had done a quick sketch of her by the tree, then a head and shoulders.

She studied the page. 'Marvellous,' she said.

'I wouldn't say that.'

'You really have the knack of catching a likeness.'

'And that appeals to you.'

'Yes. They're super. And they look like me. And that silver birch. And you were so quick.'

'You want them to look like the models and you conclude, therefore, they're good on that account. It's your first criterion.'

Fiona paused and nodded. 'You're very confident,' she said. 'You know exactly, do you, how each one will come out?'

'Not always. I'm sometimes surprised. That's partly the attraction of it all. I don't want to turn out picture after picture all looking the same. Each new stroke of the brush or pencil ought to suggest something else, something new. That sounds pretentious. May I draw you once more? In profile, I think.'

He perched her on a corner of his painting table and sat, himself, at his easel this time to work. He stared at her long enough before he made a start and paused often.

'Struggling?' she asked in one of these intervals.

'Not really. Checking's more like it.'

When finally he had done she rose from her table, but did not immediately come across to examine the finished sketch; she hung back, reading perhaps the disappointment in his face. He watched her, narrowing his eyes, before offering her the book with a flourish. She held it in front of her, before she finally raised her head to make eye contact. Before she spoke she let her gaze drop again to the paper as if the first long scrutiny had presented her with something she could not believe.

When she spoke, it was in a whisper. 'It's magnificent.'

He did not answer. She stared at the drawing almost in expectation of its disappearance, its fading from the paper.

'You like it?' he said flatly, in the end, breaking her daydream. 'Would you like it?' His second question followed after a hiatus.

'To take it away, do you mean?'

'Yes.'

'Oh, yes, please.' She did two or three skips of joy, like a small child. 'It's wonderful.'

'Do you think it's like you?'

'You say that doesn't matter, but it's important to me. You've got me exactly.'

'You've never seen yourself except through a mirror.'

'I have. In photographs. And my face is pretty symmetrical.'

'Or symmetrically pretty.'

She screwed her face into ugliness. With great care he tore the sketch from the book. She took the sheet and stared at it as if she could not believe her luck. 'Thank you. I shall frame it myself.'

'Good.'

Fiona placed the paper on the table and skipped across towards him. She flung her arms round him, standing on tiptoe, and pressed her mouth fiercely against his. Once she drew back for breath, almost desperately, then thrust her lips against his. When she withdrew herself, she moved only half a step away and gripped the sleeves of his shirt. He was shocked by her boldness. No wonder young girls were found murdered. Yet he sensed a kind of innocence in her.

'Thank you,' she said again. 'Thank you.'

Montgomery stood for a few moments, quite still, until she loosed her hold on his shirt. 'Good,' he said.

She picked up her picture again and stared hard at it, transfixed. When at last she laid it down on the table, she asked him, 'Are you married?'

'Yes.'

'Is there a sketch of your wife in any of your books?'

'I don't think so.'

'You have painted her?'

'Oh, yes.'

'Does she like it? Sitting as a model?'

'She doesn't object. She can sit very still.'

'Could you do her from memory?'

'I could make a shot at it, but it wouldn't be as good as if I did it from life. The real person is more complicated than my imagination. Or at least that needs something there, outside itself, to play on.'

'Have you always been able to catch a likeness?'

'Yes. I went on a month's course at Goldsmiths' as a student and the tutor there said, "You should spend a week or two at one of these booths at the fair where they have somebody doing ten-minute sketches of passers-by." He said he could recommend me to some friend of his who ran such a place in Porthcawl in South Wales. I went and did a fortnight there.'

'Were they, the booth owners, pleased with you?'

'Yes. They wanted me to stay the summer out, and doubled the price of the sketches and didn't lose any custom. In fact, I made quite a reputation. People would walk down from the top end, the posh part, of the town just to buy a quarter of an hour of my time, and a head and shoulders of themselves.'

'Why did your teacher send you there?'

'For practice. He was a great believer in constant practice. Or I used to think it was perhaps just to rid me of my trick of getting a likeness.'

'That didn't work, did it?'

'No. But I think the experiment did me good. Mark you, I was worn out. I had to concentrate so that I could save myself five minutes out of the fifteen, just to rest.'

'Were people pleased?'

'I think so. I needed longer to make a satisfactory job. Or at least I thought so.'

'Can you spoil a picture by putting too much detail in it?'

'I don't know', he said, 'about detail. Augustus John was always said to make his portraits worse the longer he spent on them.'

'Is that true?'

'I don't know. I never saw any of his pictures in the course of his painting them.'

'Did the critics?'

'I doubt it.'

She came across to him, threw out her arms and pulled him as he sat towards her. She kissed him with her mouth unrelaxed. He ran his hands over her back. She wore little under the thin frock.

'This is the only way I can reward you,' she said, gasping.

He pushed her gently from him. 'Tell you what,' he said. 'I've done enough for the day, so we'll run down to the beach and have an ice cream.'

It did not take them long to put his gear neatly into the back of his car. He found a large transparent envelope to protect her sketch. 'We'll put that on top and then you won't forget it.'

'That's unlikely,' she said.

They sat together on the beach to lick their ice-cream cornets. Fiona tried to explain what she'd gain from a university course. Perhaps she'd end up with a job in an auctioneer's or, more likely, teaching art in a school.

'But you say you can't draw.'

'I can draw and paint well enough for that.'

She did not lack confidence, but modestly seemed to predict an interesting life for herself.

'Does your wife work?' she asked him.

'Yes. She's a solicitor.'

'Does she like it?'

'Yes. In a way. I think she finds it rather dull sometimes, but she's careful and derives a great deal of satisfaction in doing her preparation properly. She won't miss much; that I can tell you. She knows the law well and looks things up all day even when she's at home. She's only to start on a crossword puzzle and she's surrounded by a pile of legal dictionaries and encyclopaedias.'

'You admire her, don't you?' the girl asked.

'Yes,' he said, smirking. 'Not the usual question I'm asked about her.'

'What is that, then?'

'Go on. You guess.'

'Do you love her?' She spoke without fear.

'Right. The snag with that is you feel bound to say "Yes", whatever the real answer is. And if you have to say "No", then that invites a whole battery of supplementary questions, which you don't want to answer.'

15

Later she said suddenly and childishly that she'd like to paddle.

'I have a towel in the car. You're welcome to that.'

'You won't come in?'

'No, thanks. I've had enough water round my legs for one day.'

'Will you dry my feet when I come out? My dad used to do it when I was small and I loved it.'

He duly, if awkwardly, towelled her feet, which were pale with cold, and handed over his second, untouched, thermos flask of coffee to warm her up.

'This is gorgeous,' she said, both hands round the cup. 'You're a very good man.'

About four o'clock he said he ought to be getting back. 'I like to pack my painting gear up neatly in the car, before the evening meal so I can get it out straight away the next time I need it. And I shall look through my sketchbooks tonight, then tomorrow morning I can eat my breakfast with a clear conscience and pay my dues and drive back home.'

'Where's home?'

'Derbyshire.'

'That's hilly, isn't it?'

'Yes. The bottom end of the Pennines. The backbone of England, they used to tell us in geography lessons at school. Interesting place.'

'Your part of the world?'

'Roughly. I'm from the East Midlands.'

When they reached his car and were stamping the sand off their shoes Fiona said, 'Tell you what. Let's straighten your painting stuff at the back of the car now. It'll save you time.'

'It doesn't take me long.'

'It'll give me a further ten minutes of your company.'

This surprised him and when they had finished she asked him for his address. He gave it to her without thinking. He looked at his sketch of her, which he had placed on top of the gear on the back seat. 'I'll run you home now,' he said, 'in return for that.'

'I'm a great way in your debt already,' she said, solemnly pointing at the sketch.

She lived in the Forest Arms, just off the main road five or six miles up the main road. Little traffic impeded their way there. On her instruction he turned into the car park. He retrieved the picture, and as they stood chatting and she described a repair which had just been completed on the main chimney stack, her father appeared, a stiff broom in his hand. When he saw Fiona in animated talk by the car, he propped his brush by the door of the inn and walked across.

He was nothing like his daughter in looks, but stiffer, stockier, his face a sailor's brown. The voice with which he greeted the pair was, Frank thought, one of character, being light, well modulated, cultured.

'All in one piece?' he enquired of Fiona.

'Oh, you,' she said, exaggerating exasperation. The man laughed and turned to Montgomery. 'She either comes home injured or drags in some poor creature in need of succour.'

'So I'm today's specimen?'

'It would appear so.'

Fiona rounded the car to thrust the sketch into her father's face. 'What do you think of that, then?' she asked.

He took it from her, squinted at it, turning, before snatching down the glasses from his forehead. 'That's more like it,' he said, now concentrating on the paper. He made a long, humming sound of appreciation. 'Did you do that?' he asked Frank.

'I did.'

'It's something, really something.' Mr Heatherington's approbation was immediately apparent.

'Why is it good?' Fiona asked the question almost ferociously of her father.

'You ought to be able to answer that. You're the one who's going to university to study the history of art.'

'None of your dodging. Why is it good?'

'An excellent likeness.'

'Yes?'

'It seems lively; it uses all sorts of means to make this so. There are things in it that strike me as unusually successful, which I wouldn't have thought of myself, but seem obvious once I have seen them.'

Fiona did not answer for the moment.

'Are you a painter?' Montgomery asked.

'Not really. I can slap whitewash all over the outside loos.'

'Don't you believe him,' Fiona answered. 'He's done some

17

really interesting pictures. It was he who first got me interested in art.'

'And English grammar,' he said.

'And music.' She capped it.

Her father laughed, shifted his broom from the wall, wished Montgomery a courteous good afternoon and disappeared through one of the three back doors. 'Give your friend a card,' he shouted back.

'That's a good sign,' the girl said. 'It means he'd like to talk to you again some time.'

'I hardly said a word.'

'No. But you can draw. And that impressed him. He adores doers, practitioners.'

'Has he always been in the innkeeping line?'

'No. Not at all. Only in the past three years. He organised it all so that I could begin my A level studies in a new school.'

'Were you sorry to come down here?'

'I don't think so. And the school here did me well.'

Mr Heatherington rushed out of one of his back doors to hand over a business card. 'I won't interrupt again,' he said, 'but Fi here would have forgotten all about it.'

She tossed her head but did not comment. Her father charged away, this time making use of the third door.

Fiona grinned and asked, 'What do you think he did before he went into the hotel business?'

'A teacher.'

'No. He doesn't like children enough. He was a musician.' She waited for further questions, and on receiving none said, 'He was a professional violinist.'

'In an orchestra?'

'Yes. The Hallé. He trained at the Royal College and in the end worked up to the first desk of the first fiddles.' She let him digest that. 'Then he thought he ought to settle down.'

'Spend some time with his family?'

'What's that mean?'

'It's the phrase politicians use when they've made a hash of their responsibilities and are on their way out.'

'Oh, yes. I think he was fed up with the life. The travel. Or my mother was. She'd been a teacher, but she didn't want to do that again. I think she'd have liked a bed-and-breakfast place at the seaside or in the country, here in North Wales, where she came from. But Daddy wanted something a bit bigger, with more responsibility.'

'Had he any idea what it entailed?'

'I don't suppose so. Except he'd stayed in hotels all over the country, Europe and America, for that matter. He has plenty of self-confidence.'

'Does he play the fiddle much nowadays?'

'No. Occasionally. My mother presses him. She plays the piano.'

'Is he good?'

'He says he's hopeless, but it sounds great. He thinks he ought to practise more or not play at all, but my mother won't have that.'

'Has he got a good instrument?'

'Yes, he has. It's modern, a Saunders, specially made for him.'

'And it matches your Strads or Amatis?'

'Yes. Different, but just as beautiful. He loves it. He's really proud of it.'

They talked for very little longer, kissed and parted.

'I hate the ending of holidays,' she declared.

'And I look forward to it.'

III

Frank Montgomery had no sooner garaged his car, emptied it of luggage and put on the kettle than he set off round his grounds to stretch his legs. The garden was still colourful and the heavily leaved trees and shrubs contested with each other in a marvellous variety of green, though all showed signs of recent neglect. He and Gill would have to start a blitz on winter preparations when she returned. He'd fiddle with it, play at it, until she returned, then she'd plan the campaign. He would begin by cutting and feeding the lawn, then he'd start treating the paths, ridding them of the weeds that grew between the uneven York stones he had laid himself when they had moved into this house five years ago. He looked back from the far end of the garden by its drystone boundary with some satisfaction.

The house was built on the side of a hill in three sections: the original large early nineteenth-century cottage took in the drawing room and, above it, two bedrooms. At the far end stood the modern kitchen, all in stone. The effect inside was of spacious strength. Gillian had said she thought it was too large for a mere couple, but he could tell that it had caught her imagination and he had supported her at once.

'The price is a bit fancy.' She hesitated. They were engaged in paying off the mortgage on their house in Sheffield.

'We'll live on bread and dripping.'

'No, but a place as big as this will cost a bomb to heat.'

'I've got my love to keep me warm.'

Almost immediately an aged relative of Gillian's had died and left her and her sister money, which made the task easier, the mortgage smaller.

'The Lord is mindful of his own,' her atheist husband said, efficient central heating now a possibility.

Today, four years later, they had almost decorated the place to

their liking and were buying furniture that suited the surroundings rather than their purses. The walls of the 'cottage' living
room were covered with his watercolours, drawings and prints,
and one large oil painting above the fireplace, a picture of his
father. He had painted this ten years ago, well before his marriage
to Gill, a present for his father's eightieth birthday. At the time
the old man had been delighted, but on his first visit to Avalon,
just after their wedding, he had brought the picture back. He was
grieving for his recently dead wife.

'Grown out of it?' Frank asked mischievously.

'No. It's a fine piece of work. It will honour any room it's
hung in. But I look at it, and then in a mirror at my face, and I
can see by how much I have deteriorated. My features are a
shadow, a caricature of what they were when you painted that.'

'Not true.'

'My eyes may be dim,' Herbert Montgomery had replied, 'but
nothing like as blind as all that.'

Father and son were at this time much pleased with each other.
Herbert had recovered from a cancer of the bowel and was now,
some months after the operation, beginning to feel something like
his own old self. He had not thought at the time that such was
possible, had been convinced that death was inevitable. It was all
mainly his own fault, he said to himself, because he had tried to
ignore the symptoms and had kept away from his GP until the last
minute. He had faced his imminent death stoically, fought back his
fears, or entertained them in private. He was an ideal patient when
he was in hospital and the surgeons had begun their work; he never
showed despair. When, once, Frank had confided to his father that
he was proud of him, Herbert laughed in his cracked invalid's voice
and told his son that he wanted no more of such sycophancy.

'Dad,' Frank had answered, 'you ought by your age to have
learnt to accept and appreciate a modicum of praise.'

'Modicum? What the hell will you say next?'

They glowered, each at the other and the stern frowns demonstrated the power of love.

'I don't go round praising you,' Herbert said.

'So I'd noticed.'

The old man glanced slightly anxiously at his son, but realised
this was part of the banter.

Frank had done well, at the college of art in Beechnall as a student, then at the Royal College in London. An admirable draughtsman, he lit his pictures with a brilliance of colour. His professor at the RCA went out of his way to find him a teaching job in London that allowed him time for his own painting, and within three years he had gained such a reputation with an exhibition of his portraits that he seriously considered giving up teaching. He had, moreover, married and divorced by this time; his wife's lawyers had cleaned him out financially so that when he was pressed by influential backers to accept the headship of department at a well-regarded art college he kissed the rod, hired a studio and lived in a poky room close by. He had been unhappy.

The one benefit he discovered was that he enjoyed and was successful at his work as an administrator. He spent time on it at first, to the detriment of his painting, but it suited his state of mind after the desolation of a joyless marriage. Then, again he began to paint in earnest, had two exhibitions, made such a name that he was invited to paint Princess Diana. How this came about he did not know; influence, he suspected. The Prince of Wales unexpectedly visited the second of his exhibitions and was greatly impressed. The portrait never came off; negotiations tailed away; he did not know why, though he caused a stir with three society portraits, which were featured in a *Sunday Times* magazine article on the best British painters.

While this was engrossing him his professor at the Royal College telephoned to say that he should apply for the principalship of the South Yorkshire College of Art in Sheffield. Two days later his own head of college rang to invite him to put in an application. He was frankly bewildered. Did Emrys Jones want to get rid of him? he wondered. This seemed not to be the case. He decided that Principal Jones fancied himself in the role of king-maker. Why he did not mention such a scheme to young Montgomery before was something of a mystery, but it appeared he had run across Professor Scott of the Royal College and they had spoken about their 'young' friend.

As soon as Jones praised his skill as an organiser, Scott mentioned the Sheffield post: 'Would Montgomery be up to the job?'

'He would. He has ideas, he can handle his staff well. He'd

do it on his head. The only matter that would trouble me is that it might take him away from serious painting.'

'Because he'd be so tied up with the everyday running of the college?'

'Yes. Exactly.'

'You think highly of his work?'

'With the brush, or pencil, especially. For myself, I have found that my job does not allow me to get anywhere near the clay or the stone I was brought up to handle.'

'You regret that?'

'Not really. No. I live comfortably. I've another ten years before I retire. My children are out of the way. Well, roughly. I am a hedonist.' Jones's accent became more strongly Welsh. 'I look for a quiet life. I am not the stuff of which great sculptors or painters are made. But Montgomery may well be. And I don't want to be responsible for preventing him attaining those peaks of which he is capable.'

'Yes?' Scott seemed to hesitate.

'Don't you agree with me?'

'I am one of those cynics who argues that an artist of genius will reach greatness whatever unsuitable mode of life he chooses. That's the true meaning of genius. Such people need the technical brilliance, but that is not sufficient. I have had plenty of pupils of real painterly skill, but though they might add to the beauty around us, they will never break out beyond it, will never approach the Rembrandts, the Titians, the Michelangelos. I'm telling you this, Jones, which I expect you know as well as I do, because I think here is a position that should be held by an outstanding man.'

'The South Yorkshire has a very good reputation.'

'So it has, so it has. But . . .'

'Have they approached you?'

'They have. Their Chairman is Sir Alfred Woolfe. Could I recommend any possibly outstanding candidates? He and I are old friends. He has bought several pictures from me. He doesn't think of me as an oracle, but he knows I keep my ears open for any sort of gossip in our line. The present principal, Wentworth Stainer, has held the principalship for nearly eighteen years now. He has given the college an excellent name, attracted good staff and, more importantly, good students. Like the rest of us he's been up against takeovers by universities, or antagonistic university departments and he's fought them off or joined them, talked them round with considerable skill. But he's getting on for sixty-five now.'

'The fire burns low?' Jones's voice sang like a full choir, in spite of the quietude of his question.

'To some extent. He's a clever operator. He's kept the place successful. But they're on the lookout for somebody different. And Woolfe had heard of Montgomery. He's had publicity outside our usual holes and corners. So when I mentioned him, ears were pricked up.'

'Would it interest him?'

'He's still remained in teaching, so he might as well take a few steps up the ladder. Then, if he finds he doesn't want to stay at it he'll be a bit better off, pension-wise, and . . . That's up to him, but I would like to see how he shapes. If only in the interview. There's no telling whether or not he'd get the job. You know what selection committees are like, and the South Yorkshire will be seen as something of a prize; there'll be no shortage of applicants.'

Principal Jones invited Montgomery into his study to relay this conversation. 'Edward Scott is a revered name in our profession, as teacher respected outside, as a man in touch with the world. His support will be worth much to you.'

'Shan't I be wasting my time?' Frank asked.

'I don't expect that you will be appointed, on account of your age and comparative inexperience as an administrator. But the interview will, in all probability, give you a good idea where you stand in the profession of art teacher. These days people act differently. In my time no one who had not reached his late forties would have even been called up for interview. They would most likely have seen only highly rated principals or vice-principals of other art colleges. People of ideas, certainly, but who had already been in positions of authority where they could have put some of their ideas to the test.'

'That's what I think', Frank grumbled, 'happens now.'

'You may well be right, though I was going on to say that nowadays one or two people in their thirties have been appointed.'

'I'm not as ambitious as all that.' Frank knew that within the next month the *Sunday Times* magazine would feature him and his paintings in their art critic's series on 'The Best of British Painters'.

'That's what I fear. But it will do you no harm to put such modest cards as you think you have on the table for scrutiny. I don't know who is on the committee of appointment except, according to Professor Scott, Sir Alfred Woolfe, an influential figure. You can do yourself no harm. Your artistic work has attracted more publicity than that of any already incumbent principals. That could be in your favour.'

Frank Montgomery mentally mocked Jones's choice of language, but the principal was no fool. The archaisms, he guessed, were affected. This man, with no advantages of birth, with only a moderate talent as a sculptor, had worked his way up from an obscure North Walesian village where he had not spoken a word of English until he started school at five, had burnt with an ambition that had landed him as the respected principal of a highly regarded London art college. Over the next few days Jones twice sent for Frank to enquire about the progress of the application and to offer, in all sincerity, or so it seemed, a few ideas that were at the present 'doing the rounds', finding favour in the world of art. Jones knew a great deal and was prepared to share it with his younger colleague. He confessed that a member of the board had telephoned him about Montgomery and that he had been pleased to speak to his advantage. The caller, director of education for the city, had appeared impressed by Jones's recommendation. Certainly, within a few days Montgomery was called up for interview.

If questioned by the few colleagues who knew he had applied for the post he would have claimed not to be worried nor to have prepared himself carefully. Both answers would have been inaccurate. He did not expect to be offered the principalship. The other four candidates present all seemed older, better qualified than he. Fortunately the colourful praise he received from the art critic of the *Sunday Times* and the excellent reproduction of five of his paintings appeared three days before the interview. At least two of his fellow interviewees let him know they had seen the spread.

He had worn a white shirt, a blue tie, and a dark-grey suit with black shoes, carefully polished in the hotel where he had stayed overnight. The candidates had reported at nine that morning, and the retiring principal and one of his deputies had given them a whirlwind tour of the place. The interviews began at ten, in strict alphabetical order. Montgomery was due to appear, the fourth, straight after lunch at one thirty.

He did not look forward to the interview. There were too many on the board for his liking; half of them, he decided, were makeweights, understanding little of what was happening. This shortened his temper for he could see no reason for this crowding. All would have equal votes, but he wondered if these useless nondescripts had been put in to back some favoured candidate, or were there on grounds of political fairness and would be left to vote as their ignorance led them. The Chairman, not Scott's Sir Alfred Woolfe, who was abroad, but a Mr Mee, qualifications unknown, took him without hurry through his CV. This was followed with questions such as, 'What is the Royal College of Art?' Or, 'Why did you take an MA?'

There came now questions which had been distributed to members of the board and were often read out from a slip of paper. These sometimes led to snatches of interesting discussion, led by a youngish man with curly ginger hair and blond eyelashes. When it came to his turn to put his question he began, 'I must confess that I am not a great expert on art, but I'd like to hear your opinion on something that puzzles me. It's this. For these last few years some fairly valuable prizes have been given by pundits, professors, heads of colleges, critics and the like, for objects that in my view are not works of art at all. I mean carcasses, piles of bricks, a mould laid round an empty house, an unmade bed. May I ask your opinion of these decisions?'

'You realise', Frank said, 'that when prizes are given by committee they depend on the views, prejudices if you like, of that committee. Change the group and you'll get a different result.'

'Ah, but you misunderstand . . .'

'I hadn't finished, if you don't mind.' One or two looked affronted at this and Frank knew he had done himself no good. 'You want to know why it is that acknowledged experts who have

26

spent their lives studying and teaching art, the arts, choose such eccentric exhibits. Now I can only guess. These people have seen so many hundreds – no, thousands – of decent watercolours, oil paintings, sculptures done by people of considerable skill, but between which they can't pick out one or two that are outstanding. All are good, the products of decent teaching and innate skills and constant practice, and all are worth preserving. But in that position the judges look around for originality, the ingredient missing from these productions.'

'Originality', said Ginger, 'is what they are looking for? That is a true sign of genius?'

'I wouldn't say so. Some geniuses are the final crowning completion of a certain tradition. Bach is a fine example. Whereas others throw tradition aside, will not accept the rules and begin to make their own way, guided by their own decisions.'

'Such as?'

'Cézanne. Picasso, if you want one nearer our own day.'

'I take it from your tone you don't like Picasso?' This from a cross-looking man with a moustache.

'I said nothing of the kind.'

'And you don't like committees choosing? That's what we're doing today.' Moustache again, bit between his teeth.

'Do you think, sir, that I don't realise that?'

'The Authorised Version of the Bible,' a parsonical man proclaimed, 'one of the great glories of our literature, was done by committees.'

Some heads nodded wisely at this impudent candidate being thus corrected.

'Because they had the sense to read the earlier translation of a man of infinite brilliance. Then they followed it to a very large extent; the work of a man of outstanding genius who was executed for his pains three generations before the 1611 translation.'

'Who was that?' a lady asked, wide-eyed.

'William Tyndale.'

'How do you mean they followed him?'

'They lifted, borrowed dozens of his phrases. "In my father's house are many mansions." '

'You are an expert in these matters, Mr Montgomery?' The parson.

27

'I think perhaps we are wandering a little from our declared objective,' the Chairman said.

'I am delighted', the parsonical one answered, 'to discover that this gentleman has interests well beyond the visual arts.'

The Chairman ignored him. 'Mr Stretton.' This last to the ginger-haired man.

'I take it, then, Mr Montgomery,' said Stretton, 'that if you were appointed you wouldn't be awarding prizes to students for legs of pork or piles of fabric or shapes made from ice cream.'

'I can't promise you that. I shall always be ready to award prizes for what one regards as the classical studies. What I can promise is that all students, whatever their main course, be it dress design or sculpture or computer graphics or virtual reality, at least in their first year will do a substantial course in draughts-manship, old-fashioned drawing.'

'Why?'

'Because it is useful in all these aspects. One can't draw well with a computer, in my experience, without having considerable skill in old-fashioned sketching.'

'Would that be the main reform you'll make?' the Chairman asked. 'Surely they will have enjoyed such a course at A level or in the Foundation Year?'

'You would think so, but I would want to make sure.'

'You haven't answered the Chairman's question,' the lady said. 'What would be the main improvements your period as principal would bring?'

'That I don't know until I've seen the college at work.'

'You've seen some of the college's productions in the exhibition rooms or hung on the walls of the building. What is your opinion?' The Chairman, very seriously now.

'It seemed of a high standard. I looked at these with interest, but in a hurry.'

'Did you see anything that struck you as outstandingly talented?'

'No.'

'Oh. We're disappointed to hear that.'

'You shouldn't be. The majority of your students will be good by everyday standards. It's not every year you can expect a

Rembrandt or a Titian. And though such do profit from sound teaching, their genius comes from elsewhere.'

'Where?' Moustache, snapping it out.

'Their life, their character, their opportunities, the age in which they live.'

'So you won't be out to produce men of genius.'

'No. That won't be my primary aim.'

'And what will your aim be, then, Mr Montgomery?' The wide-eyed lady, tilting her hat.

'To make sure that these good students you have here know something of the art of past times, of people working today, to practise their own particular genre and to try their hand at the admired art of their predecessors. I don't like it when people have had a sound drilling in, let's say, drawing only to find when they reach us that's all been time wasted.'

'So you'd waste even more of their time?' Ginger.

'They come to me to be taught what I know. I can't stress often enough that our students will be good, but not geniuses.'

'Genii,' said the moustachioed man.

'No. Geniuses. There are two plurals for genius. You've chosen the wrong one. But' – he humbly bowed his head in the direction of the interrupter – 'our students will produce pictures and statues, furniture and fabrics, dresses, all useful and worth looking at, beauties of an industrial society. They may not be works of art of the highest order, but they will give pleasure to thousands of people. These artists are the ones I set out to train. They are to be encouraged and disciplined.'

'Isn't that rather disappointing? To train and discipline mediocrities?'

'It's what life is like. If you'd decided that you would only appoint an artist of genius today for this post, you'd be waiting a long time.'

'You don't see yourself as a man of genius?' This time a puzzled, grey-headed man.

'One of the qualities you need in a prospective principal in your college is judgement. If I answer you with "I do so consider myself" then you have my permission to throw my application in the nearest waste-paper basket.'

The wide-eyed lady asked him what he meant by 'judgement'.

He struggled to answer, felt not pleased with the attempt and rewarded the questioner with a wide smile.

They asked a few more dull questions, as if they had lost interest in him. The Chairman said he thought that would do and thanked the candidate. Suddenly, he sat straight and asked Montgomery if he had any questions.

Montgomery ran his eye insolently along the row of the selection committee. 'No, thank you.'

'Then that is it. Good afternoon. You'll probably hear the result tomorrow. By post.'

Again, Frank bowed his head in mock-humility. 'Good afternoon.' He marched out, but to the wrong door. The committee, stretching weary limbs, paid no attention to his fumblings, left him to find his own way.

Two minutes later in the urinal he met Ginger who nodded companionably. 'Worn out?' he asked.

'Pleased it's over.'

'Yours was the most interesting interview so far. The others all knew what the questions would be and had their set answers cut and dried.' He swilled his pale, freckled hands under the tap. 'Or that was my impression.' At the door, Ginger suddenly turned. 'Do you really want the job?'

'I shan't be disappointed. Especially in view of the way the interview went.'

'Professor Scott, who is apparently very well known, his name really does carry some weight in art education, suggested that we appoint someone of real artistic standing, that it would enhance the college's already high reputation. And then you come along and tell us you'd concentrate on the mediocrities. That baffled some of 'em, I guess. It impressed me.'

Ginger waited for an answer but received none. They wished one another polite goodbyes. Driving home down the M1, Frank felt pleased that he had not answered the man's question, in or out of the interview room, because he was sure that would have killed off any chance he had. Had he spoken frankly he would have confessed that he feared he would have to spend so much of his free time on public meetings and committees that he'd have no time left for painting, and that seemed a waste of his talent. Of course, he could have comforted himself: he might well marry again and start a family in his middle age, and that might alter his viewpoint entirely.

The college office had informed him that the result would be sent to him by telephone or first-class post on the next day. He waited without hope. On the third day a first-class envelope brought a neat four lines of typescript which thanked him for his attendance and announced that the principalship had been offered to Mr T. N. Houldsworth of Colchester.

Houldsworth, a man of fifty, had a most beautiful speaking voice. Already a college principal of some years' standing, he'd acted modestly, spoken pleasantly to everybody, but had fiddled with his spectacles when left to his own devices. Frank had not heard of him in any connection, either as artist or administrator. Another applicant had said offhandedly to Montgomery that he didn't know why Houldsworth had applied for this job, which was little better, if at all, than his present post. 'A sideways promotion,' the man mumbled. 'Makes you wonder.'

'Is he well known, then?' Frank had asked.

'Yes. I believe so. Good self-publicist.'

Frank put away the letter carefully. He was disappointed, but might have known. He did not enter a competition without trying to win and if these people in Yorkshire preferred someone else he did not like it. He wished he had paid more attention to Houldsworth, who in no way stood out from the rest. He confessed his defeat to Principal Jones, who said he had met Houldsworth, a thoroughly worthy art teacher. Jones then told a story of the celebrated appointment of a third, decent, middling candidate because the committee could not decide between two who were really outstanding. 'They'd picked out these two from the word go, but then they could not decide between them. Either man would have been a paragon, a nonpareil, if I may seem to contradict myself, in the position of principal, but these provincial raddle-brains held on to their entrenched positions. Nobody would yield and so in the desperate end they elected this third, a decent citizen, a kind father, I'm sure, but nowhere near in the same league as the other two. This committee made the town a laughing stock in the art world.' Emrys Jones smacked his lips.

'It's quite likely I didn't tell them what they wanted to hear,' Frank ventured.

'They wouldn't have any idea. God knows how they come to choose their selectors.'

'And does it make much difference?' Frank asked.

'Ah, cynicism so early. It does. It does.'

'These high-flyers of yours might have caused trouble.'

'If that were the case then trouble needed to be made.' Jones waved a hand to indicate that the conversation was now concluded. 'I'm glad I'm not about to lose you.'

Three days later Montgomery received a further letter from the South Yorkshire college. This time it was in the handwriting of Sir Alfred Woolfe to inform him that Mr Thomas Norman Houldsworth had, for reasons best known to himself, decided against accepting their offer of the principalship of the college. Sir Alfred was therefore happy to offer him the post. This gave him great pleasure, as he had himself been sure that he was the best candidate. He had been unavoidably absent on the day of the interview, but George French, a man of real intelligence, had been very suitably impressed by what Montgomery had said on that afternoon. Perhaps Mr Montgomery would be so kind as to write, or phone him so that, in the happy expectation that he would accept the position, the necessary papers could be signed and they would all know where they stood. He was his sincerely, Alfred Woolfe.

Frank Montgomery made Sir Alfred wait for two days before he answered. He consulted Scott and Jones; both wondered why Houldsworth had withdrawn. Scott advised him to keep Alfred Woolfe on his side. Jones warned him not to start on new plans until he'd had a look at the place and especially – he grinned evilly – the clerical staff.

He made one or two journeys to Sheffield before the summer break and began his search for a house suitable for the principal of an esteemed college. He settled on a Victorian villa, tree-girt, on the side of a hill. Why he chose such a building for one single man he did not know. At the office of the Sheffield solicitor who acted for him he met Gillian Housley, whom he married four years later. Her father was principal of the firm, an awkward man who, no sooner had he seen his daughter settled in with her husband, proposed moving her to their Derby office. Neither newly wed was pleased. On the eve of retirement her father died and she remained in Sheffield.

IV

Frank heard the two cars draw up on his drive. Gillian and Rosemary stood outside, boot doors open. He took to his back entrance.

'Aren't you at work?' his wife called.

'No. I'm making up for the days I sacrificed in the summer.'

'Is that permissible?' His wife kissed him. 'Your governors will be giving you the sack.'

'I wish they would.' His sister-in-law put her arms round him and kissed him softly on the lips.

'How are you?' he asked.

'Well, I think. We've tucked Mama away in her nursing home and she seems, thank God, to be taking kindly to it. I thought it might all be too much for her.'

The sisters were both slim, tall, elegant and alike in hair colour. Rosemary seemed more serious of face; Frank thought he wouldn't like to get across her in a magistrates' court. Her expression at this moment was pleasant. Her use of 'Mama' to designate her mother, always 'Mummy' to her face, showed her mood. 'I'm rather proud of myself,' she said. 'We kept up together all the way.'

'You've been here before.'

'I know the route except for the last few miles. But we'd planned to have lunch here and managed it. We drove into the car park at the same moment.'

'Well done. I'll lug your cases in.'

They settled to mugs of tea and Rosemary remarked how quiet it was.

'Quiet and convenient. The main road is only a few hundred yards away.'

'I'm never sure', Gillian said, 'that I'm greatly fond of village silence. Living in Sheffield when we were first married, I can't remember being too disturbed by the traffic. We're all townees.'

'We get used to it. I knew a railway clerk who lived in a room over the station and trains were running past him day and night. He couldn't sleep at first, then he grew accustomed to it, and when he left the place to work elsewhere away from the railway, he couldn't sleep at night, he said, because it was so quiet.'

'That doesn't sound likely,' Rosemary objected.

'That's what the man said.'

'I see.'

'Rosie's going to stay with us for a few days,' Gillian told her husband. 'She needed a change, and we thought that if there was any alteration in my mother's circumstances we could talk it over and do as we thought best, together.'

'Is it likely?' he asked.

'Well. It is possible that she'll have to be transferred to a hospice or a hospital before too long. Her doctor said the hospital consultants aren't happy with her condition.'

'She might die?'

'Exactly.'

While Gillian sorted out an order to be fetched by her husband from the shop, Rosemary spoke seriously to Frank as they walked in the village. 'You know Gill's very upset about mother.'

'Is her mother really very ill, then?'

'Yes. The GP, who's a sensible sort of man, said at one stage he thought her death was a matter of days rather than weeks away.'

'Does Gill know?'

'Yes, she was there when the doctor told us. He said her heart was very weak and she'd had two strokes, which left her fairly disabled, and her dementia had really started to gallop. I think Gill was truly shocked when she saw her mother this time. She kept repeating, "It's only a month since I was here, and she's completely changed." Then she was a forgetful old woman, but with plenty of small signs of the energy that marked her out a year or two ago. The doctor was absolutely insistent after this last stroke that she went into care.'

'And Gill didn't like that?'

'Nobody liked it, least of all our mother.'

'She was unhappy?'

'Desperately. I used to wonder when I knew nothing about it, and didn't ever see anyone suffering from dementia, if that wasn't the best of solutions, if one lived on, because you couldn't remember anything and so wouldn't understand what was happening.'

'But . . . ?'

'She seemed depressed, had crying bouts, was helpless. And that was unlike her. You'll remember her bossing us all about. We'll do this today and that tomorrow. You were a great favourite of hers: "We're going along the mountain this morning because that's what Frank will enjoy." Joe wasn't anywhere in the picture. He was in the class of Daddy, poor bloody infantry, cannon fodder, as he used to say. You were not only talented, had your name in the papers, but were the principal of a college and a person who wielded power. Daddy was just a solicitor throwing his weight about in the office.'

'If only she knew,' he said.

'Until this last stroke she could just about manage at home with help. She could afford a live-in housekeeper of sorts and the district nurse came in every day. She gave the appearance of being just about on top of it all.'

'And you don't think she was?'

'No. Unless there was a catastrophic deterioration in these last few weeks. I suppose that's possible. The only good thing is that she's seemed slightly better since she went into this home.'

'Happier?'

'In a dull way, yes. The first day she went in she was awful, groaning and writhing, insofar as she could move. Then she seemed to settle; I think they'd perhaps changed her medication and she acted more calmly, as if she'd given up on us. That didn't please us either; she just sat or lay there as if she was paralysed all over and with no sort of expression on her face, except her wrinkles seemed deeper. I just don't understand how some damage to the brain can cause such devastating change in human appearance.'

'No.'

A passer-by greeted them. Had Frank been on his own it would have been with a nod and grunt, but as Rosemary, a stranger, accompanied him they were entertained with a raising of the hat, a clear greeting and a smile.

'I used to think that your father and my mother would have made an ideal married couple.'

'When they were young, d'you mean?' Frank asked.

'I don't know about that. In these last four years, let's say,

35

when they were both left without a partner. Don't you agree?'

'It never even crossed my mind. My mother died when Dad was well over eighty. He missed her, but he could look after himself and there was a whole bunch of ladies who came in to see that he wasn't lacking anything.'

'And had they matrimony in their sights?'

'He thought so. In a couple of cases. But he was determined to keep out of their clutches. I don't doubt he encouraged them to visit him and do odd jobs for him, as he did for them. He made little wooden geegaws, if that's the word, boxes, containers, candlesticks. He's still very good with his lathes and chisels.'

'He never did real carving? Figures, busts, that sort of thing?' Rosemary asked.

'No. He said it was all beyond him, so he wouldn't try. I took him to an exhibition at the college and there was quite a lot of woodcarving on display. He talked to the students and tutors, and one of them said he'd teach him, but he said "No" straight away. His mind was made up.'

'Why was that, do you think?'

'He prefers the bit he's learnt. He's managed to master elementary woodwork. And he knows that if he tries something more complicated, that will demand new techniques, different tools. His temperament is to keep up with things he knows, do them well.'

'Has he always been like that?'

'On the whole, yes. At the college, I find that there are those students who are always hankering after the new. They'll try anything. Others stick strictly to what they have already mastered. When I was a student in Beechnall there was a boy in my year who would only draw birds. He did them marvellously and certainly if he came across a bird of a kind he'd never met before he'd have a shot at it, with success, make it part of his collection. But if you asked him to draw a basket, or a boat, or a badger, or a bicycle, well, he'd do it but the drawing was nowhere near the class of his ornithological stuff.'

'What happened to him?'

'I've no idea. I think he went into teaching, but I've never heard of him since. It's possible that there's a living to be made drawing and painting birds.'

'Didn't his teachers try to wean him away?'

'Yes. They did. In their different ways. Encouragement, sarcasm, derision. One even tried to bribe him. Offered him a pound or two if he scored more than seventy per cent in the life-drawing exam.'

'And?'

'He scored sixty-nine. A close friend of the teacher, another man on the staff, graded the drawings.'

'They'd fixed that up between them.'

'I wouldn't be surprised. Anyway, our teacher refused to take the lad's pound. That made everybody suspicious. And a pound was worth something thirty years ago.'

'How many marks did you score?'

'They always marked me high. I was quick, good at likenesses and put the drawing in the right part of the paper.'

'Was your teacher any good?'

'That particular one? Not very. He went through the motions with us, kept us busy, said the right things. But he wasn't nearly as good as I was at drawing. Even then.'

'Oh, modest. Did he ever say so?'

'Yes, he did.'

'Would you have employed him at your college?'

'I expect so. He prepared his students for their exams, knew what would win high marks and what wouldn't. He could even show you little tricks of the trade.'

'You liked him?'

'Oh, yes. He praised me and I needed that. There was only one of our teachers who was anything like good with brush or pencil. And I got across him a time or two. I argued with him and he wasn't keen on that.'

Rosemary had stopped and now at the crest of a hill looked down into the river valley and the bordering trees. The sky was blue this afternoon with a bare minimum of broken cloud. 'You're lucky,' she said. 'This place is more beautiful every time I see it.'

'Yes. It is. Gill's responsible for our buying Avalon. I don't know when she first set eyes on it. I owned another house then, have still got it, in fact, but she pressed me. I wasn't exactly flush at that time, but she sorted it all out. I thought I needed the house in Sheffield.'

'And you didn't?'

'Not really. Once I'd had a fair-sized studio built on to this.'

They pushed into the village shop where Rosemary brandished

37

her sister's list. The shopkeeper treated her as if she were royalty, attempted none of the usual jovialities he saved for strangers. His wife hovered behind him as if to oversee or correct his every service, a wraith compared with her husband's broad, bucolic frame. She it was who took the money from Frank in the end, handled the till with speed while her husband fussed over the packing of Rosemary's two bags and a basket.

'Just right,' he almost shouted as he straightened the purchases in the last container. 'Made to measure.'

Frank lifted the two heavy bags and Rosie the basket. The shopkeeper made speed to the other side of the counter to open the door and almost bow them obsequiously into the street.

'He's very obliging,' Rosemary said as they set off, staggering along the main road. 'Aren't those bags heavy?'

'Like lead.'

'Gill said we needed the car.'

'I like my arms pulled out of their sockets. She's not half ordered stuff in quantity today. I went as soon as I arrived back from Wales, and filled up the fridge and the freezer, or so I thought.'

'She's made sure we'll not go hungry.'

'My father's threatening to come in the next few days. He's got a friend who's promised to drive him up here.'

'Man or woman?'

'A man. Another old schoolmaster though nothing like Dad's age. He finished up as an estate agent.'

'And they are both trenchermen?'

'I don't know about Gervase Lunn, but my father's not bad for his age. He enjoys his food, or such as they allow him. He's diabetic. He keeps it under control by diet and is said to be very good about it.'

'I hope I'm still here when he comes.'

'Yes. He's fond of you. You and Gill. "I like to see them together," he says. "They're different. Rosemary is the sort of woman I should have married. She'd have made something of me." '

'That's flattering.'

'He and my mother seemed not altogether suited. He was always quoting tags, and she thought little of his English literature and bits of the classical languages. She was a practical sort. "Get it right, if possible" was her motto.'

'Gill's a bit like that. I was very surprised when I heard she was about to marry an artist. I thought she wasn't interested in such matters. But then you didn't look like an artist. You were more like a county cricketer.'

'Thanks. And how would you describe your Joe?'

'An actor. Terence Rattigan sort of play.'

'Did he ever get on the stage?'

'Not he. He was always too busy making money.'

'Not a bad fault,' Frank said.

'If it was the only one, maybe, but it wasn't. He was the most selfish man I ever met.'

They walked along in silence. Talk of her ex-husband seemed to have knocked something of her liveliness from Rosemary's mood. Frank had only three times met J. F. R. James at any length and had not been impressed by him, or his smart clothes. The marriage was almost over, then, and the man probably not at his best. He made an effort to worm himself into the good graces of his brother-in-law, but in appearance and in voice he might have been playing a small part in an amateur comedy, before a bored audience for whom it was hardly worth making the effort. Frank wondered where James was now; he had married again, they had heard, and almost immediately his second wife had given birth to a daughter. Neither of the Housley girls had as yet had offspring and Rosemary, according to Gillian, had made it clear that in her case remarriage was unlikely. Rosie had never talked to Frank about the break-up of her relationship with Joe James. If he received a mention she spoke coolly and with balance, but Gillian had told him that her sister hated her ex-husband and the hatred seemed almost irrational, almost maniacal, so that she might well have murdered him. Gill could not offer a satisfactory reason for the virulence of her sister's feeling.

'Aren't you going to give me some advice?' Rosemary asked.

They both stopped. He took the two steps between them, weighed down by the lead heavy bags. When he reached her he kissed her cheek. It seemed cold, but she did not draw away from him.

'Again,' she said. This time she put her lips to his; she held him with one hand to his back to the soft pressure. 'Thanks, pal,' she said.

He saw her smiling and wondered at her choice of words. 'Onward, Christian soldier,' he said in reply.

V

As Frank and Rosemary began to descend the last hill towards Avalon they noticed a car standing in the road across the drive.

'Hello,' he said. 'Visitors.'

'Who's that likely to be?' she asked.

'It looks like Gervase Lunn. He's the man who was going to drive my father over some time. He visits his stepfather occasionally, at Stathern, five miles on. He's an old pupil of my father's.'

'And what does he do now?'

'He retired. He did a degree in Classics, taught a bit and then went into his father's estate agency. He's got plenty of money and is, they say, a scholarly sort of chap. Makes out he keeps up his Latin and Greek. It suits Herbert down to the ground. They do difficult crosswords together.'

As they reached the end of the drive, Lunn emerged with Gillian and Frank's father.

'Gervase is just leaving,' Gillian called out, catching sight of the two. There followed a great deal of hand-shaking and explanation. All five now trooped to the outside five-barred gate where the handshaking began again.

Lunn eased his delicate frame into the front seat of his car, wheezing. 'Five o'clock,' he said. 'Don't forget, Herbert. Tomorrow.'

'Exactly on time,' Herbert Montgomery answered, touching his moustache.

Inside, once the groceries were packed away, Frank faced his father who seemed in a particularly sunny mood. The women busied themselves elsewhere.

'Why didn't you let us know you were coming?' the son demanded.

'Gervase made up his mind suddenly, at the last minute, and invited me.'

40

'You've heard of the telephone?'

'I rang. Nobody at home. And you had forgotten to switch your answerphone on.'

'You're forgiven,' Frank said. 'How are you keeping?'

'Pretty well. As my multifarious diseases decide.' The old man, suffering from hypertension, atrial fibrillation and diabetes, looked the picture of health. 'I don't feel too good in the morning, but fine autumn weather suits me. And what are you doing?'

'I went down to Wales. I had this urge to knock off a few watercolours.'

'And did you? And are they any good?'

'One of the old ruins by the Mawddach pleased me.'

'Where did you stay?'

'Llanfachreth.'

'Never heard of it. I'd like to look at your pictures. And how about your portrait of the Duke of S.?'

'Going on nicely. I've done the face and hands. Well, nearly. In the old days I might have had an assistant good enough to paint the clothes. But now I have to do it for myself.'

'Does he come down here? At your beck and call.'

'No, they've given me a room as a studio and we arrange sittings by telephone. Now the season's over, and not so many people are traipsing round the place, he's more time. He doesn't half have to work.'

'Gah! He doesn't know what work is.'

'Of course, you know him well,' Frank said sarcastically. 'It's a pity you're not staying up here longer. I'd like to knock off a quick oil sketch of you that I can work up to a full-length painting.'

'You'd better get on with it sharp. I'm ninety now, with more ailments than a dead duck. I often think it won't be long before I'm crossing Jordan's narrow stream.'

'Are you talking about dying?'

'Of course I am. Ten or fifteen years ago in my late seventies I was bothered by the reported deaths of people I'd known well, was at school or university with. They'd seemed healthier than I was, less troubled by bodily affliction, and there they were dying, while I was much as I always had been, with some of my own teeth and a thousand of my old ideas still swilling round my brain.'

'And what conclusion did you reach?'

'That I shouldn't be long before I joined them in the choir invisible, yet inside my head I often felt and thought as I did when I was eighteen. It wasn't until I tried some physical action that my age clobbered me. Now I can barely get out of my chair. At the hospital they used to tell me to stand up from my chair without the use of my hands. Practise it, they said, and keep on at it. Make your muscles work.'

'Can you still do it?'

'Yes. Just about.'

'Go on, then. Give us a demo.'

The old man shuffled on his bottom to the edge of his chair, stuck his arms out straight so that no one could accuse him of cheating and then, not quickly but without a pause, he pushed himself up straight. Groaning, he stood in front of his chair, wiggling his fingers in half-hearted triumph at his son.

'Well done,' said Frank. 'I doubt if I could manage that and I'm not fifty yet.'

'How old are you?' his father asked. 'I forget these things.'

'Forty-seven. A great age.' The father had now sat down again and was putting on a show of comfort. 'Are you afraid of dying? Do you think about it much?'

'I can't answer that,' said Herbert Montgomery. 'I often think about it, but not altogether seriously. I tell myself that it can't be too far away, but that doesn't seem to make much difference. I'm slow now and have to think three times before I do the simplest chore, and I forget things very easily, but I'm not so ill or dissatisfied with my life that I want to die. And it all depends on the way I go.'

'What's the favoured exit?' Frank asked.

'A quick heart attack.'

'Is that possible, given your present state of health?'

'Yes, it is. I take my tablets religiously, but I might forget, or become so stressed that I overdo it all, and I'll be off, though given my usual luck I shall pass mildly away' – he waited for a sign of recognition of the quotation, but his son's face was as straight as ever – 'at a time when something particularly pleasing is just turning up in my dull life.'

'Yes,' said Frank, not thinking about the possibility.

'And what about you?' The old man's eyes twinkled. 'When are you considering giving up your job? This is the time of life when you should be at the peak of your powers as a painter.'

'Alliteration noted.'

'Never mind your sarcasm. When are you resigning? You talked about it all the time in your first three years and now you've been there ten years. Or do you like it too much, acting God Almighty?'

'You'd be surprised how little power or influence I've got over the place.'

'I don't believe it. I can remember coming to your college for some celebration and a few of your top dogs, senior men and women, were all together in your office. I don't know what we were doing there. Waiting to go down to join the lower orders somewhere. You weren't in the room, oddly enough. Perhaps we were waiting for you to lead us down. But one thing I do remember. A man standing close to me turned to one of his colleagues and said, "You can fairly smell the power in this room." '

'And could you?'

'No. What had caught my attention was how neat and unpretentious your room was. It had no great size and everything seemed packed away, out of sight, except one big watercolour. If someone had shown me a photograph of the room and asked me to guess whose office it was I just couldn't have known. It seemed small, nameless, anonymous, anybody's.'

'That's because I've a very efficient secretary who's obsessed with tidiness.'

'Very likely. But to that man in some sort of doctor's gown or official robe of office it was a centre of power, a holy of holies.'

'Steady, the Buffs.'

'We all like to throw our weight about. Even saintly old dodderers like me. The trouble is I don't get the chance.' Herbert Montgomery assumed a rueful expression. 'I often wonder when you look back over your ten years here whether you think you've done any good.'

'Why do you ask that?'

'Because when I look back at my life I seem to have achieved nothing.'

'That's nowhere near the truth. I'll flatter you with a list.'

43

'It's how it seems to me, Frank, at ninety. And so I ask you at about half my age what you'd claim for yourself.'

Frank, grinning slightly, massaged his left kneecap with his left hand. 'I started with a bit of a rush. I insisted that everybody, every student without exception, should have a first-year course in drawing. And I put a woman in charge who took it seriously. And her assistant, a new man I appointed, happened to be a very good draughtsman, so that if the students weren't getting anywhere they'd at least get the chance to see somebody doing it really well.'

'Wouldn't that put 'em off?'

'I've heard people argue that way, but on the whole, no. Some few will be discouraged, but most of the students here, though they know they'll never reach his standards, will draw all the better for watching him demonstrate how he does it. There's nothing wrong with that. That's how artists were trained in the old days. You were sent to a master's studio and there you mixed the paint or swept the floors until you worked up to dabbing in unimportant bits of the painter's pictures, and so on until you were allowed to carry out some commissions of your own. A pound to a penny you wouldn't ever be anywhere near the master painter's standards in originality, but your pictures would be, and still are, worth hanging, looking at, buying.'

'Is this man still here?'

'No. He did four years with us and went to teach in London, at Goldsmiths'. And I did hear recently that he was only teaching two days a week and was doing what you think I should do, painting on his own account.'

'Is he doing well?'

'I've no idea. I bought several of his pictures while he was with us and a year or two later when he had an exhibition up here. Just see if you can pick them out.'

'And the lady? The head of department? Is she still with you?'

'Yes. You've been introduced to her.'

'Ah, not knowing all this. That's the story of my life. But you haven't got round yet, my son, to the full recital of your achievements as head cook and bottle-washer.'

'If I'd have done nothing else, that would have been an achievement worth my time. When I look around I am often surprised how little change I've made. I have the reputation among my staff as a bit of a bastard, a chaser-up of the idle. I can manage that and, in these days of change and possible withdrawal of central, absolutely necessary funds, that does some good. My name appears in the papers, laying down the law on artistic or educational matters, and that impresses the idlers. They think I've more influence and power than I have. The younger ones hope that it will prove great for their next job.'

'But,' Herbert stressed the word.

'I've found out that people at the top ought, or are expected, to concentrate on purely administrative matters and, oh my God, money. Again, I did myself no harm by appointing a very good bursar. He'd get blood out of a stone and know how to spend it wisely. I often think the place would do better with him as principal.'

'Then why doesn't he apply for jobs elsewhere?'

'One, he knows nothing about art. Oh, he's learnt all the terms and fancy talk. He can sound marvellous when he's persuading money out of our captains of industry. But he is basically a modest man and feels that the head of an institution such as ours should be somebody who is an artist. He admires me, God bless him.'

'For what?'

'My painting. For the last few years (it was on the cards when I arrived) they've been talking of making us part of the university. It's going to happen now.'

'Will that have its advantages?'

'It'll save some money, they say. And widen our horizons. But I can't think it will do any better at turning out painters, sculptors, designers. It'll join us with the Department of Architecture.'

'And?'

'We shall be quarrelling with them, pushing and pulling, until somebody wins and a compromise is reached.'

'And compromises are in favour with you?'

'The whole of education, of any sort, is a compromise. It must be. We do our best with what we've got. In the studio. At the end-of-term exhibitions. When we dish out the prizes. I don't mind that.'

'You wouldn't compromise when you were painting, would you?'

45

'I'm not so sure. Nowadays I still get private commissions. The Duke, for instance. And his wife, the Duchess, bless her, when I've done him. I often think I should be looking around a wider world. Take this town, it's a thriving place. It's slipped, changed a few years back from the city of steel into a centre of all sorts of modern manufacture. And that's hard work these days. With sterling as it is. And if I were anything of a painter I should reflect this change. In the homes, and the faces of men and women.'

'You're getting some odd ideas.'

'How do you mean?'

'When you were younger you would have said that the value of a painting depended on how well it was done, not on its subject.'

'True. But I'd be faced with more challenges, trying to handle new concepts, all of which would be to my advantage if I were as good as my sainted father thinks.'

'So you're hanging on here?'

'Yes. I have a sketchbook on my desk, just to try things out in my spare minutes. This is regarded as eccentric, especially by those who think I ought not to have any spare time. It's the best thing I've ever done. It keeps my eye in. And the people here look on it as a kind of magic. I've found a real way through the dreary days of teaching.'

'Can you listen to somebody and draw at the same time?'

'Yes, but I never do. The worst impression I can make is that my mind's elsewhere, not on Mr X's complaints and Miss Y's brilliant schemes.'

'You're crafty.'

'Just like my father.'

VI

At dinner the four of them laughed a great deal. Rosemary seemed
especially bright, making fun of the others. Herbert Montgomery
glowered and hesitated at first, as if he found it difficult to be on
his best behaviour, but soon became cheerful. Frank felt at his
best, with three people he liked as his companions. He'd no idea
how to be at his ease at a larger gathering and tended to fall into
formality. That worked well for him, sometimes, as people
regarded him as eccentric, gifted beyond trivial chatter, the artist.
Today he was at home in every sense, watching Gillian produce
the food, beautifully cooked and served, if all plain, what his
father called 'Giotto's circle'.

'I don't want my food dowsed in fancy herbs any more than
with tomato ketchup; I like the taste of the meat, so I can judge
the standard of the rearing and cooking. I don't want it disguising.'

Frank Montgomery loved to hear his father laying down the
law. He told himself that he would soon have had enough if he
had to put up with it every hour of the day and every day of the
week. The old man, at ninety, still missed his captive audience,
his attentive class, and here was the chance to improve minds,
widen the range of their knowledge.

'You two were having a fine old chat together,' Rosemary
teased him.

'We're not dumb, certainly.'

'What was this afternoon's topic, then?' she asked.

'Setting his son on the path of righteousness,' Frank said.

'That will be difficult,' she said.

'We exhaust the same subject every time we meet,' Frank said.

'And may one ask what this fascinating conversation is about?'

'Should he resign his principalship at the college and be a full-
time artist.'

'Then you should consult Gill about that.'

47

Her sister pulled a face expressing hopeless inadequacy and passed the potatoes on to Herbert. 'I thought that teachers were so busy filling in forms these days that they'd no time to live.'

'When I started teaching,' Herbert said, 'I was in a grammar school that worked Saturday mornings. And we knocked off early, at twelve noon at the weekend, but many of us younger men were expected to be out on the games field at two fifteen to referee rugger, or watch it, or umpire until six thirty at cricket in the summer. I doubt if the modern teacher does anything like the hours we did. And we had large classes, thirty at least, all preparing for exams, all with work that needed marking.'

'And was there any advantage?' Rosie asked.

'Longer holidays. Higher pay.'

'You had Wednesday afternoon off,' Frank said, 'in lieu of Saturday morning.'

'On paper. We were all expected on the games field, or at the cadet corps.'

'Didn't you feel badly done by?' Gillian asked.

'Oddly, no. Some of the older men didn't take games. And there were one or two gifted games players on the staff who went off to represent the county, and in one case to play for England, and we had to cover for them.'

'And you didn't mind?' Rosemary.

'No. Jobs were short when I began in the thirties. We were lucky to find ourselves places in a good school. And in our way we were proud of it.'

'Were teachers more highly regarded then than now?' Rosemary pressed.

'I suppose so. By and large. Though the first school I taught in was private. Most of the parents paid and wanted value for money. And some made it clear that they didn't regard teaching children as much of an occupation, and would tell you how much they earned, just to put you in your place, for all your Latin and Greek.'

'A hard life,' Frank said, without sympathy.

'The place I was in', his father answered, 'was a day school. If you taught in a boarding school they wanted even more from you. Morning, noon and night, every day of the week, Sundays included. But jobs were short.'

'What about women?' Rosemary asked. 'Women teachers?'

'Once they were married that was the end of their teaching career. They stopped.'

'Did they mind?' Gillian asked.

'Some did, I don't doubt. And the country lost gifted women. But it was what happened. They accepted it and made some sort of life of their own, keeping a bright and polished home, and mixing with other women of their status, and bringing up children and doing good works. Your mother and I didn't get married until after the war broke out. We both were working and saving. I was forty-four when I fathered you.'

'The war had been over nine years when I was born.'

'True, but we suffered some setbacks. And we didn't seem exactly prolific. Or not successfully so. My wife lost two children, stillborn, before Master Francis John there was born.'

'Worth waiting for,' the son answered.

'I thought . . .' The old man faltered. 'Well. Your mother went back to teaching during the war. I was called up into the Navy and was away from home for months on end. I was thankful that I had no children then, though most serving men of my age were the opposite. They carried pictures of their families about with them. I don't know. They were doing, I suppose, what I was, making the best of things as they were. They couldn't alter circumstances.'

'Did serving in the Navy do you harm?' Rosemary asked. 'In the long run?'

'I can never make my mind up about that. I'd have an older family and that might have made a difference to our way of living. I'd no idea that I'd live to be ninety. I worked my full stint to the age of sixty-five and since then I've been reading, helping out in the house, gardening, do-it-yourself and, in the last months of her life, caring for Frank's mother. She's been dead seven years now. We had a good life together. She had a lot more about her in many ways than I did. Since she went, it's been downhill all the way.'

'How is that?' Rosemary again.

'I can look after myself, cook and so forth. Nothing as good as this,' he said, pointing at his plate, 'but . . .'

'If you don't stop talking it'll be cold,' Gillian worried.

Her father-in-law smiled her his thanks and began to eat, heartily for a man of his age. The sisters, when they had finished the main course, described their own mother's condition to the men. She was sixty-five.

'A mere youngster,' Herbert said, mouth full.

'You get on with your grub,' his son warned. 'We've all done.'

'I know I'm slow.'

When he had finished Herbert thanked Gillian with courtesy and beamed down at the table. He had chosen trifle and cream for his pudding, and had done his very small portion justice. He helped clear the table and load the washing-up machine.

'What did he teach?' Rosemary asked Frank, aside.

'English and Latin.'

'Was he any good at art?'

'He'd lay down the law about it. As he did about most things. And I suppose he could draw a bit. He had something of a reputation with his pupils for his blackboard sketches. And he bought, when my mother pressed him, some decent pictures for the house and some books on art.'

'Was your mother gifted that way?'

'Yes. She could draw. Not that she did very often. But she worked some marvellously complicated embroidery pictures, and made very colourful quilts and cushions. That sort of thing. She'd a very good eye at sewing. She rarely boasted about it. The old man regarded art as something for other people. He'd have much preferred me to be a doctor or a lawyer.'

'You had to fight him about that?'

'In a fashion. But my mother used to support me. When I made a bit of a name for myself, then I think he began to be proud of me. The picture of my mother which I did when I was a student he had framed in a very elaborate way. When he shows it to people, he says that he wouldn't part with it for a million pounds.'

'Is it good?' Rosemary asked.

'Yes. At least I'm not ashamed of it when I see it now. It's not at all bad for a nineteen-year-old.'

Rosemary went out to help her sister with the coffee.

Herbert Montgomery returned and sank blowily into a chair. 'I've eaten too much as usual,' he groaned. He closed his eyes and folded his hands over his belly.

'Good,' Frank encouraged. 'Have a quick nap. I'll wake you when your coffee's ready to drink.'

Herbert slept, quietly and easily, for nearly half an hour. Waking, he looked puzzled by his surroundings and his companions. He finally, not quickly, pulled himself together. 'I'm with you now,' he announced, sitting up straight, cup and saucer in hand.

'That coffee will be stone cold,' Gillian said. 'Let me get you another.'

'No, thank you. I like it like this. In the war, when they let us loose ashore in some Eastern port, Bombay, even Aden or Melbourne, there was nothing I enjoyed more than iced coffee. I loved it. I'm right as nine pence, isn't that so, Frank?'

'Thik hai, sahib.'

'He used to press me all the time to tell him about the war and the Navy.'

'Does it seem a long time ago to you now?' Rosie asked.

'Well, it's fifty-seven years. Memory is very odd. Some things are really sharp and others vague or gone altogether.'

'Is that because some incidents were more exciting?' Gillian asked.

'They meant more to you at the time?' Rosie.

'On the whole, yes. Though some trivial affairs stick in my mind, and I can't understand why. Perhaps it is that they were important at that period, but don't seem so now.'

'Such as?'

'Buying, that is haggling like mad for, my first pair of chaplis. They're those sandals we used to wear. I can still see that man's face, and his pan-stained teeth as we argued. I don't know why I recall that particular instance. I must have done it more than once.'

'The first time?' Rosemary put it.

'I suppose so. Can't even tell you where it was. But I remember his face and his voice and his teeth.'

He drank his coffee, and took great care to place his cup and saucer safely on the low table by his chair.

'More coffee?' Gill asked.

'No, thank you. I shall be up all night as it is, chasing out to the lavatory.'

In the room all was warm, if rather dark. They sat comfortably, comatose even. Occasionally someone asked a question, but the silences were long and soothing.

'Have you still got your Sheffield house?' Herbert asked his son.

'Yes. We've let it out to a professor at the university. A doctor, an oncologist, a cancer man. The agent says he looks after it very well and he's a keen gardener.'

'Why doesn't he buy a house?'

'He's already got one. In north Oxford. I think he hopes to get back there before too long. And I don't want to sell it. It's on the cards.'

'Are you quite comfortable in your house?' Rosemary asked Herbert.

'Yes. It's a bungalow we bought when first Edina was ill. It's big, and has central heating and double glazing. Warmth's absolutely a necessity to old people.'

'Do you get help?'

'I have a gardener and a cleaning woman. They keep me spick and span. I don't have meals-on-wheels, not yet, anyhow. I can cook and I go down to the shops pretty well every day. I bring back a little on each excursion. If I didn't go out there'd be days when I'd speak to nobody.'

'Not to neighbours?'

'No. On both sides they're youngish people and are out at work. And our gardens are organised so that privacy is maintained.'

'You don't feel lonely?' Gillian asked.

'Yes. Sometimes. I've television, and radio, and telephone. I don't encourage visitors these days, because I can't cope with them. I'm so slow. It takes me ten minutes to get up out of my chair to make a cup of tea.'

'Old age isn't too much of a burden?' Rosemary asked.

'When I was seventy, say, I was pretty lively. I could walk and even ride a bike. I never used a car unless it was absolutely necessary. We took quite long holidays abroad. I continued to take a class on English literature at the WEA. Sometimes at weekends I'd get the tent out and nip off to the seaside for a day or two. If some snag arose, it didn't faze me. I got on sorting it out and even enjoyed it. My memory was beginning to go, slightly.' He paused.

'I find myself', Gillian said, 'running upstairs and when I've got there I wonder what it was I came up for.'

'And how old are you?' Herbert asked.

'Nearly thirty-nine.'

'I think that's inattention rather than memory loss. I find I can't remember names or words. Not just new words, but words I've been conversant with all my adult life. And now they've gone, or worse, they're on the tip of your tongue, you know you know them, but they just won't come. It's getting so bad with me that I often reframe my sentence before I actually speak it.'

'If you know what you want to say, can't you think it without the words?'

'Yes. "How much is that thingamajig?" And you point at it. Now it's got to a stage when I seem to be baffled by my own lack of knowledge. When I was younger there were great hosts of facts or theories I didn't know, hadn't heard of, but to which I had access if I did something about it, access to dictionaries or other books of reference. These seemed, if I can put it like this, part of a coherent corpus of knowledge. Now it's not so. The whole is beginning to dissolve. I acquire a new piece of knowledge and try to put it alongside the rest of what I know in that department or topic, only to find that I'm adding it to something that's already disintegrating and that facts which would help me to understand my new acquisition no longer exist for me.'

The three listened in silence.

Rosemary it was who spoke first. 'I don't quite follow you,' she said. 'Can you give me an example?'

Herbert looked helplessly at her, searching. 'Talleyrand,' he said finally. 'Does that name mean anything to you? I came across it again recently. I did European History for Higher School Certificate, and thus the name rang a slight bell. He lived at the time of the French Revolution, but when I tried to connect him with Robespierre and Danton or Marat I found I could not. What they did had also disappeared. Marat was murdered in his bath, but the others were names, nothings. I read that Talleyrand was banned from entering France during the period of the Revolution, but why and by whom I hadn't the foggiest notion. I also connected him with the Congress of Vienna, but again why and how I had no idea. This was because my knowledge of the Revolution, Napoleon's wars, the Congress no longer existed.'

'That's not surprising,' said Frank. 'You've not thought about the subject for seventy-odd years and however great your knowledge as a schoolboy, it's disappeared. I can barely remember something I learnt yesterday.'

'It has never seemed like that before,' his father objected.

'Seemed, seems,' Frank answered. 'We were all marvels in our youth. Never made any errors, always masters of our subject. It's not true. We weren't, or at least I wasn't, and I don't kid myself that I was.'

'When you're young' – Rosemary spoke hesitantly – 'you're always on the lookout for something new, exciting, unexpected.'

'That's right,' Herbert answered her. 'You don't think at my age that some marvellous surprise is just round the corner. You know there isn't such a thing. The only surprise, and it's only that because we don't know the day and the hour, is death.'

Frank now stood by the bookshelves from which he had taken and opened a volume. The mention of death had temporarily quietened the others.

Gillian recovered first and stared at her husband. The other two copied her. 'What have you found there?' she asked.

'Charles Maurice de Talleyrand-Périgord, 1754–1838,' he read portentously in his best French accent. He then quickly gabbled through part of the encyclopaedia article.

'Some name,' said Rosemary. 'I'd never remember that in a thousand years.'

'That's just the sort of name that would have embedded itself immediately in my mind when I was young. And you mentioned the Congress of Vienna. I'm glad you did that, or your book did. I've not forgotten everything. But I couldn't tell you much about it. The name Metternich. It took place after the Napoleonic Wars. After Waterloo, 1815, yes.' Herbert sat mumbling. The women watched him.

Frank turned over the pages, reading idly, it appeared. 'What's Telugu, then?' he asked.

'How do you spell it?' Rosemary wanted to know. Frank gave her the letters and repeated the word.

'I know that,' said Herbert. The women sat up. 'It's a language of south India. There are Tamil and Telugu and Kanarese. It's a Dravidian language.'

'What's that?' Rosemary again. 'Dravidian?'

'It was the name, the old name, in Sanskrit of a province where these languages are spoken. That's right. Dravidian. I wasn't sure; it might have been Davidian, but no, Dravidian. That's the word.' They listened until he suddenly burst out. 'Malayalam.'

'I beg your pardon,' Frank said. Rosemary crowed with laughter.

'That's another Dravidian language.'

'How do you know all this?' Rosemary.

'I was out there for a time in the war.'

'Did you learn to speak any of them?' she pursued him.

'No. Not a word. I wasn't there long enough.'

'Still, the old edifice of learning's not altogether in ruins,' Frank said, putting the book back on the shelves and returning. 'Well answered, Father.'

Herbert, pleased, replied modestly, 'I can remember another thing. I was out there, ashore, for a time. It was in Bangalore, I think, and in one of the Indian villages thereabouts I saw a little boy playing with his friends. These south Indians are dark-skinned, and so was this lad, except that he had a thatch of really blond curls. It looked artificial. Like a wig. The other kids had straight, thinnish dark hair, so this one really stood out. And yet he chattered away exactly like the rest.'

'Presumably his father was a fair-haired European?'

'Presumably. I never worked it out. I'm no sort of biologist and I had a vague notion that the darker traits were stronger. This child's skin was much like that of the rest of his playmates. It was only the hair that was springy and really bleached. He was the only one like it that I ever saw. Odd. That's why I remembered it. He'll have been dead for years now. They grew old quickly. I wish I knew more about inherited traits.'

'Couldn't it have been dyed or bleached by his mother? For some religious festival or something of the sort?' Frank.

'Possible. It seemed unlikely. The village was a poor place. Not much spare cash for modern chemicals or wig-wearing.'

'There's not much wrong with your memory,' Rosemary said. 'I'd never heard of Telugu.'

'Yes, but my memory of contemporary happenings is hopeless.'

Herbert drew a hand in despair along his forehead. 'When I look in the magazine that my newspaper puts out on Saturdays, and even more so on Sundays, I read about all sorts of celebrities, famous people I've never even heard of.'

'Such as?'

'I can't recall their names. They are actors in the cinema or on television. I've not only never seen them, but I've never heard of them.'

'You move in the wrong circles,' Rosemary said.

'I certainly don't go to the pictures much.'

'But can you recall the names of film stars of your earlier life?'

'Yes. Clark Gable. Spencer Tracy. James Stewart.'

'No women?' Frank interrupted, laughing.

'Yes. Jean Harlow. Greta Garbo. Bette Davis. Katharine Hepburn.' With a grin: 'Betty Grable.'

'I bet you know who Marilyn Monroe is,' Rosemary said.

'Yes, I do. Though I never saw her in a film. All I can remember was a snapshot of her standing over a grate with her skirts blowing up.'

'That was a still from a film.'

'What about pop groups?' Gillian suddenly asked.

'I've heard about the Beatles and the Rolling Stones, and that's about it. They all have daft names and you can't hear a word of what they're singing. I once went to a wedding reception and they had a local group blasting our ears. "Blasting" is the word. It was painful in the extreme.'

'What were they called?' Frank asked.

'No idea.'

'Do you remember the pop songs of your youth?'

'Some. Some fragments. A line or two came into my head the other day. I wondered why.'

'What were they?' Gillian asked.

'"When I pretend I'm gay / I never feel that way, / I'm only painting the clouds with sunshine," ' Herbert sang tunefully. 'It's from my young manhood and from a film. *Gold Diggers of 1933*. Something like that.'

'The word "gay" dates it,' said Frank.

'That never entered my head,' his father replied.

'Do you know any more of it?' Rosemary asked.

'"When I hold back a tear / To let a smile appear / I'm only painting the clouds with sunshine."'

'Not one of the most memorable bits of English literature,' Frank said.

'It must be. He's remembered it all these years.' Gillian sounded judicial.

'Do you remember why you remember it?' Rosemary.

'No, I don't. Perhaps I liked the tune. God knows that's trite enough.' He hummed a tuneless snatch.

'I wonder', Gillian said, 'which came first, the tune or the words?'

'The tune,' Frank said brutally.

'Yes, that's probably right,' his father agreed. 'You know, I can see the office where this masterpiece was concocted. Greasy men in braces. A piano or two. And somebody knocks off a tune that they think catchy, and some other man puts words to it.'

'Is that right?' Gillian asked.

'No. I'm making it up. I guess somebody writes a lyric and somebody else puts a tune to it. Then the professionals play around with it. I've no real knowledge, but I've often thought of the dozens and hundreds of songs of love or grief turned out in dingy offices. And nowadays it'll be worse, because there are all these amateur groups howling through their songs, drummers going mad, guitarists banging at their three chords.'

'Weren't there amateur groups in your day?'

'Yes, bands. But they'd all learnt to play their instruments. In the Salvation Army or elsewhere. They made a satisfactory sound. Nowadays the top pop groups hire professional players to come in when they're recording to make it approximately worth listening to.'

'Did you ever play in them?'

'No. I had some piano lessons, but I wasn't very talented.'

'Weren't there talented people writing good popular songs in your day?'

'Of course. There'd be talented people at any sort of human endeavour. Some of these activities will offer more opportunities than others. Pub pianists will be more likely to display an outstanding gift than, say, a man on a corporation dustcart at his job. Some dustmen will carry out their duties better than others.

That's obvious. The strong, the supple, the agile will excel at emptying dustbins, but not so obviously.'

'I've never thought about that,' Rosemary said, then, turning to Frank, 'Is it so with your sort of art?' she asked him.

'It's never been quite so popular. You didn't find young men of hardly any talent making a good living by drawing cartoons, let's say. The public doesn't want pictures as they want groups at their disco or on the record. As a student I used to do head-and-shoulder sketches of people at the seaside for a pound or two.'

'Did you sign them?'

'Yes. If they asked. It put the price up.'

'Had they heard of you, then?' Rosemary asked.

'No, they hadn't. Nor will they have heard of me now.'

'It's not a fair world,' his father said. 'Luck plays a great part. If you're at the right place at the right time, you may do well.'

'Do you mind that?' Rosemary asked.

'Sometimes. In my own poor profession it wasn't always the most gifted who rose to the top.'

'What was it, then?' Rosie again.

'Luck, as I've said, or influence, or ambition, or even the loud voice?'

'Perseverance?' Frank asked.

'Occasionally.'

They talked into the night. Herbert dozed from time to time but defended his arguments with some skill and much anecdote.

In bed, Gillian said to Frank, 'Your father's been enjoying himself.'

'He always does.'

'You wouldn't think he was ninety, now, would you?'

'No. Do you like him?' Frank asked his wife.

'Not altogether. I try to make allowance for his age, but he doesn't seem to know much about the modern world. It's as if he hasn't changed his mind since the war.'

'So he's not always right in his opinion?'

'No. He isn't. And sometimes he's nasty with it.'

Frank lay, surprised.

VII

Gervase Lunn called in for a light lunch before he took Herbert Montgomery back home. Frank noticed that his father had inveigled Gillian into a corner and had harangued her with much finger-wagging. She listened with her smooth, beautiful lawyer's face unmoved. The old man grew red in the face and afterwards ate his salad, boiled ham and huge potato in its skin with a gentlemanly savagery. He took out his ill temper on Lunn, making fun of his stepfather. 'How is he?' he groaned out.

'Pretty well for his age.' The stepfather had married Lunn's mother in his late seventies, soon after Gervase's father had died. An accountant, he was said to have accumulated a great deal of money and as Gervase was his sole heir, the 'young man' paid him due homage.

Herbert Montgomery disliked him. 'What's the old fathead up to now?' he asked.

'He's had a garden designer in to reshape the garden so that he'll still be able to handle it on his own.'

'Why doesn't he employ a gardener to do it for him? He can afford it.'

'He needs exercise, so he says.'

'He needs his head examining.'

Frank and the two women saw the guests off from the front gate. Rosemary hurried back indoors. 'Where's she off to?' he asked.

'You sound just like your father,' Gillian said. 'She'll be straightening out the kitchen and the dining room. Sweeping up the crumbs you and your father have scattered.'

'Uh. I saw the old man was giving you the benefit of his advice this morning.'

'Yes. He was. And, as usual, it was all about you. He doesn't seem to trust your judgement somehow.'

'Let's hear it,' he said ruefully.

'I am to tell you not to resign from your job until you've piled up a decent pension. Old age without money is the worst of life. You don't need a great deal, but if you can't afford the bit you do need you're in real trouble.'

'And what did you say?'

'That I was a working woman and younger than you by eleven years, and am easily able to support you. He said he wasn't so sure. I said I'd be senior partner next year when Uncle Frederick retires.'

'You didn't tell him that I thought I could earn more money by painting than by running the college?'

'I did, or hinted at it.' She smiled. 'He wouldn't have it. He'd been reading, he said, a book on Rembrandt, how he was extremely popular, all the rage with moneyed people as a young painter, but as he grew older his style of painting went out of fashion.'

'He didn't draw any moral from it, did he? That the lack of custom left him to paint himself and those around him, and demonstrate to posterity what a great genius he was, having no one to please but God and himself?'

'No. All he seemed concerned about was the state of your finances.'

'That's always concerned him. He fought me tooth and nail to keep me away from art, particularly painting. "You'll not be properly rewarded," he'd tell me.'

'He thinks highly of you,' Gill said.

'He thinks he wasn't properly paid for all the work he put in at his various schools. And art teachers were well below him, in payment, status and everything else, on a par with woodwork men and PT instructors.'

'It's different now, is it?'

'Not in my view. They all have degrees now, but that's typical of today's educational system. You can get a BA in cookery or blacking boots.'

'Does it worry you when he talks to you like this?'

'No. Should it? I'm pleased he thinks I'm an influence for good and that you'll listen to me.'

'I think', Frank muttered, scratching the crown of his head, 'he still sees me as a boy, not much bothering what I do or say and living a bohemian life to cap it all.'

'What's bohemian about your or our existence?'

'We own two houses. "You can only sit in one chair and one room at a time" was his favourite advice.'

'You haven't told him we're considering buying a property in France, have you?'

'I might have mentioned it. I can't remember doing so. He'll be a bit envious. He was never in a position to buy foreign homes. He'll boast about it. To other people. But he'll wonder how much it costs us and whether it's a waste of hard-earned pelf. His parents hadn't a lot of money and so he feels we are tempting fate. It's like buying a piano. There it stands, polished up to the nines, and the kids plinking on it after expensive lessons. And when the axe falls and the bailiffs come in, that'll be the first thing out of the door and into their van.'

'He never talks about a deprived childhood.'

'His father always had a job, so did his brothers. He was the first in his family to go to a university and to teach in what they called a secondary school. He'd come up in the world. A Bachelor of Arts. That was something.'

'And you've got to climb a step higher.'

'I've already done so.'

'But you've to be careful not to fall off the ladder.'

Later, on a shopping expedition he and Rosemary chatted.

'Your father's a remarkable man,' she said.

'In what way?'

'He says he's lost his memory and the next minute he comes out with all this stuff about Dravidian languages. I'd never even heard of them.'

'He lived out there.'

'I suppose so. How does he spend his spare time?'

'Reading his newspaper and the odd book or two. He was going through *Vanity Fair* again, he told me. I guess that he spends rather more time in front of the television screen than he cares to let on.'

'Can he get out? To walk to the shops?'

'Yes. And he can still drive. He doesn't go too far because his eyesight's not good.'

'Has he friends?'

'Yes and no. He'll talk to anybody. People in the street, the man inspecting his gas meter, but close friends who visit him regularly, no. They're either dead or gone away. Most men don't live to ninety.'

'So he's no intellectual acquaintances?'

'Well.' Frank paused, sighed. 'The man next door to him in the close where he lives is a lecturer in physics at the university. But he's nowhere near Dad's age and the old man says that his general knowledge is very severely limited. He can't even explain in straightforward English what it is he's researching into. And when the old man quizzes him about, for instance, quantum mechanics, he's nearly incoherent. Or at least my father can make nothing of what he's told.'

'Does he question him in an aggressive way?'

'I expect so. And some of his explanations when they're put in simple English seem to be self-contradictory or nonsense. Or, at least, in father's old-fashioned view.'

Rosemary, who walked quickly and kept Frank moving at his smartest pace, now asked, 'Does he do any artistic work? Does he paint or write, for instance?'

'No. He thinks that's beyond him. Apart from his bit of wood-work. I guess he'd like to do these things. I don't know whether he's tried and failed at some period of his life and now hasn't the energy to make another attempt. He's not very good, either, with his hands, knocking a nail in or, let's say, doing a straight-forward job about the house. My mother was miles better than he was hammering a nail into place.'

'Did he mind?'

'I guess he did, but he'd deny it. He'd tell himself that it was a workman's job and beneath him, and for that reason he'd never bothered to acquire the skill.'

'He's an intellectual snob, then, is he?'

'No doubt about it. But I don't hold it against him. He's worked his way up the social ladder. He didn't ever like to be called a "teacher". He taught in secondary and grammar schools, and thus was a "schoolmaster". I told him that "teacher" was the title with which people greeted Jesus, but he said that was two thousand years ago, and usages of words change every few decades, or sooner.

Nowadays every magician or conjuror calls himself "professor", and that when the government and the city authorities link us up to the university I shall be called "professor" with them.'

'Has he come round to accepting you as a painter?'

'He's pleased that I'm principal of the college. That's a position salaried by the government.'

'But when the newspapers feature you as one of our better painters?'

'He's pleased. He draws people's attention to the article. And he'll lay down the law about art. In some way he guesses that it's a kind of knack, which I've somehow acquired. Or at least he used to think like that. Now he looks on portrait painters as interpreters of the sitters' characters. That's a mouthful. And when the university in Sheffield awarded me an honorary D.Litt. he was pleased as Punch. When Gill, on the big day, said that the colours of doctoral robes didn't match my complexion I think he was quite shocked. There are some things you don't joke about.'

'And you argue with him?'

'I used to. Not so much now. In some ways we could do with more old fogeys like him in the present-day schools.'

'Expound.'

'He believed from the top of his head to the heels of his boots that the things he taught were important. Not in themselves always. To learn the conjugations of Latin verbs isn't educational in itself, except perhaps that it teaches you to sit down and slog away until the tenses are all fixed in your head, like the multiplication tables. But they will lead on to something else, some higher learning, Virgil or Horace. And he'd knock Shakespeare into their brains until some of the great speeches were second nature to his pupils. He was a good reader himself, in a rather parsonical way, which was the fashion of his youth, and he made them learn lines they'd never forget.'

'"Friends, Romans, countrymen . . ."' she said with ironic emphasis.

'I expect so.'

'But they wouldn't understand it, not young boys?'

'Nor some adults. But he gave his pupils the benefit of the doubt. They were the intellectual cream. And they'd grow into it. And some of them believed him.'

'But there must have been some who weren't interested in words and rhetoric?'

'I don't doubt it, but they had to learn with the rest in the hope that some of it rubbed off on them. He knew what was good and he did his best to catch their interest, but he thought they were children, immature, without too much in themselves until people like him had got after them and taught them the errors of their ways.'

'Is that right?'

'It's the way we look on children's pictures nowadays. They may show unusual talent, but they are nowhere near the works of the great masters; we should be mad to expect that.'

'But they have some sort of worth?'

'Oh, yes. They show some kinds of skill. But I remember when some young American girl did pictures that were like Picassos, so that people were prepared to pay good money for them, somebody delighted Herbert by writing to *The Times* to say he'd be more impressed if the child did things that could be mistaken for Titians. "I wish some of these Turner Prize judges would begin to think like that." He delights in taking somebody to task.'

'Is he happy? Now he's really old?'

'Content. He wishes he could go off to Italy or Switzerland or Austria every holiday.'

'Not Thailand or Burma or Borneo?'

'No. He wants connections with European culture. He loved Vienna or Salzburg or Florence. These oriental places that are all the rage now have no attraction. "I went to such places at the King's expense in my youth," he'll say. "I'll go now where *I* want to go." But he's rather slow and he hates that. "It takes me a whole week to do an afternoon's work. I haven't the will sometimes to get out of my chair." '

'But the deterioration is slow?'

'It is. I don't think he'd want to live if it started to quicken up.'

'In my mother's case it's begun to gallop. Soon after Daddy died Mummy was up here with me to see Gill and your father was staying with you. They seemed so lively together and got on so well that I thought, idly for a start, they would make a good married couple. He was nearly twenty-five years older than she was, but one would never have known it. I thought as she was sixty or so at the time, she'd be physically strong enough to look after him if ever he became ill. They argued, I remember, once about who was the greater composer Mozart or Beethoven. My mother was in favour of Mozart and he called her a Platonist because she believed that inspiration came from outside the person. He wouldn't have it. Beethoven had learnt his greatness from experience of human life. They used to play your CDs and listen hard, the pair of them. It made me think that old age wasn't so bad. They argued like young students when I was at the university and enjoyed every minute of it.'

'I missed most of this. We had some long-drawn-out meetings at the time and I was hardly at home. He told me how well your mother and he hit it off. By the time I came home for dinner the polemics had died down. Gilly was pleased as Punch that the pair of them were so immersed in controversy. She said to me one night, "My mother's coming alive again. I never thought she would, after Daddy's death. That seemed to have kicked all the life out of her." '

'It was sudden, wasn't it? Your father's death?'

'Yes. If you remember both Gill and I were married the same year. There was only a month between the two weddings.'

'I remember it well,' he said, solemnly facetious.

'I used to think the pair of them would be glad to be relieved of us, though in fact neither of us was living at home. Daddy said that two weddings so close would ruin him financially, but straight after our wedding they sailed off to Egypt and Greece for a cruise, so they must have had money left. I know they had. The amount Daddy left quite took my breath away. They had an outstanding year together travelling, reading, weaving in my mother's case. Then Daddy had his first heart attack, was in and out of hospital several times and died there, less than three months after he began to be ill. It knocked my mother sideways. I thought she'd never recover. She didn't seem to want to. She was seriously depressed, didn't eat properly, didn't look after herself, never went anywhere. She had plenty of money so she could have all the help she needed and in fact she had one very good home help who kept her alive. But she was low, missing Daddy. Gill and I couldn't understand it. I mean, she had been well used to occupying herself. He was often away and she was perfectly content. I know he kept coming back. But now she seemed helpless, with crying fits and threats of suicide. It was awful to see her. It was as if she'd changed character.' Rosemary delivered this slowly against the sharp rhythm of her walking.

They paused in their conversation though, again, without slackening pace.

'When did the dementia start?' he asked.

'Not long, a month or two, after she stayed with you. Her memory had been shaky for a year or more even when Daddy was alive. They used to pull each other's legs when they couldn't immediately lay their tongue to a word or a name and tell us that that was one of the drawbacks of old age. But while she was over here, staying with you and Gill, she appeared perfectly normal, much as she was when Daddy was living. She argued with your father as she did with her husband and seemed to enjoy it, and from the way she spoke she was full of plans for holidays and schemes for learning.'

'And when did that come to an end?'

'Not long after she got home. She must have had a stroke, or a seizure. We never found out because it had so affected her memory and speech that she wasn't able to tell us. She was also paralysed, could not even shuffle about at first.'

'When did this happen? I mean, was she on her own?'

'No. Mrs Steadman, her cleaning lady, was there. She came in every day except Sunday. She apparently heard a bump and found my mother lying on the floor. She'd fallen from her chair when she'd been watching television and knitting. Elsie – Mrs Steadman – phoned the doctor who lives less than a hundred yards away. He came round immediately, examined her and put her in hospital.'

The two now entered the small superstore.

'You push the trolley,' she ordered and drew out her list. For the next ten minutes she concentrated on her slip of paper and the shelves, barely speaking, except to complain than even in a minuscule place like this they regularly changed the goods about to make it difficult for shoppers. He wrote a cheque at the checkout counter.

'You shouldn't be paying,' she said. 'One or two of those things are private purchases.'

'You can visit me in the workhouse.'

'My father used to say that.'

'We're old-fashioned.'

She packed their bags and they marched off.

'Thank God it's mainly downhill,' he said.

'My mother, now,' she said. 'She spent some weeks in hospital before they sent her home. She was physically better. She could just about make her way around the house from one piece of furniture to the next. She arranged for Elsie Steadman to live in five days a week and a nurse called twice a day at the weekend. I didn't think she was fit to be on her own, but the doctor thought otherwise. I asked him if she understood where she was living and what she was capable of. "It's next to impossible, at least for us amateurs," he said, "to make out how her mind functions. One moment she repeats a question, sensible in itself, that you answered not two minutes before. And yet sometimes she has passages of common sense, so that someone coming in at that moment would think she was normal." '

'Was her speech clear?'

'I wouldn't say clear, but it improved during her stay in hospital.'

'But it soon deteriorated, didn't it? I was quite shocked, I remember, when I came down with Gill. She might have been speaking Hebrew for all I could understand of it.'

'Yes. Nor could she remember anything about the stroke or whatever it was. That part of her life seemed completely obliterated from her memory. But she was visibly getting worse; the doctor said so. That's why Gill and I went down together and spent some time with her, to see if anything could be done to make it possible for her to continue at home.'

'But it wasn't?'

'Absolutely not. We were all devastated at her state. I expect Gill told you. Elsie Steadman was a treasure. She's at least sixty-five, but fit and strong, and genuinely fond of my mother. When she became doubly incontinent Elsie would clean her up as if she were a baby. And she took such care. Mother was never to be uncomfortable. And she seemed to enjoy the job. I think she took pleasure living in my mother's big house rather than in her terraced cottage. I hope Ma has left her well provided for in her will, but I doubt it because Elsie came to her best when my mother was both physically and mentally feeble. She wouldn't know what a will was.'

'Did dementia run in your family?' he asked.

'Not that I know of. Why? Are you wondering what Gill's old age will be like?'

'There are years between us. I shall be off my trolley, or dead, well before she's ready for Alzheimer's.'

They arrived back red-faced and breathless. Gill was nowhere to be seen. They emptied their bags and put the food away. Rosemary seemed particularly good at deciding what went where in a strange house. When they had finished they made themselves cups of tea.

'I frighten myself to death thinking about old age,' Rosie said. 'My mother's case has been so quick and remorseless. She didn't deserve it.'

'That has nothing to do with it,' he said.

Suddenly Rosemary fell from her high stool. She had just put down her empty cup on the table and appeared to be sitting perfectly still, but this could not have been so. The rubber-capped feet of the stool scraped from under her as it toppled. She tumbled backwards. Her legs flew into the air as she fell. For a moment she lay spreadeagled with her eyes closed. She breathed heavily. Momentarily shaken, for he had been concentrating on his teacup when the stool went from under her, he rid himself clumsily of the tea and pushed up to his feet. As he moved towards her, she twisted the upper part of her torso as if she was trying to rise, but failing in this she sank back and groaned quietly.

He knelt by her, uncertain what to do next. 'Are you all right?' he asked, stupidly, he thought.

She gave no answer, but lay flat back, face pale.

He pushed himself upright, made for the sink, picked up a glass which he filled from the tap. He knelt by her again. 'Rosemary,' he said. She gave no answer. He repeated her name fruitlessly. He stared at her colourless cheeks, her closed lips. Again he said her name. Nothing. Somehow he gently pushed his right arm under her shoulders and lifted her up to lean on him. Her head lolled; he raised the glass to her lips.

'Have a sip,' he commanded the dead face. 'Try a drink.'

She opened her eyes, but the expression on her features was

one of bewilderment, of amaurosis. She took in a snatch of breath and sipped at the water. Now she slightly moved her head, as if her sight had been suddenly restored and she was trying to understand what she saw.

'Another sip,' he said. She readjusted her head to drink, succeeded to such an extent that she began to cough. He held her tighter.

'Oh dear,' she said. He unfolded an unused handkerchief from his pocket. She took it to wipe her lips. Now she looked down as if embarrassed or ashamed of her coughing fit. He waited.

'Are you hurt?' he asked.

She considered this, looked herself over, pulled down her skirt. 'I'm not decent,' she said and tried to smile.

'Do you think you could stand? With a bit of help.'

'I think so.' Her voice was still feeble, lifeless.

'Don't rush. I'll get up, but first of all we'll prop you on that cupboard.' He paused but she did not answer. 'If it hurts when I move you, shout. I don't want to aggravate any injuries. Just keep still until I get myself up and on my feet.' Her head drooped sideways, her chin on her chest. 'When you're ready I'll lift you and we'll make for that chair by the table.' He pointed towards it. He picked up the glass and handed it to her. 'Wet your lips again, while I get the chair into a better position to hold you.' He did this slowly, very deliberately, to give her time to reconsider her position. He courteously took the glass from her.

'The big moment,' he said. He put his arms under hers and lifted her. She leaned hard on him as he drew her up. He felt the softness of her breasts. She must have been stiffening her legs, if only a little, for she came up swiftly, easily, almost catching him out. They staggered the two steps towards the cupboard, where she supported herself with his help.

'Good,' he said. 'There's no great hurry. Try another sip. Can you move your arms? Separately.' She made the required movements. 'Now your legs.' Again she experimented. 'Can you feel any pain?'

She moaned slightly. 'I must be bruised,' she murmured.

'Can you stand without supporting yourself?' he asked. Again she tried, and succeeded. 'We'll get you over to that chair by the table. That will give you time to recover.'

They shuffled to the chair where she collapsed, resting on her arms.

'I'll get you a cup of tea,' he said. She did not answer but sat, pale as death, mouth slightly open. She kept her eyes closed. While he prepared the drink she remained silent.

He placed the mug in front of her. 'I've put sugar in it,' he said. 'I know you don't take it, but treat it as medicine. Sip away.'

He left her for a few moments and circled the kitchen. Outside the pathways seemed damp in the cloudy light. The morning had begun bright, with frost and sunlight, but now the weather matched his low spirits. He took a turn along the corridor and again gloomed out of a small window. The woodwork of the house and doors creaked and he cursed. Now he made for the kitchen and his sister-in-law. As he stepped beyond the threshold he saw that she had barely moved. She had, he noticed with pleasure, taken perhaps an inch of the contents of the teacup.

'How are we?' he called.

'Fine, thank you.' She half lifted her head.

'Good. Have another sip of the tea, and then we'll see what we can do about moving you out to somewhere more comfortable.'

'I shall be all right.'

'Are you in pain?'

'Yes. In a way, but I don't think it's too bad. I expect I'm bruised, but perhaps a hot bath will set me right.'

'I've heard, or read, though I don't know how much of it is true, that the reason why a doctor or a physiotherapist always accompanies a footballer who's been injured off the pitch is to stop him getting into a hot bath and doing himself a great deal of harm.'

'You needn't accompany me,' she answered, the first sign of her old spirits. She sipped again at the tea. 'I hate this sweet taste.' She looked up at him, twinkling. 'It's doing me good.'

At this moment the door was opened and Gillian came in, wearing her outdoor clothes.

'Where have you been?' he asked brusquely.

'Ten minutes tidying up a couple of shrubs at the far end of the garden.'

'Rosie's had a fall.'

'Outside? I said you should take the car. It's stupid to have to carry all that stuff back when it only meant a five-minute drive.'

'It was in here,' he corrected her. 'Rosie fell from the stool.' He pointed at the offending object.

'How did that happen?'

Neither answered her.

'Were you fooling about?' Gillian's voice was edgy.

'Don't be ridiculous,' Frank answered. 'We'd put the groceries away and we were drinking a cup of tea.'

'That stool looks pretty stable,' Gillian said. 'What happened, Rosie?'

'I tried to move it back just a little, and somehow the stool went from under me and I fell off backwards.'

'Are you all right? Have you hurt yourself?'

'I'm bruised, I think.' Rosemary reached for the healing cup. 'And shocked. It happened so suddenly.'

Gillian looked about her. 'That's not very comfortable. Would you like to lie down? In the parlour? Or on your bed if we can get you up there?'

'Perhaps.' She looked up helplessly.

'Right. Let's see if you can stand up.' Rosie worked her chair back and, hands down on the table, pushed herself upright.

Gillian came across at speed.

'Frank, get that tartan blanket out of the ottoman in our bedroom. Away you go.' She sounded impatient. He obeyed. Gillian took Rosemary by the left arm; they swayed as they reached the door. 'Steady now. Don't rush. Short steps and lean on me.'

'I'll push you over,' Rosemary protested.

'Get away with you.' A few more hobbling steps before the next rest. 'Does it hurt?'

'Not much. Not specifically. I ache all over and feel so weak. The stool just seemed to slip from under me. And there I was, flat on my back with my legs up in the air.'

'Did you bang your head?'

'No. I don't think so. I went over backwards and I felt the jar right up my spine. For a minute I thought I'd done myself some real damage.'

'But you don't think so now?'

'No. I hope not.'

71

They negotiated the parlour door, made gingerly for the sofa where Rosemary, under instruction, laid herself down. Though the room was warm from the radiators, Gillian turned on the electric fire standing in the hearth. They smelt the burning dust.

'Where has he got to?' Gillian asked. 'I send him up for a blanket. I could have knitted one quicker. Typical of a man. Only half listens. Let's have your shoes off. Are your slippers downstairs? Yes? I'll get them. Here's the blanket.'

Frank had come in, stood staring.

'Nip along to the kitchen and get Rosie's slippers. They have red bows.' He did as he was told. When he returned, Gillian pulled on the slippers, rearranged the cushions and tucked her sister in with the blanket.

'That's better. Give us a shout if you want anything.'

She and Frank left the room, walked the corridor in silence, but on the closure of the kitchen door she walked swiftly over to the stool, shifted it with an ill-tempered movement or two, tested its stability and wheeled to face her husband. 'How did it happen?' she asked.

'No idea. I wasn't watching or saying anything. She suddenly went backward. I didn't see the fall and it wasn't until I heard her hit the deck that I noticed. Her legs were up in the air.'

'Oh, yes?'

'Oh, yes, what?'

'And what next?'

'She lay there with her eyes shut. On her back. She seemed to have knocked herself out. I thought perhaps she'd cracked her head on the table or the floor.'

'But she hadn't?'

'So it would appear. I fetched her a drink and helped her sit up, and then got her over to the table. By that time she seemed more like herself.'

'She wasn't showing off, was she?'

'In what way?'

'Well, falling off the stool for a start.'

'I didn't see her fall. I've told you that. And I could think of safer ways of falling off a stool than by going backwards.'

'Was it an accident?'

'I've no reason to think otherwise.'

'Did she play up much when she was on the floor?'

'No. I thought for a moment she was unconscious. Then that all the breath had been knocked out of her. She was shocked, quite badly. She hardly spoke. She'd be in pain.'

'What were you talking about on the road to and from the grocery store?'

'About her mother. And she asked questions about my father.'

'And did that', Gillian asked, 'in any way upset her?'

'Not noticeably. She was puzzled by the speed of your mother's decline. Are you trying to connect that in some way with her fall?'

'I wondered.'

'Was she, is she, very fond of your mother, her mother?'

'Not particularly. They didn't get on too well with each other when Rosie was at school. She was glad to get off to the university. My mother used to talk to me about her when she'd gone and she'd say that this was a fine chance for her, studying the law, but she didn't put it past her to spoil her opportunity. If she does well Uncle Philip will take her into his office. He's said as much. And he's not short of a penny or two.'

'But it wasn't Rosie, it was you who went into your uncle's firm?'

'Yes. She was bolshie. She was going to do it her way, without any help from relatives. I heard her use the word "nepotism" to my mother, who was very angry. "If help's there and is offered, and you go and turn your back on it you're a fool." But she did law at Newcastle, and after she'd got her degree she worked as an articled clerk in that city and stuck with the firm after she'd qualified. She was clever, was our Rosie, and got on well with men, as long as they didn't try anything on with her. Later she joined the family firm in their Beechnall office.'

'Did you and she get on?'

'On the whole. Especially when we were older and she didn't try the big-sister act on me. Not that she ever did all that often.'

'And recently? When you stayed down with your mother, the pair of you.'

'It upset us both. We agreed there was nothing for it except to put her into a nursing home where she had full-time care, but both of us had dealt with cases of ill-treatment of elderly people, so we wanted to be as careful as we could. And she didn't want to leave her home, as far as we could tell. Rosie was harder than I was. "She doesn't understand what's happening to her. It just upsets her that we are arguing about her. Look at the fuss she made the other day when we wanted her to wear her pearls instead of the glass string of beads she's apparently so fond of. You'd have thought we were murdering her. And I would have said that she was too gaga to notice if we put a string of carrots round her neck." '

'And what was the outcome?' His most professional voice.

'We left her to her beads. But we saw to it that somebody else was responsible for moving her. We stayed down there, and visited her for the first two days after she went in to make sure she was settled and being looked after. We were surprised how easily she seemed to take to the place. And she even made improvements in the first week or two. Then she began to lose touch with life. The change had stimulated her for a short time, but after that she sank into a sort of torpor. She hardly spoke, understood nothing and lost such physical strength as she had left.'

'Yes.'

'Rosie took it badly. She's the sort who'll keep her spirits up if there's anything she thinks she can do, but as soon as she realises she's helpless will drive herself mad with worry. That's why I wanted her to visit us here.'

'Hasn't she friends?'

'I should think so. She's a sociable being.'

'No young man in sight?'

'I don't think so. She'd had enough of marriage to Joe James.'

'Yes. Not a nice man.'

'A bastard.'

'Didn't she have any inkling of how he'd turn out?'

'I think she did. People warned her. But she thought she could master him. She couldn't.'

'Where is he now?'

'He's living and working as a barrister in Manchester. He'll make a living; he was good in court. It's just that he wasn't fit to live with.'

VIII

A week later Frank Montgomery was sitting in his office at the art college when Gervase Lunn telephoned. There had been a meeting that morning to discuss how next year's courses would be arranged when the college joined the university. Some sort of compromise had been reached. Satisfactory, according to both sides, it left Montgomery with the feeling that he had been stranded. The Vice-Chancellor, in the chair, had been, as usual, complimentary and friendly, but Frank was dissatisfied. At the preliminary meetings eighteen months before Frank had been sharp, arguing that on the whole art colleges and universities had radically different aims. When the two converged, as in the training of teachers, there might be sense in the writing of learned academic essays on the effect of Greek culture on Italian painters of the Renaissance, but the purpose of an art college was to encourage talented people to draw, paint, sculpt, design, not to write about these arts. This led to argument which Montgomery enjoyed, and during which he believed he more than held his own. Once this initial period of polemics was over, and it never quite was, he lost interest and rudely pointed out that they had more than discussed these differences in every meeting so far.

The Vice-Chancellor was an interesting man. A physicist by training, he dressed like a chairman of a company or a banker. He had been on the committee which had appointed Montgomery and had always been affable, if diffidently, to him, though Frank had put this down to the low status the V-C awarded to art.

Once or twice he asked questions. 'What would you do if you had a painter, let's say, of real genius who entered your college? Would your course help or hinder him?'

'Both, I expect.'

'Would you alter the course to suit his development?'

'If he was the genius you suggest then he'd alter what we

75

offered to suit himself. There'd be plenty of things, at least for a start, for him to pick up. But the chances of a real genius coming our way are small. He'd make his or her own way. We have to give three years' hard training to the people who have talent.'

'Are there many of them about?'

'Oh, yes. You must have come across plenty in your own subject. People who will add their modicum of knowledge. They're not likely to cause trouble. They'll work hard and do as they're told. They'll clear up corners of sciences, add to the beauty of our houses, leave the world more efficient than it was. Not by much, but that little is not to be ignored.'

'What proportion of your students are they?'

'How many firsts do you give in physics?'

'Varies. One in ten, some years.' The Vice-Chancellor did not often walk; he looked out of place swinging his arms in the sunshine. 'It's very rarely I talk about people. It's usually money that I have to worry about. Mark you, Montgomery, it's all I'm fit for these days.'

'Do you wish you'd stuck with pure physics? Research?'

'No. I did quite well in that line for a start, but I saw I was better suited to administration. I knew as soon as I was made professor in my early thirties. I knew I should make steady progress. I was V-C, not here, by the time I was forty. I was lucky. Opposition fell away. I appeared to have the qualities people wanted.'

'Luck plays a big part with genius.'

'Luck plays a big part, full stop. I shall be glad to have you at the university, Montgomery. You don't want my job for one thing.' He rubbed his fat, capable hands together as if in delight. 'I'll call in the physics labs while I'm over here.'

'Frighten 'em to death?'

'Not they. They headed our lists, both teaching and research, at the last assessment. They're pleased with themselves.'

'And Professor Christie and Sir Thomas Jordan have Nobel prizes. Luck, do you think?'

'If when I came here and was told that Christie would win the prize within five years, I wouldn't have picked him. Tom'd already done the work that was to win him the prize.'

'Didn't you know?'

'I knew what he'd done and I knew how good it was. But it has to get into the public eye. Christie was already FRS, but his collaborator at Cambridge knew his way about the publicity circuit. They, Christie and Rawlings, were lucky and received their prize early. Usually the committee leaves the scientific prizes until some years later when there has been time to adjudicate on the effects of the discovery. They have made mistakes, you know.'

'And Jordan?'

'A different kettle of fish, altogether.' He laughed, but said no more.

The Vice-Chancellor made his way into the physics block. Montgomery watched him, wondering if he was cheering himself, or if at any time earlier when he was a physicist proper he had hoped himself to be a Nobel Laureate.

Now, back in his own office, Frank Montgomery lifted the telephone. 'A Mr Gervase Lunn for you, sir,' one of his secretaries announced.

'Put him through.'

'This is Gervase Lunn.' The voice sounded tremulous.

'Yes. Montgomery here.'

'It's your father.' Lunn paused, hesitating, making small noises in his throat. 'He's had a fall.'

'When was that?'

'This morning about ten thirty.'

'Where?'

'At his home. He fell downstairs. Luckily his neighbour, Mrs Wynne, had just called in to see if there was anything he wanted from the supermarket. She phoned the ambulance and then me. I was about to go out. I'd already put my overcoat on. When the ambulance came I was able to go with him to the hospital.'

'Was he conscious?'

'Stunned, dazed, shocked. He tried to say something but I couldn't make out what it was.' Again Lunn murmured to himself, appearing to cast about for the next few words or a topic. 'They're keeping him in. I was expecting to be asked to drive in and fetch him back. But he's broken an arm and a leg. And has other minor injuries. They weren't too busy and they had a bed to spare.'

'Have you seen him since this report?'

'No. I wanted your advice. I've tried twice to ring you.'

77

'I've been over at the university at a meeting.'

'So your secretary said.'

'You could have left a message with her about my father's accident, or any other important matter.'

'I did think of it, but I decided it would be an invasion of your privacy. Your father was in good hands and I didn't know whether you'd want it spread all around the college that he had fallen down his stairs. There seemed no hurry. You could perhaps come down tomorrow; it's the weekend. I hope I did right.'

'Yes. Most thoughtful of you. Very many thanks.'

'I turned it over and over in my mind. Between the first call and the second. I wasn't sure what you'd want. People in the public eye often don't want their private troubles talked about by all and sundry.'

'Yes.'

'I could have left my phone number with your secretary and asked you to give me a ring. But I tried to put myself in your position. I would have been needlessly worried. There was no desperate hurry in this case; your father was being properly cared for. I guess you would have thought me unnecessarily panic-stricken. So.'

'Thank you, Gervase. You're very kind.'

'Oh, not at all. To tell you the truth I didn't know what to do for the best.'

'You did well. Could you give me the name of the hospital, and the ward, and I'll get in touch with them?' That took long enough for the man to sort out. 'Thank you. And your phone number, please?'

'Mrs Wynne and I both have keys. We'll look into the house to see all is well.'

Montgomery thanked Lunn again. It seemed that now responsibility had been shifted from him, the man wished to continue the conversation, to be thanked and praised. In the end Frank put the phone down. He then called his wife's office and she said, immediately, that she would accompany him.

'Shall we set off tonight?' Gillian asked.

'No. First thing tomorrow. It's only just over an hour's run. We'll start, but I must be back for Saturday night. The Duke has cleared the whole of Sunday for me to get on with the portrait. I reckon I'll have the features and hands done.'

78

'Your father might be very ill,' she said. 'Two fractures and the rest at his age.'

'That wasn't my impression.'

He spent the remainder of the afternoon in a foul temper, but apologised, as he left, to his office staff, blaming his father's accident.

His secretary changed her lugubrious face immediately and put her hand tenderly on his arm. 'I'm so sorry,' she said. 'I couldn't make out from the old gentleman who rang what had so upset him. He seemed all at sixes and sevens. Is he very ancient?'

'Sixties, but odd. His wife left him thirty years ago and he's been in chaos ever since. He's gay.'

The phrase cheered him; they parted smiling.

Next morning he and Gillian left at about ten o'clock. He had rung the hospital in Beechnall the evening before and they had given him a favourable report. The surgeon had decided it would be best to keep the old man in on account of his age. 'I'll pass your message on to Herbert,' the girl ended cheerily. 'He'll be pleased to see you, I'm sure.'

They found Herbert Montgomery sitting at the side of his bed, the broken arm and leg in plaster. He gruffly told them that they were looking after him well, that he could get about and that he could just about eat his food, though it was not exactly palatable. He was still in pain, he claimed, as he opened his pyjama jacket to show them his quite frightening bruises. No, he said wryly, he had not fallen the full length of the stairs, only a mere seven or eight steps. He gave them utterly clear-headed instructions about what necessities he wanted from home and where these were to be found. The doctors had left him with no idea when they'd send him out. The orthopaedic wards were moderately empty and they'd kept him in, but if a whole lot of accident victims flooded in this weekend, out he'd go. 'There are a great number of motor-cyclists, young people, dashing about the roads and landing their riders in the hospital.'

Soon after midday, lunch was served to the patients and Frank checked his father's lists, and the younger Montgomeries set off to retrieve the articles.

'If there's anything of interest you see lying about bring it along when you come back this afternoon.'

'Such as what?'

'The mail, for example. A book or two Gillian thinks I ought to read. Three quarters of the books in my house just stand on the shelves gathering dust. I never read them.'

The bungalow where his father lived was in surprisingly good order. Gillian had already queried how one could fall downstairs in a bungalow.

'It has a couple of bedrooms up in the roof. It's unexpectedly roomy. Four bedrooms. My mother always dreaded small houses. "When you come to your senses and get yourself a proper wife," she told me, "I'll be able to put you and your family up without trouble." "If that's the main consideration," I argued, "you should have stuck in your old place." "This is not out in the country. It's healthier. In a new suburb. I shall be able to send him away on walks to keep him fit." "Yes, and have no doctor within miles." '

The old man had been content and suited there even after his wife had died. He'd kept the place spick and span, so that they had no difficulty finding the possessions he wanted in the neatly kept drawers. Gillian remarked on the cleanliness of the windows.

'That's his pride and joy, to keep them clean.'

'He does them himself?'

'Yes. Inside.'

'It's a wonder he hasn't fallen before. He should get his cleaning woman to do them.'

'If he has to give up one of his jobs, he regards that as a defeat, a sign that he's getting old and useless. He's talking of going back to his old house. The tenants have just vacated the place. Then he'll feel he's capable.'

'He's ninety.'

Back at the hospital they found Herbert grateful. He congratulated them on the completion of their tasks. They'd followed his instructions to a 't' and he hadn't expected it. 'It's no use, these days, issuing instructions to people, I find. Either they can't read, or if they can they think I'm incapable of instructing them properly and pay no attention.'

They talked pleasantly. The father thought he would be able to manage on his own when he returned home. Mrs Wynne was efficient, provided one didn't want anything complicated out of her, but Gervase Lunn was just a fusspot. Sometimes he was interesting to talk to, but ask him to do anything and he panics.

'He got you into hospital.'

'Yes. I suppose he did.' Herbert looked at Gillian, then asked, 'You aren't thinking of coming back here tomorrow, are you?'

'No. Afraid we can't . . . Frank's giving the Duke's portrait the whole day tomorrow.'

'Is it nearly finished?'

'Pretty well advanced. I want to make a real start on the Duchess as soon as I can. I've done most of the preliminary work.'

'You weren't supposed to be there today, were you?' Herbert asked.

'No.'

'I'm glad. You're daft enough to give up a good working day. And painting's' – he now turned again to Gillian – 'what he does outstandingly well. Nothing should stand in the way of his brushes and canvas.' Herbert spoke loudly as if he wanted the rest of the ward to hear what he said. 'And how's the university? Have they swallowed you up yet?'

'That's cut and dried.'

'And do you call yourself professor yet?'

'When all the legalities are out of the way, and Parliament and the Queen approve.'

'When's that?'

'Ten months or so. The next academic year.'

'And you'll still be with them?'

'Other things being equal.'

'You lack fire, Frank.' The old man puckered his eyes.

'I'm sure. "Cool" is one of the highest adjectives of praise today.'

'There's no use in speaking sense to him, is there?' Herbert asked Gillian, who stared steadily at her father-in-law. 'Don't you find that?'

'Oh, I don't know. He quite often amazes me by how near to the truth he gets.'

The old man grinned. 'Well done,' he said. 'You stand up for him. Not that he needs it. You should bully him more.'

Herbert began on a meandering tale of how his wife used to hector him or trick him into doing what she wanted. 'She was very beautiful, you know. I was proud just to be seen next to her. I'll show you some of my photographs of her. Frank could perhaps use them some time.'

'Frank made a very good painting of her.'

'Yes, yes. He was only a youngster then. It was well done, I admit. It must be wonderful to have a gift like that. Most of us don't. I didn't, for certain. Do you know what I'm going to do when you've gone? That Sibelius CD you brought. I shall listen on my earphones to the Sibelius Fourth; I want to get to know it really well. He thought he was dying when he wrote that.'

'Of what?' Gillian asked.

'Throat cancer. Something of the sort.'

'Was he old?'

'No. Because the next symphony celebrates his fiftieth birthday. And he didn't write much after his sixtieth. It was always said that the manuscript of his eighth was about somewhere in his desk. They never found it.' He looked on the CD case. '1865–1957. Ninety-two. But he composed little or nothing for thirty years.'

'Perhaps he thought he'd said it all,' Gillian suggested.

'Some people blame strong drink,' the father offered.

'They can't in your case,' Frank said.

'No. I'd nothing of importance to say in the first instance. That was, is, the trouble.'

'Don't you believe it.' Gillian again hurrying in. 'We came across a man just a month or two ago who'd been taught by you. And he said how beautifully you read Shakespeare to them. If he'd learnt nothing else, it would have been worth attending school just for that.'

'And what was his name?'

Gillian looked over to her husband for information.

'Frederick Rowley. Sir Frederick Rowley now.'

'Rowley, Rowley,' the old man repeated. 'No. I don't remember him, neither the name nor the face. Not even the title.'

'He remembers you,' Gillian said. 'And you old schoolmasters shouldn't ever forget the effect you've had on some lives.'

'Effect, effect, e-bloody-ffect,' the father said, but wearily, before his face fell. 'I'm sorry,' he added, 'I shouldn't have said that.'

'Frank sometimes swears at me,' she said.

'It's not the swearing. You're doing your best to cheer me up and you get insulted for it.'

She took his hand and pressed it. He looked at the movement in surprise, as if it involved two other people.

'My wife would have made me pay for those remarks,' Herbert said. 'She'd a ruthless streak in her. She'd made me a bit careful what I said to her. She was like Frank.'

'Soft as butter,' the son answered.

'But thank you, Gillian. When you're gone I shall remember what you said with a certain amount of pleasure, as well as remorse at my graceless reception of it. When you're old and immobile and things are getting on top of you, occasionally something rallies, uplifts you. Does that sound pi to you? You're not too young to know what pi is, are you? The word's gone out of fashion. It's an abbreviation of pious, I guess, and it means sanctimonious, too religiose for the occasion. I'll tell you what came into my mind as I was talking to you just now. You don't object, do you?'

'No. Go on, please.'

'One day last week I was feeling very down. The weather was rotten, horribly damp and foggy. I could barely see the houses across the close, and no trees. We have quite a lot about. Our builders, or his architects, weren't vandals. They didn't chop trees down for the devilment of it, or to clear a few square yards so they could squeeze more houses in. Well, I couldn't see them, only the two silver birches in my garden from the kitchen window and the shrubs with their trunks and branches all slimy wet. Things were getting on top of me. I knew I shouldn't bother to go for a walk or do a few jobs out in the garden in such weather and, besides, I'd left this day to pay my bills. And I forgot where I'd put them down and couldn't find them when the moment came. So I went round the house swearing and kicking the furniture, and by the time I'd got at them, and my chequebook – I don't use credit cards – and the stamps and stationery and envelopes, I felt thoroughly useless and hopeless. I'd not done my usual morning chores. Everything piled up on top of me. If I as much as walked across the room, I cracked my knee on a table leg.'

The old man's face had grown animated. He must have been like this when he was a teacher, and knew he was coming to the

point and that his pupils were with him, had grasped where he
was leading them.

'I sat by the table, took out the first bill. They don't just send
you the bill these days. The envelope is chock full of offers or
brochures. And they seem to clutter my mind, baffle me in case
I'm missing something to my advantage. I spread them out, found
the bill, filled the cheque in, sealed the envelope and felt a bit
better that at least I'd made a start. And as I sat there I remembered these lines:

> St Agnes' Eve – Ah, bitter chill it was!
> The owl, for all his feathers was a-cold;
> The hare limp'd trembling through the frozen grass . . .

Now do you know the first thing that came into my head, perhaps
because I was feeling so off colour, was what a daft thing to say
about an owl, and then suddenly my mind changed gear, and I
was grateful that I could remember these lines, that Keats had
written them. I felt as I did as a sixteen-year-old and was reading
this for Higher School Certificate. And Keats was the greatest
poet there had ever been to me at that age. It's years since I read
"St Agnes", and I would have said I didn't clearly remember all
of it, only odd lines here and there, and an impression of marvellous words drawing the perfect picture.

> While he from forth the closet brought a heap
> Of candied apple, quince, and plum, and gourd,
> With jellies soother than the creamy curd
> And lucent syrops, tinct with cinnamon . . .'

Herbert Montgomery repeated the lines without embarrassment,
not over-emphasising but giving each word its due weight. His
eyes sparkled as he spoke another line: '"And the long carpets
rose along the gusty floor." It's a marvel, isn't it? Exactly right.
You can see and hear it. But what's even more wonderful is that
I, ninety years of age, should be rushed back seventy-four years
by these words and become momentarily not an inefficient, rheu-
matic old man, baffled by a few bills, but a schoolboy with the
whole world before him and an example of what might be possible,

if a young, ill, cockney doctor could compose poems that would not only last for years, but which would alter the lives, if only briefly, of other people, or of one man at least.'

They waited for him to continue but he stared ahead, stroking furiously at his white tubby chin. His silver hair retained its straight schoolboy parting.

'What difference did it make?' Frank asked cautiously.

'Only an hour or two, for a start,' his father answered, 'but it would have been miraculous if it had only been for five minutes. It made me into myself of seventy-four years ago. That's a hell of a time. Beyond the Bible's three score years and ten. When I speak of something that happened in politics, say, while I was at school, it's ancient history to most people alive today, even elderly folks. And yet a few words of Keats transformed me. I don't understand or deserve it, but it happened.'

'Did it help you fill in cheques more efficiently?' Frank asked.

'You're facetious. But yes, it did. Any lifting of the spirit at my age makes life that bit more negotiable.' He looked, almost imploringly, towards Gillian. 'I'm afraid', he said. 'I didn't . . . I haven't explained this very well to you, I'm a bit at the mercy of my words nowadays, can't remember them, but it happened, I assure you, and was so strong.'

'Yes,' Gillian said gently.

'What James Joyce called an epiphany.'

'Yes.'

'Do you ever feel like that?'

'Yes,' Gillian answered. 'I don't know if what I experience is as strong as what you have, but it's true that suddenly something quite ordinary becomes transfigured, transcended into something else that's magical, or which lifts your spirit.'

'That's exactly it,' the old man said, slapping his hands on the arms of his chair.

They talked on excitedly for a few minutes while Frank grew glummer. He hummed to himself, walked a few small steps, rattled the money in his trouser pocket, seemed in a hurry to be away. 'Let me know if there's anything I can do,' he said.

'I shall be home tomorrow. But thinking again of moving back to what really is my home.'

'Don't you be in too much of a hurry. It'll do you no good to get back home, wherever that is, all plastered up and then do yourself some more damage because you're not fit.'

'It's my arm and leg that are damaged, not my brain.'

Outside on the way to the car park Gillian said to her husband, 'He's a brave man. A good many people of his age would be shocked silly after a fall like that.' She thought about this. 'I don't know which is worse, to know the extent of your injuries or to be like my mother not knowing what's wrong with her at all.'

'No.' he said grimly. 'My father's always been a bit of a fool. Carry on regardless is no sort of way to behave. He'd never have a day off school even if he was dying.'

'I think people were like that in his generation. You felt your-self lucky to have a job at all, so you turned up for it whether you were fit or not.'

Once in the car and beginning their journey home she asked him, 'Was your father a strict disciplinarian as far as you were concerned?'

'Not really. Not unless I broke something he valued or some-thing of the sort and he lost his temper. I remember I was larking about with a golf-club in the garden shed and I knocked a favourite vase off his bench. He was supposed to be mending it. My mother had taken a little chip out of the rim and he said he could glue it back. I belted it with this club, a putter, I don't know where it came from because he never played, and he snatched it out of my hands and set about me with it.'

'Did he hit you with the head?'

'No. He walloped me with the handle. I howled so loud my mother came in.'

'How old were you?'

'Seven.' Frank laughed, but silently. 'I saw my mother standing at the door of the garden shed. She said, "That'll be enough." Which one of us she was talking to I don't know. He stopped beating me, and my mother brushed my coat down and said, "Don't make such a fuss" and sent me indoors. I went in and waited for her. What she said to my father I don't know. When she finally came back into the house she led me, none too gently, to the sink and washed my face, and read me a lecture. I knew, she said, that he was fond of that vase, that it had been a present from his mother and that I ought to have been more careful. She dried me up, gave me a biscuit and told me to keep out of his way.'

'Were you hurt?'

'Yes. To some extent. But by shock more than anything else. He usually didn't lose his temper, just ticked me off or bawled me out. I was much more likely to get a clout from my mother than from him.'

'And what happened?' Gillian enquired.

'And the consequence was,' he intoned, 'when he came in for lunch he was polite to me and pressed me to have second helpings. I could barely bring myself to answer him. Next day, by chance, I found the putter in two parts in the dustbin.'

'Did you hold it against him?'

'Not for long.'

'But you've not forgotten it? You've held it against him ever since?'

'No.' He drew out the vowel.

'And when you think about it now, who was right and who was wrong?'

'We were wrong all round. I was an only child and they spoilt me. The thrashing did me no great harm and taught me to respect other people's property. It was only later that I concluded she'd pitched into him when she'd sent me out of the way. My mother thought I was going to be somebody, different from other children, to be treated differently.'

'But you said she smacked you.'

'So she did. She lost her temper from time to time. I was no angel. But I guess that my father's attack on me with the golf-club made her afraid he'd do me some permanent damage.'

'Physical or psychological?'

'Don't know. I don't suppose she did.'

The pair were silent during the next few miles of their journey.

IX

As Christmas approached the weather grew colder, with frost each clear night and on one or two days snow showers. The college of art held exhibitions, one of which was featured on television. The head of the dress design department, inflated with pride, strutted about the place like a monarch. In an interview with *The Times* he claimed that the next 'world-class' designers would appear from the English provinces and instructed the *Guardian* that the effect of oriental ideas had changed the face of British haute couture.

Frank had now finished the Duke's portrait and had persuaded His Grace to open an exhibition of watercolours by senior students. The speech he made was short and distantly witty, and described to the undergraduates what it was like to be painted by their principal. 'It is a lesson I shall not forget,' the Duke pronounced, 'because, though I have been painted before, I was on the watch this time, but still could not account for the effect of apparently random dabs of paint which in themselves seemed nothing, but somehow enhanced the realism.' His wife, the Duchess, went in each day to inspect the completed painting and said that as the oils gradually dried, more and more of his character was revealed. 'I wanted', the Duke said, 'to be made to look young and handsome.' This proved impossible as he was neither. He asked his wife what she thought he looked like and she had said a well-to-do estate agent. She was now being painted, but he had not made up his mind who or what she resembled. He promised that both portraits would be put on exhibition at the college for a few days in the spring, if his wife gave permission – that is, was satisfied with her portrait.

Her Grace smiled and bought two watercolours, both outstandingly good in Frank's eyes; she congratulated him on the teaching of the difficult art and he introduced her to Graham Walker, the man who instructed in the subject. Unused to praise, the teacher flushed and writhed; when he spoke his voice was strangled. One

88

councillor, well known for throwing his weight about, asked Frank what the title of a small picture, *Aquarello*, meant.

'Watercolour,' he answered.

'What language is that?'

'English,' Frank said. 'From French or Italian. Originally from Latin.'

'Why give it a foreign bloody title when there's a perfectly good word in English?'

'It starts up interesting topics for conversation.' The councillor snarled his derision. 'Well,' Frank said, 'you've added a new word to your vocabulary.'

'One I could do without.'

'You must be the judge of that,' Frank answered politely.

The Duchess must have overheard this, for she whispered to Frank, 'Mr Montgomery, I think you're a mischief-maker.'

Frank on the whole enjoyed these public appearances, especially if they were short, which they normally were. The meals accompanying them were boringly longer, but he was usually seated next to someone worth talking to and the college kitchens provided excellent fare.

The brief appearances on television seemed to waste a great deal of time in preparation in multiple alteration of useless detail. One of the producers noticed his expression and asked, 'You think we overdo it here, but you should see them in film studios.'

'Is that so?'

'I wonder', the young man continued, 'if the subjects of your portraits don't think you play about too long with the paints on your palette before you put them on to the canvas. I know painting's different from photography; you can move more things about to suit yourself, as we can't. We have to shift them. A good picture is our sine qua non.'

'But your people can speak, put arguments, give us their ideas.'

'You'd be surprised how little that counts.'

'Expound.'

'These clips of ours will appear in local news programmes. And I'd guarantee that you'd be amazed how many people will be bursting to inform you that they'd seen you on the telly, but they wouldn't be able to repeat to you even vaguely what it was you said. So we need to make the picture do for both seeing and hearing. I'll tell you what. We'll put you up with the Duke and Duchess, and you can tell us – I'm giving you time to think about it – what you set out to do and how far you succeeded with the portraits.'

'You'll have to get their permission first.'

'I've begun to soften her up. They like their touch of genteel publicity.' The producer, if that was his title, suddenly looked up at Frank. 'They say you're the best portrait painter in England, so I shall be doing my bit for posterity by having you talk about your picture. Think what it would be like to have a film of Rembrandt talking about his work.'

'If you'd been around you'd have been interviewing some fashionable young man rather than the old master.'

'Such as who?'

'I can't name him. His name, in any case, will not be familiar to either of us. There were plenty of painters about.'

'I'm going to think hard. There's an interesting half-hour to be made out of this. What d'you say?'

'I agree, but you will have forgotten about it inside a week. And if you remember your masters will veto it on the grounds that they haven't the money to throw away on a feature nobody wants to watch.'

'We shall see,' the young man said portentously.

Over in Beechnall Frank's father had spent three more days in hospital before they let him free. He'd learnt to get about and manage things 'half one-handed'. He did not find this easy, and seemed disappointed in himself. Gillian visited him each Saturday, taking with her sandwiches and a large cake. 'He can provide his Earl Grey,' she said.

Though the old man complained, he set his face steadfastly against Frank's coming over. 'He's plenty to do with those portraits. I don't want him here making trivial conversation to me when both of us know we'll be worrying about paintings. Besides,' Herbert rallied his social skills, 'I prefer having you here on your own.'

'Thank you,' she said, 'kind sir.'

'Aren't you busy in your office?' he asked her.

'Run off my feet. I shall be taking over as principal next summer when my uncle retires.'

'Doesn't that mean you just sit back and watch the others do the work?'

'It does not. We've no end of tricky business on hand. People are using their solicitors more these days.'

'They've all grown suspicious? Or merely litigious?'

'That's about it. And more money, some of them, to throw in my direction. We have to make some of our appointments at eight in the morning, because people can't get in during their working hours. You'd be surprised how many.'

'Why's that?'

'I suppose they think they can't afford the time off. Or their bosses won't give it to them. And with more and more women working, you'd have thought they would have taken an hour off if the trouble was serious, but they want to keep their cake and eat it. I don't understand it, but we have to fit in with it.'

Herbert laughed. He appreciated his daughter-in-law's attempts to keep him in touch with the wide world outside his bungalow.

'And we've a big murder case coming before the Court of Appeal.'

'Is that particularly interesting?'

'As a slice of life, very much so. As a piece of legal work, pretty well cut and dried.'

'Will you win?'

'We expect so. It's not always exactly a matter of law.'

'And does a big case like that bring you kudos or more work?'

'It gets you known. The QC is a bright boy and he seems pleased with us. He's doing a case in the House of Lords and he says he wishes his solicitors there were as careful and sensible as I was.'

'Good.' The old man enjoyed this. 'Are there any other snags?'

'In the office, you mean? Well, we've taken on a new girl and she needs quite a bit of looking after.'

'Is she a fully qualified solicitor?'

'She's passed all her exams. But she's rather nervous. Won't trust her own judgement yet. She's careful and quite clever, and very industrious. In my view she'll be a first-rate lawyer in two or three years' time, when she's had more experience as to how matters work out in the courts and elsewhere. She knows more about pure law, if I can call it that, than I do. She remembers all sorts of out-of-the-way judgements that most of us have neither seen nor heard of. She'll be good. Once she's done a year or two with us at the dull sorting-out that we beaver at all day, I'm going to suggest that she does a Master's in law part-time. I know the professor and I'm sure he'll take her on. But I'll get her boots dirty in our everyday mud before she flies on angel's wings.'

'Will she be any good to your firm once she has done this extra study?'

'You can't know too much or be too clever, but I see what you mean. It will depend on personal circumstances. Most likely she'll want to go and join some very large group where she will be able to specialise.'

'Is she married?'

'She'll marry next summer.'

'What's her husband?'

'He's a teacher, a historian. I don't know how long he'll stay at it. He's ambitious and he's already doing research. He's nice. There they are with their first-class honours, both of them, and when they're together they're like a pair of schoolchildren. They walk on air.'

'Clever people are not always sensible.'

'I agree.'

'Witness your husband.'

'Tut, tut, tut.'

Frank received a short note from Fiona Heatherington. He had not heard from her since that afternoon in Wales in the summer and, to speak the truth, had not expected to. She had almost finished her first term at university and had learnt a great deal. Some of the classes were dull, but the man lecturing on the history of art was very bright. 'We're doing the Renascence,' she wrote, 'and that's how he spells it. He spends all his summers in Italy and his wife is Italian. His children are trilingual, Welsh, Italian and English.' She had taken the sketch of herself which he had done for her, now properly framed, and showed it about. One of the staff had recognised the signature. 'I became quite a talking point. They all wanted to know how well I knew you, and how long, and all the rest of it. And then how many hours had it taken you to do it? They hardly believed me when I told them.'

The professor and head of department had condescended one

day to stop and speak to her in the corridor. She had been invited to his room to show her treasure.

'I have met Montgomery,' he said. 'He's at, or under the aegis of, the University of Sheffield. A brilliant man, but I thought he painted only the aristocracy.' I told him that wasn't me. He asked where we had met. When I described to him how quickly you had knocked off that sketch, he was amazed, but said in these days of photography catching a likeness wasn't of supreme importance and had I noticed how often the camera seems to lie. 'I don't mean when the photographer does it deliberately, but when somebody takes a clear photograph of someone you know well, and you look at it and yet don't recognise the person.'

'Why is that?' I asked him.

'Hello, a philosopher,' he said, but he had a go at saying that we, unconsciously, set up ways of recognising people, and if these don't appear, then we're puzzled. He was quite interesting. Then he asked me if I kept in touch with you and when I said 'No', he said it was a pity.

That's why I'm being impudent and writing to you. I've never met anybody famous before. You didn't seem so to me. Just a marvellous draughtsman. At least, I recognised that. I delayed writing to you until the Christmas break and I read just a day or two before I started this that Thomas Hardy (we read *Tess of the D'Urbervilles* for A level) kept a whole room full of his books which people had sent to him for signature and which he wouldn't either sign or even pick up and return to them, because his time was too valuable. Anyhow, I've written my letter now. And to think I asked you to dry my feet. Oh, dear. Forgive me.

Yours sincerely,
Fiona

Frank smiled as he read this, picked up a postcard and thanked her. With his pen he sketched in a few deft strokes the outline of a man squatting in front of her, drying a foot. He initialled this, put it in an envelope and asked Gillian to post it the next time she went out.

'And who's Miss Heatherington?'

He briefly gave her the story and handed over Fiona's letter, which she read with a straight face. 'How old is she?'

'Eighteen, nineteen.'

'She sounds bright. Is she Welsh?'

'Her father didn't appear so. Nor she.'

'And what's this feet-washing business?'

'She had a paddle. Said she used to like her father to dry her feet for her, because he really did get rid of the sand between her toes.'

'You do some curious things.'

'Agreed. But she'd sought me out; she thought I was good at painting.'

'If she'd been an ugly, middle-aged, WEA class painter?'

'I probably wouldn't have sketched her.'

Gilian went about her expedition, the letter-card on the top of one of her bags. She wouldn't forget it; she was well organised. He wished he knew what she thought of his dealings with the girl. Not that he felt guilty, though it was true that they had exchanged kisses.

He met Fiona two days later. Her department had arranged a bus trip to see the two exhibitions in Sheffield. She had enquired if the principal was in that day and he had invited her up to his office. She sat with her cup of coffee very nervously answering his questions.

'We do visit other departments. Yes. Mostly to London. But this college has had a good lot of publicity in the newspapers and on the television. Most of the people here today are dress designers and the lecturer who organised the trip used to teach here. John McGeachie.'

'Yes, I know him.' Frank tapped at his teeth. 'What did you think of our exhibitions?'

'You've really dazzled our designers. I was more interested in the watercolours.'

'And what did you decide about that?'

'They're very good. I walked round with Helen Freeman who teaches us, and she was impressed and she takes some pleasing.

94

"They're talented and well taught," she decided. Do you teach them?'

'Very little. I do take the odd class.'

'Do your ideas clash with the teacher's?'

'I expect so.'

'Does it matter?'

'No, the man who teaches watercolour painting here gives them a sound basic training: where to put the picture on the paper, how to use paint, to mix it, to be realistic or non-realistic, to make combinations of shapes and colours, all the things they've already taught you. Our man is good, strict but encouraging. He's a very good painter himself and that helps. They try his ideas, but if they decided to disregard him and experiment then they have to be prepared to defend what they're doing. When I make one of my infrequent excursions into the classroom, and that's after they've had a thorough drilling in his principles, it doesn't much matter what I say. In any case I'm not likely to contradict him. They think sometimes that I am doing so, but that's because they haven't grasped Graham's basics.'

' "There's a wideness in God's mercy," ' she quoted confidently, surprising him.

'I beg your pardon.'

'It's a hymn we used to sing at school.'

He harrumphed and nodded, acknowledging her momentary superiority, then said he must now turn her out. 'I've letters to check and sign, and in half an hour I'm due at a meeting down in the city. That's the drawback with being an administrator. I'm always off somewhere else at a meeting. I'm going today to help appoint a professor of physics.'

'Do you know anything about physics?'

'No more than you.'

They shook hands and she left. She'd been in his office no more than fifteen minutes. His secretary appeared with a handful of letters for signature. He read each, signed it, said he might be back by four thirty, instructed her to close the office if he hadn't shown up and to leave important messages (she was to interpret that widely) on his answerphone at home if he wasn't back before she left.

'We're appointing a new professor. That makes some of them argumentative.'

95

She laughed. 'That was a pretty young lady,' she said gently. He continued reading and signing. She inserted the letters into their envelopes.

When both had finished, he said, 'Yes, she is.'

'She was very self-confident. In a quiet way. She came into my office and asked if it would be possible to see you for just a few minutes. I said you were busy and asked her if it was important. She looked at me as if I was something the cat had brought in and said, "Yes, it is for me." '

'I met her on holiday.'

'Is she applying for a place here?'

'No. She's at Cardiff. She's here with that party looking round the exhibitions.'

'Were you pleased to see her?'

'Not particularly.'

'Well, she'll be better looking than these professors of physics you'll be interviewing.'

'You'll be delighted to know that one of the candidates is a woman.'

'Any good?'

'As well qualified as the rest. On paper. None of them is any good, really, or they wouldn't be applying for this job. This is a dead end. He or she won't go any further. They'll draw a professor's pay, but they'll end their life here, unless they come up with some piece of research that gets their name known, and judging from their curricula vitae that's not likely.'

'You sound cynical today. How will you decide?'

'I shan't. The Vice-Chancellor will. And the likes of me will ask a few awkward questions, just to give the appearance that we're alive and kicking and not to be tricked. The other members of the panel are mostly scientists.'

He went out, washed his hands, combed his hair, put scarf and coat on, and was surprised to see Mrs Salcombe still there on his return. His face demanded a reason for her delay. She did not speak.

'Are you all right?' he asked.

'Charles has cancer.' Her husband's brother. 'The doctor told him yesterday.'

'Can they do anything for him?'

'They're going to start chemotherapy. Next week.' She gathered the envelopes, straightening the pile.

He approached her, rested a hand on her shoulder, having no idea what to say. 'Does he feel ill?'

'Yes. He has done for a month or two; there's pain. This is what he feared.'

'They're getting on top of cancer these days.'

'People still die.'

Charles Salcombe would be in his early fifties, a decent man, worked in the City Treasurer's Department and lived next door to his brother.

'Let me know if there's anything I can do.'

'Thank you. Yes. It's not the sort of Christmas present he'd want.'

'Still, he's had the sense to go to see a doctor. He hasn't kept it to himself. A good many do.'

'He's a sensible man. And a good man. Goes out of his way to do anybody a good turn.'

'Yes.'

'He's the last person you'd want to see this happen to.' She tapped her wristwatch. 'You'll be late,' she said in a different voice.

He touched her upper arm again and made for the door. Outside in the corridor he passed two typists, wished them good afternoon and found his left shoelace undone. The girls turned into their room and, as he bent over his shoe, he heard one say, 'Monty's got his glad rags on this morning. Where's he going?'

'Some sort of interview at the old Poly. Jean said he'd be out most of the day.' Jean was Mrs Salcombe.

'I wouldn't mind going out like that now and again. Nice change and they feed you up, as well, on glasses of wine.'

'Ah, but you don't know anything.'

'You speak for your bloody self.'

The door closed. He grinned and set off on a twenty-minute walk.

He arrived home that night at about six thirty. He had been back in his office before Mrs Salcombe left. There had been little argument about the appointment. They chose the youngest of the candidates, chiefly because the Vice-Chancellor wanted him. 'He's the only one who seems engaged on anything like real research,' the V-C had told him in confidence before the interview, in the urinal. 'Might come to something.' The young man had spoken well for himself, politely refused to be bullied, said he was up for another chair the day after next. There was hardly any disagreement, and when Frank asked his fellows to list the points against the man the question fell flat. When the Registrar asked, 'You presumably have some matters you'd hold against Dr Lowe?' Frank shook his head. 'Are you suggesting', the Registrar pursued his devil's advocacy, 'that we have deliberately drawn up a short list with only one candidate there worth considering?'

'No,' Frank answered. 'I was mischief-making. I just didn't like to see such unanimity among us.'

'Are you perhaps hinting', the V-C, a man Frank hardly knew, now entered the lists, 'that we have chosen the wrong man?'

'No,' Frank answered, 'I was merely demonstrating my ignorance. Lowe's research to my untrained mind seemed no better or worse than that of the rest.'

'Yes,' said the Vice-Chancellor, politely, deliberately, obtuse, 'I'd agree nobody knows what will ultimately happen to a research project in anything much larger than Ph.D. size. We have to follow what they call these days "gut instinct". In a few years, if you are still about here, you may be able to chide us if nothing much has come of his work and we shall remember that you warned us against it, if gently. But, I warn you, we shan't feel grateful to you.' The rest of the table tittered. This passed as wit in these circles. 'Has Principal Montgomery sown any doubts in your breasts?' His eyes unfortunately seemed to fasten on the large and untidy bosom of the sole woman on the board, a political nominee. Frank wondered if this was by chance. The Vice-Chancellor, knowing that he had won his way, generously proposed to take the vote again. The result was as before, 12–0, with no abstentions.

'You enjoyed yourself,' the Professor of Inorganic Chemistry said to Frank on the way out.

'I didn't think so.' The reply was almost boorish.

The Vice-Chancellor made a point of coming across specially to thank him. 'You keep us up to the mark. It is always as well to have an outsider with us, someone with an insight into character, into the humanity, if I dare use the word, of the candidate.'

'You're appointing a scientist not a saint.' He'd had enough of academic good manners.

'I see what you mean. What we can get, at best, is a man who will build up a department that gets us a good name for research, attracts and then looks after students, both under and postgraduate. I sometimes suspect that other heads of department choose a mediocrity so that their efforts will not appear in too bad a light when they're compared, as they will be, with the new man.'

'Oh, dear.'

'It used to worry me at first because it seemed impossible to handle properly. I think we did the right thing this morning since an old colleague of mine was Lowe's referee. He knew I'd be on the qui vive, and there they were, all the aspects I'd be on the lookout for duly mentioned. Ah, Mr Montgomery, I know what you're going to say.'

'Is this ex-colleague a vice-chancellor?'

'No. He was head of a large physics department, but left to work in industry. He's at Cambridge now, enjoying himself rather than making money.' The V-C shook his hand. 'Thanks very much. I'm always glad when you're present on these occasions.'

Frank could not deny his flush of pleasure. The V-C was a cunning devil, he knew, who would tell people, if it didn't interfere with his own designs, what they wanted to hear.

Back in his office he sat and listened to Mrs Salcombe outline the phone calls they had received that afternoon. She seemed more cheerful, taking satisfaction from the acknowledgement that while she had been in charge, a position she enjoyed, she had managed it without egregious error.

'What are tonight's plans?' he asked as she left.

'We shall have to go in and sit with Charlie and his wife.'

'Yes. I suppose so. Is that hard work?'

'Not with him. He's cheerful enough, but his wife's the weepy sort.'

He nodded, uncertain what to say. 'What will you do? Just sit and talk?'

'Since he's been ill, we've taken to playing dominoes. It's a daft game, even fives and threes, but you can talk in between; there's no hurry the way we play it. It fills the time up. I'm surprised, really. We sometimes play Scrabble. They're religious,

99

both of them. I think she'd have us all on our knees praying, but Charlie knows that neither Cyril nor I are churchgoers, so he rarely mentions it. He likes his little jokes and quips. This last few months since he's been ill he's not been quite so cheerful, though you never hear him complain.'

She adjusted her top button and left. Through his windows he saw her walk out briskly to her car.

At home, over their light evening meal, Frank described his day's work.

'Not very creative,' his wife commented.

'No. And though I try to poke my oar in I'm not really qualified. Nor even gifted or interested. The only thing I can say in its favour is that it makes a change from the everlasting bits and pieces I'm grubbing over at the art college. That's dullness itself.'

'You should thank God you're not a solicitor. Dullness all day and every day.'

He described Fiona Heatherington's visit.

She seemed to have forgotten her and to be barely interested. 'Had she anything of interest to say?'

'Not really. She'd found out from her teachers who I was.'

'Is she talented?'

'I've no idea. I've not seen any of her work. She talks well. And her face is lively all the time, even when she's nervous. I should have done better to have taken my sketchbook out and had another shot or two at her face. It was young and innocent and secretive, but not in any bad sense. She was full of ideas and hopes and ambitions, but I didn't know what they were.'

'You ought to. You've been long enough with students.'

'I begin to think I've had just about my bellyful of students and their teachers.'

'Now you start to talk like your father. He thinks that all the new ideas and departments and disciplines you've introduced into your college aren't worth a half-page from your sketchbook.'

'That's not true. A day like today puts me where I belong, among the mediocrities.'

'Are you resigning, then?'

He drummed on the table with his right hand, violently. She watched him, with eyes scared and wide open.

X

For the first two days of Frank's Christmas break the Duchess arranged to give him a sitting or two. She had been loath to grant this 'favour'; as the house was still open, and they were desperately busy. He began painting from first arrival, about ten o'clock, when she had done her initial hour of office work. She kept a notebook by her side and every time he declared a break she stood up, took a few steps and wrote. Her energy was manifest each time she marched away from the podium.

'I can't afford to idle about,' she declared. 'I'll have to use this as thinking time.'

'You're one of the best sitters I've ever had. You really can sit still.'

'Can't Gerald?'

'Not really. He twitches.'

'Why is that?'

'I imagine he's slightly embarrassed by it all.'

'He's been painted before, you know.'

That put him in his place.

She smoothed her voice. 'Does the fact that I can sit still mean that the finished portrait will be all the better for it?'

'It should do, but I'm not sure. That depends on me. You make the whole thing easier for me, but painting pictures, as with any work of art, sometimes comes out better on account of obstacles.'

He did not allow her to look at the morning's work, but promised that she could examine the day's effort after the hour she promised him in the afternoon. On instruction she had dressed in the ball gown for the first session.

'You haven't painted any of it, have you?'

'No. But it affects the face, which I'm busy with.'

They made a curious couple, she in her magnificence, and he in his dirty painting smock and his spattered brown trilby.

She returned at half past two, absolutely punctual, and he worked furiously for just over the hour.

'May I inspect it now?'

'Yes.'

She came round. He had worked at tremendous speed. 'The likeness is there already,' she announced. 'That is if I really know what I look like.'

'Yes. Of course you do.'

'I often wonder how close to reality our pictures are.'

'I guess that a portrait done in Elizabeth the First's reign which would seem a really good likeness to contemporaries might well seem mannered or lifeless to us, and thus unlike the original.'

'So you can't win.' She whirled the hem of her gown imperiously as she moved towards the door, but stopped again. 'My favourite is Holbein,' she announced. 'We have two. I look at them most days.'

'And what is it that makes them so pleasurable to you?'

'They look like human beings. In spite of the clothes, and hats, and the background.'

She marched away and he continued to paint. He thought deeply. She was not a tall woman, but she had remained slim. He guessed that she'd be one of those rare creatures who could still at sixty wear their wedding dresses. Clearly she expected her orders to be carried out exactly. The set of her shapely shoulders and breasts spoke power. He had no idea who she had been before she married. It did not much matter. Duke's daughter or dustman's, she carried her rank now to perfection. Her voice, her accent, placed her. There was nothing of the modern plebeian about her. Her whispers carried weight.

Looking at the painted face on his canvas, he wondered if he admired her. He ought not to be impressed. He'd come to like the Duke as a human being, capable of error, carrying out his duties, though occasionally stumbling; in spite of good bearing, his voice lacked authority; his position had not left him quite sure of himself. She was almost violent with energy under her quiet appearance, her still form under his painter's eye. There was nothing of Shelley's Ozymandias's 'frown and wrinkled lip and sneer of cold command' – he'd learnt that by heart at school – about her. Her expression was pleasant at most times, but calm, because she knew what she wanted, and why, and how to achieve it. She did not look her age; she laughed easily, if curtly, a handsome woman, though one would hardly use that word for one so slim and lacking in height.

Carefully, as always, he covered up his palette, paints, cleaned his brushes so that he could begin work without trouble next morning. He stared at length at her face on the canvas and was satisfied, even as he saw the possibility of adding improving touches which he would not make until his model sat in front of him again. He hung his smock and hat on a hook; at home in his studio he would have shaken them out and dropped them to the floor. Here, he supposed, had he followed his usual untidy custom a servant would have appeared, picked them up and hung them in place. He had asked Her Grace to have the room locked. He did not want people poking around, stirring up dust, tidying rags, shifting paints about, straightening bottles, emptying jars. His day's work had satisfied him. Now, in the north-facing room, darkness was almost on him; he could barely make out what he had done. He tiptoed down the stairs and out by a back door. He climbed into his car, chose B roads for his return.

At home, singing to himself, he began to prepare an evening meal: cottage pie that needed only warming, more potatoes, frozen runner beans, gravy. He searched around for dried fruit and prepared custard. Uncertain of how he'd manage if Gillian came home late, he was relieved to hear her car outside just as the potatoes tested to perfection. 'Hello,' he called out. 'We'll be ready in five minutes.'

'Goodness. Are you cooking? Oh, great. I've been busy and only had dry biscuits and cheese spread at lunchtime.' She sniffed the rich air, opened the oven door. 'You found the cottage pie. Well done.'

'I'm just keeping my eye in,' he said. 'The Duchess and I have been in close communion most of the day. And now I'm back among the plebs.'

'"Or walk with kings, nor lose the common touch".'

'I don't know if that's quite what a painter needs.'

'I can see you had a good day. What's she like?' Gillian asked.

'Used to her own way. But can sit very still. That means, of course, that I have to provide any signs of life.'

'Where do you get them from?'

'The intervals. When I'm giving her a break. Then she comes alive. She's not very tall; you could give her an inch or two, but dynamite.'

'She flares up, you mean? Explodes?'

'No. Shows that there's tremendous power about.'

'Was she nobility? Before she married?'

'Yes. She was brought up to the large country house, park, servants and all the rest.' He rubbed his chin. He had just looked her up. 'The Earl of Ludgrove's daughter. She's artistic, paints a bit herself. She's decorated one of the bedrooms with a mural. I found this out only recently.'

'She showed you, did she?'

'No. The Duke took me up to see it. He seemed proud enough of it.'

'Was it any good?'

'Not bad. Amateurish. She'd profit from a few drawing lessons.'

'Did you say so?'

'I did not. The original sketch, which she'd squared up and then transferred to the wall, I thought very attractive. I'd have been inclined, if she'd been a nobody applying for a place at the college, to have offered her one if that was her usual standard.'

'Did she ask questions of you as you were working?'

'Not really. She can't see what I'm doing.'

'Do you talk at all? While you're painting?'

'Yes. The usual English topic. Weather, the garden. Price of petrol. That sort of thing.' He smiled. 'She's used to making small talk.'

'And how's the painting going?'

'Fast. Really fast. Two or three weeks will suffice. I find I'm painting in a lighter way, less paint, than with her husband's.'

'Deliberately?'

'Partly. I'm not sure. I keep comparing the two paintings. His is still in the same room. We call it "the studio" now. Drying out.'

'And how do you like full-time painting?'

'Great. What I was trained for. Which reminds me, I must finish that head and shoulders of you this holiday.'

'I'm not like you, with a great long holiday. I only get Christmas Eve to New Year's Day.'

'More than a week.'

'We're visiting your father and my mother. I phoned your pa again but he won't consider coming up here. "I've got a system," he said. "And I don't want to spoil Gervase Lunn's festive goings-on." '

'That won't take much doing.'

'No, but he's got a lady.'

'Who, Gervase? I don't believe it. He's bent as a corkscrew.'

'No, your father. She's some sort of voluntary worker for a society befriending old people.'

'He's not mentioned it to me.'

'No?' Gillian was all sweetness. 'He's afraid you'll tell him not to make a fool of himself.'

'No. Any more talk of his moving back?'

'You should go and make an oil sketch of him.'

'When you're hard at the grindstone. But he's a fidget. He can't sit still. I'd have thought he was always dropping off to sleep, whenever we're with him.'

'It's the nature of our conversation.'

In the next two days he made great progress with the Duchess's portrait, taking his wife with him to comment.

'Does he always ask your advice?' the Duchess asked Gillian.

'Always? Almost never.'

'Then why are you here?' The Duchess's benign delivery excluded rudeness.

'I think it must be to meet you. He's obsessional and while he's painting you he's obsessed with getting you right. I think he trusts himself as far as the painting side goes, but he thinks he might have missed something of you in the laborious process of putting paint on canvas. So he gets a boring lawyer, one as far from the artistic eye or temperament as he can, to come and look. And he hopes if he's missed something I shall spot it, if only by chance, and point it out.'

'I can see you're a clever girl. I never thought of painting in that sense.'

'Nor does he. I don't for a moment imagine that he reasons it out. He lets ideas flash through his brain and hopes that he can somehow transform them into a full work of art. He's always had the knack of catching a likeness, but that's not everything.' Gillian laughed as if suddenly seeing the ridiculous nature of her own reasoning.

'I don't know that I quite follow you.'

'I'm not surprised. I'm not explaining it very well. In fact, I'm not sure that I understand myself what I'm trying to say. I'll put it in baby language. Painting a portrait is a lot more complicated than observing the sitter and then trying to imitate what your eyes see.'

'That's difficult enough as it is.'

'Yes. It is. But . . .' Gillian left it to her interlocutor, interlocutrix, she thought pedantically and grinned. The Duchess would think she kept herself well supplied with amusing tags which raised grins and baffled the people to whom she spoke.

'Is being a solicitor what you'd call a philosophical occupation?'

'Depends. On the whole it's rather dull. You need to know the law and to understand the language of the documents you're studying. That needs care and knowledge. I suppose to think historically how the law in our society came to be as it is could be philosophical as well as ethical or sociological. And then, if you're like me, you ask yourself, when some client's outlining what wrong his neighbour has done to him, whether pursuing the case, even successfully, will not so stress the man that he'd do better to go home or to the pub and forget all about the wrong that's been done him.'

'Does that happen often?'

'More often than you think. The best way to stop people from going to the courts is to lay out the costs. Money's important to most people.'

'And they withdraw?'

'We fall back on the solicitor's letter. I explain politely to the neighbour or wrongdoer where he's infringing the laws or by-laws, and why my client objects.'

'That sounds like a matter of psychology. Or common sense.'

'Right. The laws are drawn up to help us to live peaceably together, not to grab our swords or guns every time someone tries to take advantage of us.'

'Isn't going to law a long-drawn-out and expensive job?'

'It can be. Things like the small-claims court can speed us up in minor matters. But you must have read in the papers about neighbours pretty well ruining themselves over the height of a hedge.'

'Doesn't that say more about the people concerned than about the law?'

'I'm sure that's so.'

They noticed Frank standing watching them, listening, dressed in his paint-splashed smock and hat.

'I am ready when you are, Your Grace,' he said. Her lips curled at his mock-formality; she sat down rather hard on her chair, allowed him to rearrange her dress and make slight alterations to her position.

'Thank you,' he said and, tight-lipped, settled to paint. His wife watched for a strong moment or two. She had seen him at it many times, but never lost her wonder at his confidence. He chose and added colour to and from the palette at speed, never showing annoyance, hesitation or apprehension. When she had questioned him about this he'd said his palette was prepared for what he had determined to do. 'Do you often make mistakes?' she had asked.

'Often, but constant practice keeps me away from any fault that's too drastic.' She watched him so that she could see his face and his hands, not the canvas. Sometimes he hummed or sang, tunelessly, it must be admitted, but not this morning.

She enjoyed her time of observation, then said, 'I must go now. Anything you want from town?'

'No, thank you. Are you going to the office?'

'I'll call in. Otherwise mainly shopping.'

'Right.' Frank did not cease painting.

'Goodbye,' Gillian said to both.

'One moment.' The Duchess, quietly imperious. 'May I move?' She did not rise; merely turned her head towards Gillian. 'May I phone you some time? I'd like to visit you if I may, and talk to you again.'

'Yes, surely. We'll be glad to see you.'

'Once Christmas is over.'

'Yes.' Gillian wished them goodbye again. Frank had not ceased to dab and stroke at his canvas. The Duchess settled again and once outside the door Gillian found that she was lost. She stared out of a small window, got her bearings. A workman approached, carpenter's bag in his hand. She asked her way. He pointed it out rather than spoke, though he did make some throaty social sounds. She thanked him. He touched his cap, a hundred years behind the times.

That evening he arrived home soon after five to find his evening meal, home-made vegetable soup, then salmon, peas, potatoes and parsley sauce, a great plateful, almost ready.

'Are you going back this holiday?' she asked as he went upstairs to the bathroom.

'Don't think so. I'll concentrate on you.'

'You'll only get two or three clear days.'

'Yes. I understand that.'

'I've another proposal.'

He came back to the end of the small corridor to the bathroom and paid attention. 'Yes?' he said. 'What is it?'

'I'm thinking of inviting Rosie down and I wondered what you'd think of the idea of painting us together.'

'Um?'

'Don't give me your answer now. Later on. When you've thought it over.'

'Right.' He slumped off to the bathroom, beginning to whistle. He'd clearly had a good day.

As they sat down to their soup he announced (they had spoken little as both were hungry), 'I'll set a canvas up for you and Rosemary.'

'I'll ring her first. She may not want to spend her break sitting for a picture.'

'You think not?'

'I think she will. She'll love it.'

'Interesting.' He concentrated on his soup. When he'd finished his second bowl he breathed deep and said, 'You seemed to be getting on well with the Duchess.'

'Yes. I did my best for you. I didn't want to queer your pitch.'

'What did you think of her?'

'She seemed to say straight out what she thought, though I think she made a bit of an exception in your case.'

'And why would that be?'

'She didn't want you to be annoyed with her and ruin the picture. Or make an old bat out of her.'

'Not likely. How old do you think she is?'

'Late forties, fifty, perhaps.'

'She's sixty. She doesn't look anything like that.'

'She didn't do it with make-up. You surprise me. Unless I'm easily impressed. Did I look at her and think, "This is an aristocrat? A duchess? Isn't she young?" '

'There's something in that, but I do think there is something extraordinary about the woman, even if I can't pin it down. Perhaps she's used to her exalted rank, and all the admiration and sycophancy it brings with it.' He spoke cautiously. 'And can accept it.'

'If you saw her on the bus and didn't know who she was, would you be equally impressed?'

'I wouldn't say "equally", but I'd see something out of the ordinary in her.'

'Why is that?' Gillian asked. 'And are you trying to get it into your picture?'

'Yes. No.' He smirked. 'If I said I was trying to paint her as I see her, then that would be about it. It's not so much cerebral as aesthetic. I don't find it a matter of logic where she appears on the canvas. One could say it was a matter of proportions and that's mathematics, but I put it down to my looking at hundreds of pictures.'

'Thinking does harm, does it?'

'No. It's good to sit down and puzzle out what you want to do. I'm always at it, but when I set about the actual work it may turn out to be different.'

'Why is that?'

'Because I'm a poor thinker, and I need to be stimulated by the charcoal, and paint, and paper or canvas to know what to do.'

'That has to be learnt?'

'That's what the college is for. I should like a philosopher on the staff to discuss these matters with the students, but while money is short it'll never happen. It might be possible when we're part of the university.'

'Will it', she asked, 'make your people better painters or sculptors or designers?'

'Technically, no. But I'd like them to listen to somebody who's not teaching how it's done, but who makes clear what one can say about the finished work. It might frighten some students, but I don't want people who are good at only one or two things. I was at college with a man who was marvellous at painting birds. But it was all he could do really well. For the rest he was average.'

'It's better to be good at painting birds than at nothing, isn't it?'

'Yes. Most people aren't even that. Ordinary.'

'D. H. Lawrence said, "I hate ordinariness." Was he right?'

'I'd need to cross-examine him. When you see those scenes of everyday life depicted by Vermeer, they're not ordinary. If somebody thinks they are, then he doesn't know anything about art. It's difficult, I know, to say exactly why Vermeer excels. You can talk about his treatment of light. But that can mean nothing as well as something. When you've painted as many pictures as I have you begin to realise that compared with your efforts there's a lasting quality about a Vermeer. My view is that one becomes tired of any picture if one studies it for months on end, even the best of paintings, as one does with a piece of music. And if the picture is small enough then it's more likely to pall than if it were large. There's less to look at. Remember I'm talking only about masterpieces. I haven't tired of Vermeer yet.'

'Which picture do you look at seriously hour by hour for months on end?'

'None, of course. But if I did, I'd be less tired than with any other great master.'

'Rembrandt? Titian? Poussin?'

'Yes, I think so. I may be wrong, but I haven't the time, or inclination to try to test myself out on any such experiment.'

'Full-time painting does you good,' she said happily.

'There speaks your father-in-law again.'

'Very likely.'

'Very? Certain.'

They ate with pleasure, drank a glass more than they ought.

XI

Rosemary arrived after teatime on Christmas Day.

She explained that she had spent the morning picking up old people, helping to serve them at dinner, in a church hall, and getting them back before dark.

'Were they pleased?'

'On the whole. Some of 'em have no idea of time. You knock at their door. They say they're all ready and then they begin to look for the brooch their granny gave them and without which they can't appear in public. So I have to join the search, leaving the couple waiting in my car to sit and complain.'

'What time do you have to get them there?'

'We try to manage a full house by eleven thirty, but it's always midday. They're down at the tables by twelve fifteen. Old folks seem to want their lunch early.'

'And you take them back?'

'Yes. They have a piece of Christmas cake and a cup of tea just before three and then it's home, James.'

'Do they talk to each other?' Gillian wanted to know.

'It varies. Some are as garrulous as you like. Others, mostly men, won't say a word. And the majority like to drop off after a good meal. They don't need entertainment. Last year we had a pianist in and tried to get them to sing carols. They said they enjoyed it, but . . .'

'So you haven't had much to eat?'

'Oh, yes. We have our snack once we've cleared away and got them settled down. It's mainly standing up, but I ate as much as I could manage.'

They discussed the picture, and he did two pencil sketches before supper and asked their opinion. On the morning of Boxing Day, when they had washed up the breakfast crockery, they took a ten-minute stroll in the garden before he settled them together.

111

He had already done his charcoal outline, though Rosemary did not know when. Presumably he had used his memory and pencil sketches before breakfast, or on Christmas Day.

By nine thirty he was painting hard.

After an hour, in almost complete silence, he asked Gillian if she would make coffee for them.

'Where shall we drink it?'

'In the kitchen. And we'll break for no more than twenty minutes.'

They swilled out their cups and were back in the studio exactly on schedule. At twenty past twelve he allowed Gillian to warm up the soup, and prepare the cheese and salad to go with the potatoes she had baking in the oven.

Rosemary sat, rather embarrassed at her sister's brisk busyness. 'I ought to help her, you know,' she told Frank.

'She knows what she's about. She doesn't need our help.'

He painted grimly on. His concentration was frightening. He made no big gestures, though he occasionally closed an eye, or muttered as he reached for a new tube of paint.

'You can relax,' he said suddenly. 'It's background time. I have to know roughly what sort of wall you will appear against. I think I know; but I find, even after all this time, that when I start putting the paint on all kinds of new ideas appear.'

'From where?'

'God knows. I thought I knew what I wanted, but fresh notions come sidling in and I try some of them.'

'But you gave Gill exact times to have lunch ready to serve. What happens if you come to some crucial decision as we get up for lunch?'

'If that happens you'll stay here with me. I shall be just as annoyed as you are, believe you me. But the painting comes first. Especially on winter days like this, when daylight is at a premium. You can stand, if you so wish, walk about.'

'And may I look at your picture?'

'Yes. As long as you don't say anything about it, or ask any questions. That's mere superstition on my part, but it's what I always demand.'

'Even with the Duke and Duchess?'

'Sure. They don't mind. I let them look at the work in progress at the end of a day's final session. I told them when I started that I didn't want any comment from them, or any conversation between us about the portrait until we were getting near completion. I realise that sitting still on a dais is extremely boring and that the sitter is bursting to say something.'

'And what did she say?'

'The Duke just nodded and agreed. He's spent time in the Army, and is used to being told to do things that aren't altogether sensible. The Duchess, mildly enough, just said, "But if I think at the end of a day's painting of some point that seems to me to be important, what am I to do? Forget about it?" ' His face creased into amusement, though his brush assiduously continued its work.

'And how did you answer that?'

'I told her to think about her important point for an hour or two, and if it seemed still as crucial, then she should write it down and hand it over to me the next morning.'

'And how did she take that?'

'Calmly enough. Queenly. She said she would do just that.' He looked about for a painting rag, found it, dabbed with it. 'She clearly thought that all her ideas were important.'

'And are they?'

'I shouldn't think so. Especially about painting. She didn't write anything down for me. But she's an intelligent woman and may say something useful from time to time.' Now he used the rag on his hands. 'Would you tell Gill that I'm scrubbing up now and I'll be down for lunch in a few minutes?'

Rosemary stared at the painting. He'd hardly made a start on his wife's head, but her own was painted so that no canvas showed. There were as yet no easily recognisable features, eyes or mouth, but Rosemary thought that the set of the head exactly caught her likeness, almost miraculously so. Those flecks, and dabs, and strokes of paint meant nothing in themselves so far, and yet by their total shape were her.

Frank had taken off his smock and stood there, his wide braces over a khaki pullover already splashed with paint. He was staring back at the picture now with intensity. 'It's coming,' he said, and pushed out and into the lavatory. She could hear the taps running as she left the studio.

When he came into the kitchen downstairs he had donned a

tweed jacket over the pullover and braces. The three sat down to beef casserole, rather than Christmas leftovers or oven potatoes.

'I have to keep his strength up,' Gillian said. 'It's his favourite. He doesn't much like poultry.'

They chaffed each other. Gillian even asked her sister what she thought of the picture so far.

'I'm not allowed to say,' she said, gesturing towards Frank.

'Never mind him.'

'I'm not listening,' he growled.

'Well, it reminded me of a very early spring day, February perhaps, with the sun shining but there's a really cold, biting wind blowing over the snowdrops, and the crocuses and iris are shaking like the grass. It's rough, the boughs and branches all of a bounce, patchy and erratic but full of energy and promise.'

'How about that, then?' Gill asked her husband.

He nodded grudgingly. 'There speaks the poet.' 'Amen,' his wife mocked.

Later during the lunch break Rosemary enquired after Herbert Montgomery, saying she had expected to see him there.

'No,' Gillian said. 'We wanted him to come, but he's obstinate.'

'It was the usual story. I ought to be painting not entertaining old people. He said he'd come up to the exhibition of the "ducal oils", that's what he called them; he's always on the lookout for some daft phrase, and demanded that the portrait of Gillian I was doing should be finished. We hadn't asked you about this little bit and piece we're on with now, or he'd have wanted that done and dusted.'

'He sounds lively enough.'

'I don't know,' her sister answered. 'I was worried. You can't go falling downstairs at his age and not damage yourself. He was quite badly bruised and so does little exercise. He only gets out of his chair with difficulty. You can see he's in considerable pain, and he's shocked and depressed. He's talking now about moving house.'

'Does he get any help?'

'Yes. His doctor, a lady, organised social service people round to see him. He has meals-on-wheels now; a nurse comes in every day; he has a woman in twice a week to bath him and friends visit him. And Gervase Lunn is very good. He says Herbert fancies some woman; I don't know the truth. His housekeeper looks after all the washing, and Mr Lunn shops for him and gets his stuff from the chemist's. Not that father's very grateful. Lunn's a fool who will never get anything right. He seems a very decent sort to me and rings me regularly to let me know how the old man's making out. I tried to get him to persuade Herbert to spend Christmas with us and I believe he did his best, but he was insulted for his pains. "I want to stay here, where everything is at my finger-ends and I don't have to chase about at anybody's behest." I expect his cleaning woman and his nurses and Lunn's housekeeper move him about.'

'I understand all that, but my impression is that he's getting no better. He's in considerable pain and depressed with it.'

'I guess that's right. That's why he wants to move. It won't cure his aches and pains. If you give him advice he mocks you. I said he ought to try to walk about the house and garden to unstiffen his muscles. He just answered, "You've no idea of the extent of the pain." '

'So he won't listen?'

'No. I know it must be awful,' Frank muttered. 'I said as much, but warned him that he ought to try to build up the power in his legs and arms. Then the old man sang to me in his cracked voice, "Tell me the old, old story." That cheered him up a bit. He used to say that when he was in the Navy, and the authorities came up with a spurious excuse for not allowing something the sailors wanted to do, they'd hum that together. And that led him on to one of his usual complaints: soldiers and sailors wouldn't be able to do it nowadays, because they wouldn't have learnt any hymns in their childhood. "We used to sing 'Why are we waiting?' to the tune of 'O Come, All Ye Faithful', when a meal was late, or a pay parade." "Didn't you get into trouble?" I asked.'

'And did they?' Rosie asked.

'He tells the tale how some tar got hauled up and punished, and wrote to his MP complaining that he had been given CB for singing hymns.'

'And what happened?'

'Nothing much. He had a reply from his MP, a bland sort of letter that he showed all round the barracks, thanking him for his service in HM Forces, and saying that there was perhaps a more appropriate place to sing hymns than the drill square, and promising him a parcel, which never arrived, or did so after the man had been posted on.'

'What's CB?' Rosemary asked.

'Confined to barracks. You weren't allowed out in your free time and you had to parade in your best uniform to be inspected, then take that off and put your denims on and go down to the cookhouse and peel spuds for tomorrow's meals.'

'And did the commanding officer get into trouble?'

'Not that they heard of. Most MPs would do nothing about it. One or two of them the authorities didn't like, because they did kick up a stink. A QC, KC then, called Pritt, a Communist. He was a tartar.' Frank grimaced. 'Going through this lot cheered the old man up a bit. He was back in his thirties. I'd heard it all before, of course. But he soon lost his spirits. The only other time he was anything like himself was when he ticked me off for wasting my gifts in the college instead of painting full time. "God gives you the talent and you, what do you do? Throw it back in His face and sit in your office deciding whether you'll hold a meeting for the staff in room two or room three." '

'I didn't know Mr Montgomery was religious?' Rosemary ventured at the end of this.

'He isn't. But he'll use any argument.'

'Frank was very clever with him. He asked him if he'd come over to Derbyshire with us and inspect his son while he was painting you and me. But he wouldn't hear of it. "It'll take too much out of you, all three of you," he said, "looking after me instead of working on the painting. You've spent hours preparing all this lovely food for me today and I can't eat it. No. I shall just be in your way." I don't know what we shall do with him. He doesn't make the best of the help we do get him. In the end,' Gillian said, 'he'll be in such a state that he'll have to go into a nursing home.'

'And he'll dislike that?'

'So he says. But I have known people who have fought, really battled it out, not to go into a home and then when they get there are much happier. If they've kept their brains and their limbs in good order, they boss the other people about and the carers encourage them because it means they have some of their work done for them.'

The afternoon's painting went well. Frank concentrated on Rosemary, but was careful to give both women short breaks. He concentrated, almost frighteningly to his sitters. Rosemary saw him as a different man, a demon, unstoppable, wild with effort. He dismissed them early in the afternoon, though he continued almost until it was dark.

'Surely he can't see?' Rosemary asked her sister once they were out of earshot.

'Only just. But he hates finishing so soon. He won't be doing anything too important.'

'Is it heavy work?'

'It tires him, for sure. He's on his feet all the time. And would be all day if the light allowed it. But it's the concentration and the constant experimentation that takes the steam out of him. He goes at it like a madman, sometimes. And yet he can paint as if he's in a trance, easily as sliding on ice.'

'He seems a different man.'

'So he is. Make no mistake about it. I sometimes think his father's right that he should spend all his working day at a canvas. Whether it would pay off in the long run I don't know. I think he'd shorten his life.'

'Could he afford to give up his day job?'

'Look, if he didn't earn a brass farthing from his painting I earn enough to keep us living at our present standard. And he's in now. People will pay big money for both his portraits and his landscapes.'

'How many pictures does he paint in a year?'

'At present? At most between half a dozen and ten. I'm not counting sketches and so on. I mean reasonably large pictures. If they're commissioned, of course, they go off, but the rest I keep. I want to see his stuff on my walls.'

'And he doesn't mind?'

'Doesn't seem to.' Gill took her sister's arm. 'I don't altogether understand him. He likes lording it as principal of his college. He'd miss it. It's different.'

'Is he good at it?'

'I guess so. The staff and students don't put it over on him, and he doesn't make unreasonable demands on them. He's strict if he needs to be, because he's pretty hard on himself. And he takes classes. Just next term he's going into the life class to paint with them. He won't have the time at it that they will, but they'll see how he goes about it and how successful it turns out to be.'

Rosemary left them three days after Christmas 'to straighten' her house and get ready for work the day after New Year. Frank had spent more time on her than on his wife and she was delighted with the result. On New Year's Day in the Queen's Honours List he was appointed CBE to the pleasure of his father. They had not told him this was to happen and the old man sent him a card: 'She should have made you a knight, but I don't suppose that will be long.' Frank and Gillian, who'd known about the decoration for some time, got surprisingly drunk on their own that evening. He felt so ill the next morning that he added nothing to either of his unfinished paintings.

Gillian went primly off to her first day of work, advising him to go easy. It had been a really, really profitable holiday, she said.

He groaned and sketched distant hills through the window until his hands grew too frozen to hold the pencil.

XII

Frank Montgomery tramped round the college grounds on the day of the arrival of the students. The January weather outside was cold, foggy, with low cloud.

'It makes you glad of having a really warm workplace to come to,' his secretary said.

'Isn't it warm at home, then?'

'Yes, but I shudder when I think of the gas bills we have to pay.'

People seemed genuinely pleased to see him, to congratulate him on his decoration, which had been heavily featured in the local newspapers. Two cuttings fluttered on the noticeboards together with a photograph taken at least six years ago.

'We'll have to change the heading on the college stationery,' Mrs Salcombe said. 'Shall I set it in motion?'

'Don't bother. Let me get used to it first.'

He guessed this modest word would have been passed round the clerical staff, and probably the teachers, before the day was out. There was plenty to do, but he felt in no mood for speed. The Duchess had sent him a card from Venice telling him she'd be home before the end of January, when she would arrange to attend further sittings. The weather in Italy, she wrote, was comfortably warm.

'How's your brother-in-law?' he asked his secretary.

'He's been dreadful in the holiday. This chemotherapy must be very powerful. He's had to spend some days in hospital.'

'Is it doing any good?'

'We don't know yet. He looks awful. He's lost weight. We know he's in pain even though he doesn't say much. He's very down, I can tell, because this treatment makes him feel so ill. And he just slumps in his chair when he gets up in the morning and sits staring at the wall. He doesn't want to read, or look at TV, or listen to the radio.'

'Does he have visitors?'

119

'Yes. But he can barely raise the energy to speak to them and that's not him. I go in every evening every day and at the weekend after breakfast as well. But it's more for his wife's sake than his.' She looked down, morosely sorting the papers on his desk. She took a grip on herself. 'Is your father any better?'

'I couldn't say one way or the other. His pain must be less, must be, but he's very depressed. He wants to move house.'

'So would I in his place.'

'From a convenient bungalow to a sprawling Victorian house?'

He spent an hour dictating answers to the many letters of congratulation. He attempted a fetching modesty, as he did to the Vice-Chancellor, who added oral praise to a well-expressed letter. 'You deserve it,' he told Frank, 'not only for your administrative skills but for your real interest in art teaching. You've made the fusion between the university and the college a lot easier than it might have been.' Frank knew the V-C liked the word 'fusion' to describe the new status, especially as it allowed a gentle play with 'confusion' in his public utterances. 'And the museums have livened themselves up since you began your series of exhibitions which showed them how it should be done. Somebody has noticed and put a word in at the right place.'

'That's about it. It depends on knowing the right people, or knowing somebody who has access to the right people.'

'I wouldn't know.' The V-C sighed. He was reported, especially by his enemies, to be waiting for his own call to knighthood, which never came. Frank thought the man had more sense than to be distressed by such a snub, if it existed. 'Are you still considering leaving us here?'

'I don't honestly know. I think about it.' Frank laughed. 'Especially when I see my father who tells me to stop larking about in educational institutions and get on with my painting.'

'I've heard you say that before. Is there any sense in it?'

'I might go out of fashion and not sell anything.'

'Is that likely? I mean, with painters as good as you?'

'It happened to Rembrandt.'

'Oh, there speaks my ignorance. Of course, their economic situation would have been different from ours.' The V-C was smiling. 'When you join us full time, Frank, I'll have you made pro-vice-chancellor.'

'Thank you.' He was surprised to hear this. The V-C knew how to bait his hooks. 'Wouldn't that mean public appearances and plenty more useless meetings?'

'Nothing you need be afraid of. When your college joins us you'll add to our good name. Your place is known, approved of. It attracts publicity in the media, as does its principal. This university – I know I say it often enough in public, but I mean it – has some outstandingly good people on its staff. We've three Fellows of the Royal Society. But take somebody like Tom Jordan. He's not only at the forefront of his field in physics and astronomy, but his particular line draws praise and raises interest in the wider world. And Tom attracts good young men to his department. We're lucky. The medical school has done itself proud in the past few years. And we have our high-flyers on the arts side. Frederic Corder, for instance. I expect you know all this, but it does no harm to get it straight from the horse's mouth. So when they plan tacking on another department from right outside to us I do not shudder. At first, perhaps.

'But I've known you for a year or two and I know what I'm getting. Your college chose you early, so the legend goes, and I was there to vouch for its truth, because they knew you were unusually gifted as a painter. That was a dangerous move, or could have been. You might have been useless as a principal, however skilful with a brush. And there they'd be, stuck with you for twenty-five or thirty years. Thank God it wasn't so. They've had you nearly eleven years now and know what improvements you've managed. You're gifted in that direction. And I'd like you with us for a year or so when we become attached. You can fight your corner, shoo away those among us who'll write your courses off: wallpaper design, high-fashion frocks, interior decoration, or MAs in cartoon drawing or nude photography or preserved parts of beasts. And when you've settled in then you can think about leaving us for the higher artistic life.

'I was very loath myself to leave research for administration, but I threw my hat into the ring in the end and found what I was really good at. I get called out to chair committees these days, government schemes that I used to mock at when I was hard at research. I tell you all this not to praise myself, just to warn that the fact that you excel at something means that you shouldn't stick with it all your life. I changed, against my better judgement, I thought then, but found my true métier. You're not fifty, yet.' The Vice-Chancellor blew out his lips, slapped the change in his trouser pockets. 'That's a long sermon, you'll think. I'm fifty-two. I don't know how long I shall stick at it, but I want this place to be better for my tenure here.'

Frank made vague noises of agreement.

'I like talking to you. You give the impression of weighing up what I'm saying. This is not always the case. Some write me off, ex officio. No vice-chancellor ever talks sense. Others resort to sycophancy and peak-touching. The majority let it in one ear and out of the other. They have their schemes; they've in many cases thought them out carefully and don't want my interference never mind blockage. Take Tom Jordan, for instance. I know exactly what he's thinking. "I'm a better scientist than you ever were, so when I come to you, Mr Vice-Chancellor, with some project for research, it's your job – no, your duty – to skedaddle round and rake in the money to pay for it. Yes, and if you have to get the cash at the expense of some half-baked scheme emanating from the heads of these mediocre professors, you must grab it without a second thought. We bring honour to this place. We expand the bounds of science and it adds to your kudos." '

'He's as arrogant as that, is he?'

'He'd be shocked' – the Vice-Chancellor was smiling now – 'to hear me put it in words as plainly as I have to you, but that's exactly what he thinks. Haven't you met him?'

'Just. I hardly know him. He was on the appointments committee not long ago for a professor of physics at the ex-Poly.'

'And you were?'

'I was.'

The V-C nodded approval of the choice. 'And didn't he seem about half a mile above the heads of the rest of you?'

'Not that I noticed. He hardly said anything. About halfway through the interview he chased the candidate we finally appointed about some research the man said he would follow up here. I didn't know what they were talking about, but I could see his questions were awkward. He wasn't going to let the candidate get away with any cock and bull. But I'll say this for him, the chap, his name was Lowe, didn't seem unduly put out and appeared to be giving satisfactory answers. And when it came to the choice, Jordan just said there was no doubt in his mind that Lowe was the best.'

'He didn't give the impression that it didn't much matter who was appointed?'

'No. He just said it very quietly, unemphatically. "There is no doubt in my mind." '

'Did no one argue with him?'

'One of the politicos, as far as I remember, had a shot at it. Jordan didn't seem to mind and hardly bothered to answer. He'd given his opinion, and if we chose to ignore it then that was our affair.'

'Yes.' The V-C drew out his one word. 'Makes you feel about an inch high.' He stood to his six foot two. 'I like to talk to you, Frank. Lonely job this, sometimes. I look forward to seeing you up here when you're one of us.' He moved across, threw an arm about Montgomery's shoulders and ushered him out of his door in no time. Frank smiled to himself. By the time he arrived as part of the university it might not take him long to be numbered among the enemy. Frank did not know how seriously to take the Vice-Chancellor in this new guise as a human being, a confiding friend. He was a crafty devil, and if this proposal to appoint the new man to the position of pro-vice-chancellor was serious it would certainly be to keep some other ambitious colleague out of the job. It might have been mere flattery, hot air. This seemed, nevertheless, a good day.

That morning, immediately after Gillian had set off for work and he had washed up their few breakfast crocks, the phone had rung and a woman's voice checked on his name, and asked if he would hold the line for the moment because the President of the Royal Society would like to speak to him. He waited, wondering. The Royal Society of what? Arts? Literature? Painters in Water Colours?

The President spoke, named himself and the place from where he was speaking, Carlton House Terrace. 'I hope this is not too early for you. I'm here this morning preparing myself for a meeting and I've been deputed to speak to you. This, you will understand, is all in the strictest confidence.'

'I can't promise that I shan't tell my wife.' Frank felt bound to show independence.

123

'I understand that What I am about to put to you is at present a mere suggestion. Nothing has been finalised. A well-known man of business has written to us saying that he is willing to donate to us a considerable sum of money for a new portrait of the Queen to be given to the Royal Society in this jubilee year. You'll understand all that. That was an offer.'

Frank kept his mouth shut.

'Now, we on the committee called a meeting. This was a generous gift, if unusual.'

'You'd have preferred it to be offered for some scientific project?'

'Oh, come, Mr Montgomery. We're not as philistine as all that. If we could we would play our small part in the production of a work of art. To cut a long story short, we made our enquiries from various experts, civil servants, heads of museums, gallery owners, journalists. You know. We acted at speed, we had to, and as you can well imagine we received a wide variety of answers. *Quot homines, tot sententiae.* But, you'll be glad to learn this, your name stood high on many of the lists. I suppose you're not surprised?'

'People come in and go out of fashion,' Frank answered glumly.

The President seemed unsettled by this ungenerous reception of his praise. 'We put the following questions: one, who'd do the best portrait? I know that depends on fashion.'

'And', Frank continued for him, 'nobody has any idea how posterity will judge your choice.'

'Yes.' Frank imagined lips growing thin. 'The second was: would the cost be within our means? And number three: will the artist we choose be amenable to reasonable demands?'

'Which is what you're trying to find out now?'

'Yes. And, of course, will Her Majesty be agreeable to be painted again, this year, and by the painter we name? Now, can you answer me this question straight off? Are you interested?'

'When would you wish this to be done?'

'In the next three or four months?'

'And how large will it be?'

'That depends. We're willing to take your advice. We'll show you where we'd like to hang the finished portrait. Are you interested?' The question followed the reasonable proposal with a sharpness Frank enjoyed. This man did not waste time.

124

'Yes.'

The President, this dry voice, gave him a little time to reflect on what he'd agreed.

'There is no telling what will be the reception by the Palace of our proposal. It's possible that a good number of other societies and corporations have made similar applications. That's why I am so vague. I'd be grateful, I can't stress this enough, if you'll not broadcast our approach to you.'

'I understand that. It must be difficult to make a choice.' Something of his pleasure sounded in his voice.

'I was surprised how many of our Fellows seemed knowledgeable about as well as interested in contemporary portrait painting. You are well known, Mr Montgomery.'

'Certainly the newspapers have been featuring me recently.'

'That's where most of us depend for our information.'

'Yes.'

'And one other fortuitous happening recommended you to me. I ran across Sir Thomas Jordan the other day and mentioned our scheme. I leave no stone unturned. And I've known Jordan for some years. He supervised me for a year or so at Cambridge. I mentioned your name and he said you were from his part of the world. "In fact, I've met him once; he seemed rational enough," he said. He also told me that those in the know up in Yorkshire had no doubt that you were the most outstanding portrait painter in the UK.'

'Thank you.'

'You must have made a good impression there. Tom is an obsessed man. He's kept at his research and teaching, and for the last twenty years in the same place. Apart from a few times over in America, where he's highly respected. He's been offered chairs at both Oxford and Cambridge, and at Imperial and in the USA, but he's decided he can live most pleasantly where he is. His wife's a Yorkshire girl and the university provides him and his assistants with the machinery he needs, the laboratories. He's done well, made a name. He's a somebody with us scientists. He doesn't go searching for honours. If learned societies present him with gold medals he'll just about bother to receive them. Or he will sometimes. He gives the impression of a modest but blunt north-countryman, living the simple life and doing what he wants to do. But, of course, you've met him. He's a very considerable scientist and there are not too many of whom that could be said. When he recommended you, that moved me in your favour. He's shrewd. And he doesn't make out that he knows what he doesn't know. Good, good. There are one or two questions my committee has instructed me to put to you. How many sittings would you require?'

'Four or five. Perhaps fewer. I'm supposed to be quick.'

'And would you be willing to travel to London for these?'

'Yes. I imagine they'll have some little corner of the Palace where I can work.'

'I'd think so. This is not the first time she's sat, you know. Have you any notion, just off the cuff, of the size?'

'Depends where you're going to hang it. What I'm thinking of is a head and shoulders, perhaps two feet by eighteen inches.'

'On canvas?'

'Unless for some good reason you want it otherwise.'

'Would such a picture fall inside the two hundred thousand we've been given?'

'Yes.'

'And you'd be prepared to travel outside London?'

'Within reason.'

'We'll put this to the Palace as soon as we can. I may as well tell you that the Surveyor of the Queen's Pictures was one of those who recommended you.'

'I've forgotten his name, if I ever knew it.'

'He's not forgotten yours. Right, I'll have to go now. My secretary will give you my various phone numbers and e-mail addresses, and you can perhaps leave me yours so that we can easily make contact. I'll be in touch as soon as I can, but you'll understand that the arrangements are not easily made. The Queen is a very busy woman. And this is not yet an offer. It's not mine to make. And discretion, please. It's been good to talk to you. I have to undertake a lot of tasks quite outside my ken. I'll hand you over to my secretary now.'

'She knows all about this transaction?'

'Yes. She knows why I wanted to talk to you. But I wouldn't discuss the details with her at this stage. Or with anyone else. Your wife, yes. But it might all come to a sudden full stop.'

That had been two days ago and he smiled still. 'Painter to Royalty and the Aristocracy' he mocked himself. He'd not heard from the Duchess. Perhaps she was still in Italy. He kept his hand in at the weekends on the two unfinished portraits of his wife. She was notably impressed by the royal project.

'She seems rather shy?' Gillian ventured.

'I've no idea; I must have seen her in the flesh four times in my life. For a few seconds. At a distance.'

'But hundreds of times in photographs in newspapers and magazines. And you'll see her when you collect your CBE.'

'I suppose so.'

'Aren't you pleased?'

'Flattered. It means my name is getting known. And publicity is good. But I don't want to be known as painter to the high and mighty.'

'No. Have you gone down to that life class yet?'

'Yes. Last Thursday. I did a whole afternoon and enjoyed it. I wanted to see how quickly I could get along.'

'You did well there?'

'Yes, I think my speed surprised the students. They'd already had a class just doing pencil sketches and making their minds up.'

'Were you pleased?'

'I couldn't tell, really. I hadn't done long enough on it. If you're any good you'll come upon new ideas all the time as you're painting. You don't just repeat the old tricks. That's what the students are supposed to be doing. Finding out what's important in the picture and why, and concentrating on that and learning to leave the unimportant pieces, not allowing them to take attention away from the main picture. Knowing what's important and what's not is the first demand on an artist intent on doing well. And what's important changes in some ways as you paint.'

'I thought some old masters put on coat after coat, on, let's say, an arm to get the exact flesh tints.'

'I know. But they had to bear in mind what they were about. And mix their own paints. Madonna and Child, not the floor covering. And if you look at the incidental details with some of the great painters they are marvellous little masterpieces in themselves, and yet are never allowed to draw attention away from the centre of the picture.'

127

'Isn't that a waste of time, then?'

'No. They satisfied themselves by making each small part as perfect as they could, but still not interfering with the main thrust of the picture.'

'Like Bach's second-fiddle parts?' she asked, to put him down.

'If you say so. Have you seen Rosemary recently? Tell her I'd just like another hour or so on her face.'

'Which will then be perfect?'

'Sometimes, madam, you seem to be trying to rile me.'

'Don't you get talking to the Queen like that.'

XIII

Frank kept himself busy.

The Duchess gave him two more sittings, then had the canvas and easel sent over to his studio at home so that he could finish it when he found time. He completed his wife's head on the sisters' double portrait and spent a further afternoon in the life class. The students stood amazed at his speed, and he felt so pleased with himself that he went round the whole class, evaluating and even over-praising, he guessed, each picture. He had one telephone call from the President of the Royal Society informing him that negotiations had begun, but that no definite agreement had been reached with the Palace. The Queen had been pleased at the choice of the painter, but the snag seemed to be that her officials had this year committed her to such a heavy programme that they did not feel they could make any more demands on her at present. When Frank asked the President if he believed the excuse, there was a longish pause, and then a diplomatic answer: 'I don't know enough about royalty. Life in the Palace must be very seriously kept, well, within limits. I don't think this delay, if that's what it is, by any means reflects on your competence or suitability for the commission.'

'Are they always like this?' Frank asked.

'I don't know. But don't be too disappointed. One of these officials will pull his finger out and we shall be away.'

'They don't make any allowances for the artistic temperament?' Frank asked.

'What do you mean?'

'If they trifle too long with the painter, he might get his own back by withdrawing himself or uglifying them.'

'Uglifying? Yes, I see.'

They talked thus for a few minutes. The President said he would keep in touch. By way of encouragement he told a story

129

of how his professor had taken, appropriated, a piece of apparatus he had made when he, a Ph.D. student, had been called away by a family tragedy. When he returned it meant that several weeks' work had been wasted and had to be repeated. The young researcher had been furious, but he had not uttered a word of protest to his professor. In the end, however, it all turned to his advantage because he had omitted some vital statistics in his first calculations, which would have meant that in any case he would have had to repeat the whole sequence of operations. 'It did me no harm,' he said virtuously. Frank took no comfort from this story, which barely seemed to have a relevance to the present situation. He grunted his dissatisfaction.

Almost immediately after this conversation Gillian rang from work to say she had heard from her sister that their mother had been taken seriously ill.

'What's wrong?' he asked.

'They think it's pneumonia. She has great difficulty in breathing. They want Rosie and me to go over today in case anything happens. Is that all right with you? We should be back later this evening.'

'You don't need my permission,' he said.

'I know. But you might want to get yourself a meal in town before you go back home.'

'I'll look after myself. Anything you want me to do?'

'No. I'll phone you from the nursing home.'

He ate lunch in the refectory at college and decided he should do this more often. The food was edible, and his colleagues looked on him without suspicion and talked freely to him about the move to the university. He watched a young, attractive woman fascinating her head of department. He breathed deeply, in envy, for the man was at least ten years older than he. For the rest of the lunch break he sat in one of the two armchairs in his office and neither opened a book nor picked up a pencil. He did not sleep, but allowed casual musings to drift past. He thought of Gillian who would clear her desk, instruct her subordinates what to do in case of emergencies, not that she'd expect any, and then ring Rosemary to say at what time she could be ready. He guessed they'd leave between half past two and three, in Gill's car. The afternoon ebbed away pleasantly, and he and his secretary left the building together at five.

At home, in the dark, he made toast, grilled bacon and ate almost greedily. The college food had no great sustaining power. Here, but not quickly, disciplining himself, he ate six slices, a piece of fruit cake and drank two cups, large-sized, of Earl Grey. He then washed the dishes, slipped on his thickest anorak and walked out into the garden. The night sky pleased him. It was clear; that would mean frost. The stars, larger than usual, caught his brief attention. He marched to the end of his land and stood staring down the road. Footsteps approached. He did not expect to hear pedestrians at this time of the evening. Though the clack of the shoes on the road sounded clearly enough, he had to wait for the visual evidence. He guessed it was a woman or child, but was not exactly sure.

Finally the black figure came into view. A woman, bundled up, elbows working strongly.

'Good evening,' he called out.

'Good God, you frightened me.'

He did not recognise the voice. 'I'm sorry. I was just taking the evening air.'

'Isn't it a bit cold for that?'

'Oh, I shan't stand out here too long.'

'I don't expect you will. Goodnight, Mr Montgomery.'

'Goodnight.'

He thought she might be the lady in the post office, but he wasn't certain of it. Why would she be out at this time of the night? She continued to hurry away. His phone rang from the house. He dashed back, knocking one leg against some dark obstacle he could not name. Indoors, he answered his wife, who had patiently waited. 'Sorry,' he said. 'I was out at the far end of the estate.'

'I wondered where you'd got to. I thought perhaps you'd been delayed at work.'

'How's your mother?'

'Slightly better. They've had a doctor and she'll send her to hospital tomorrow if she's no better, but they think she's improved during the day. She looks in a poor way to me. I guess she's unconscious all the time. She doesn't recognise us nowadays, even when she's perfectly well. But in a coma, like this? The matron said she thought she'd die before the morning was out. That's why they sent for us.'

'I see. Are you coming home now?'

'Yes. And I'm bringing Rosie back with me.'

'Why's that?'

'This has really hit her. When we set off this morning she seemed perfectly normal, but we hadn't been sitting long in Mother's bedroom before she broke down. And I mean broke down. The sobs tore her apart, really shook her. After a time she went out to the cloakroom and cleaned her face up, but she hadn't been back ten minutes before she was off again.'

'Is she better now?'

'Yes. I think so. I went and saw the matron and made sure she had both my addresses, and said that Rosie would stay with me. I told her how upset Rosie was and she was very sympathetic, brought us cups of tea, that sort of thing.'

'Right. I'll turn the heat on in the room she usually has. Did this come as a surprise to you?'

'Yes. Her weeping was violent; it frightened me.'

'I thought she and your mother were more often than not at loggerheads.'

'They were. We'll talk about it when I get home. I've got her sitting out in the car wrapped in a blanket.'

'How long will you be?'

'Something over the hour.'

'Will you want supper?'

'We've not eaten anything substantial since lunch. There's a big pot of soup in the fridge. Unless you've had it all. That'll be fine. 'Bye, now.'

He set about preparations for Rosie's arrival, but they did not turn up until after eight thirty. The rooms were welcomingly warm, the soup was on the stove, the slices of brown bread he had delicately cut were ready for toasting. The entry of the sisters seemed uneventful; Rosemary showed no signs of distress. Within ten minutes they were seated at the table enjoying their meal.

'You've lit the fire,' Gillian said, pausing from the soup.

'It's a cold night. And there's nothing more cheerful than a log fire.'

Both women had second helpings and he demonstrated his knifemanship on more bread. When they had finished he made them sit either side of the fire, while he prepared coffee and packed the crockery into the dishwasher.

'The service in this hotel is excellent,' Gillian said as he brought in their coffee and a plate of chocolate mints.

'Are you all right, sister?' he asked Rosemary.

'Perfect,' she said. 'I can barely keep my eyes open I'm so comfortable.'

'We'll put you early to bed, then. I'll run up now and turn the electric blankets on.'

'Will you be able to run Rosie in to work tomorrow morning? If you can't, I can.'

'Yes. My presence at the college is not altogether necessary. It all goes much more smoothly when my secretary's in charge.'

He noticed now that Rosemary looked fagged-out, her skin pale, her eyes heavy in the firelight. 'When you're thoroughly warmed through, you can have a bath and bed.'

She could barely conceal her yawns and Gillian hurried her upstairs.

'She's really fatigued,' she told Frank. 'I would have said that she was an imaginative type, but it wasn't until she actually saw our mother than she cracked up.'

'Why was that?'

'She might have felt she ought to have taken Mother into her own home. She's still living in the fairly large place that she and Joe had when they were married. He went back to London after the divorce and she stayed behind in the house. He's in Manchester now, I think, but I don't know for how long. She probably thinks now that she should have taken Mother in when Father died. They had separated by then. My mother never recovered from my father's death, though, heaven knows, that was expected. She had her first stroke while she was actually staying with Rosie. It wasn't serious and she insisted on going back home as soon as she was able, to be, as she put it, among her friends. That was a gross exaggeration. She had no real friends. And before the stroke she and Rosie had been niggling at each other. Mummy was left knocking about in that big house all on her own all day and that did her no good. Rosie suspected that the anxiety might well have contributed to her stroke. She was particularly busy at that time, often brought work home at night or at weekends and Mummy didn't like that.

She thought Rosie ought to be devoting all her spare time to her. We spoke about taking her in here for a short time and you agreed, but when I mentioned it to my mother she was scathing. "It will be worse than at your sister's. She at least lives in a town where a few of the amenities of life are available, not stuck out in some boring, cold village." And then she looked me straight in the eye and said, "I expect you'd be as bad as Rosemary. You can't be worse than that selfish cat. She'd tell me straight to my face, 'I've my life to live, Mother, and my career to make.'" '

'And she was much worse when she got to her own home?'

'Yes. She seemed settled once she arrived back. Then dementia and a second stroke all piled on her inside weeks. But you saw how she hung on to her own place. We had to force her to go into the nursing home. And Rosie feels guilty about it.'

'And you?'

'I wish I could have done more, but I couldn't. I wish my mother had not been ill in the way she was. That's not impossible. She was only sixty when Daddy died. That's no sort of age these days.'

'Why has it hit Rosie so badly?'

'She's lonely. She works too hard. She never quite got over Daddy's death.'

'That's five years ago.'

'Five or fifty, she still misses him. Especially since her divorce.'

'I'd think she'd be glad to be over that.'

'I don't doubt it, but it still left her on her own. And her ambivalent feelings over Ma topped the lot for her.'

'Is she physically fit?' he asked.

'I doubt it. She won't eat properly, if I know her. When Joe was there she prepared big solid meals in the evening. He was as greedy as he was selfish. But it meant she ate properly. And I intend to hold her here for a day or two. She can easily go to work and back from here. And I'll see to it that she eats. And just make sure that you talk to her.'

'Yes, sir,' he said.

'She admires you. You're somebody. She would have done better to marry you.'

'I was too busy courting you. And Joe was a sight more attractive than ever I was.'

'He was about as attractive to me as a rattlesnake.' Gillian's twisted lips illustrated her distaste.

'Has she tried anyone else since she divorced?'

'Yes. I don't know how seriously. Except for one. Frederic Shakespeare. Did you know him?'

'No, except by name. He's a barrister, isn't he, like Joe?'

'He's retired now. He was years older than she was. His wife died about the time Rosie and Joe split up. She'd always been something of an invalid, so they said. I didn't know her. They had a daughter who stayed at home and looked after her mother. As soon as her mother died, leaving the girl some money, off she went.'

'Where?'

'Abroad somewhere. Australia, I think, though she doesn't live there now. She married someone she met out there and they moved to Cape Town. And poor Fred seemed lost.'

'From what I recall of him he was too important to be lost.'

'That goes to show. He made his usual court appearances and presided on committees as he'd always done, laying down the law. But once he was out of the public eye he went to pieces. He'd sit in his armchair at home and cry like a child, so Rosie said. It all proved too much for her. He was like a great baby What he needed was a dummy.'

'Did he deliberately overdo it?' Frank asked.

'Probably. I don't know. Whenever I saw him he was on his best behaviour. I was a young solicitor and he was a leading light in the local courts. He spoke at legal dinners and was very good. I was greatly impressed by him, but I couldn't see him as a husband for Rosie. It would have been like marrying her grandfather.'

'He couldn't have been all that old?'

'No. He'd be in his early sixties, but he seemed to be living in a different age. He was a Victorian Father-knows-best. Somebody dubbed him "the Law and the Prophets".'

'It all proved too much for her.'

'Yes. She needed somebody to look after her. Father spoilt both us and our mother.'

'I don't suppose Joe went out of his way to cosset her?'

'No. I don't know why she chose him. I've often asked myself why a shrewd and clever girl like Rosie should choose somebody like him.'

'He could be charming. And he was certainly clever.'

'He thought too highly of himself. Anyhow, Rosemary threw Frederic Shakespeare out in the end.'

'And that upset her?'

'She doesn't do anything' – Gillian spoke slowly, as if to make sure that her judgement was exactly right – 'she considers important, without what you call "upsetting" herself. She turns it over in her mind for days on end.'

'Do tricky legal judgements affect her in the same way?'

'Not really. Not unless she becomes emotionally involved. Usually she can stand back. She's clever; she knows the law; she works hard. But she needs somebody to make a fuss of her. I did hope that Fred would do, because he was older and might replace my father. Another thing, she found she couldn't look up to him. So you know now what's needed for the next day or two.'

'Will she agree to stay here?'

'She might object, telling us that she has no right to interfere with our lives.'

'I see.'

'We might persuade her to stay here and take it easy for three or four days. She can get in touch with her cleaning lady who'll see to it that the house is in good order and that the bills, milk and papers and so on, are paid. We'll aim for a week.'

'Will she not want to go down to see your mother again?'

'I expect so. But with two of us against it she'll yield, for a short time, at least.'

'You don't half organise the world,' he told her, laughing.

'I wish I could.'

'You're a good girl, Gillian Montgomery.'

Rosemary seemed almost pleased to accept their offer of hospitality. Frank drove her to work the first day and checked her car for her. Gillian would take her to see her mother and then back. Both were home before six, and Rosie helped prepare the evening meal, which was on the table by seven. Frank had arrived home after a lengthy afternoon meeting. They talked leisurely together over the meal and Rosemary chatted with cheerful normality.

'Anything interested, interesting in the office?' Frank asked her.

'We have a murder on hand and we're trying to overturn a verdict that's nearly twenty years old. They're not interesting as matters of law, but fascinating as far as the people are concerned. I'm not technically in charge of either. Two of our young men, both with their wits about them, are dealing with these and they both know what to do, legally speaking, but they talk to me about their cases. It's surprising. The barristers need guidance, it seems. One' – she turned to her sister – 'is from Frederic Shakespeare's chambers, and the other is so patently nervous, as it's his first big case.'

'So they come to auntie for advice?' he asked.

'You could put it like that. They mostly tell me what they've done and ask whether it's suitable or right.'

'And is it?'

'Yes, because they're both good at their jobs.'

'Doesn't the principal partner get asked for his advice?'

'They did, at first. The trouble is he thinks these cases are quite straightforward. As they are. And he will claim that both of them are quite capable of handling them. Again, as they are. So they come to me.'

'A sympathetic ear?'

'Yes and no. They know I'll think about their cases and make suggestions, most of which they'll ignore, but they'll know somebody's keeping an eye on them.'

'Why didn't you take the cases up yourself?'

'I'm better employed with the humdrum and with money. It's all boring and rarely gets into the paper, unless we do something utterly stupid or criminal.'

'Such as?'

'Helping ourselves to our clients' savings. It's our job to see to it that the firm's well supplied with such business. It gets us a good name. The majority of citizens are not murderers.'

'They need conveyancing and the like?'

'Exactly. And there are some biggish transactions on our books. Not merely houses, but large properties in great stretches of land. Not difficult, but the clients don't want mistakes and sometimes they want us to make haste with it. So John, the principal, and Matthew, even older and more staid, and I handle that side of the business, and when some desperate case that'll be splashed all over the tabloids as well as the broadsheets comes along we get one of our young Turks on it.'

'Are they as wild as all that?'

'You wouldn't think so. But compared with us wrinklies, yes.'

'You speak as if you're ninety.'

'I'm forty-three.'

'You don't look it. You'd pass for thirty-three anywhere.'

'"In the dark with the light behind me."'

'Do you like this bread-and-butter work that keeps the firm solvent?'

'We're used to it. We do it every day. Our job is to do it properly,' Gillian interrupted.

'That's right. It's dull, but every job has its *longueurs*, its tedium. Even yours, I suspect.' Rosemary laughed. 'It's true that sometimes I think to myself, "You've got another twenty years or more at this." And I wonder if it's worth it.'

'We do some good,' Gillian said.

'The general public wouldn't give you much of a vote of confidence. They seem to think that lawyers complicate and drag out cases to line their own pockets.'

'That's the public who on the whole don't use solicitors, except in the case of house buying.'

'The opinion of the ignorant may be a nuisance, but we mustn't provide evidence that appears to give credibility to it.'

'I always see my solicitor as a trusted friend.'

'It's not Gill, then? Or her office?'

'No, I stick with the man I started with up here. George Carter. You'll both know him. Old-fashioned, but as honest as the day's long.'

'He had a reputation as a ladies' man,' Rosemary ventured.

'Has he tried it on with you?' Frank asked.

'No. Or yes. I always think I can recognise that sort of man and I can detect signs of it. I suspect he's watching me for the slightest evidence of encouragement and then he'll strike.'

Frank enjoyed these exchanges with his wife and his sister-in-law, and said so. 'It's easy to talk to you, I must say,' he told Rosie.

'It's part of my job,' she answered, 'trying to talk sense into troubled people.'

'That's me,' he said cheerfully, 'tousled and senseless.'

She put her arms round him.

Rosemary settled easily with them. The two women drove over one evening to check on Rosemary's empty house and to talk to the charlady. They made arrangements and plans for emergencies. The house looked splendidly clean, each piece of furniture polished, windows shining.

'It looks better while I'm away,' Rosie said.

'Yes, but unlived in. That's what I like about the place, the bits and pieces of untidiness, things slightly out of place,' the cleaning woman answered. 'It looks like a home then and not a museum.'

'She's quite a philosopher, is she, your Marina?' Frank said when he heard the comment. 'Is she married?'

'Yes, a good man, but wedded to his garden.'

'He knows what he wants. And that's more than some of us do.'

XIV

On a bright Saturday morning at the beginning of February the
three drove over to Beechnall to visit Frank's father, Herbert
Montgomery, and the sisters' mother, Frances Housley. First, Frank
drove to the nursing home where they found Mrs Housley in bed,
neatly prepared for them, with brushed and beribboned hair, finger-
nails varnished, but apparently sleeping.

'Is she asleep or unconscious?' Frank impatiently demanded
of the matron after a series of euphemistic sentences.

'Asleep,' the matron brusquely answered. 'She'll wake for the
lunch. In fact, she'll wake for you.' She went through a grimly
gentle pantomime of rousing the patient, who in the end opened
her eyes, small now and piglike; she did not recognise her daughters, who spent some minutes trying to entice their mother to
drink a glass of orange juice. Frances drank grudgingly, lolled
heavily on the women, murmured so quietly that they had no idea
whether she thanked them or complained.

They spent an hour there without result. The sisters talked inces-
santly to stimulate their mother. They recalled incidents from
their childhood, talked with animation of their father's skill at
castle building with bucket and spade on the beach at Swanage
or Bournemouth, but without success. Their mother did not attempt
to speak, sagged in her bed with eyes closed, breathing heavily,
a bubble of spittle on the corners of her mouth. Frank admired
these attempts to rouse their mother, the change of subject, the
laughter, the pointed questions, the gentle hands laid on the body
to caress or comfort. It was a virtuoso performance in which he
could play little part, but in the end failure remained: an inert
body, a collapsing face, a sagging mouth.

At the end of an hour they gave up, tidied the bed, kissed the
wrinkled eyes and left, calling in on the matron's office on their
way out.

'Did she show any signs of recognising you?'

'No. Not at all. We managed to get all her orange juice down her.'

'Good. We mustn't allow her to become dehydrated.'

'Is there anything we can do for her?'

'Not really. Stimulation is what's needed, but she may well be past it.'

'How long will she live?' Gillian, bluntly.

'Ah, that I can't tell you. If she passed away tonight, it wouldn't surprise me.'

'Will she have to go back into hospital?' Gillian again.

'It's possible. Another stroke or some other crisis and we'll have to send her back. I think her life is pretty well over, life of any quality, that is.' The matron's voice was low, almost a sigh. 'We won't allow her to be in discomfort. We'll take care of her, because we like her. She wanted to give us no trouble.' The past tense rattled Frank. 'I am quite sure that she is in no distress. We'll look after her and if there is any change in her condition I'll let you know immediately. And if you ring I'll tell you if ever there seems a chance of improvement; or make a visit and I'll tell you how things are. I can't promise much. It's hard for you. We have to look facts in the face. But we can never be completely sure.'

They thanked the matron, almost fervently, Frank thought. As they tiptoed down the wide flight of stairs and into the foyer, he noticed the glistening of tears on Rosemary's face. He took her arm and she clung to him. Gillian walked stoically ahead of them. Out in the car park, Rosemary wept openly, leaning on the car bonnet. Gill helped her into the back of the BMW and borrowed a freshly laundered handkerchief from her husband to dry her sister's eyes.

He did not immediately drive away, but gave Rosemary a few minutes to recover as she sat in the back holding her sister's hand like a child. She seemed calmer, but suddenly blurted out, 'It's not fair.'

Gillian threw an arm round her, pulled her in close so that their faces lay together.

'She was an intelligent woman, knew her mind and what was going on in the world. Now look at her. She might as well be a corpse. She's all but dead. She didn't know her own daughters.'

Gillian murmured banal comfort to Rosie, whom she hugged. When she had straightened her sister, physically and emotionally, she spoke plainly to Frank. 'We'd better get on now or your father will be worrying himself.'

'Right. It will only take ten minutes.'

It took twice that because of traffic deadlocks and by the time they reached Herbert Montgomery's house Rosemary sat quite calmly.

He was waiting for them, in a smart suit. He had moved back only a few days before.

The whole thing had been kept secret from Frank. His cleaning lady's husband had hired a van and had moved such pieces of furniture as he wanted. They were few because both the bungalow and house were fully furnished. They moved his favourite chair, his desk and its contents, his food from the fridge, kitchen utensils and his clothes. This entailed one journey only. Gervase Lunn, put under a vow of secrecy as far as Frank was concerned, had taken the old man back in his car and had seen him settled.

After Mrs Wynne had cleaned the bungalow and brought over anything they had forgotten on their first raid, they had instructed the estate agent who had dealt with the house over these last years to put the bungalow on his letting list.

Three days after he had settled, Herbert Montgomery had rung his son to announce the *fait accompli*.

'Why didn't you tell me?' Frank asked. 'I might have been of some use to you.'

'And you might not. You would have been telling me how foolish it would be to move in the middle of winter. But here I am now, settled and snug.' The old man could not keep triumphalism out of his voice. 'I organised all this, you know. And here I am, back in touch with civilisation.'

'Are you sure you're all right?'

'Of course.'

'It didn't knock you up at all?'

'Not a bit. All the bedclothes were well aired by Mrs Wynne, and both places have central heating. Moreover, the estate agent told me, to my surprise, that I shall get more for letting the bungalow than the house. It's modern, you see.'

'Is that so? Good. The house is still a big place for one old man.'

'I shall be nearer to Mrs Wynne, and Gervase Lunn, and the doctor. And we arranged for the nurse and the lady who baths me to come to the new address, and the meals-on-wheels brigade. And the rest. It will be easier for them all or all of us all round.'

'And you're pleased with yourself.'

'I am.' He chuckled. 'I spent some time making accurate lists of the things I wanted moving. Either way. Like a military campaign.'

When Frank announced this to Gillian she looked abashed and concerned. 'The crafty old devil. I hope it doesn't end in tears.'

'It may not.'

He was uncertain, but had arranged the present outing.

'You've taken your time,' Herbert grumbled. 'I've sat here waiting with the kettle boiling and the coffee cups out and ready since before eleven.'

'We've been to see my mother,' Gillian explained.

'Oh, how is she?'

'Not very well. She's had two strokes, you know.'

'Of course I know. She's in a nursing home somewhere, isn't she?'

'On Claremont Road.'

'Oh, yes. I know where that is. How old is she?'

'Sixty-five.' He looked hard at her. 'Not yet three score years and ten,' she glossed.

'That's no sort of age, especially for a woman, these days. She's not fit to go out?'

'No. She seems to be asleep or unconscious most of the time.'

'I see. Well, are we ready, then? Do you want to use the lavatories and washbasins?' His legs were aggressively wide apart. 'I hope you're not taking me to one of your Thailand restaurants.'

'We wouldn't think of it. We've booked a table at the Robin Hood, not a quarter of an hour's walk from here.' Frank spoke peaceably.

'That's a pub not a restaurant.'

'Have you ever been in it?'

'No.'

'It's reported to provide admirable lunches.'

'I've never heard that.'

'You never go out on your own for meals. Anyhow, you've been away from the district for some time. Rosemary here not only works in this city, but lives just outside, and she carefully quizzed the young people in her office about the best place to take a discriminating old gent of plain tastes, and the answer was unanimous.'

Herbert looked at Rosemary and smiled. She made a slight inclination of the head in return and asked to use the bathroom 'to repair her face'.

'If I had a face as comely as yours I would leave it as it was. It needs no repairs.'

Obviously pleased, the old man issued directions and offered to accompany her to provide a clean towel. She said there was no need and when she had left the room the three sat down.

'How are you keeping?' Frank asked his father.

'Only fair. I've settled back here without trouble. I'm getting old. It's almost weird. I read obituaries in the paper of old men, old enough in their photographs to be my father, and I see the date of their birth.' He picked up an open newspaper he had been reading before they arrived. 'Look at that decrepit, bearded old piece of senility. Born 1923. I was at grammar school then, and can remember things that happened there as clearly as if it were only yesterday. Cricket matches and holidays and examinations. And this old wreck was a squalling newborn baby. And now he's a corpse. It doesn't seem possible.'

The thought seemed to depress him.

'Moreover,' he began again, 'I can't get about easily now. I have to take walking sticks to do a few yards up the street.'

'Do you try to get out a bit each day?'

'No. It's winter. The north-east wind doesn't do my heart any good. And it rains, icy-cold rain. And the pavements underfoot are treacherous. These York-stone slabs don't sit together properly and trip up the most athletic, never mind old cripples like me. And that's on dry days.'

'You'll manage to get out to the car?'

'None of your sarcasm. It's no laughing matter.'

'Do you feel dizzy?' Gillian asked.

'Often. Especially first thing in the morning, and I have to sit

144

on the side of the bed for a few minutes before I can stir my stumps safely to get washed and shaved and then dressed. It's a long-drawn-out operation, I can tell you.'

'I'm sorry.'

He glared at her, but she spoke again, softly, enticingly. 'Has Frank told you his news yet?'

'No. What's he been up to? Has he decided to pack in his principalship?' His scorn scalded the word.

'That's not it. You tell him, Frank.'

'You tell him.'

'It can't be good news if you're both so anxious to avoid putting it into words.'

Gillian took in a deep lungful of air and stood. Rosemary came in from her make-up session, all smiles, almost dancing.

'The Royal Society in London . . .' Gillian began.

'What Royal Society's that?' the old man snapped.

'*The* Royal Society, the top scientists.' She made her father-in-law wait.

'What have they been doing?'

'They have decided they would like a portrait of the Queen to hang in their headquarters.'

'Haven't they got one?'

'I believe they have, but they'd like another. It will be the fiftieth anniversary of her coronation in a couple of years. And they want Frank to do it.'

'What does the Queen say?'

'Nothing to us, of course. But she's delighted with their choice of painter, or so we are led to believe.'

'And when does he start?'

'It will be some little time, they think. Nearer the anniversary. Then the arrangements will be made for the sittings.'

'Sittings. You don't need sittings for a portrait of the Queen. You've seen a thousand and one photographs of her.'

'Shows what you know about portrait painting,' Frank said. His father looked slightly abashed by the rudeness. 'And don't go talking about it all over the place.'

'We're keeping it to ourselves,' Gillian said emolliently.

'I didn't know about it.' Rosemary added her peace-offering.

'There, you see.'

145

The short journey in thick traffic lifted the old man's spirits. When they had, with difficulty, found a place in the car park, he struggled out and the two women took him by the arm and helped him indoors. In the restaurant, still broad-minded, he inspected the room, the other diners, the table decoration and approved of the menu. He chose chicken with tarragon sauce for his main course. By the time his minted pea and ham soup arrived he sat comfortably at ease with the world.

He questioned his son about the Royal Society commission, and before long was suggesting the probable dates and places of the sittings. He spoke with confidence as if he were a personal friend of royalty. Frank said little, unwilling to spoil his father's obvious delight. The old man clearly revelled in his son's success. By the time he was into his main course, he was questioning the ladies about points of law they had recently met at work. He specially quizzed Rosemary, pleasuring himself in her company.

'Would you say that your life as a legal luminary' – he paused on the expression, which showed his gratification with the food and company – 'is becoming more interesting or not?'

'A solicitor's work needs care,' Rosemary answered, 'knowledge and care. I could not get my former husband to understand that.'

'How did he earn his daily bread?'

'He was a barrister. But he took a romantic view of his work. He saw it as reaching its climax in public, in the courts, where he had to convince a jury that his client was in the right. He liked that; he was good at it.'

'But not at the law, the legal aspects.'

'He knew a fair amount of law, or could swot it up without difficulty. But' – she laughed suddenly, nervously – 'it was the adversarial side he liked.'

'The cut and thrust?'

'I suppose you could call it that. It is, sometimes. But he used to say it was knowing the right simple points that would convince a jury.'

'Did you ever appear with your husband? In court?'

'Not often. And on one occasion I greatly admired him. It was a case of grievous bodily harm, as the papers call it, wounding with intent. I thought our case was not too strong but he, by his cross-examination, made the jury think that the other man was just as much to blame as our client.'

'And you think he wasn't?'

'It's hard to say. They were both lying as hard as they could, making their own side right. But Joe, my husband, by his cunning questioning of the men, the victim and our client, made the jury, twelve decent men and women, conclude that both men were as bad as each other. It worked.'

'Did you' – Herbert Montgomery's eyes sparkled – 'not feel guilty that you and your barrister's efforts had resulted in the jury's conviction that an innocent man was a liar, or that they had released into society a man who should have been sent to jail?'

'One sometimes felt a twinge, but our job was to convince a jury and we did this, sometimes against quite formidable opposition.'

'Opposing counsel?'

'Yes, and sometimes the judge. It was possible to deduce what the judge thought.'

This kept them arguing until the arrival of the pudding, in Herbert's case a small swirl of ice cream with a dash of brilliant red jam. The ladies ate fresh fruit and cream, while Frank indulged himself with treacle pudding and thick yellow custard. These delicacies silenced them for a few minutes. The waiter enquired whether they would have their coffee at table or, he pointed showily, in the conservatory outside.

'Is it warm?' Herbert asked. 'Some of us have old bones that crave heat.'

The waiter obviously approved the phraseology of the question. 'Beautifully warm. Central heating and double glazing are more than adequate, sir.'

They had no sooner settled outside to sit overlooking the crowded street when a tall, distinguished man rose from his table and walked across. He greeted Rosemary, who introduced him to the rest of her party: 'Lord Whelan.' He made pleasant conversation for a few minutes, then arranged to meet Rosemary in her office next week over some legal matter or meeting. They spoke in low confidential voices, which made the subject matter almost incomprehensible to the rest. Both conspirators made notes in their diaries.

Lord Whelan was about to turn away when he fastened his eyes on Frank. 'Are you Francis Montgomery, the painter, sir?' he asked.

'Yes.' Frank gulped an answer.

'I saw your portrait of my relative by marriage. The Duke. At Lockesley House. It was magnificent.'

'Oh,' said Frank, mildly surprised. 'Thank you. It hasn't been on exhibition yet.'

'No,' the man answered. 'I saw it at the house. I don't go too often, but the Duchess is my sister. I saw the early work you put in on her portrait. Last time I was there they told me you'd had it taken over to your studio in Derbyshire.'

'That's so.'

'Is it complete, now?'

'Every so often I put in an hour or two at it. No picture is ever finished in the eyes of the painter. I look and I dab.'

'And improve,' said Rosemary.

His lordship looked at her with approval.

'Sit down for a minute,' Gillian invited him.

'I mustn't stay. I had to come across to fix up a date with Mrs James. Between us we are attempting to improve the lot of solicitors in this city. Whether they think we are succeeding is another matter. And then I recognised her famous relative.' He spoke now with a deep-voiced dignity in the direction of Gillian and Herbert. 'And I had to come across and voice my admiration for his magnificent portrait of my brother-in-law.'

'You are something of a connoisseur?' Herbert.

'Not a professional. But I was brought up, as was my sister, among oil paintings and my interest was stirred; I was about to say "aroused", but I do not wish to claim too much for the expertise I have.'

'And the portrait was to your liking?' Herbert asked.

'It was admirable. The first thing was the likeness. It had caught Gerald in one of his slightly arrogant moods. He is the kindest and most generous of men, but he succeeded to his title in his early twenties and has never been allowed to forget his rank and status.'

'And the result?' Herbert was excited at this opportunity to quizz a member of the aristocracy.

'He sometimes talks to other people as from a great height. Even when he is agreeing with you, or about to do you a favour. But the portrait caught this trait, without exaggeration. Apart from that, and some would claim that was the most important task of the painter, to depict the character of his sitter, stander in this case, the actual beauty of the paint on the canvas, the skill, the variation, the thousands of strokes and touches, with not one wasted, would make this a marvellous work of art even if it were nothing like him.'

'One has to be careful in these days of photographers,' Herbert said.

'I often wonder about that,' Gillian offered her view. 'If one looks at two authentic snapshots of someone one knows well, they often look quite different, one quite unrecognisable.'

'We interpret what we see. A camera cannot do that,' Herbert pronounced.

'I suppose so,' Whelan said pacifically.

'Was the Duke pleased?' Herbert now asked.

'Yes. He didn't look a fool. He carries himself well. That's sufficient. Unlike his wife, my sister. She's utterly different.'

'Wasn't the Duke brought up among oil paintings?' Herbert asked, enjoying himself.

'Yes, but I don't know how often or how carefully he looked at them.' He glanced at his watch. 'I must be on my way. I have a few hours' work to complete. I've enjoyed this exchange. We must all meet again. We'll get Mrs James to arrange it.'

He shook hands with them, one by one, Frank last. He spoke only to him. 'Thank you, sir. It has been a privilege.'

When he'd gone Herbert voiced his pleasure. 'I liked him. Straight. But clever. Is he a good lawyer, Rosemary?'

'Oh, yes. Excellent. Humphrey Whelan has always been good. His firm is now very large, one of the biggest in England. The Labour government made him a life peer. It's said he's a valued adviser to the Cabinet and not only on points of law. His father was also in the Lords. The Earl of Ludgrove. But Humphrey was the third son and always knew he would have his own living to earn. He has done well financially. Now I think he spends his time on good causes and trips to advise influential people.'

'Politicians?' Herbert asked.

'Yes. On the whole. But he's many irons in the fire.'

'And a friend of yours?'

'Friend? We have met several times. Joe thought highly of him. He's recently become a large figure in these parts.'

'Why does he have his lunch in a pub?' Frank asked.

'He's no side. Doesn't throw his weight about. He'd know where to get the sort of lunch he likes. And this place is near his headquarters. He lives out in one of the villages. He's bought a big country house.'

'Lives like a lord?'

'Exactly. Whenever we meet, and that's not often, he tells me he's trying to ease off. He's going to retire from his legal work in a couple of years when he's sixty. Then he thinks he'll travel. Or learn to paint. All his acquaintances think he'll become a fairly full-time politician.'

'That will mean living in London,' Frank said.

'Don't you worry. He has a flat there already. In fact, his firm has two or three.'

'He must be a millionaire. Isn't that so, Rosie?' Gillian asked.

'Yes. But there are plenty of millionaires about these days.'

'Every day *The Times* publishes up to a dozen wills of people you've never heard of, living in towns and out-of-the-way villages who have left more than a million. With the price of property as it is, it's not surprising.' This was Herbert, a man who kept an alert eye open on the world.'

'Didn't you know Whelan, Dad?' Frank asked mischievously.

'I've heard of him and his various concerns, but I've never seen him before. That's one of the drawbacks of old age. I can't get about. If they held a Lord Mayor's Show in my own street, it would be on a day when I couldn't totter out to the front gate. And it's only in the past few years that Lord Whatever-his-name-is has come into public prominence.'

'I see.'

'Would you say he was in some way outstanding?' Gillian asked Rosemary.

'Yes. He was a very good lawyer, very practical. He built up his predecessor's firm, and then they combined with two other large practices and he always came out near the top. They've been expanding ever since. And he had a great many political acquaintances to whom he was useful. They didn't make him a baron for nothing. He'd strengthen their team in the House of Lords; he's an excellent speaker and he'd always be on hand with sound advice. They like to know, our London politicians, what people in the provinces are thinking. Or a few do.'

'Is he married?' Frank asked.

'Yes. I know Elaine, his wife, better really than I know him.'

'Is she a lawyer?' Herbert.

'No. I don't know what she did before she was married. She went to university somewhere, but I don't know what she read.'

'Was she pleased about his title?' Gillian asked.

'I don't really know. She doesn't make a great show about being Lady Whelan. I find her very easy to get on with. She's been ill recently. She'll be about my age.'

'Thirty-one,' Herbert said, beaming roguishly.

'I wish, I only wish,' she replied to his compliment.

They finished their coffee and drove straight back to Herbert's house. The place they found not only tidy and dustless, but warm on this bleak afternoon. The old man's spirits were high all the time at the Robin Hood, but now, in his chair by the fire, he seemed grimmer, preparing for his next calamity. The women, at his command, made cups of tea.

'Will any more visitors come in today?' Gillian asked.

'No. I don't expect so. This is a cheerless house. People are not likely to show up unless they have to.'

'I was just thinking how cosy it was,' Rosie said.

'Yes, it will be when there is a group of intelligent, lively people here. I shall have a woman in later this evening who will help me to undress.'

'And put you to bed?'

'No. She comes in about eight thirty and I'm ready by nine. Usually I don't go to bed immediately, unless I'm very tired. I sit about the house and read or watch the telly. I can't read for too long. That's another drawback.'

'Doesn't the lady stay with you?' Gillian asked. 'For half an hour or so?'

'No. She's one or two other calls after this. She's efficient, folds my clothes very neatly and talks all the time.'

'What about?' Frank asked.

'Her home, her husband, the dog, her grandchildren, her shopping. She's not short of subject matter.'

'But is it interesting?'

'It depends on my mood. Sometimes I'm quite taken by what she's saying, while at other times it takes all my patience not to bawl out, "Shut up, woman, for God's sake." '

'Does she think you're interested in what she's saying?'

'I think she'd talk whether I was paying attention or not. I get the impression her husband doesn't listen overmuch. She likes the sound of her own voice. But she's useful; she makes dressing and undressing a sight easier than it would be.'

'Did you know her before?'

'No. To the best of my knowledge I had never met her. But since she's been coming I have run across her once or twice when Gervase Lunn has taken me out in the car or the wheelchair.'

'Does he come often?' Gillian asked.

'Once or twice a week. At least once he takes me shopping. I make a list. He gets stuff off the shelves. I just stand or sit about and instruct him.'

'He's a good man,' Gillian said.

'I suppose he is. I pay for his petrol. And I think he's another short of company. You'd think with the radio and television and the Internet nobody could be lonely these days, even those who live on their own, but I tell you I'm often sick of my own company. It's time, as I keep saying; I can't read for long periods now and I belong to the age of books. Which reminds me, I saw one of your pictures in a book on modern English painting. Did you know?'

'I suppose I did. Was it a good reproduction?'

'Excellent. And the man said one or two flattering things about you.'

'Good,' Frank said. 'Now, is there anything we can do for you, because we shall have to be on our way soon! I'm getting less and less fond of driving in the dark.'

'You sound just like me,' Herbert said. The girls laughed out loud.

When they set off it was already dark. They had left Herbert with all his curtains drawn and the cake Gillian had baked laid out on a glass dish with a doily.

'Your father's not lost his wits,' Rosemary said. 'He talks sense all the time.'

'I don't know about that,' Frank grumbled.

'You don't know? What do you mean?' Gillian asked.

'The old man was always a good talker. Now he seems all turned in on himself and his troubles. When he was on about the woman who helps to dress him, he knew what she cares to tell him, but that's all. At one time he'd have made something of her anecdotes about her husband and grandchildren, brought them alive.'

'Perhaps', Gillian said, 'he feels embarrassed about being helped on and off with his clothes. It must make him feel helpless and hopeless. He's no longer himself. He doesn't know how to fill in his time. He can barely get up and down stairs, and has to have women in to dress him and bath him.'

'He'd have enjoyed that at one time.'

'I never thought of him in that way.'

'I'm telling you that at one time he'd have had the woman in the bath with him inside ten minutes.'

'He was a ladies' man, was he?' Gillian.

'He was.'

'You surprise me. He always seemed so proper to me, asking intelligent questions, telling me what he'd read and thought.'

'He was in his eighties by the time you met him.'

'He's still very attractive now he's ninety,' Rosemary said. 'He has lovely hair and a marvellous complexion.'

'Did your mother know?' Gillian asked.

'Yes. They were married late. She was getting on for forty before I was born and he'd had several women of one sort or another before they were married. My mother used to bring their names up from time to time. And one of them used to visit us occasionally. They'd been engaged for years. She was an actress. I used to call her Auntie Ella. She always brought me interesting presents, so she was in my good books.'

'When did she act?' Gillian said. 'This is all news to me.'

'In London. She'd married. A widower. He was a something to do with tobacco. He was, moreover, a knight.'

'So she was Lady Something or other?'

'Lady Holmes. As an actress she'd been Ella Steadfast.'

153

'I seem to remember that name,' Rosemary said.

'I wouldn't think so. She'd be well before your time. It was quite interesting to watch them, Mother, Dad and Auntie Ella. You'd have guessed that those last two were the man and wife.'

'How could you tell?' Rosemary.

'They seemed genuinely fond of each other. Touching, smiling, recalling incidents. My mother used to look on them like exotic animals in the zoo.'

'She wasn't jealous?'

'Not as far as I could make out. They weren't as she and Herbert were, but that didn't surprise her. My mother was a quiet, clever, secretive sort, whereas Dad was a typical schoolmaster of the period, extrovert, always ready with the right word, anecdote, required piece of information.'

'And what about the knightly husband?'

'Sir Harold. We never saw him. He was getting on a bit. I think Ella was older than Dad but not by much, and her husband even older. I don't suppose he fancied seeing his wife making a fool of herself with my father.'

'He never talks about her,' Gillian said. 'At least, not to me.'

'Had they children?'

'No. Holmes had two children from a first marriage. I did see them once when we were taken to the Theatre Royal here. She brought them along to see *The Tempest*, which one of them was doing for some exam. We all went round to the dressing room afterwards to see Robert Edison who played Prospero. Ella had acted with him at one time.'

'All very exciting,' Gillian said.

'The thing that impressed me most was that I stayed up so late. I fell asleep in the taxi on the way home.'

'What a life of luxury you lived.'

'You might well think so. But the Holmeses are dead now and the old man's abandoned inside his house, unable to get out. That's what has finally done for his morale. Until this last accident he could get out for a walk if he felt down in the mouth. It mightn't be very far; just round the local streets. Now he's stuck; he can barely scramble to the front gate or the dustbin or the back lawn. He's dependent on people coming in to see him, bringing him the news or to take him out. And there's nobody

154

about with his eye for scandal or something a touch different. His life's ended. And nobody will help him out of his predicament. His doctor's pessimistic. "You're ninety, Mr Montgomery. You can't expect to gad about even as you did at sixty." So he thinks he's finished. He enjoyed it today. He found his tongue again. He loves feminine company he can impress. It's difficult to impress somebody pulling your vest off or sponging you down. And he was pleased to meet your notable lawyer. He'd feel he could still hold his own with a titled professional man. I was pleased because it kept him off my back. "Give up your daytime job, and do what you do best." '

'Do you think then, Frank, that we did him any good on this visit?'

'I think so. It stimulated him. For an hour or two he felt something of his old self. He'd something to think about outside his deficiencies. The snag is, if I'm any judge, in the many hours he's left on his own he'll compare himself with the lively man he was this afternoon and realise he can't find such pleasure on his own.'

Frank, driving, delivered his judgements slowly to the women on the back seat, as if he considered every word before he released it.

'Do you think, Frank,' Gillian asked, 'that your father's had a happy life?'

'Hard to say.' Frank paused long enough. 'He was good at his job as a grammar school teacher, and at a time when schoolmasters in his sort of school were well regarded. They were, within limits, people of some consequence. There were some really clever graduates in such schools in the thirties. In this part of the world there was a great deal of unemployment or short time. Industries kicked out their research people, Ph.D.s, and they found places in the grammar schools. So Dad lived comfortably, could buy books and take us on foreign holidays, not nearly so popular at that time. He did a spell in the Navy during the war, but was invalided out on account of two quite serious accidents. So he came back after a couple of years, or perhaps a bit longer, and was made head of department perhaps rather more quickly than he would have been in the ordinary way. He moved schools twice and ended up as head of department and then deputy head of a good academic school.'

155

'What did he teach?'

'English. And some junior Latin. He taught on to sixty-five. That's unusual nowadays. The school seemed pleased with him. He was invited back for plays, speech days, Founder's Days and so forth. A successful career. My guess is that a good percentage of his pupils would express satisfaction with his classes.'

'But?' said Gillian solemnly from the back.

'But.' Frank said nothing while he negotiated a piece of country road under repair. 'Well, after the war I think he imagined it would be like the old days. They had employed women teachers during the war, but they'd all gone, and people were back from the Forces. And their attitude was different, as was that of the new young men, fresh from the university. They weren't so pliable as he was as a young man. I'm not saying they were bolshie, but they'd speak their minds rather more openly than their predecessors. And my father thought that standards weren't so high. He certainly often complained recently about it. His last school did well all the time, continues to do so, as you'd expect. And if it was competing against the comprehensives then there was no comparison. Later, when the government abolished grammar schools, he thought that was a tragedy, and said that if he had been a young man he'd have gone after a job in one of the grammar schools which were left.'

'So he felt educational standards were low.'

'He was convinced.'

'But his pupils didn't suffer.'

'No, but he felt that he and his like had shown the way, set many children from poor families, for instance, on their way to universities, and then governments and local councils had thrown all his pioneer work away.'

'Do you think it's true?' Rosemary asked.

'Something in it. But he regarded teachers as experts in their subjects and pupils as pots to be filled with that knowledge. Nowadays I believe education is child-centred, and one part of it claims that children have opinions worth noting, ideas which are to be encouraged.'

'Wasn't that always so?' Rosemary asked.

'To a much smaller extent. You learnt the groundwork of Latin or chemistry at school and then used that basis to make further discoveries. Or the clever pupils did. And I guess some, a few, were already as schoolboys beginning to develop their own ideas, whatever the topic.'

After another pause, he took up again the subject of his father's disappointment: 'He always felt that he was not sufficiently appreciated for his experience. If the local teachers had a conference or meeting on some educational topic he'd never be asked to speak. The officials would invite some young shaver from the education department of the university who'd hardly spent ten minutes in a classroom but who was full of the latest jargon or who'd baffle them all with fancy statistics and notions of probability. And so he left the profession slightly disgruntled. He missed the classroom and the common room. He didn't miss the last two headmasters he served under. They were years younger than he was and their ideas were not his. He didn't exactly claim they were ignorant, but they did not themselves value the education they were offering. They dropped Greek from the syllabus without compunction. He left before the craze for IT set in.'

'Oh, dear.' Rosemary with a large histrionic sigh.

'I guess all old-fashioned teachers retired feeling they were unwanted.'

'Wasn't he glad not to have to get up early and mark books and all the rest of it?' Rosie.

'No. He'd fill in his time, he thought. He wasn't short of occupation. Or not until a few years ago and Edina, my mother, had died, and he realised how much of his success, in and out of school, had depended on her.'

'Was she clever?'

'Yes. Not academic, but she knew what was what.'

XV

They reached the Montgomery home in the dark. A north-eastern wind cut into them as they walked the thirty-five yards from garage to front porch. Gillian hurried indoors, but Rosemary accompanied Frank on his trek to close the five-barred gate at the end of his grounds. 'It's bitter,' she said.

'You should have gone in with Gill.'

'No. I'm grateful that you've allowed me to live here. It's made my life more tolerable.'

'Not at all. It was Gillian's idea, and what she says goes.'

'I don't believe that for a minute.'

He closed the gate and turned to stare down into the valley with its irregularities of lights. He tried to recall the shapes of the trees, the buildings, the hills beyond, none of which seemed to bear much resemblance to the lamps there, either in windows or out of doors. The darkness was moonless and coldly unwelcoming.

'You're fairly isolated up here,' she said.

'We should be if we hadn't the use of cars.'

'Do you prefer it to your Sheffield house?'

'I don't much mind. It's quieter. I have slightly more room. And after a day in the college I recover my spirits as I drive back.'

A gust of icy wind rattled the hedges and the bare branches of shrubs.

'Let's get in,' he said, 'before we're blown away or frozen into the ground.'

She took his hand, surprising him. She held on to him right to the porch, like a child, and when she let him go, she stretched up to kiss his cheek. He understood this as a token of her thanks.

As soon as they passed into the hall, the warmth of the house hit them with comfort.

'That's better,' he said. 'The wonders of modern science. I set the heat to come on at three this afternoon, but we're back later than I thought.'

'It's lovely,' she said, taking off her coat and hanging it. 'Like strong medicine.'

'Gilly will have the kettle on and boiled by now,' he said. 'Let's go and see. And we're glad to have you here. As long and as often as you like.'

'I must be in Gillian's way.'

'She's not said so to me. And while this winter weather's here, an hour or two's conversation doesn't come amiss.'

'But you and Gillian want your own private time together.'

'We can have that in bed.'

When they reached the kitchen Gillian asked what they'd drink. She did this each night, listing the beverages. Frank chose his usual coffee, saying it wouldn't keep him awake. Rosie opted for Horlicks and Gill for Ovaltine.

'I thought they were going to stop manufacturing that,' Frank said.

'They wouldn't dare.'

'They've been making it long enough. I remember my father telling me that he used to tune in to one of these Continental stations to get the cricket score from the test matches in Australia. I think it was Hilversum. And they had advertisements, and the one for Ovaltine was a song "We are the Ovalteenies, happy boys and girls". Or girls and boys. It's quite possible that there was a children's club, badges and all.'

'When was this?' Rosemary asked.

'Between the wars, I think. When Dad was a young man. They were simple souls in those days. Though I remember he used to talk about a German brother and sister who lived with the people next door. Dad was living in London then on one of his first jobs. They used to come in from next door and Dad used to talk to them to improve their English.'

'Were they Jewish?'

'Presumably.' He raised a finger to Gillian. 'Nor can I remember what happened to them. I seem to recall that they went in time to America.'

'And their parents?'

'Don't know. Dad moved after a year or two. And then went into the Forces. He was invalided out. I don't quite know how long he was in the Navy. Two years, perhaps. He injured himself and had no sooner begun to recover from that than he had a bad crash on a motorcycle. He was in hospital for some time, then they sent him back to civilian life. He disliked talking about it. He was about to go for officer training and he felt that a valuable part of his life's experience had been taken from him. He served at sea for part of his time and I think he regretted not having done his full stretch. He went back to the school where he was teaching when he was called up. They were glad to have him.'

'Why did he want to finish off his Navy service?'

'He didn't like to leave a job half done. If he had to be in the Forces, he'd make as much of it as he could. He felt he could have done well. I once was ill-advised enough as a young man to say that surely he was better qualified to teach English than to drop depth charges or to bang shells up in the air at raiding bombers, any fool could soon learn to do that and it was less important than instructing the young.'

'He was angry with you?' Gillian asked.

'Furious. He just told me I didn't know what I was talking about. He was romantic about it. It was a young man's duty to serve his country in a time of need. I read somewhere that Enoch Powell, the politician, who did remarkably well in the Army (he joined up as a private and ended as a brigadier), felt he would have done better to die for his country.'

'That's ridiculous,' Rosemary said.

'They think differently from us.' Frank stroked his cheek. 'Anyhow, it was a loose end in my father's life. One other thing he hadn't properly completed. If he'd ended as headmaster of Eton or High Master of Manchester Grammar, and neither was at all likely, he'd have chided himself for not going further.'

'What would he have wanted to be?'

'Secretary of State for Education, perhaps?'

'That's not any better than the other positions.'

'Maybe not. But he thinks so.'

They sat silently, luxuriating in the warmth. Gillian began the questioning. 'D'you know, I'd never have guessed that your father was a disappointed man.'

'Why's that?' he asked.

'He showed no signs of it. He was always confident in his opinion and well prepared to defend his views.'

'When you first met him you were a teenager. He was for a man in his seventies very fit physically. And, moreover, my mother was still alive. She looked after him well. He didn't, in my view, appreciate all she did for him. His clothes were always clean and ready; he didn't do much about the house; if there was a clash of engagements, it was she who gave way. The result was that he always seemed smart, could keep up with his reading, could attend meetings, stay in close touch with friends, choose holidays abroad in places he wanted to visit. When she died, near his eightieth birthday, he became a different man. It didn't happen quickly; we were all surprised how well he dealt with the bereavement. He hired a home help, but he couldn't lay down the law to her as he did to my mother. I guess he tried, but she wouldn't have it. At least two of them gave up the job. Then his health began to deteriorate. He had aches and pains; he had bouts of flu; this had never happened before, though he was delicate as a child. He'd never take any time off from school. But now he had to stay in bed for some days; the old accident wounds began to trouble him so that he wasn't able to walk about as he did previously. The doctor put him in hospital twice. He hated that. He was never in for more than a few days, but he felt dependent on the young nurses and that didn't suit.'

Frank sighed, shook his head.

'And he's grown worse?' Gillian asked.

'Yes. When we were married seven years ago he was mobile still, and lively. He made the speech of the afternoon at our wedding. He looked young and resilient. But he'd begun to consider his life and was concluding he'd got nowhere. There were no medals from the Palace, no honorary degrees. The school occasionally made a bit of a fuss of him and that was about it. I even think he was jealous of me.'

'Why was that?' Gillian.

'Was it because you were young, so much younger than he was?' Rosemary, hesitantly.

'That came into it. He was forty-three when I was born. He was a good father.'

'Strict?' Rosie.

'Yes. In a way. But he'd put in time instructing me, reading to me, getting me to read to him, or describing what I was reading. All, I think, to my advantage. But I guess he knew that my mother had more influence on me than he did.'

'And that was right?'

'I'd say so. She was artistic as he wasn't. He'd tell you Vermeer's dates. My mother loved sketching and had no end of books about artists. To my father artists were oddities. The art master was like the PT man or the handicraft teachers, one rung above the caretakers. He wanted me to go to university to study some more academic discipline. I disappointed him. Then I began to make something of a name for myself and when I, or my agents, charged what he considered ridiculous prices for my pictures he was reconciled, or, at least, easier in his mind. Finally, I got this job here at the age of thirty-six. Head of a well-known college, highly spoken of, so young, well, it was a schoolmaster's dream come true. It was most unusual. I didn't expect it, I can tell you.'

'Why did you, then?'

'It's rumoured that some influential governors argued that they should choose an artist, somebody who had proved himself as such, instead of some dull teacher or administrator. They said it would attract students, pull them away from the London schools. That's why they'd give me time off for artistic work, as long as I didn't take advantage of them.'

'And you didn't?' Rosemary asked.

'I did not. And they found, and I found, that I wasn't so bad as an administrator. I quite enjoyed smartening the place up. I appointed some very good teachers, youngish men and women who had their way to make. That's where I really scored.'

'And that's the secret, is it?' Rosie.

'Isn't that so with your office? You employ clever youngsters. With us, I discovered soon enough that they'd learn, if they were any good, after a year or two.'

'All of them?'

'A fair proportion. But I soon realised that nobody was indispensable. As long as they gave three years' hard inspiring work it made all the difference to the place.'

'Where did they go?'

'Most of them wanted to go back to London. That's where they thought the action was. True, to some extent. A few make for some picturesque place, Cornwall, the Lake District, Walberswick, abroad even, where there's a living to be made. Some have decided that their future lies in teaching and they go off for promotion.'

'Aren't they learning their job with you?'

'Again, to some extent. As with you. But if they're any use they'll soon be giving more than they're taking. They have ideas which are worth trying.'

'Are there some dependable old people who'll see their time out in your college?'

'One or two.'

'Are they not useful?'

'If they're good. Most of them aren't. They aren't total disasters, but if we're to get a high reputation, you don't want too many mediocrities, passengers.'

'Would you sack all of them?' Gillian asked.

'The place would be better off rather than the opposite if I did.'

'Do they know you think that?' Gillian again.

'They know that I favour young men and bright ideas.'

'So they're fed up with you?'

'They were when I was appointed. I was a young upstart who knew little about it, who hadn't the remotest notion where our students would end their working lives, who'd got the job because at the time the appointment was made, I was being written about in the newspapers as one of the bright hopes of British painting.'

'And now?'

'I'm edging towards the old dependables' stage.'

'And have lost your early enthusiasm?'

'My enthusiasms now are different. Let's put it like that.' He laughed. 'And my registrar is great at publicity. He's hard on staff and students but they know if they come up with something worth seeing he'll move heaven and earth to get it a big spread in the newspapers and radio, and above all the telly.'

'Was he one of your appointments?' Rosemary enquired.

'He was. He came a year after me. He came from Liverpool University where he was deputy assistant registrar. I knew

163

somebody who taught there, and he said that Wilfred Melton knew a great deal about art and was the best man at publicity he'd ever seen.'

'Didn't they want to hold on to him at Liverpool?'

'I expect they did. But he was well down the line of administrators. And I think he wanted to have his talents stretched on the arts, rather than on strictly academic subjects.'

'Had he trained as a painter?' Rosie.

'No. He did Classics in Part One at Cambridge, then Fine Arts in Part Two. He gave a first-rate account of himself in his interview, and my friend John Priest was not the sort to praise without good reason and he said that young Melton was not only brilliant, but honest. "An Israelite in whom there is no guile." Even so I had not a little trouble convincing some of the old brigade. They thought they'd done wrong in appointing a principal who was still wet behind the ears and didn't want to compound the error by making his second-in-command another such upstart.'

'How long was it', Gillian this time demanded, 'before he made his presence felt?'

'About three years before we made the papers in a big way. *Sun* and *Mirror* as well as *Times*, *Guardian* and *Independent*. He knew people on these papers. He worked up a controversy in the letters columns arguing that people who could draw in a traditional way were just as interesting as some of the Young Turks who were carrying off the London prizes. He was lucky, in a way, because we'd some good painters among the students, and teachers who stretched them.'

'All new people?' Rosemary asked.

'No. We hadn't had too much time. But it roused fire in at least one of the old laggards, once they saw what Melton could manage and saw their photographs in the national press.'

'He was lucky, you say,' Rosie pressed.

'Wasn't it Napoleon who said he wanted generals who were lucky? We had a college that was decent, hard-working if old-fashioned. Pupils who came had been looked after. Their teachers were, on the whole, literate, which is more than one could claim of the staff at some of our rival institutions. We had something of a name. Good, solid place. Respectable courses, conscientious instruction. Students could be put on show anywhere. And when you fling this fluffy blanket of publicity over a well-established foundation it works. The number of applicants, always respectably high, became astronomic. Governments know what they're doing when they appoint their spin-doctors.'

'Will he stick with you when you become part of the university?' Rosemary asked solemnly.

'I'm not sure. Depends what the university wants him to do. He's introduced and developed all sorts of new dodges, and then got them recognised and copied elsewhere. If the university make it known to him that they take him seriously he might well stay on. I think he'd like to go back to Cambridge or Oxford if there's half a chance.'

'Wouldn't they be seriously fuddy duddy?'

'I shouldn't think so. He'd liven them up if they were.'

He enjoyed talking with this woman, though he was never sure how near the truth he was.

Rosemary made a point of taking Herbert Montgomery out to lunch once a week. 'He's an interesting man,' she said. 'He soon loses his gloom.'

'Does he give you advice?' Gillian asked.

'Now and then, but it's Frank he's thinking about. "Has he made up his mind when he'll take up full-time painting?" is asked each time I see him.'

'And what do you say?'

'I tell him that Frank's as good an administrator as you'll find, because I know that will set him off. "Even if he's as good a college principal as he is a painter, he should give the job up." It riles him inordinately. "If there aren't more principals of genius than there are painters of equal status I'll be surprised. Frank Montgomery has real genius." He puffs his chest out. You should see him. "You don't know what it's like to realise suddenly that your son is world-class. He was good at school subjects, English and Maths and Languages. He did English and French and Latin for A level. His school wouldn't provide any A-level teaching for art. He entered himself and did a few classes at the local technical college on Saturday morning and one evening a week. He got a distinction and a prize for the highest mark in the country. I still thought he should go to the university, but he'd made up his mind. Art college. He went to the one his mother had attended.

165

It was his own choice, but she was pleased. He won prizes by the dozen there and then he went to the Royal College. I asked him recently if the teachers were any good. A few were inspiring painters or critics. The reason I did so well, Frank used to say, was that I could do it much more quickly than they could. It took them aback. They made sure he went to a good first job. He was already exhibiting, making money as a student." '

'I think he was pleased,' Frank told his sister-in-law. 'But the reason he's so pressing now is on account of his own case. He's lonely, hasn't too many friends, has nothing much to show for his life's work except an inadequate pension. I shall leave pictures behind me to witness whether or not I was any good. He depends on the memories of his pupils for his immortality. And they, he fears, don't think of him very often, and when they do don't write or phone to tell him.'

'Would he like to be praised?' Rosemary asked.

'Yes. Or at least he'd like to have his hat in the ring for a chance of worldly reward.'

They both laughed at his old-fashioned phraseology and then sat in comfortable silence.

After a time he took up the topic again. 'My father feels his inadequacies. Up to the age of eighty his memory was good and he had a lifetime's learning at his fingertips or his tongue's end. Now he still follows his old procedures. If he doesn't know something he immediately drops whatever he's doing and looks it up. A few years ago he remembered what he'd found. Now within five minutes it's gone. He tries to remedy this with a little notebook. He immediately writes down what he's just found out in a little hardback notebook he always carries about with him. But he finds, when he goes for another look at the book, he's forgotten what, let's say, "entropy" or "hendiadys" is.'

'What is hendiadys?' Rosie asked.

'Using two words or expressions instead of one.' She looked puzzled. 'With might and main. Nice and warm.' He nodded. 'Now he thinks, and I guess that there's some truth in it, that your mental or physical and creative powers run down, so that I at forty-seven will shortly lose my strengths as a painter. I shall be able to put on a show as an educationalist, but I shan't be able to work at full stretch as an artist.'

166

'And you agree?'

'Human beings are so complex and so different from one another that I wouldn't like to say. Titian painted on superbly until he was getting on for a hundred. Or so they used to think. I might suddenly decline, especially if I don't continually practise. The only thing I needn't worry about is that my father won't be there to see me. That's one advantage of having your children late in life.'

'But you'll miss their successes?'

'I suppose so. I'm a pessimist.'

'Do you admire your father, Frank?'

'Yes.' He stroked his forehead, frowning. 'But not altogether. He's laying down the law as to what to do now, but he never exactly encouraged my mother. She could draw beautifully. She could play the piano well and she had a superb singing voice. But in his prime, when he was swanking around in his school, she was the woman who cleaned the house, prepared the meals, looked after me, stood just behind him at school functions. The little woman.'

'He didn't admire her, then? Love her?'

'It was his way, his upbringing. He'd fling a few crumbs of praise in her way in public, but in the same manner you'd praise a precocious child.'

'Didn't she mind?'

'She was never asked. And he was so wrapped up in his own concerns that she was left to do as she liked once her domestic duties were over.' He dug his hands furiously into his trouser pockets. 'I tell you what. I'll show you something.'

Frank ran upstairs to his study, unlocked his desk and took out a sketchbook. He opened it at a drawing of a cottage and two trees by a pond. 'Look at that,' he said.

'It's beautiful. Where is it?'

'My grandparents' house.'

'Done by you?'

'No. By my mother. It's a marvellous little sketch, so economical. It was from this book I first learnt what could be done with a pencil.' He turned over a page or two. 'Now, how about this?'

'Is it your father as a young man?'

'It is. And just see how she suggests his character by the set of his shoulders and the expression on his face.'

167

Rosie stared long enough at it. 'You can tell it's your father,' she said. 'But he seems different.'

'He was somebody, then. In his own eyes. That's where it counts. Now he's had all the stuffing knocked out of him.' She looked harder. 'Turn over. Here's a beauty.'

Rosemary did as she was told to find the sketch of a small boy seated on a tricycle.

'That's me,' he said, 'aged five, preparing for the sixties.'

'You seem pretty pleased with yourself.'

'I'm pleased with the trike.'

'My word, you look bright.'

'Unlike the present appearance.'

'Children can appear really bright as adults can't.'

'Why?'

'Heaven knows. They don't realise, perhaps. Whereas if adults want to look intelligent, they frown, screw their faces up.'

Rosemary screwed up her face as if testing the truth of his assertion. 'Has Gilly seen all these?'

'Yes. They're not secret. In fact, she asked me if she could take a page out and have it framed.'

'And where is it now?'

'Somewhere in her bedroom or study, I think.'

'What did she say?'

'Oh, she was impressed. It was something she could never do, not in a thousand years. She did art at school, but . . .'

'Did she meet your mother?'

'I'm not sure. She died three years before we were married. Only a year or so after I came to Sheffield. Gill, and you for that matter, used to come to the college. That's where I first met the pair of you. So it is just possible that you met, either or both of you, at the college.'

'No. I think if I'd been introduced to the principal's mother I'd have remembered. Was your mother like you?'

'In character? No, I don't think so. I've had the opportunities to show off my idiosyncrasies as she hadn't. She had to play second fiddle to her husband.'

'And you regret that?'

'She knew what she was in for when she married. She'd been teaching art and music in a girls' school. She was thirty-eight when she married and almost forty when I was born. But she sank all her peculiarities, if she had them, to be a perfect wife and mother. She ruled the roost at home sometimes, ticked my father off.'

'Didn't he mind?'

'You bet your life he did. He'd blow his top if she went too far. But they were always careful about what they said in front of me. And my mother always defended him if, when I got older, I complained about him.'

'She must have been able to put up with him?'

'Yes. And the house, the home was comfortable enough. She saw to that.'

'My husband went beyond all reason. It came to a stage where we couldn't stand each other any longer. I was lucky. I had a job and no children. When he went off to London, I refused to go with him. That added to the other grudges he bore me. I wasn't prepared to support him in his career.'

'As you weren't?'

'As I wasn't. I was only too glad to get rid of him.'

'Was he a good barrister?'

'Quite good. He was intelligent, spoke well, was sharp in court, but he didn't work hard enough to climb to the top of the tree. I did help him several times. I knew a lot more about the law than he did. I think he realised that. That's one reason why he wanted me in London with him.'

'Is he doing well?'

'He's making a living. He'll never be a QC. He's always likely to put his foot in it with some legal luminary. He's in Manchester now.'

'Why did you marry such an unpleasant character?'

'He wasn't unpleasant when we first met. In fact, the very opposite. Charming, suave, putting himself out to please.'

'After you were married did you think that some of his worst characteristics were there to be spotted while he was acting so agreeably?'

'Yes. In a mild form. I blame myself in part for our quarrels. I wasn't averse to pointing out the defects in his knowledge of the law. He disliked that. In his view women not only knew nothing, but lacked any kind of judgement. So. He felt doubly betrayed. But I will say this for him. When I straightened him out on some point of law he made good use in court of his new knowledge.'

'But never thanked you?'

'Not really. I think he convinced himself that he had somehow used some bit of knowledge I had acquired by chance but that he had used it to the advantage of his client. He had a high opinion of himself. He got across one or two judges.'

'He wasn't brutal?'

She hesitated before she answered. 'Not at first. But later I so enraged him he did beat me once or twice. He tried to make it up when he'd calmed down, but by that time I'd had enough. I just moved out and lived in the office flat until such time as he'd taken off for London.'

'And then?'

'I went back to the house. It was in my name in any case. I'd bought it, partly through some money I'd come into. But I was earning more than he was when we married. By a fair amount.'

They sat comfortably. She talked freely, it appeared to him, without embarrassment. She was intelligent, even learned, he guessed, in her own sphere, but open, speaking easily of her difficulties. When he asked her what she thought about his father's opinion that he should throw over his principalship at the art college and spend his time painting, she pursed her lips. 'That's beyond my power to answer. I don't know you well enough for a start. Nor can I judge the relative status of these jobs, if I can call them that, in your mind. Your father was delighted when you were appointed to the art college at the age of thirty-something. He could barely believe that an education committee had made such a bold decision. And then you've made a success of it. It's considered to be one of the top art academies in the country, and now it's to join with the university and will be one of their most highly regarded departments. When the broadsheets publish their lists of the best places to study, your place will be among them. This is what I'm told, but by knowledgeable people whose judgement I trust. Now why should you give up a position you've done so well at? You've another thirteen years if you decide to retire at sixty. If you still have a relish for the work and it doesn't bore you stiff and you're still full of ideas you want to try out. Why, there are even vice-chancellorships to be had these days, if you turned your ambitions in that direction.'

She paused, smiling.

'So that's the answer,' he asked, 'is it?'

'No. Because I can't speak for you. Your father thinks that you are at the peak of your powers as a painter now and should be turning out pictures at speed. In a year or two, or so he tells me, you'll have gone off the boil, or lost some of your physical thrust. So you'll never have the chance again.'

'Do you agree with that?' he asked.

'It sounds plausible enough, but I don't know. It perhaps just reflects your father's own loss of energy and his physical decline.'

'That's probably right. He thinks he's left nothing to show for his life's effort. A few famous pupils and he can't be certain that he is the sole cause of their success. He's pretty sure that he isn't.'

'You've done some pictures this last year. And now there's the Queen coming up.'

'But I ought to be painting landscapes, widening my range.'

'Do you paint landscapes, then?'

'I've one on the go now. I'll show you tomorrow.'

When Gillian poked her head round the door to announce that she was off to bed, they made a move to go.

'I'll see that all's locked up,' he said.

Rosemary accompanied him on his round of the doors and windows. 'I do enjoy these conversations with you,' she said. 'They really have edged me back nearer sanity.'

'That's good.' Gruffly.

'Our Gilly's very lucky to have a husband like you. You're not only very good at your work, in fact, outstanding, but you don't throw your weight about. You talk like an ordinary sensible man.'

He put an arm round her waist and they kissed, more deeply than was proper.

XVI

When the college resumed work in January, Frank found himself busier than he expected. He had thought that the union of university and college had been sealed, signed and delivered, but found himself forced to attend meeting after meeting, where people argued either over useless minor detail or for purposes of self-publicity. It's true that when occasionally he saw the point of these arguments, the participants seemed invariably to prolong them needlessly. When he said as much to the Vice-Chancellor, he agreed, but seemed surprised that his colleague was so put out.

'You realise, don't you, that some of your heads of department are staking their claims as members of the university staff. They like to hear the sound of their own voices and they hope they are impressing their personality or their vigour or their ideas on the rest of us.'

'What good does it do?'

'It gives the appearance, at least, that their opinion has been asked for and listened to. That keeps them on their toes. And they can't complain afterwards. All the important decisions have been taken and made known. They realise now there'll be only three chairs, of which you'll have the senior one, and that means that one of your heads of department will be without. That's bound to cause trouble. I expect they've already been on at you enquiring what their chances are.'

'They have. I told them that I have written glowing references for them all and they will be judged by a committee of the Council or by fellow professors in due course.'

'You know who'll be left out.'

'I know whom I wouldn't appoint. I've made it clear to you. You presumably will have passed it on.'

'You're firm in your opinion?'

'Absolutely. Miller deserves it least and will kick up the minimum of fuss once he's not appointed. You can appoint him to a personal

172

chair in due course, if you so wish. He'll be retiring in four years, and will be delighted when eventually he's allowed to take the nameplate off his door and change it for one calling him "professor".'

The Vice-Chancellor edged Frank into his room, where he poured glasses of dry sherry. 'It's rumoured', he said, 'that you are considering retirement.' He spoke confidentially.

'Untrue.'

'And that you are to paint the Queen for the Royal Society.'

'That's so. How do people get to hear these things? I don't know.'

'These matters, which show you in an excellent light, are allowed to leak. Whether it's the Palace or the Royal Society, and remember they both have underlings who are in the know and can pass the good news on without any repercussions.'

'How do they reach you?'

'God knows. Haven't you noticed it at your place? We've two Fellows of the Royal Society, but it wasn't from them I heard it. I think it was at a meeting of vice-chancellors, but I can't be sure. I was interested at once when I heard your name, but it was in a conversation I was not party to. I thought somebody might come over later and ask about you. When do you start?'

'I've no idea. Some official at the Palace will fix the dates or argue with me about them.'

'Will you need a big number of sittings?'

'Four, I guess. Unless I run across some snag.'

'What sort of snag? You mean it doesn't look like her and you'd have to begin all over again?'

'I don't anticipate that in particular, but something of the sort.'

'And if she doesn't like it? What happens then?'

'She'll make it known to the Royal Society. Tell them she doesn't want to see it hung in their headquarters.'

'And they'll do as she wishes?'

'I've no idea. They might. Or hide it away in a vault in the hope that its value will increase. Perhaps they'll even show it secretly to a few hundred people. "The picture the Queen found too honest." Get a legend working. It'll be even more valuable to them than if it were hanging on their walls.'

'Why did they want it in the first place?'

'Some millionaire offered them the money, made the suggestion. After all, it is a Royal Society.' He stressed the adjective.

173

'Do you find yourself feeling threatened by the commission?' the Vice-Chancellor asked.

'No. Not at all.' He smiled. 'Suppose you were the President and you had a message that she didn't like it, what would you do?'

'I'm not even a Fellow. So it's utterly unlikely. But, if . . . It would depend what I or my committees wanted out of the Queen. I'm no judge of pictures, so I wouldn't have the qualifications to say whether it was good or bad. But if the Queen expressed her distaste and offered to do the Society some good, I'd fall in and toe the line like the other creeps. That must sound feeble to you.'

'No. Especially as you say you don't know much about painting.'

'I suppose', the V-C. spoke softly, as to himself, 'if I were an expert and judged it a great work of art, then I would face a dilemma.' He patted the painter's shoulder. 'There's no evidence, is there, that the Queen comes down against this painting or that? I've never heard or read as much.'

'She must like some more than others. But she, or her advisers, never let the news out to the press.'

'No. Didn't Clementine Churchill burn the Graham Sutherland portrait of her husband?'

'So it's rumoured.'

'You'd think that a shame?'

'Yes. Sutherland was talented. Not that I thought that one of his best pictures. But in principle I'm against the destruction of works of art. Even on economic grounds, because we never know what future generations will admire and want to buy.'

'Great to talk to you, Frank,' the Vice-Chancellor said. Talk about art had run beyond its allotted time. Montgomery slipped out, wondering how many people the V-C would tell about the proposed commission.

He was not surprised when a few days later a local journalist rang to ask about the portrait of the Queen. 'I'll talk to you when it's duly commissioned, if ever it is.'

'Would you be prepared to do it?'

'Yes.'

'That's very short.'

'You asked a question and I answered it. But there have been no formal negotiations and so I'm not prepared to talk about the matter. Come back to me when you hear the business is finalised.'

174

'Are you painting much these days?'

'As much as ever I do.'

'Is your painting of the Duchess completed now?'

'Not quite.'

'How long will it take you?'

'That depends. A month at the outside, unless I'm ill or something else interrupts.'

'Does she like it?'

'You must ask her.'

The man was not to be put off and piled one question on another. Was it an exaggeration to say he was the best living English portrait painter? Why had he concentrated on portraits? Did he prefer to paint the nobility? Could he come to the studio and see examples of his recent work? Frank answered each briefly and seemed hardly polite, though the journalist took no umbrage, but came up cheerfully with his next query. When the interview was finally over, Frank immersed himself in his administration, though his temper was short. He even complained to Gillian when they were eating their evening meal.

'It's all publicity,' she said.

'Then I can do without it.'

'Can you? I thought these days it was the hype, the spin that made reputations.'

'Yes, that's right to some extent.'

'But it doesn't apply to you?'

'It does, alas. But I don't like it.'

'Why is it so?'

'People can read. And so they follow what the newspapers and magazines tell them. And especially the radio and telly. I guess this wasn't always so. In the good old days' – he laughed at his cliché – 'pictures were for private owners and their friends.'

'Did they know anything about it?'

'I guess so. Painters had an élite clientele, all able to commission their own portraits. The nobility could tell a good painting from a bad in the same way that they could sing a part from a musical score. That was one of a gentleman's accomplishments. They learnt to do it because their friends could. It was like the days when, let's say, miners acquired a bit of money and bought pianos to stand in the parlour. I'm told that they not only sent their children for lessons, they tried to learn themselves.'

'Successfully?'

'I've no idea. Some who had some innate musical talent got somewhere, I expect, in spite of the fact that a miner's hands got terribly knocked about on the coalface. But children learn more quickly.'

Gillian listened thoughtfully.

'Has Rosie settled back in her house again?' he asked.

'I guess so. Though it means she has to, or thinks she has to, visit Mother more often.'

'And that's a waste of time?'

'Yes. She doesn't recognise anybody, but lies only half-conscious in her bed all day.'

'But Rosie still insists on going?'

'Yes.'

'Does she expect some dramatic change for the better?'

'I don't think so. She knows Mother will never come out of that home.'

'Do you think it did her good to stay with us?'

'Yes and no. The company here certainly cheered her.'

'What was the drawback, then?'

'Don't you know?'

Frank looked startled, frowning. 'No, I don't know.'

'Oh.' Gillian pulled a solemnly wry face. 'She thought she was getting too interested in you.'

'What does that mean?'

'Exactly what I say. Didn't you notice anything?'

'No. Did you?'

'Of course I did. She was all over you. She couldn't keep her eyes away from you.'

'And so you spoke to her about it?'

'No, I didn't.' Gillian now talked slowly, as if afraid of saying anything untoward. 'I thought sometimes I ought to. We usually discuss things very frankly. After all, we're grown-up women, and lawyers, used to plain speaking. We're sisters and very close. But I didn't on this occasion.'

'Why was that?'

'I'm fond of Rosemary. She's clever, and decent, and had a rough time recently one way or another. She's my sister. Eighteen months older than I am. She's always led me. She decided on law and I followed her. And recently my mother's illness had scarred her terribly. She felt guilty. She hadn't done enough. That was quite wrong, but I couldn't convince her. I thought when once she was in with us it would settle her to some extent, but then she became, well, obsessed with you. Did you never notice?' He shook his head. 'Are you sure?'

'No. How are you so certain?'

'I believed the evidence of my eyes and ears. I can't understand how you could be so dim. She followed you about the house and brought every conversation she had with me back to you. In the end she told me, confessed it.'

'What?'

'That she was in love with you.'

'In those words?'

'Yes. She also told me it was time she went back home before she said or did something foolish.'

'Did you think that she had any sort of encouragement from me?'

'No. She said as much. "I don't think he notices how I feel about him." '

'Um.' He confined his puzzlement to a long-drawn-out monosyllable while he collected his wits. Gillian watched him. She seemed calm, in no way upset, slightly amused by his discomfiture. 'What', he asked, 'am I supposed to do about it?'

'Were you attracted to her?' Gillian's question was swift.

'I liked her. I admired her. She reminded me in many ways of you. Not in looks; you're not very alike in appearance. You walk as she does and you talk similarly. I would guess – I've never put this into words before – she's more curious than you are, more inclined to ask questions. You'd think about it first, try to anticipate conclusions before you started on questions or observations.'

'I don't know whether that's true,' she said, without emphasis.

'What do you suggest I do about it?'

'What do I suggest? It's your decision that counts.'

'If it were left to me I'd do nothing. Go on with life as usual whenever I see her.'

'Do you feel flattered?' Gillian asked.

He scratched his nose. 'I suppose I do. She's an attractive woman. But why should she fall for a man getting on for fifty, nothing much to look at, and married to her sister and thus forbidden?'

177

'You must realise that you are a personality of some note to her. You're not only principal of a very fine college of arts and crafts, but, moreover, famous for your own work. You've featured in the newspapers and are frequently mentioned on radio and television. You have appeared on television programmes. And thus she finds you attractive.'

'You always speak of her as eminently sensible.'

'So she is. But she's had bad luck now for three or more years. She blames herself for the divorce from Joe.'

'That's not sensible. From all you tell me he was a nasty bastard.'

'Did you not find him so?'

'No. I didn't like him much. He seemed too fond of himself for my liking. But otherwise I'd noticed nothing out of the ordinary. He was quite a good-looking man.'

'He beat Rosie.'

'Often? Regularly?'

'Whenever he lost his temper. And that was fairly frequently. He'd go mad, then, and set about her. Now, though she was terrified of him, she felt in some roundabout way that she was responsible for his violence. And she'd not been married long, less than two years, when our father died.'

'Had the beatings started then?'

'Yes. He was growing frustrated. He didn't get enough work and that which he had didn't bring him any opportunity to shine. Then he had this offer to join Wilfrid Woodward's chambers in London. Rosie refused to go. He thought he could bully her into it, but he failed. She had enough sense to hang on here. The house was hers, in her name. But it troubled her. She has old-fashioned ideas of loving, honouring and obeying her husband.'

'Once he got to London did that settle him?'

'I don't honestly know. I doubt it because he's in Manchester now. He wouldn't leave Woodward's firm unless he wasn't finding there what he wanted. He's married again now. Rosie, by the way, paid for all the divorce expenses.'

'Does she ever see him now?'

'No. Not so far as I know. He doesn't come back here, slumming it.'

'Nor does he harass her?'

'Not as far as I am aware. He did at first. But she refused to

178

meet him and she slammed the receiver down whenever he phoned. That seemed to work. Now he's started a family.'

'How do you know all this?'

'I still run across Hugh Pearson down at the courts. He was Joe's best friend for a time and they still keep in touch.'

'And all this plays on Rosie's mind?'

'I thought she'd got over it, as much as anybody could. She works hard at the office and is senior partner now. She never went out socialising a great deal, but she met men, seemed happy enough. I thought she was seriously considering Frederic Shakespeare as a husband.'

'And you approved?'

'It wouldn't have been my choice. He was too old for one thing. It petered out. I was pleased rather than otherwise. But then my mother began to be ill. Rosie organised help and made it possible for her to remain in her own home. Ma was never very grateful; she hated her illness, said it was unfair. It all seemed in the end too much for her. She took Mother out at the weekends, arranged little get-togethers for her, with relatives and friends, but strokes became more frequent and there was nothing for it but to put her in a nursing home. Rosie fixed her up in a very suitable place, not half a mile from Mother's house, so that it was easy for her friends, such as she had, to drop in and visit her, and for Rosie to take her for little outings, shopping, the odd matinée and the like.'

'Was your mother grateful?' he asked.

'No. There was no pleasing her and she told Rosie so. Rosie was always Daddy's girl and I think now that that made Mother jealous of her. She did her best, I believe, to hide it when we were small, but not now. Her constant pain, her heart trouble, her crippling strokes took away any self-restraint she had. But it had told on Rosie. Every time she went to the nursing home and saw my mother there, pretty nearly unconscious, she felt she was responsible, that if she had taken more trouble in the first place Mother wouldn't have been in this state.'

'That's not true, is it?'

'No, but Rosie knew she disliked her mother, made no secret of it, to me, for instance, and that therefore she had never extended herself.'

'But all this seems a far cry from the sensible Rosie we know.'

179

'That's so. If you met her in her office as a client, you'd have found her quick, intelligent, courteous, helpful. But alongside there existed this other area of unreason.'

'Can anything be done about it?'

'I've tried to argue her into seeing the doctor, or a psycho-analyst, oh, anybody who could help.'

'But she won't?'

'No. She thinks she knows what's wrong and doesn't believe it can be cured by drugs.'

'How can it be cured?' he asked.

'I've no idea. I think a few hours with an analyst talking it all through would probably sort her out because basically she's sensible.'

'And?'

'And nothing. She regards these analysts as charlatans, out to make money. I tell her, "The same could be said of lawyers," but she laughs and says she's sure there are some good, honest prac-titioners in the business, but the few people she knows who have consulted psychologists become dependent on them. They now need their weekly sessions, as some people need their medicines or drugs, legal or illicit. They go off every Thursday or whatever for their hour on the couch and boast how much good it's doing them, but they're no different, they're not getting away from their obsessions and guilts. If these counsellors were any good they'd cure their patients, wouldn't they? She talks very reasonably about all this to me, but it's all a façade, a cover. Deep down inside herself she feels she's incurable. The poet William Cowper, and you couldn't have found a quieter, unpushing, delicate, more attractive man, said of himself that he was "damned below Judas".'

'He'd be a case of clinical depression?' he suggested.

'The result of chemical imbalances in the brain, you mean?'

'Exactly.'

'I guess she is now. I don't know.'

'Do you think I should speak to her about it? Not go out of my way, but next time she visits us here?' Frank asked.

'I don't know,' Gillian answered. 'If I were in her place I wouldn't want it. It would embarrass me terribly. No. I think your first idea of keeping mum is what I'd suggest.'

They left it there, but the topic occupied them over their spare time for the next fortnight.

XVII

Rosemary's obsession troubled Frank Montgomery. He would suddenly think of it while he was in the middle of some dull meeting or the writing of testimonials, which he hated; or even when he was painting. Not that the latter took up too much of his time; the days were short and he had a prejudice against painting by electric light.

His portrait of the Duchess was now complete, stood drying in his studio. Her Grace had been across to see it and had expressed her satisfaction. 'It has something of me about it. Gerald will approve. He thought his was superb, but that was partly because you gave him what he calls "a believable *gravitas*". He sometimes hits the nail bang on the head, does my husband. He's quite interested in painting; I tell him he should try it for himself. "You have the eye," I say to him. "Yes," he answers, "but not the hands." He's quite good in his way. He told me, for instance, that your painting of him looked exactly like him from the word go. After an hour or two's work, "you'd recognise me, immediately," he said.'

The Duchess enjoyed questioning him. 'Would you say that you painted our portraits quite differently? What I'm getting at really is: have you one technique for men and a quite different one for women?'

'There's just a touch of truth in that, but my technique, if that's the word, varies from person to person, irrespective of gender.'

'You don't think of your women sitters naked?'

'Sometimes. But clothes are interesting, too.'

'Even men's?'

'Yes. The way they fit, or merely hang on a man will give you clues as to character.'

'And women's?'

'Yes. They have a wider choice.'

The Duchess pulled a wry face, laughed and congratulated him again on the portrait.

181

February was cold, wet, miserable. He painted in the short daylight hours of each Saturday and Sunday. Gillian, as usual, overworked during the week and they dined late most evenings. His wife did not now seem at all curious about his painting, neither approaching the studio, nor asking questions. He worked up some of the summer's North Wales sketches, but the results seem uninspired, the unimaginative products of a well-trained mediocrity. He blamed the time of year, and the unsettling interim between art college and university department for his disappointing standard. 'It's journalism,' he told himself, 'not art.' He wondered if this was mere wordplay, comfortable lying to himself. His dexterity had not failed, nor his eye for colour; he had taken care, made meticulous, fastidious choices but these left the paintings without attraction or individuality, clever enough, but in no way out of the ordinary. He painted on; he sulked. Nothing seemed to go right. Depression ruined his spare time.

He saw nothing of Rosemary, though she and Gillian went each weekend to see her mother, usually in the nursing home, once in hospital.

There was, she reported after her last visit, no observable change in Mrs Housely, though there must have been some alteration, for her transfer to hospital. The matron of the home explained that their mother had been in such distress that the doctor tried to send her back to the NHS hospital to see if they could make some improvement. Her screams had so upset the other occupants that the matron and the doctor had seen the transfer as their only way out of the difficulty. The hospital had been reluctant, pleading or rather boldly stating that their beds were all occupied at this time of the winter. In the end the sisters had placed her in a private hospital where the same consultant succeeded in quietening her down. The matron of the home muttered, unsure of the nature of the distress, though she was unwilling to admit as much, and appealed to the pity of the daughters. 'It was heart-rending to hear her screams,' she had said, 'and she could by no means tell us what was wrong.' After the hospital had silenced her, she was returned to the nursing home, where her sleep or coma was now deeper than ever.

'How's Rosemary taking it?' Frank asked.

'Well. It has amazed me. Two things have. First, why my mother suddenly changed from this comatose barely moving body to a

violently tossing and screaming maniac. It doesn't seem possible.
I would have said that she hadn't the strength. It made me wonder
if the doctor hadn't been playing around with her drugs or they'd
taken her off medication altogether. She's had all those minor
strokes so I'd have thought – I'm speaking without the book –
that such hellish frenzy would have brought on a fatal seizure. I
questioned the matron about her drugs and she ripped through a
list the consultant at the hospital had prescribed. "It's not ever so
different from what she was on before, one or two small changes,"
she said. I don't really think she was trying to cover anything up.
I guess she didn't understand how the hospital had calmed Mother
down. "It was", she said, "as if the ambulance, the journey, the
new surroundings had shocked her out of it." '

'She's not returned to this' – he hesitated for the telling word
– 'vehemence since she came back?'

'No. She's more like a corpse now than a living being.'

'I see.' Frank spoke slowly as if helping his wife back to calm.
'And what was the second thing that amazed you?'

'Rosie. She took all this in her stride. I'd have guessed that she
would have been completely shattered by it, but it isn't so. She
was running between this hospital and that home, as though it was
for a client. There was a whole series of calls between hospitals,
the consultant, the doctor and the matron, and from what they say
it was Rose who sorted it all out. She suggested the private hospital
and got that fixed. She is so much better balanced than she was.'

'I'll go over with you on Saturday or Sunday to see my father
and call in with you and Rosie to see your mother.'

'Good.'

'That won't upset Rosie?'

'Why should it?'

'There was,' he answered in a sarcastic voice, 'if you remember,
your story of her obsession with me. You'd better give her a ring
and we'll fix the day, and perhaps take the old man out for lunch
again.'

'I'll do it tomorrow.'

Arrangements were duly made. Herbert Montgomery said he'd
be delighted to see the two girls again and to go out to lunch.
He judged the last restaurant they had visited to be excellent and
a return there would win his approval.

'But are they open on Sundays?'

'You'll have to ask them, won't you, professor?'

They met Rosie at Mrs Housley's nursing home. He thought his sister-in-law looked pale, haggard, somewhat withdrawn. She said she was perfectly well.

'You've been overworking,' he said.

'I have my living to earn.'

'Not at the expense of your health.'

'This weather gets me down.'

'Come and have a week or two of the air of Derbyshire with us.'

'I'll think about it,' she answered brusquely, but smiled at him. She was an attractive woman.

They sat for perhaps twenty minutes at Mrs Housley's bedside, attempting to wake her gently, to talk her back to life. It proved useless. The stertorous breathing seemed to fill, almost shake, the room, to mock their whispers. A girl assistant looked in and said that the 'old lady' was like this all the time now. She didn't think she felt any pain. They moved her, both in daytime and at night, to prevent her getting bedsores. 'Not that she'd know,' the girl commented with innocent cruelty.

Rosemary made another attempt to rouse her mother, holding her hand, stroking her arm. When this failed she said, 'It's no use stopping. We'll call in on the matron if she'll see us.' As they walked down the wide stairs she said, 'Her arms are like sticks, not human flesh at all. They're just warm. That's all you could say about them. It's a wonder she's alive.' She almost choked over the words, but efficiently made her way, collecting herself. By the time they reached the matron's room her face had regained normality.

The matron grudgingly gave them ten minutes. She, too, was amazed that Mrs Housley still lived. 'We do our best to keep her from pain and discomfort, but she eats very little. Her constitution must be very strong.' She would let them know at once if there was any change, even slight. As a sign of her respect she abandoned the pile of papers and the biro on her desk, and walked as far as the front entrance with them. There she formally shook hands, wished them goodbye before adding in a pious whisper, 'We'll see to it that she doesn't suffer.'

When they reached Herbert Montgomery's home he answered the door in his best suit, but hurried away, calling behind to them to drop the catch. He was listening, it appeared, to the slow movement of Bach's Concerto for Two Violins being played on the radio. They stood around in their outdoor clothes until the final movement concluded, when the old man rose and with a movement like a clergyman blessing his congregation turned his wireless off. 'I once heard Antony Hopkins talking about that second movement,' he said, standing feet apart on the hearthrug, head back, lecturing the ceiling, 'and he said that he could describe that movement in technical terms, but we would, and he was truthful, understand it better if he said of it that it was like two angels singing together. He was right, you know, exactly right.'

'Well done, Bach,' Frank said sarcastically. 'Get your coat, Dad.'

'Is it cold out?'

'Very.'

'I keep it warm in here. I don't mind spending money on heat.'

The women congratulated him. He went out to the downstairs cloakroom where he spent a long five minutes.

When he returned, topcoat, scarf and hat on his arm, Rosemary helped him dress. 'There you are then,' she said. 'Fit to appear before the Queen.'

'I'm still', he answered, 'caught up with that Bach.' He made a movement, half swaying, half conducting with his right hand, presumably to convey to his visitors the music that was running through his head.

Once in the restaurant, waiting for a table, he forgot Bach and became a man of the world. He laid down the law about money; in his view the people of Beechnall were spending far too freely for the economic health of the country. The banks were always sending him by post offers to lend him money. Plastic cards, with countless financial advantages, were his for the filling in of a short form. 'If I were poor and needed monetary help from the government, I'd need to fill in a form as long as your arm with questions that I couldn't understand except with the help of a lawyer, but to obtain one of these golden or platinum or whatever cards I just fill in a half-page of simple questions. But they would ruin me.'

'Why would that be?' Rosie asked.

'Because I'm old and daft and forgetful. One would need to put down somewhere every transaction. And I'd lose my record and get into debt.'

'You don't do that now.'

'No. I've devised a simple method. I have three accounts. One for my old age pension, one for my teaching pension and one for my savings, such as they are. I own two terrace houses that my father left me and which I let out. An agent handles these for me and pays any profits into my savings. If I have to spend money on them I take that out of the same savings account. Now I'm sure there are ways of making more money, in interest, than I do, but as long as I'm easily solvent, I don't bother myself.'

'What if you weren't?' Frank asked.

'I'd try to borrow from you.'

The girls laughed. The old man preened himself.

Once at the table he continued to talk. This meant they had all finished their courses while he was still only halfway through his. They waited patiently, seeing this as part of his enjoyment.

'I'm sorry I'm so slow at eating,' Herbert apologised. 'I like the sound of my own voice far too much.'

The ladies forgave him at once and said so.

'What about Frank, though?' Herbert asked. 'He doesn't want to sit there listening to me. Do you, now?'

'If you don't mind your food being half cold, I don't worry myself.'

'That's kind of you.'

The senior Montgomery chatted on, chiding the government who wanted us to save more.

'With interest at the level it is?' Frank asked.

'I could. That's because I make no demands. My life is dull. I hardly drink and I don't smoke. I don't go on holiday. On the fortunate side my houses are all well built and don't need a great deal of attention. I've two wardrobes and countless drawers full of clothes and shoes. I live like a miser, not out of either choice or necessity, but because I can't do otherwise. I'm near the end of my days and I don't, therefore, go chasing after pleasures or luxuries. They wouldn't satisfy me even when I tried them. Sometimes, when the weather's fine, I tell myself that I'd just like to go down to the Council House Square and look at the people and the shops, and then sit on one of the streets and watch the children or talk to other old people.'

'Not at this time of year, surely?' Gillian said.

'No.'

'But why don't you do that when the weather improves? Give yourself an hour or two of pleasure?' Rosie.

'I can't do it physically. Getting on and off buses and walking more than a few hundred yards is physically beyond me these days.'

He finished his soup. They had already ordered the main course. He had chosen, to his son's surprise, liver and bacon, with mashed potato and cabbage, but had warned the waiter that he did not want too much. When the meal arrived it was laid out beautifully on his plate, but the aesthetic appeal seemed to take, to Frank's mind, the strength out of the plebeian dish. He grinned to himself. The old man called for mustard. 'This will warm me,' he said to the ladies.

They began to eat. All were hungry. Herbert smiled, enjoying himself. He had not eaten, he said, such a tasty meal for months. 'It reminds me of the time when I'd come home from school fainting with hunger. Now, I pick at food, play with it. That's what you're like when you're old. You eat on your own.'

'Can't you get food brought in?' Rosemary asked.

'I do. They've decided I'm sufficiently disabled or dysfunctional to have meals-on-wheels. I didn't want them, but one or two ladies pressed me. I can see it's a good thing. I don't have shopping or preparation and cooking. I just have to warm it up sometimes if they happen to come early.'

'And is it palatable?' Rosemary asked.

'Yes and no. Institutional food. Airline grub. It's in cardboard packaging. I don't say it tastes of that, but I don't find it like this.' He indicated his nearly empty plate with a hand stretched like a compass. 'This has come straight from the frying pan or saucepan, straight from the stove. You can taste the difference.'

They waited for him to clear his plate, which he did with a kind of genteel reluctance. He immediately set off on a criticism of the performance of Mozart's *Marriage of Figaro* to which Gervase Lunn had ferried him. The singing and orchestral playing had been magnificent, but the production had been foolish, seeking to impress for no reason.

'Did you find it too long?' Frank asked.

'No. Why?'

'It's an act overlong for me.'

187

'I see.' Herbert, face in left hand, elbows on the table, obviously did not. 'When it comes to music, Frank, I'm afraid you're something of a philistine.'

A pause followed. The women looked apprehensive.

'That's me put in my place,' Frank said.

Again the sisters laughed, but Herbert looked abashed, shifty, as if he knew he'd gone too far.

'You can't have too much of a good thing,' Rosemary ventured.

The situation was saved by the arrival in the restaurant of Lord Whelan, the lawyer. He stopped at their table, an expression of comic surprise on his face. 'How do you do?' he greeted them. 'Do you live here? The last time I was in here I saw you.' His voice was deep, well modulated.

'We could say the same of you,' Rosemary answered.

Whelan looked at Herbert. 'Are you well, Mr Montgomery?' his lordship asked.

'I can't complain,' the old man said, 'and I'm all the better for the company I'm in.' He was clearly flattered that Lord Whelan had remembered him, and his name.

'Good, good.' Whelan nodded. 'I had better go and see to the needs of the inner man.' He placed a beautifully manicured pair of hands lightly on Herbert's shoulders before he wished them goodbye and moved, like the important person he was, away.

Herbert's smile broadened, and he addressed his ice cream, plain vanilla, as if it were the most rare dish. 'He seems a good man,' he said, looking up, 'no side about him. Do you meet him often?' To Rosie.

'About once a fortnight, one way or another.'

'An acquaintance worth cultivating.'

Herbert accepted a brandy with his coffee and arrived home in high spirits. This took the form, as was often the case with him, of asking serious questions. As they sat in his 'parlour', he suddenly demanded of Rosemary, 'Do you often think about death?'

'Yes,' she said, taken aback but cool, 'I do.'

'Why?' he asked.

'Because of my mother.'

'Yes,' he said irritably. 'I didn't mean that; I meant your own death.'

Rosemary did not answer at once, but sat upright. Gillian and Frank watched her. 'I don't think very often of dying. It would be morbid at my age when there's nothing, or seems to be nothing, amiss with my health. Even when I'm depressed or low in spirits I don't particularly think of dying.' Again a pause. Frank waited for some tactless comment from his father, but none was forthcoming. 'There is one thing, though,' Rosemary said, and waited. She continued when once she was convinced that she held Herbert's attention. 'I have thought recently of a girl I was at school with. She was my age, in my class, pretty and a superb runner. She always did outstandingly well at the school sports. Every year after the fourth form she was victrix ludorum. After school I lost touch with her. She went to a different university and neither of us went back to reunions at school. Most people thought she'd be there because she was so popular both with the staff and fellow students. About three years ago – I was very down at the time because I was at loggerheads with Joe – another friend took me along to a reunion. I quite enjoyed it, though I didn't know too many of the people there, but it was pleasant. And this girl, Eileen Fowler, was mentioned. Somebody asked me if I remembered her, and when I said I recalled what a good athlete she was, I was told she was dead.'

'How old was she?' Frank asked.

'My age. Married with three children.'

'In an accident?' Frank pressed.

'No, Breast cancer. She'd had a mastectomy. She lived in Essex somewhere, I believe. The girl hadn't any detailed knowledge and the telling of the tale didn't much affect me at the time. But in these last few months, perhaps because of my worry about my mother, I kept thinking of her, couldn't get her out of my mind. She'd been so healthy, so athletic, so competitive, it seemed wrong that she'd died so young.'

'What would she have been?' Herbert.

'Forty-one. That's all. Her eldest was sixteen. She'd married straight after university.'

'Happily?'

'As far as I know. A solicitor. I've forgotten how the girl who was telling me all this had got to know. Her husband had, she said, looked after her and the children really well when she was so ill. She went off to a skeleton. I've been thinking of her recently, because I remember her at school. She was so strong then. She could have run through a brick wall.'

'Was there any specific reason why she had this cancer?' Frank asked. 'Anything they could trace?'

'I don't know. Nothing of that sort was mentioned to me. I remember how she'd charge up the steps at school. We tiptoed up them very ladylike, one at a time, but she'd do two leaps up a whole flight.'

'It's sad,' Gillian said. 'I remember her winning all the races and jumps. It's haunting to think of her wasting away, helpless and leaving a family.'

'Yes,' Herbert agreed. 'It's amazing what does haunt the mind. Last week the wireless was on and I was doing some little job about the house. And some man was singing Ivor Novello: "We'll gather lilacs in the spring again". And I was back at the end of the war, after the war, at a cricket match, with my wife. She wore a white dress. It was before Frank was born. They were playing this song on a sort of tannoy system the physics master had fixed up. And we were drinking tea outside the pavilion; it must have been an old boys' match, Founder's Day, something of the sort.' He stared around, bemused, as if he'd lost his train of thought.

'What's that to do with death?' Frank asked rudely.

'Death? Nothing, nothing. But that tune brought that day at the cricket match so vividly to my mind. I hadn't been married long. It must have been the first time I took Edina to such a function. I was utterly proud of her. She was so talented and beautiful. I felt, well, fulfilled. It was a highlight in my life. I'd left marriage alone for so long. I was forty. I can't say that I often recalled that occasion. I didn't. But the sound of that Novello tune made me remember the sunny afternoon fifty years ago.'

'Noël Coward said something about the emotional power of cheap music,' Rosemary said.

Herbert paid no attention. 'The tears rolled down my cheeks. This is unusual with me. But I was knocked sideways.'

'Why do you think that was?' Rosemary asked.

'That afternoon, recalled so long after, seemed one of the highlights of my life, a day of supreme happiness. This was a year or two after the war; there were a good number of really bright young men on the staff, most with attractive, well-dressed, or so they seemed, wives, and Edina outshone them all. The headmaster and the chairman of governors both made a point of talking to her. I had arrived. I was delighted. But only fifty years later did I see this as one of the great days of my life.'

'And was it?'

'I've tried to compare it with the other little triumphs. That ranks with them, not least because it took place, was born or seen, inside me. The others were judged by people outside. I was invited to tea with the Lord Mayor when I retired. Services to education, they said. It meant that somebody, some friend with influence, had recommended me. Earlier I had been elected deputy head, by a committee of the head's appointment. I strutted about after that. But this sunny day brought me the purest joy.'

'That's great,' said Rosie.

'Why did you feel it so strongly?'

Herbert considered this, gnawing a knuckle. 'Old age. Just as your bodily muscles lose their strength and suppleness, so do the controls, whatever they are, of your emotions become feebler and, to quote the poet, a spontaneous overflow of powerful feeling results. I haven't the strength now to suppress my feeling and tears resulted. I would have been ashamed of this at one time, but now I boast.'

By the time they left the house, Herbert had resumed his usual tetchy self. He managed to kiss the women and shake hands with his son. 'Don't leave it so long next time,' he ordered.

As they drove out towards Derbyshire, having delivered Rosemary at her home, Gillian said, 'I felt really imprisoned in your father's house. It's dark as hell and claustrophobic. Why does he keep his curtains halfway across?'

'Perhaps he hasn't the energy to pull them right back?'

'I don't think so. It's deliberate choice. He's determined to live in the shadows. He's a remarkable man in many ways. I don't just mean "eccentric". He seems to be putting a life together out of the bits and pieces, now he's cooped up in his own home. Does he talk to his cleaning ladies and nurses as he did to us, do you think?'

'I doubt it.'

'You don't seem to like him.'

'A little of him goes a long way with me. He likes to lay down the law and loves a captive audience. He shows off to you and Rosie.'

'You mean about that Novello song?'

'Yes. At one time he would have complained bitterly how banal it was, with its English country lanes and the rest. Now that doesn't suit his mood. I don't doubt for a minute it reminded him of that afternoon at a cricket match, but he worked it up into a song and dance act to impress you and Rosie. And perhaps you've noticed. He changes his mind.'

'Was he a strict disciplinarian when you were young?'

'Yes. He thought he was. I was fairly careful not to put a foot wrong. But I think I realised then that my mother ruled the roost.'

'He seems proud of her.'

'I think he was. She was a talented woman and good-looking. I'm not saying he was without grey matter. He was a good teacher, well organised, marked strictly and kept a tally of the marks and issued monthly form lists. But you did it his way. He'd deduct marks if you didn't underline the title as he had instructed. It succeeded. His public examination grades were admirable. You knew if you were in his English set, your chance of getting an "A" mark was high. And he could be interesting. About the books he read. Or about words. He'd tell them where words like "kiosk" and "coach" came from.'

'Where do they?'

'"Kiosk" is Turkish, "coach" from the name of the place coaches come from, Kocs, in Hungary. Or he'd get on to slang: how the Roman soldiers called the head "testa" a pot, and that became tête in French. Oh, his lessons were full of interest to clever boys who thought in the way he did.'

'Was he fair, or did he have favourites?'

'Fair, but he had his favourites.'

'Did he teach you?'

'Yes, he did. And I had to call him "sir" like the other boys, not "daddy" as at home.'

'Was that difficult?'

'I got used to it. It meant the other boys looked on me as a bit of a freak. But on the whole they respected him. He was a somebody. And he delivered the goods. He should have died at his retirement instead of dragging on another twenty-five years.'

'What an odd thing to say.'

She got out as she spoke and opened the five-barred gates into their grounds.

XVIII

At the end of February the college opened its doors to the public for the exhibition of Frank Montgomery's portraits of the Duke and Duchess. The newspapers, local and national, splashed it over their news pages and, to everyone's surprise, people crowded in.

'What price the theory that nobody's interested in art or the aristocracy?' one of his colleagues wanted to know. The staff were amazed but impressed by the fuss the exhibition caused. The artist was interviewed at length on radio and television. The Duke and Duchess were introduced in their great hall where the pictures would next be exhibited. The Duke sat in his chair in almost complete silence while his wife seemed at her most lively, acidly dismissing the patronising comments of one of the interviewers. He was shaken by her frankness, overawed. She finished, staring him hard in the face, with, 'I am honoured to be painted by Montgomery, as I would have been to be portrayed by Holbein or Rembrandt or Velázquez or Reynolds.'

In the exhibition were hung five of his landscapes, a dozen watercolours, the picture of Fiona Heatherington and, in a place of honour, the largish portrait of the two sisters, Gillian and Rosemary. These two were not altogether pleased, because journalists rang them at awkward times to enquire what it was like to be the wife or relative of a famous painter.

'Did you know he was a genius when you married him?'

'I knew he was a painter, yes.'

'But one of the finest of all English painters?'

'You say so.'

'It's largely agreed. Even critics who find his kind of painting old-fashioned can't help admiring him.'

'I'm in no position to judge,' Gillian said. 'I'm a lawyer not a critic of art. I am pleased that he is so well reviewed, praised. I would be that if he were a doctor or a footballer, especially so in these days, when celebrity seems to be all. The girls who give the television weather forecasts or the people who appear in soap operas are all better known to the public than my husband. It's their opinions that are sought on all manner of subjects, not because they know more than most, but because their faces and voices are recognised. That my husband is now allowed to pick a small apple from your tree of celebrity pleases me. It shouldn't, but it does.'

'Is your husband a difficult man to live with?'

'No. Why should he be? You want him to demonstrate the artistic temperament. He's very good at his day job as head of an art college. Like everybody else, he can be a bit short if things aren't going exactly to plan. But he's not used to being courted and flattered and quoted at every verse end on the television or in the newspapers. His head isn't turned.'

'Not yet. But he's getting very good publicity now. Won't that affect him?'

'That remains to be seen.'

'What do you expect, though?'

'If, as you seem to be suggesting, his head is turned by it all, then he won't be the man I married.'

'And?' the journalist asked impertinently.

'And nothing. And would you please pass the word round to your colleagues that I don't take very kindly to having my work interrupted.'

The man got something off his own back by describing Gillian as Montgomery's 'formidable lawyer wife'. This was accompanied by an old photograph which, in the words of its subject, 'made me look about thirteen'.

At around this time Rosemary approached Gillian about spending a fortnight or so with them.

'Yes, you come. What's wrong?'

'There's nothing really wrong, but I feel so depressed.'

'About work?'

'No. That's going really well. The firm seems to be getting itself together. No, it's nothing specific. I just feel so low, and tired, with so many aches and pains.'

'Have you seen your doctor?'

'She's trying me on some new antidepressant.'

'And it's making no difference?'

'I only started the course yesterday.'

'And we'll form part of the new strategy?'

'That sounds unkind.'

'I'm sorry. I didn't mean anything by it. You make arrangements for your house to be looked after and come up here any time you like.'

'You must ask Frank first.'

'He'll be only too glad to see you. His little burst of fame is getting on his nerves. His phone's going all the time here and at the college.'

'Doesn't he like it?'

'He did at first, but he's tiring of it. They ask the same old questions time and time again. And now somebody's told them that he's going to paint the Queen. Where the news came from originally we don't know. But nobody seems capable of keeping his, or her, mouth shut these days.'

'Is he painting more?'

'To the best of my knowledge he's not had a paintbrush in his hand these last three weeks. And, like you, he's depressed. Not badly, but enough to make him awkward. Your presence will make a change. He likes talking to you. "Rosie has ideas," he says. He means it.'

Thus, the following Saturday Rosemary arrived just before lunch. Frank was out, at a meeting at the university, had gone off with ill grace 'to be bored'.

'Is he?'

'I don't think so, but he likes to paint all the weekend, so Saturday meetings don't appeal much. "I spend all my life learning to use paint and then have to waste my time listening to academic gasbags polishing their egos." I ask him if he can't learn anything from them, and he grunts, "How not to act." '

Frank returned just before one when lunch was just about ready. The two women served him at table and he seemed much at ease.

'You're pleased with yourself?' Gillian suggested.

'Yes. The meeting was short and afterwards the Vice-Chancellor invited me into his room.'

'For a drink?'

'He offered me one, but I refused. I was driving. So he put the decanter away and we both remained sober.'

195

'What's he like?' Rosemary asked.

'A decent sort. Wily. He has to be. He's not sorry, I think, to have given up his scientific research. He feels that he can still do plenty as an administrator. They're very concerned with fund-raising, but he never seems overwhelmed by it. He can stand back.' Frank shaped up to give an imitation. ' "You, m'dear Frank, are one of the glories of this university now. I make a fuss, there-fore, of you when I've half a chance and boast about our close acquaintance when you're not to be seen." '

'And what had he got to tell you this morning?'

'A trip to Italy among other things. This summer.'

'To do what?'

'Just to paint. He can talk the hind leg off a donkey to squeeze money out of people and some tycoon – no, I'm not going to name names – who's given a couple of million to the university, thought he'd do the arts some good by giving me a month, August, in Tuscany.'

'And you said "yes." '

'No.'

'Oh. What are the drawbacks?'

'None that I can see. I'm like my father, always suspicious; to us there's no such thing as a free lunch. Besides, I must first of all consult my dear wife.' Both women laughed out loud, slapped their knees, but Frank kept his face serious. 'She might decide that a fortnight in Skegness would suit her better.'

'You can depend on that,' Gillian said.

'What's the snag?' Rosemary asked.

'There isn't one. I'm not used to these free gifts that seem to come the way of celebrities. Do you know some firm wanted me to take a part in a commercial advertisement on telly. They pay rather better than academe.'

'I'm glad to learn how to pronounce that word. Three syllables. I always thought it had four,' Rosemary said.

'He turned the offer down,' Gillian added, 'without consulting me.'

'What would you have said?'

'There would have been no use in waiting for my answer. He'd made up his mind not to do it. Straight off. No hesitation.'

'Why?' Rosemary.

'He thinks highly of his art. It's not to be prostituted to big business.'

'That's good,' Rosie said and took Frank's hand.

'Don't encourage him,' Gill reproached her sister laughingly.

'Ah, you women,' Frank said, not displeased.

'Why', Rosemary asked, 'did this tycoon of yours not approach you personally with his offer?'

'No idea. I guess he wanted to please the Vice-Chancellor, but within reason. It wouldn't be some large donation. He's given plenty to the place already and that won't be the last. But he thought a thousand or two would give somebody pleasure and if he did it through semi-official channels, word would get around. It's meant to be hush-hush, but they can't keep anything secret. I let the V-C off the hook by refusing. Had I taken it there might have been some jealousy. I'm a Johnny-come-lately to some of them.'

'What will he do with the money?' Rosemary again.

'I don't know. Invest it and give an annual prize to a student. He might even found the prize in the arts and design faculty. He can claim that it will encourage the newest department and our rich friend will have his name attached to it. But he'll have plenty of worthwhile plans that could encourage unsung corners of the place.'

'You're as bad as he is,' Gillian said.

'I know, I know.' Frank looked at his two lawyers. 'In my position I'm always searching for compromises and second-best choices. And I guess the V-C is congratulating himself that I let him loose. Now he can regard me as a man beyond earthly prizes.'

'A month in Tuscany just painting would have been perfect for you,' Gill murmured.

'And you.'

'You know as well as I that I can't afford more than a fortnight in summer and that probably outside the month of August.'

'Skegness, here I come,' Rosemary crowed.

Rosemary settled down quickly with them. She and her sister arranged to leave work so that they arrived home at much the same time. They prepared the evening meal together, chattering in the kitchen over their glasses of sherry. The weather seemed warmer and this suited her. She'd snatch an opportunity to walk round the grounds of the cottage. Gillian was delighted and reported a small fraction of their talk to her husband.

'I saw that Lord Whelan we met, this morning,' he told Gillian. 'I rather liked him.'

197

'He'd been in Sheffield and had made a special point of calling in at the college to see your exhibition.'

'Oh?'

'Does he know the Duke?'

'Didn't I tell you he was a brother of the Duchess? He praised the portraits, said they had (now what was his word?) real grandeur. But the picture he liked best was the one of you and Rosie. It caught you exactly, he said.'

'According to Rose he appears to know something about painting. And he said to her that if ever he had the money or the vanity to have his own portrait done he'd want you to do it.'

Frank did not reply, but nodded.

'And do you know what else he said?' she continued. Here comes the point of this talk, he decided. 'He asked Rosie if you wanted to paint her in the nude, would she allow it?'

'And?' He was interested now.

'She asked why you'd want to do that? He said because she was beautiful.'

'Is he interested in her in that way? Sexually?'

'I wouldn't be surprised. He's married, though.'

'Isn't adultery seen nowadays as the saviour of a good many marriages?' he said.

'I read something to that effect in some newspaper. Is it true?'

'What was her answer to his question?'

'No, she wouldn't allow it. She said her body was not so attractive that she'd want to preserve it for posterity.'

'But what if it attracted, inspired, the artist?' he asked.

'Does it?' She spoke as if about somebody else.

'Yes, but not so madly that I'd do anything to be allowed to paint her naked.'

'You'll have to discuss it with her,' his wife said primly.

'Gillian Montgomery, you're a mischief-maker.'

'Have you only just found out?'

She left him to find his way to his studio; she grinned savagely to herself. Later she sent Rosemary over to see if he'd like his morning coffee out there or back in the house. He chose to stay where he was. Rosie returned with a tray.

'Would you put it down, please? If I know Gill, the coffee will be boiling hot.'

198

He was working, she saw, on a largish landscape, four feet by three. The expression on his face had set grim. She looked hard, but said nothing.

'What d'you think?' he asked stonily.

'Very good.' She kept her answer near to moderation.

'Um,' he grunted his dissatisfaction, continued painting.

She watched him for a minute, then said, 'I'll leave you to it.'

He made no answer, concentrating on his canvas. When Rosemary got back to the house, she mentioned Frank's taciturn rudeness.

'He must be struggling,' Gillian answered. 'He'll fight his way through it.'

'Is he often like that?'

'Not really. But at odd times I have found him down in the mouth, fighting with himself. I don't know how often it happens because I don't make a point of interrupting him too much when he's at work. I always have a good look at what he's doing, because I'm curious, but I make no comment. When he's finished, or nearly so, he'll ask me then what I think of it. Not that he'll take a blind bit of notice of what I say, because he considers I know nothing, am ignorant of painting.'

'And is that so?'

'Well, you can't be married seven years to a painter and learn nothing. I've heard him lecture; I've been round exhibitions and listened to him chat to other painters. Some of them are quite brilliant talkers about art. He's not. He's clear and he holds ideas, and if other painters' works don't fit in with his ideas he says so.'

'He thinks he's always right, does he?' Rosemary asked.

'I wouldn't put it like that. He knows what *he* wants to do. If other people want to do otherwise, he'll listen to their principles and tell them in simple language where they're likely to fall short. It makes him feared.'

'And disliked?'

'He has his enemies, but he expects that. There was one man who said Frank painted far too quickly. He said this to Frank's face. I remember it as plainly as anything. We came across this man at an exhibition of portraits of English people. I think it was the Tate, but I'm not sure. And this fellow, Henry Cornwallis, a Royal Academician, and Frank began to argue about a Holbein. And Cornwallis suddenly came straight out with it. "You're too quick with the brush for your own good," he said in a lofty, disparaging way. "You've no idea how long I spend on any one picture," Frank answered. "No, I don't, but it's the impression I get." "Slap-dash?" Frank said. "Is that the expression you're after?" "Not exactly," Cornwallis said, not a bit put out. "But it's a phrase that's edging towards the truth, though as yet it's a long way off." '

'Was Frank cross?'

'You bet. Especially as he thought Cornwallis was quite a good painter in his academic way. He said he wouldn't have minded if Cornwallis had just said that he didn't like Frank's paintings, but to put their failings down to speed or careless workmanship seemed wrong to him. "He doesn't know. He can't. He thinks everybody paints in exactly the same way that he does. It's not how you do it, but the result that counts." '

'Is there any truth in it, do you think?'

'Well, he doesn't seem to spend the enormous time some people take over quite a small painting. I mentioned this criticism to a painter I knew, and he was dismissive of Cornwallis. "Oh, Henry Hugh", he said, "is jealous of your husband's success. Old H. H. will put on a dozen or more coats of paint to get the right flesh tint or the exact colour of a piece of velvet or satin, whereas Frank will get it in a quarter of the time, without this constant trying." This man said painters were just like other "lesser mortals", envious of superior skills.'

'Did he think that Frank was superior as a painter to Cornwallis?'

'Yes, he did. And he said Cornwallis knew it. That was the trouble.'

When Frank returned for lunch, neither woman questioned him about the morning's work. He did not speak much, but ate heartily, now and then starting back from the table and sighing loudly, but as if he'd no idea what he was doing or of its effect on the others. When Rosie went out to make the coffee he sat like stone at his end of the board. 'I'll take mine out to the studio,' he said, when she returned with it. She poured his cup. He stood up. 'What time do you want me in for dinner?'

'Six thirty, seven.'

'Right.' He swept his cup upwards, spilling some into the saucer, and made his way out.

He returned just before six, and dropped into an armchair. 'Good day?' Gillian asked.

'I can't complain. I hit a snag or two this morning. But I've managed.'

'A glass of sherry?'

'Why not?'

He drank this slowly, savouring it, like a mathematician who has just solved a difficult problem, or a punter who had laid and won a bet at long odds and can barely believe his luck. At dinner, while not exactly cheerful, he talked to them and even introduced topics of his own. At the end of his meal he put down his pudding spoon, squared his shoulders, and with the air of a Victorian head of the family prepared to make an announcement. The women watched the performance with ill-concealed amusement, wondering what he'd say.

'I think I've earned a day off,' he said. He received no answer. Tomorrow is Sunday, so we'll have it together.'

'Where? How?' Gillian asked.

'That depends to some extent on the weather.' They listened. 'I would like an easy day. That means we don't go too far. I don't see a day of heavy driving as anything of a rest.'

'Have you any suggestions,' Gillian asked.

'I have given it some thought.' He pursed his lips as if he knew their intention to mock. 'First, we'll be in no hurry to get up. Then a leisurely breakfast and then we'll run out to Southwell. There we'll walk about if the weather allows, have lunch and then in the afternoon go to evensong in the Minster.'

'Evensong?' Gillian queried, surprised.

'That will mean an hour's sitting down, more or less, on a hard chair in a beautiful, powerful building. The choir I'm told is good.'

'What time is it?'

'I'm not sure. Fairly early at this time of the year, I should think. But I'll ring up and find out this evening. Then another walkabout. The days are getting longer now. Then back home for a cup of tea and sit about until we go out to dinner. Perhaps this new Thai restaurant in Sheffield What do you think?'

'Yes,' said Gillian.

'That sounded like half-hearted approval.' Frank turned to Rosemary. 'What do you think?'

'Very good. Gilly won't be chasing about all day preparing meals for us. I must admit that I'm a bit surprised by our attendance at evensong.'

'Why, may I ask?'

'You've not shown a great interest so far in your life in religion.'

'There is a building nine hundred years old being used for the purpose it was built. It is worth our attention.'

'I wonder if God would approve,' Rosemary said. 'It's merely for our entertainment.'

'I don't see why not,' Frank answered.

'We're none of us religious. You'll enjoy the music and the great pillars around you. And I suppose I shall.'

'I'm not proposing to bring you out of the place a born-again Christian.'

'I see.'

Later he spoke to Gillian about her sister and her objections. 'I didn't know Rosemary was religious,' he began.

'She isn't, or not any more than I am.'

'Then why does she seem so concerned about our going to evensong?'

'Concerned? I don't think she was that. Surprised, more likely. Startled. Like me.'

'Why? She knows I listen to music.'

'It's as if', Gillian spoke gravely, 'you'd suggested that we attended a public execution somewhere.' His wife watched him. 'Out of character somehow.'

'She won't mind going?'

'No. She might even enjoy it. As long as it doesn't drag on for too long and bore us to death.'

Sunday morning grew brighter, with great clouds pushing through wide, irregular areas of blue. The three rose at nine, breakfasted at leisure, rang the Saracen's Head to order lunch at one.

'When are we getting out?' Gillian asked.

'When you ladies are ready. There is no hurry today. We dawdle everywhere. We're resting our weary limbs.'

'Weary limbs and tired minds,' Gillian said.

'You speak for yourself,' Rosie answered. She had dressed herself in style, resplendently, out of character. Just as they were about to set off soon after eleven, they were delayed by a vigorous shower.

'Has that altered our plans?' Gillian asked.

'Not at all. It's the time of the year. I've put out three umbrellas.

We'll wait until it's dry again. As long as we're at the pub before one.'

'I've not been to Southwell since I was a girl. Do you remember we went with Aunt Wendy in her limousine.'

'I don't remember that,' Gill said.

'Wasn't the bishop at the door to welcome you?' Frank.

'Not that I remember. Though Wendy probably expected it.'

They set out later than they expected, Gillian finding all kinds of small domestic tasks to be completed before she was ready to enjoy herself. Frank complained about this, but occupied himself with the pile of Sunday newspapers he'd fetched from the shop. Rosemary, still gaudily dressed, sat in a corner with a magazine trying to appear inconspicuous At the Saracen's Head, after a twenty-minute sharp walk round the damp Minster grounds, they dined on roast beef and most delicious cabbage. 'I hate cabbage,' Rosie said, 'but this is fit for heaven.' Between them they drank a bottle of red wine, quality indifferent, Frank pronounced, but welcome to his parched mouth.

They ate slowly and talked a great deal. Rosemary spoke freely about her mother. 'I don't think she's suffering,' she said. 'In fact, I don't think she has any idea of what's happening. She's like a baby in that she cries out when she's uncomfortable. There's nothing to be said in favour of her quality of life, except that she's kept clean and out of pain. It's made me think about euthanasia. If the doctors came to me and said that they could legally put her painlessly to death I'd agree to it, and think they were doing Mother and Gill and me a favour.'

'You've no idea what she's thinking about?' Frank said.

'Not the slightest. She hasn't spoken a coherent word to me or shown any sign whatsoever that she recognised either of us during the past month.'

Frank looked over at his wife, who kept her eyes down to the tablecloth. She did not speak or move. Her stillness bespoke fear. Rosie, on the other side of the table, seemed not to notice the effect of her confession on her sister. People at contiguous tables did not appear to be interested in, or to be taking notice of, her urgent voice, but continued stuffing their own mouths, or laughing, braying rather, like third-rate actors.

'I've always feared old age,' Rosemary continued. 'I hate its weakness, its impotence, its utter dependence on others, its incontinence, its lack of enjoyment.'

'Can they not enjoy some things?' Frank asked. 'Food, for example?'

'I doubt it. Their taste buds lose their virtue. And other treasures. I remember an old client of mine, dead now. He was a doctor of music, was at one time organist and master of the choir at a cathedral. He conducted choral societies and orchestras, examined for the Royal Schools. He retired in his early seventies after a fairly serious illness. This kept him indoors most of the time, but his interest in music lasted. He had a large collection of records and CDs, and an excellent music centre so he could listen, and did so, for hours a day to those and to radio programmes. His legs were the problem. He used to joke about them. 'I know a good many organists who can still chase about in their dotage. I used to think it was throwing their feet over the organ bench and pedalling away which kept them in such good nick.' And his wife, his second wife, was much younger than he was and looked after him really well. I used to think how lucky he was in spite of his immobility to be able to fill up his life with his music, and his memories.

'But in his eighties he lost it all. I think he had a stroke, or a series of strokes, and afterwards music meant little to him. He had the means still, but it meant nothing. He'd tried in his earlier retirement to keep up with contemporary trends. He bought a good many modern works and scores. He used to complain that much of it was beyond him. "I was too well drilled in the Baroque and the Romantics to allow this stuff much scope." But then, I say, in his eighties, not long after I got to know him, he was ill again, and when he'd recovered, or so it appeared, his appetite for music had gone. He could hear it in that he wasn't deaf, but he didn't seem to know it in any shape or form. His wife, Alice, used to say to me, "Music might all be the same now, 'The Teddy Bears' Picnic', for all the effect it has." If you played something for him that you knew he had known back to front in his old days, he neither showed signs of remembering it nor even enjoying it as a new piece of music in a style he knew. It used to annoy Alice. She'd question him and, though he answered plainly enough, it was as if he didn't understand what it was all about.

'One day she asked me to question him. She put on Bach's "Air on a G String", a piece he knew well because he'd conducted the suite it comes from times without number. Anyhow, she played it. Nobody spoke while it was on. He seemed to listen. "You know that?" I asked. He thought, shook his head, finally said, "No." I told him the title, and it did not seem to mean anything to him. "He was one of your favourite composers," I said. He looked puzzled. "Bach," I said. "J. S. Bach." He shook his head. It was pitiful. If I'd have said Duke Ellington or Mick Jagger it would have been just the same.'

'Did he miss Bach?'

'Not as far as we could tell. He'd sit there and seemed contented enough in a dozy sort of way. Alice said he was more like a rag doll than a human being.'

'She knew him in his prime?' Frank asked.

'Yes.'

'It must have been awful for her.' Gillian.

'It was awful for everyone.'

They finished their lunch and walked out. The weather threatened, but all had umbrellas. They found their way to the Minster with ten minutes to spare before evensong. Grey cloud with a few spots of cold rain darkened the last fifty yards.

'Who's preaching?' Frank asked.

'Neither the bishop nor the dean,' Rosie said. 'I looked at the notice. "The Rev. T, Smith".'

The service which they followed in the prayer books was spoilt for them by the voice of the young clergyman. The choir sang with power, but Frank did not know the Introit, the setting of the Magnificat and Nunc Dimittis, the short anthem. Even the hymns were unknown to him, but the organist seemed to enjoy himself.

When Frank complained to the women about this, Gillian replied snappily, 'It's not surprising. You don't go often enough.'

The Rev. T. Smith, who wore an Oxford MA hood, gave them an interesting seven minutes of introduction to a sermon, then suddenly stopped, saddened, and nodded towards his congregation in apparent satisfaction. His text was 'My grace is sufficient for thee'.

As they stepped out it was fine, but the air was chilly.

'What's the programme now?' Frank asked.

'Up to you?' Gillian answered.

'And you, Rosie?'

'I'm game for anything,' she said.

'In that case we'd better get you home before you do damage elsewhere.'

She slapped him with the gloves she had not yet pulled on.

'Will you children remember where you are,' Gillian mocked.

At home they sat with large cups of tea and he announced that they'd drive into Sheffield for a meal.

'I've decided on a popular choice,' he said.

'What's that?'

'Chinese. I shall have sweet and sour, which has ousted all the Indian dishes in a recent poll.'

'I don't feel in the slightest bit hungry,' Gillian said.

'In a couple of hours you might. What about you, Rosie?'

'I'm like Gill. A sandwich and a thin slice of cake will more than satisfy me.'

'Are you sure?' They were. 'Then I'll go and put the car away.' He pushed out, leaving his cup half full. 'Don't get changing your minds.'

'Is he cross with us?' Rosemary asked.

'He doesn't like to be opposed. Especially as he's going out of his way to please us. He thinks it's a great treat for us not to have to prepare meals, or sit stewing over papers from the office, as I often do on Sundays. He's giving us a rest. He doesn't see that it's just as much strain going out, all dressed up, as slopping around at home or in the garden.'

'What would he have been doing if he had stayed in?'

'Oh, painting.'

'Has he got something on the go?'

'Two pictures at least. He's always painting nowadays. It's partly him, but it's his father's nagging to produce works of art, and not to sit at a desk filling in all sorts of bureaucratic forms and questionnaires. So he feels disgruntled now.'

'Will he get over it?'

'Oh, yes.'

'With your assistance?'

'Probably. But he's always on the lookout for something new.'

'But what we did today was nothing out of the ordinary. We had a very decent meal and a couple of little walks round the streets, and then evensong in the cathedral.'

206

'We usually eat at home on Sundays at midday. That's my treat to him. I quite like steady all-morning cooking. It soothes me. And I feel so pleased when he compliments me on the dishes I think up. You don't like to hear all this, do you?'

'I don't mind. You're really sensible and so I'm glad there's pleasure in serving your husband. I had such bad experiences with Joe. He'd never think of throwing a word of praise in my direction, even though he'd wolf the lot down. It put me off cooking, and I gave him rough and ready meals, thrown together any old how.'

'Did he still eat them?'

'Yes. He'd a good appetite. But I made no attempt to present the meals in an attractive way. I'm not saying that I put the saucepans on the table and served from them. No, I just slapped the stuff on his plate and let him get on with it.'

'Did he complain?'

'Yes. From time to time. He'd look at his lunch and say he'd seen more attractive cookery thrown away in dustbins.'

'Did you answer him back?'

'In time, no. I'd smile and nod as if I'd not quite heard or understood what he said.'

'Did that work?'

'Obviously not. But he was a brute. He'd beat me sometimes.'

'And then?'

'I'd just run away upstairs and lock myself in my room. He didn't come after me. The doors were good and solid. And he'd bang about the house or the garden and then he'd cool off. I think he wasn't sure what I would do about it.'

'I don't know how you put up with it.'

'I had plenty to do at the office, so I was out of his reach most of the day. I slept in my own room and locked the door on him. At the weekend he might well go out or even away. It made it possible for me to live my own life, as I couldn't have done if we had had two or three children and I was continuously bound to the house. Even so, it was unpleasant. I shan't be in any hurry to marry again. I've had offers.'

'Have you, by God?' Gillian giggled.

'Mr Shakespeare.'

'He was far too old for you.'

207

'Yes. And I wasn't physically attracted to him. And he had a family who were everlastingly poking their noses in.'

'That could have made it even more interesting.'

'My life is interesting enough, thank you. What I need is peace. And now Dominic Whelan's advancing his claims.'

'He's married, isn't he?'

'Yes. But these days adultery's regarded as one of the strengthening factors of a long and happy marriage.'

'Do you fancy him?'

'I like his company. We can talk easily. He's a very astute man. He has a great deal of influence in the town. But I haven't the slightest idea what he'd be like as a lover.'

'You know, surely,' Gillian objected, 'whether he attracts you physically?'

'No. I don't. He's not repulsive, but he doesn't overwhelm me. As Joe did when we first met. Even as Frank did.'

They heard Frank return.

'He's been a long time putting that car away.'

'Yes. He's been down to the studio to consider work in progress. Or, more prosaically, he's been talking to somebody at the gate.'

Frank pushed open the door. 'Did you see somebody to talk to?'

'The post office queen. Mrs Parks.'

'And what had she to tell you of interest?'

'Usual village gossip. The new man at The Rowans is a professor of architecture at the University of Manchester.'

'Do you know him?'

'Not at all. I didn't even know his name.'

'Which is?'

'George Brailsford. According to her he's built things all over the world: China, Singapore, Australia, Germany, Saudi Arabia.'

'Whose house has he bought?'

'The Watcyn-Jones place.'

'That's a big place,' Gill informed Rosie. 'Will he be altering it?'

'No. He can't. It's listed.' He sat down and rubbed his hands together. 'And Mr Cotterill, he's committed suicide.'

'Who's he?'

'A jobbing builder in a small way. He's the man who mended Irvine Smart's garden wall.'

'No. I don't remember him at all. Why did he do it? Money troubles?'

'Love. According to her.'

'Well, go on,' said Gillian in mock impatience. 'Don't leave us with half a story. Who's the lady?'

'Unknown. Said to live somewhere down Hucklow way. Mrs Parks was vague. Somewhere on the Buxton side.'

'And?'

'He was a widower, she a widow. They met. Or perhaps he did some work for her. He's always busy: he's a good workman. Anyhow, he fell in love. She did not.'

'Yes.'

'That was that. He chased her, wrote her letters, constantly phoned her. It got so bad that she complained to the police. Said she was being stalked. That didn't win her much sympathy, at least with Ma Parks, who said it wasn't every hour of the day or night. The police gave him a polite warning and the story got around the village. He seemed very down in the mouth at first, but then they all thought he was getting over it. He'd always plenty of work to occupy him. But this morning his neighbour saw the garage door open and wandered across. He thought Cotterill's garage had been broken into. And when he looked in, the car was there and Cotterill was hanging from one of the beams at the far end. He must have done it Saturday night, because this neighbour had spoken to him at teatime on Saturday. He seemed pretty well normal, stood talking there for five minutes or so.'

'What did he do? The neighbour, I mean. When he found him?'

'Cut him down. Tried to revive him. He was dead. Phoned the police and one of Cotterill's sons who lives in Sheffield.'

'Did he leave a note?'

'Yes, apparently. Inside the house. One to his son, one each to his two daughters and one to the lady.'

'What did they say?'

'In the son's note it just apologised, said life wasn't worth living. That's all. Very short.'

'Was he well liked?'

'As far as I could make out. Kept himself to himself. Mrs Parks said her paper girl delivered his Sunday newspaper as usual. Didn't notice whether the garage door was open or not.'

Gillian and Rosemary both sat in silence.

'Would you like another cup of tea?'

Gillian slipped out of the room, leaving her husband to his cross-examination.

He squared his shoulders. 'How did you like evensong, then, Rosie?'

'It was strange to me. A lot of the words I recalled in a vague sort of way. "Dearly beloved brethren, the scripture moveth us in sundry places" and "Lighten our darkness we beseech thee, O Lord" and we used to sing the Magnificat and Nunc Dimittis at school, but to simple chants, not the fancy settings they had. It was rather like going to a secret society, or Masonic ceremony, not that I've ever seen one, where the initiates were saying all sorts of out-of-the-way prayers or mantras, going through motions which had no sort of relevance or meaning to me. I tried to join in the singing. We sang hymns at school. But I knew neither words nor tunes of most of these.'

'Yes. So it wasn't worth going?'

'I wouldn't say that. It took less than an hour so I wouldn't complain. I was interested but it didn't mean much to me, even in a place as old and powerful as that.'

'I try to think what they'd do when that nave was first built. The service would be in Latin, wouldn't it?'

'Yes. Which would be even more unintelligible than the present one was to me.' She looked guiltily about her. 'I had nothing to bring to the service,' Rosemary said.

'What do you mean?'

'They believed in God, who looked after them. It pleased God to hear this gibberish and they would gain favour with Him. I suppose there'd be little sermons. And they'd be in Old English, Anglo-Saxon. But the services would be almost wholly given over to the monks. I don't know if they let the plebs in on Sunday and holy days. Or did they have to go off to their own village churches? With a place the size of the Minster they must have had others there besides the comparatively small community of monks. Unless' – Rosemary paused – 'they built these places with no regard to the number of worshippers in the congregation, but to be a fitting house for God.'

'That seems right,' he said.

'Wordsworth wrote a sonnet about it, didn't he? "Tax not the royal saint with vain expense." About building King's College Chapel at Cambridge in such splendour for so few people.'

'I don't know it.'

'I'll look it up when I get home,' she said.

'We're an ignorant pair,' he said. 'But that's where they say we should start. With ignorance.'

'Who are they?'

'Well, the mystics. Really religious people. That's why they had stone churches for God, while they lived in caves and daub-and-wattle sheds. Not at first, of course.'

'And is that, do you think, satisfactory? A fair division?' she asked.

'I guess they thought differently from me. But their lives were short compared with ours. Men nowadays on average live to seventy-five and women to eighty. And that age is getting higher than at any former time, never mind the Middle Ages. If we feel ill, we rush off to the doctor's surgery. They didn't exist in villages.'

'What did they do?'

'Went to the local wise woman who knew about herbs, if the body failed to cure itself.'

'And they died?'

'We all do that. Death comes much later to us. When my father was a young man in the twenties and thirties all these cures, books full of them, which we have now, didn't exist. Doctors had to depend on a mere handful of medicines and then on bedside manner and common sense.'

'And that didn't work?'

'Very often not, I suspect. Penicillin wasn't used until some time in the last war. And when something like the plague, the Black Death, hit them they were helpless, their only option to run away. They'd no idea of the cause and so they'd no idea where to start to contain the disease.'

'Some people think Shakespeare died of the plague, don't they?' she interposed.

'I've not heard that. I thought he'd been visited by Ben Jonson and some of his actor friends and an evening of heavy drinking had done for him. He wasn't all that old.'

'Early fifties. And he started late. But he didn't waste his time. He wrote quickly.'

211

'I wonder if he was a churchgoer?'

'They think his father was a recusant, a Catholic. He knew about religion, said the right things, but didn't show much real interest. Not personally. He didn't tell us a great deal about himself.'

'I did *Hamlet* in the sixth form,' Frank said, 'and I always took it that when he wrote . . .'

'Go on. Let's hear you.'

'". . . The oppressor's wrong, the proud man's contumely . . ." ' He broke off. 'I've forgotten what "contumely" means. Do you know?'

'"Insolent scorn",' she said in a low voice. 'Go on, I'm enjoying this.'

> 'The pangs of disprized love, the law's delay,
> The insolence of office, and the spurns
> That patient merit of the unworthy takes . . .'

He drew in a large loud breath of satisfaction.

'Wouldn't these be troubles that most sensitive people suffer?' she asked.

'"The law's delay?" ' he questioned, laughing.

'Not in our office.' She sat straight. 'I wonder if Shakespeare ever visited Southwell?'

'There are no local tales or rumours to that effect.'

'Too far away?'

'No. I don't think it would be that. I'm always surprised how far people would travel in those days. But he had no local connections as far as I know.'

'Not even your Mr Shakespeare?' Gillian, who had returned and stood listening to the last part of the conversation.

'No. He boasts about his achievements, but I've never heard him mention that he was descended from William.'

'He had no male offspring who grew up and married. Poor Hamnet died young, sadly.'

'What are you two chattering about?' Gillian reseated herself.

'About what we got out of our visit to the Minster,' Rosemary answered.

'And how does Shakespeare come into that?'

'One thing leads to another,' Frank said. 'Even with you legal

212

eagles. What we're really trying to get at is what we gained from our churchgoing today.'

'And what was that?' Gillian asked.

'A great deal of puzzlement. We both seemed on the wrong wavelength.'

'And was Shakespeare on the right one?'

'He never let on.'

'Have you ever done any sketches at Southwell?' Gillian asked her husband.

'No. That heavy Norman architecture doesn't suit my free and easy style.' She guffawed. 'In fact, the experts say that the Gothic parts are the best of the architectural features. But it's the nave I remember. It's small, and even flat, but it's powerful, heavy, represents some plain, serious early belief.'

'The Anglo-Saxons?' Rosemary asked.

'No. I'm not a great expert, but the Anglo-Saxons weren't much good at building with stone. Our first great cathedrals came from Continental builders and architects.' He looked across at Gillian. 'I could just sink a glass of whisky.' He stood, striking an attitude. 'Will you ladies join me?'

They agreed to do so, and he made a show of fetching and setting out their glasses, a jug of water and the three-quarters-full bottle.

'No decanter?' Rosemary asked.

'No. We don't drink enough to use a decanter. Nor do we have a soda siphon.'

'We're like the cathedral,' Gill said, 'rough, low, raw.'

Frank poured their drinks, all three whisky and water. They toasted each other silently, proud, perhaps, of the earliness of the occasion.

'Going to evensong was like receiving an unexpected letter,' Gillian said.

'From God?' Rosie asked.

'I wouldn't say that. From some far-off time. I'm uncertain where it originates, because the correspondent has never written before or at least not for years. And I can't read the handwriting. It's impressive, even beautiful. It wasn't as if it was in a foreign language; the script made every word, even in my own dialect, strange. It wasn't like the monks' Latin; I'd have recognised that for what it was, even if I couldn't translate it. This was my native tongue, but disguised by the writer. Or say it was as if my eyes were incapable of making it out.'

'"My eyes are dim; I cannot see; I have not brought my specs with me".' Frank said solemnly, emphasising the rough rhythm of the couplet as if to compensate for his lack of tune.

'That's right. Exactly.'

'And what are you going to do about it?' Rosemary asked.

'Judging myself from past performance, nothing, absolutely nothing.'

'I tell you what I think you should do.' Rosemary spoke earnestly. 'That is, take your father along to see what he thinks about it.'

'He'd be complaining about the hardness of the pews on his old bones,' Frank answered.

'I've never heard him speak about religion,' Gillian said. 'Has he any views?'

'He has views on pretty well everything. Even though he changes his mind. I've never known him attend church, except for weddings or funerals. But he likes to stir the waters. If he thought he could upset us or get us arguing, that would be his line. He'd call it education. I doubt if he has serious views now on anything, be it politics, morality, religion. He lives out of the world.'

'Was he always that way inclined?' Rosemary asked.

'No. He was always interested in his job. His English and his Latin. They in part kept his pupils and thus the country from barbarism. He grew out of his admiration for sports as he got older. *Mens sana in corpore sano*, he used to tell them. But after the age of sixty, when his body wasn't up to these marvellous movements, he said he regretted the time he'd wasted in his life on cricket and rugby and tennis and running. And what about painting? I ask myself. He always takes the line that we improve our lives by looking at great pictures. He has his usual grouses and objections. Showing works of art hung in rows on bare walls in museums and galleries is the quickest way to put any sensible persons off them. Great paintings should be seen in smallish rooms and in twos or threes surrounded by all sorts of domestic trivia.'

'Such as?' Gillian asked.

'Vases of flowers, biscuit barrels, family photographs, clocks, bric-a-brac, books. The usual domestic clutter.'

'Wouldn't they distract?' Rosemary.

'If they did, either you weren't fit to look at good pictures, or the pictures had no real value in themselves. Of course, he'd tell you that you had to learn to appreciate pictures as you had to practise and learn anything else worthwhile.'

'So he'd say the same about our evensong?'

'We went in unprepared, so we didn't get out of it all that we might have done.'

'What would he have got out of it?' Rosemary asked.

'The opportunity to lay down the law. Now he's old and immobile he doesn't get the chance so often.'

'Does he resent it?'

'Yes. Retired schoolmasters always miss their captive audiences and so lecture their wives. Dad did, I know. Whether my mother paid attention is another matter. She was a lively woman and had plenty to occupy her mind.'

'Would you say', Gillian came in solemnly, 'that your father thinks he's had a successful life?'

'Why do you ask that, Gill?' Rosie's voice was faint.

'Frank speaks as though he were only moderately good at a few unimportant tasks or hobbies.'

'I'm a pessimist,' Frank answered. 'The higher your class, the less successful you feel.'

'How do you mean?' Gill.

'On his deathbed, Beethoven is reported as saying, "Strange, I feel as if up to now I have written no more than a few notes." And he's not the only one. While my father was working he took great satisfaction from his daily grind. Old pupils used to congratulate him on the marvellous lessons he gave, which opened their eyes. That pleased him. As he grew older he became less certain. The world was a place where second-rate, popular rubbish was not only respected, but highly paid. Schoolmasters, and I guess he'd include women teachers, if grudgingly, were badly rewarded, regarded with less and less respect in society today.'

'Did he think highly of women?' Rosemary asked.

'He gave the impression he didn't, that they were mere dim imitations of men, but I think he was afraid of my mother. She didn't know Latin and Greek, but there were dozens of things, drawings and paintings, yes, but household tasks, DIY, she could

215

do much better than he could. He'd try to ride the high horse with his academic pretensions, but she went her own way. I think she saw him as some mothers see a gifted child. Not that she treated him as if he wasn't grown-up. She'd listen when he was spouting on about something that had caught his interest and say not a word. Only now and then, when he went over the top about something he knew little about, did she interrupt. "Don't be silly, Bertie," she'd say and kill his argument with just a few words.'

'And what did he say?'

'Oh, he'd huff and he'd puff, but he was sharp enough to know when she'd got him.'

'Did they quarrel over you?'

'Not in my hearing. She was pleased that I'd chosen art school over university. She'd been at Goldsmiths'.'

'Did she teach?'

'Yes. Before and during the war, and then when they first married. After I was born she gave it up except for a few courses she taught for adults. In some curious places. I wasn't ever quite sure whether she thought painters could be taught. I suppose she had decided, as I did later, that she wasn't here to produce geniuses, though even they needed teaching like anybody else in the first stages. I've heard her say that time and again. After that they'd teach themselves. She said she could teach mediocrities like herself to make a good workmanlike job of their pictures.'

'Did she ever give you advice?'

'She used to praise what I'd done. When I was a boy. Very generously. Occasionally she'd ask why I'd chosen a certain design, or group of colours, presumably because she thought I hadn't been as successful as I might have been.'

'And was she right?'

'I didn't think so at the time. But I was arrogant as well as nervous and diffident when I was young.'

'I didn't know her very well,' Gillian said. 'She was ill when I first met her. And she died soon after we were married. I was a bit afraid of her. I was only a young girl when we first met. And she looked ill even then.'

'She liked you,' Frank said.

'She would have thought I wasn't good enough for you.'

'She came to our wedding,' Rosie said. 'And she must

216

have been very ill then. She died about a month afterwards.'

'It's odd how she came to marry anyone like your father,' Gill said.

'They'd be suited when they were young and could put up with trouble. They both worked, they weren't under each other's feet the whole day. When I came my mother stayed at home full time. She probably didn't like it, wouldn't have chosen that. She had waited some years after he came out of the Forces, before she married him. I think he thought he'd lost his chance with her.'

'Why was that?'

'He considered, I guess, that she was wedded to her job as an art teacher.'

'And he used to lecture her?'

'Yes. He'd always have some pet subject at the ready. His school was very lively and he'd bring the topic of the day home and try a few ideas out on my mother. She didn't seem to mind. She perhaps even approved. It made her feel that she wasn't cut off from the world of the intellectual. It may even have amused her. I remember one of his lectures. I thought of it earlier when you asked me what he would have made of the service in the cathedral. It shocked me at the time. I was about eleven, as I remember it, just starting at the grammar school. It took place when they had cleared away and washed up after the evening meal. Usually this was his quiet time with the newspaper. He was a very conscientious marker and would clear up his day's marking until fairly late, but only after this period of quiet. But on this particular evening he seemed to be excited, ready for argument. Apparently at school they'd been discussing the nature of God. A fair number of his colleagues were atheists or agnostic and said there was no evidence on which to draw conclusions. He argued that they claimed there was nothing existent without a cause and therefore the universe must have a cause, and that cause, or its causer, must contain within itself its own cause. He called that God '

'How did your mother take all this?'

'She listened. And murmured agreement as she knitted away, just to keep him talking.'

'Apparently they had then asked him how this causeless cause could be described as, for instance, the God of love, or the Father of Jesus Christ.' Frank paused for them to consider this.

217

'He said he himself could not draw any such conclusions. He pronounced, and I can see him now with his brows knitted, his hands clasped, and an expression of, oh, extreme earnestness on his face, "I believe that God is so great, and so unlike us, that these notions of God purveyed by the churches are wrong."'

'"Why?"'

'"The doctors of the Church in earlier times thought out what would be the most laudable qualities a human being could have and then claimed that God, being Himself perfect, must have these attributes to the nth degree.'

'"And He hasn't?" my mother asked.

'"I'm not saying that. We just haven't the mental and emotional means to grasp how great and different He is."

'"Are you saying that because God allows terrible accidents, like earthquakes or volcanoes or typhoons or floods, He doesn't love the human race?"

'"I sometimes used to think that, but if He's omniscient He may see beyond these events, terrible and tragic as they are to us, to some greater good to the human race or the universe at large which needs, in some mysterious way, these accidents."

'"What they used to call providence?" my mother asked.

'My father was surprised that she knew such a word and showed it by his facial expression. "Yes," he answered. "Exactly."

'That seemed to have caught him out, showing that my mother had considered all this before ever he had.'

'Had she?'

'I doubt it. She showed no sign of triumph, but went on with her knitting needles clicking away. She'd pulled this one word out of her education and used it, and it seemed to stop him in his tracks.'

'Where had she learnt it?'

'Church or Sunday School or even in her reading. I remember my old English teacher, Nobby Clarke, explaining to us what the word meant when we were just starting to read Milton's *Paradise Lost* in the Lower Sixth:

> That to the highth of this great Argument
> I may assert Eternal Providence.
> And justify the ways of God to men.

218

He told us all about that, and "theodicy".'

'My word,' Rosemary said, 'you must have paid attention to what they were teaching you in school. What's "theodicy" mean?'

'Justification of God. A theory that vindicates God's action in allowing evil in His created world. We all used to argue with old Clarke that if God was all-wise and all-knowing He would not had allowed evil in the world He was creating.'

'And how did he answer that?'

'He used to put his head back and look upwards, and then close his eyes. "I know", he used to say, "that you would all have made a better job of it than God did. Some people argue that it is because He allowed free will to the human race. That never seemed very convincing to me. He could, had He so wished, have made us all incapable of evil. But the last snag is that evil undoubtedly exists and there's no use acting or talking as if it did not." '

'Goodness,' Rosemary said, laughing. 'And it upset you?'

'Not that, particularly. It was when he argued that we don't get anything near the full nature and power of God, even if we knew a thousand or a million times as much as we know now, and by that he meant not just the bit he knew, but what all the scientists and saints knew, all put together.'

'Was your mother impressed by these arguments?'

'Mildly, I suppose, if she wasn't thinking about tomorrow's meals or her next day out sketching.'

'Your father always seemed a bit pompous to me, setting himself above other people,' Gillian said.

'That's fair enough. Less so recently. But he always set great store by education, and if he could convey some knowledge to you as you listened he felt that was what he was good at, if not what he'd been put on earth to do. If he knew something you didn't, and he was trying to teach you this, it was no use being diffident about it. You delivered it as if you meant it, knew its importance. A stuttering, shy delivery makes a teacher's class uncertain. They don't believe you It doesn't suit everybody, of course, but it works with most, especially if the subject matter is new to them.'

'You seem to admire your father,' Rosemary said.

'I said he was good at what he did, that is, teaching boys.' Frank coughed. 'The method of addressing equals as if they were a class of boys wasn't always acceptable, so that he wasn't exactly popular with everybody. In the last eighteen months or so I've seen a change in him. He hasn't the energy nowadays, nor, I guess, the conviction. The world is not what it was. Information technology is not the equivalent of the classics of our language or of Latin and Greek. Young people are much more likely to be seeking out porn channels than the views of poets or philosophers, historians or scientists. He has bursts of energy now and again, as when he tries to bully me away from educational administration and into the production of works of art.'

'That's good,' said Rosemary. 'He looks on you as a primary source of culture, not a second-hand purveyor of it like himself.'

'I suppose so. But it's not always been his view.'

'Is that because he sees himself as leaving little of his work behind, except in the uncertain memories of pupils who themselves will shortly die, while your pictures are there for generations to come?'

'I hope you're right,' Frank growled.

'Of course she is. Well said, Rosie.' Gillian spoke loudly.

'The old man may have been a pompous prat,' Frank said, 'but his pupils could spell accurately, put sentences together properly, knew how to pronounce words, which is more than one can say of the television reporters I hear. Moreover, his boys read widely and could remember what they'd read and learnt years later. He passed some of our cultural heritage on to two or three generations of boys. They possibly didn't like it, but profited from his teaching. He made them learn poems. They may have resented it at the time, but now they have a little anthology of verse in their heads.'

'Do they ever use it?' Rosemary asked.

'I expect so. We all like to shine and these days such a talent will be unusual.'

'A good man?' Rosie asked.

'Yes, I should say so. And what worries me most is that he often seems so low nowadays, with no expectations from present or the future, and no pleasure or even insight or appreciation of those things he's managed in his long life.'

'Yes.'

'Of course he came from a working-class family. He was the first in the family to go to university in the days when to put BA after your name meant something in these parts.'

'Would you say he was in some measure responsible for what you are?'

'I'm sure. He gave me a basic education and, better still, something to rebel against.'

'And you convinced him he was wrong?' Rosemary asked.

'I think so. He has his doubts still, but yes.'

They sipped their whisky.

'We've given your father a real going-over this evening,' Gillian said. 'Is that the result of our churchgoing? Our father.'

No one answered the question.

'I bet he'd be pleased we've talked about him so much.'

'I think that next time we go to church we should take him with us.' Rosemary.

'Wouldn't it be better', Frank asked, 'to drag him into a Salvation Army meeting?'

'Why?'

'He'd feel impressed in a cathedral, but an army barracks with tambourines and cornets and songsters rattling the windows would seem vulgar to him. There ought, he'd say, to be a certain beauty and decorum about the worship of God.'

'I think I agree,' Gillian said.

'I'll give him a ring later this evening to tell him how we've spent today.'

Frank refilled his glass; the ladies nursed theirs.

'Two lawyers and a famous painter dissecting his character,' Rosemary said. 'He should be flattered.'

'One misguided son, a daughter-in-law and her sister,' Frank said. 'He'd be pleased you young ladies thought about him. Even critically.' Frank raised his glass. 'His health,' he said in a loud voice. 'His good health.'

XIX

In June, within three days of each other, Frances Housley and Herbert Montgomery died.

Mrs Housley died on Tuesday in the early hours. There had been little change in her condition of the past months and certainly two days earlier Dr Milner had seen her, according to the matron, and had expressed his surprise that she was still alive. When the nurse on an early round had found her, the doctor, who lived not far from the nursing home and was on night duty, came over at once, examined her and certified her death. This information was telephoned to Rosemary, who rang her sister and she and her husband drove over to Beechnall before nine o'clock.

Rosemary had been, it appeared, over to the nursing home and had seen the body of her mother, which had now been taken to the undertakers. There would be, it appeared, no inquest in that the doctor had visited her so recently and had been expecting her death for some months.

'What do we do now?' Gillian asked.

'There's nothing much you can. They've been telling me, as well you know, for the past weeks that she might go at any time and so I've been preparing a list of people who'll need to be informed. You can phone or write to some of these once we know when the funeral is. The undertakers will see that the body is prepared and, if you wish, you can go in and see her in their chapel of rest. They'll also insert a notice in the local newspaper, as from us. Did you want to go to see her?'

'I suppose so,' Gillian answered uncertainly.

'She looked no different from when we last saw her, except she was still. There was none of that heavy breathing that so upset me.'

'Is there nothing else I can do now? I'll see to the death certificate, if you like.'

222

'No. I don't think so. You go back to the office and I'll ring you there. There's no sense in two of us hanging about. Perhaps one afternoon you can help me to let people know. We'll have a reception afterwards, tea and sandwiches and buns after the service, but at my house. That's more convenient, there's more room than in here. I'll get in touch with the caterer we usually use.'

'Where will the funeral be?' Frank asked.

'St Augustine's. She occasionally went there. She knew the vicar. We've been in touch with him.'

'Is she to be buried or cremated?' Gillian.

'Buried. In the Northern Cemetery next to Daddy. It's all in the will. Her property is divided equally between us, once a few knick-knacks have been given to some friends and charities. About fifteen in all. That won't be difficult.'

'And what about clearing her house?'

'I haven't thought about that yet. We'll decide what we're going to do with the place. Sell it or let it. There's nothing of very great value. I have looked it over while she's been in hospital and the nursing home.'

'I'll ring my father,' Frank said, 'and go over to see him.'

'Is he well?' Rosemary asked.

'As far as I know.'

When he returned from the phone, Gillian was ready to leave. 'How was he?' she asked.

'Grumpy. As he usually is first thing in the morning. He said he was sorry to hear about your mother. He said he'd be glad to see me, but it didn't seem like it.'

On her way back to the office Gillian dropped Frank at the end of Victoria Avenue where his father lived. He rang the front-door bell at least three times and waited. It was no use trying the high gate to the back of the house because his father always kept that bolted and barred.

At last, slowly and laboriously unfastening the defences, his father let him in. 'Welcome to Fort Knox,' he said.

The house smelt stuffy as if no window or door had been opened for days. They made an uneasy, senile progress to the living room.

'Can I get you a cup of coffee?' the old man asked.

223

'I'll get it.'

'No, you won't. You won't be able to find the right mugs, or the coffee, or milk or anything else.'

Herbert took so long over the preparation that Frank wondered if he'd collapsed out there. Finally, he brought in two mugs on a tray. Coffee had spilt from both. He set them out. 'I was sorry to hear about Frances Housley,' he said, wrestling with the lid of a biscuit tin. 'How are the girls taking it?'

'Pretty calmly. They've been expecting it for weeks. She's hardly been conscious these last two months.'

'Yes.' The lid came off; the open tin was placed before Frank, who thanked his father and took a biscuit at which he stared suspiciously.

'She wasn't very old, was she? Sixties?'

'She would have been sixty-five in October.'

The two played with their coffee, which was far too hot to drink.

'And how are you keeping?'

'Much as usual.' Herbert wore neither collar nor tie, but his shirt was newly washed, and trousers and pullover were clear of marks of dropped food. The old man had shaved and his cheeks were rosy. His parting ran straight and he had made his white hair flat with a hairbrush and tap water. 'I'm in pain.' He lifted a leg; he was wearing shoes not slippers.

'When you're up and about?' Frank enquired.

'And when I've been in bed for a short time.'

'In your legs?'

'All over. Some days I can hardly get about. But what do you expect at my age?'

'Do you take painkillers?'

'From time to time. I don't like to have too many. I feel sleepy and dizzy if I overdo them. I wouldn't be able to get on and off buses these days without fear of an accident.'

'Are you going out somewhere this week?'

'Not this week. I put my name down for a trip to Stratford-on-Avon the week after. If they can fill the bus.'

'Who organises these outings?'

'Some man at Gervase Lunn's church. I usually try to go. Makes a change from being cooped up here.'

'Decent people in the party? Nice conversation?'

'"Nice" just about describes it. You never heard such meaningless chitter-chatter.'

'But it's better than silence?' his son asked.

'You might think so. I don't.'

'Can you get out on your own? For a walk or to the bus stop?'

'I don't use the bus service at all. It's too difficult to get on and off. I've just told you. And making up my mind to go for a short stroll is a long job. There's the dressing up for it, and the locking up to make sure the house is secure. Twenty years ago I could have been into the car and halfway out to, say, Sheffield or Birmingham in the time it takes me now to get out of my front gate and into the street. And though I'm convinced exercise is what I need I'm never sure I'll do more than two streets without incapacitating myself in some way or another. And yet ...' Herbert broke off.

'What?'

'In my head I'm much as I was thirty years ago. I went out last week, on that very sunny day we had. I'd just heard some music on the radio as I left. I put it on to make intruders think there's somebody at home. And it was ringing in my mind. The minuet and trio from Mozart's G minor symphony, I stayed back a minute or two to hear it to the end. And for the moment as I stepped along the street I forgot that I was an old man, who couldn't see too well and who needed a stick and whose every step hit me with a twinge of pain. I was young again. I could walk fast for miles on end. I was likely to meet somebody interesting or see or learn something I hadn't seen or known before. It didn't last long, a minute or two at most, and I was back to my useless old age. But it was wonderful.'

'And disappointing?' Frank.

'Of course.'

'How do you spend your time?'

'I have these nurses and women in to help me dress, or give me a bath, or clean the house.'

'Aren't they here today?'

'No. There'll be somebody before too long with my meals-on-wheels. They come early and I have to heat it up. They give me instructions. Reheating doesn't improve the food, but it's better

225

than nothing, I expect. They all give me my orders as if I'm a four-year-old and half daft at that.'

'Does that annoy you?'

'Not particularly. They have to make sure and I imagine quite a number of their patients are far from compos mentis.'

'Do you read much still?'

'No. My eyesight doesn't allow me to read for more than a few minutes at a time. I'm squinting and peering even if the light's perfect. And then my eyes begin to droop and I just can't go on. It's the same with the newspaper. I try to get through it every morning, but I never get near finishing it and however many times I pick it up during the day I never read it all.'

'Nobody reads everything in the paper. They're all so huge these days.'

'But I don't manage to pick out those things I'm interested in. I'll pick up an old newspaper to put under a cup and I come across something fascinating which I'd never noticed before.'

'Can't you get these big-print editions from the library?'

'Yes, of things I don't want to read. In any case they're too heavy to hold.'

'What about the radio and television?'

'The radio used to keep me interested, but not now. Some days I hear a news bulletin and can't give you the news headlines two minutes after they've been read.'

'There's music,' Frank objected.

'That's where I feel most deprived. At one time I could listen to music all day, given half a chance. Now some of the greatest classics pass me by, pieces I've known all my adult life. My mind drifts off; I find I'm not paying attention, that the greatest music in the world doesn't hold me any longer. I used to sit there a few years ago with a pencil in my hand, conducting for all I was worth. These days I sit there, my mind blotting out these great achievements of men with my trivialities of pain, or worry, or even with lassitude. I'm liable to drop off to sleep.'

'You don't mean to say you get no pleasures at all?'

'I do find pleasure. But not much and very briefly. I think my greatest delight these days is looking at the faces of small children. Some of them are so beautiful. And when they skip along or giggle or act with such spontaneity I am cheered. I think that

226

these are our successors and pray that they will make our world a better place. But that doesn't last long either. I know that in a few years' time they'll be vulgar adults like their parents and will end up like me as useless old drags on society.'

'Have you always been interested in small children?'

'Not particularly, though I remember how a smile used to spread over your face when you were pleased as a baby. And that reminds me. Has the Queen said any more about that portrait?'

'Not a word.'

'And why's that?'

'I've no idea. She's probably had so many societies and communities wanting her to sit that she's decided to do nothing about any of them. She's had several painted recently.'

'I know, I've seen some, in the broadsheets, and I didn't think much of them. Do you make enquiries from this President of the Royal Society about what's happening?'

'No, I don't.'

'Why not?'

'I imagine he's got plenty on his plate. Organising an oil painting of the Queen is not what he was trained or elected for. Besides, I've plenty to do without chasing work.'

'Don't you realise that such a commission would be publicity, big publicity for you? And these days that's the heart of the matter. Who makes the big money or ends up with best jobs? The best persons, the most gifted? Not on your life. It's those who blow their own trumpet, get their name in the newspapers, appear on the television. Celebrity. That's what you should be after.'

'I don't think so.'

'I know you don't. That's your trouble.' The father's face was red with excitement. He rattled his mug on its mat. 'There you crouch, the modest violet. And whom do you choose to paint? Some unknown schoolgirl you meet on holiday. Who's interested in that?'

'I am, for one,' Frank answered.

'And I'm not saying it was a poor drawing, or not worth doing. And I know you did the Duke and Duchess. That's what got the Royal Society enquiring after you. Throw your weight about. You can be too modest. You've got to make your name known.'

'I'll think about it.'

'You know damn' well you won't.' His father rarely swore; he must be strenuously serious. 'You'll sit there in your office, filling in forms.'

'Yes. There's some truth in that.' He looked at the clock. 'It's eleven o'clock. And your lunch hasn't been delivered. Does that happen often?'

'Very rarely.'

'I tell you what.' The phone rang. Herbert signalled his son to answer. 'Your meals-on-wheels. The system's broken down. Three people away and now the van's kaput. They wonder if you could manage without today.'

'Yes, I can.'

'You're regarded as one of the more capable, they say. They'll deliver to such as can't do without their help, though it will be very late. Is there a bit of a restaurant or shop around here where we can get a meal?'

'Just round the corner. On the main road. I don't know what the food's like. The place looks clean. I imagine it's for working men who want a midday snack.'

'Can you walk there and back?'

'I think so. I feel a bit better today. Perhaps because of your visit.'

They hobbled the two hundred yards or so to the place, where they ordered roast beef and Yorkshire pudding. They waited perhaps ten minutes, though there was no one else in the place. Herbert said he wanted a very small portion. He then made this order precise. One slice of meat. One roast potato. One spoonful of carrots and one of cabbage. No, thank you, he did not want boiled potatoes or peas. Yes, he would have horseradish sauce if they had it and if they hadn't he'd have mustard. The food was bland and plainly served. Neither man had a 'sweet', so described by the menu, 'afters' by the serving man. A cup of tea was served as soon as they had completed their course. Herbert Montgomery ate slowly, but cleared his plate. By this time the five tables were full, with women out for shopping, and by two small groups of men in overalls who talked loudly and made it clear that they'd visit the bookmaker's next door as soon as they'd finished eating.

Frank and his father made their slow way back. The son helped his father off with topcoat and scarf, and sat him down in his sitting-room armchair. 'Anything I can get for you?' he asked.

'No, thank you. I'm replete.'

'Shall I turn the heating up?'

'No, thank you. I've enjoyed that little outing. It made a pleasant change.'

His son put a stool under his father's feet. 'I'll have to be off,' Frank said. 'I believe there's a bus at one thirty that I shall just about catch.'

'No car?'

'No, I came down in Gillian's. She'll pick me up tonight.'

'You're going back to the college?'

'I am.'

'Will they have missed you?'

'I told them I'd be back this afternoon. And I've an absolutely efficient secretary. She'll deal with any contingencies.'

The old man laughed, a phlegmy, thin sound. 'If a class teacher is missing,' he said, 'they have to chase about to replace him. But when the head is not there, all goes on as smooth as clockwork.'

'How right you are.'

Frank took his father's hand. The old man pulled feebly at his coat. Frank started to go.

His father weakly reached up and kissed the son's cheek awkwardly. He had never done this since Frank was a child. 'Thank you, thank you,' he wheezed. 'My sympathy to the girls. They're to let me know if there's anything I can do and when the funeral is. Let yourself out and drop the catch.' He smiled. 'Thanks for the lunch. I shall have indigestion all day.'

They were his last words to his son, for two days later his cleaning lady found him dead in his favourite chair. He'd had his breakfast and washed up, and had sat down to read the *Guardian*. The newspaper had fallen and tented itself round his feet. His eyes were closed and his expression relaxed. The wrinkles in his face seemed cut deeper, the woman told Frank later. It was as if he had died in his sleep. A trace of spittle hung at the corner of his mouth. She had, she said, phoned the ambulance, which arrived within five minutes. The paramedics confirmed that he was dead, after a brief attempt to resuscitate him. She then phoned Frank at the college.

Frank, overcome by the unexpected death, called his wife, who immediately drove round and took her husband to the hospital in Beechnall. During the journey they barely spoke a word. Once, he found his teeth chattering. Gillian seemed calm, composed as she had been since her own parent's death. She stood by his side, often holding his arm, while they completed formalities. In this case, it appeared, there would be an inquest. The undertakers inserted notices in the local paper, in *The Times* and the *Guardian*.

At the weekend Frank and Gillian drove over to look in at Herbert's house. The place was spotless. The cleaning lady had been in again. Rosemary joined them; she had intended to start on an inventory at her mother's place, but came to support her brother-in-law. As Frank expected, his father's papers were in order. The old man had had several 'clearings up' in preparation for his death since an illness some three years before. Herbert had installed a safe, bolted into the floor, and had given Frank a key. The safe was as tidy inside as the room outside. They found his will, bank books, bank cards, the deeds of the house, papers detailing his few investments and finally a large envelope addressed to 'Francis John Montgomery', which detailed his wishes for the form of his burial service, and then a letter, dated three years back, a time soon after he had recovered from his first serious stroke.

The letter was sealed. Frank poked around the living room for a paperknife to open the envelope neatly. The whole house demanded it.

'I guess the cleaning lady came in yesterday,' Gillian said, 'and dusted and polished as usual.'

'It's all so neat,' Rosemary said. 'I always had the impression that old people were careless about dirt, couldn't see it. My mother was beginning to get a bit like that.'

Frank had to go into the kitchen for a knife to open his father's papers. He sat down to the table and drew out the differently sized sheets: a typed copy of his will, instructions as to where he was to be buried and the order of service with music in a church three streets away. The final sheets, separately sealed, in Herbert's small neat handwriting was a letter to his son, dated three years earlier while he was recovering from his stay in hospital.

Dear Frank,

I have felt so near death in these last weeks that I
fear my next illness may kill me quickly. I therefore
will try to express to you what has been beating about
in my mind. I feel particularly privileged in that I am
allowed by our relationship to say to you, who has
made so great a success of his life, what I think, I a
comparative failure, about your status and, perhaps,
your future plans.

First let me say how proud I am of you. When I read
in the newspapers or catalogues of exhibitions or books
on modern art what the experts write about your work,
I am astounded that you have won such a reputation
before the age of fifty. I say to myself, 'This is my son'
and then I immediately remember that I opposed your
decision to become a professional painter. Fortunately
you, and my wife, your mother, had more grasp of
reality, as well as greater inclination to the use of imagination, than ever I had. This is perhaps not the place for
it, but I must record the enormous debt that both you
and I owe to that generously gifted, modest woman.

When now I press you to leave your position as principal of your art college and concentrate on the aston-
ishing gifts you have been endowed with, I realise that
you have achieved in the educational world a much
higher rank than I ever reached and that you may think
I am talking ignorantly or even enviously. Indeed, I feel
this myself, but I want you to realise that it is because
I so greatly admire your artistic work. The economics
I do not understand, but you, my son, have in the eyes
of acknowledged experts the talents which will place
you in the years to come among the immortals. I can
see the wry smile on your face as you read this. It will
read as pompous and exaggerated rubbish in your eyes,
if not utterly ludicrous, but I wish you to grasp how
highly I regard you, and what an honour it is to me to
be the father of such a genius.

My own life is a failure. Perhaps it is this which
compels me to wish you to achieve success which few

231

others can contemplate. When I look back on my eighty-eight years, I think of Virgil's words: *O mihi praeteritos referat si Iuppiter annos* – O that Jupiter would restore to me my past years – and yet I know that if they were brought back ten times over I'd never touch the heights which you reach with such ease. I know my limitations. I've learnt to think modestly now that such small gifts that I once possessed have dropped away from me in old age. I do not complain, or I try not to.

I have just read this through. You'll decide that it is the usual old man's whining rhetoric. In some ways I have prospered: an excellent wife, a son of genius, a job I did more than adequately and which I enjoyed. I have until recently had excellent health, and only just begun to realise what effect illness has on character. My life has been prolonged well beyond the average length and I have kept my mental faculties moderately intact. I should be thankful I can still walk; a strong pair of legs is one of the greatest boons a man can have as he grows older.

I write all this down in the hope that you will not see this letter as the result of an old man's envy or transient pique. You have gifts that are beyond price. I write this because you won't be able to argue with me, and throw the compliment back in my face. People of outstanding talent, from the few I have known, need praise. If they do not receive it, then the nature of their work is altered. It may be altered for the better, as I believe happened with Rembrandt, but their life is unhappy. You may think I know nothing about painting, though I'd answer that by saying that no one could be married to your mother for forty-odd years and remain ignorant of art. But my view is backed by so many expert critics (yes, I know you despise many of them), and such unanimity must demand respect, though you might easily argue the opposite that I am convinced of your outstanding achievement in your forty-five years.

In this brief and badly, baldly laid-out note I, therefore, ask you not to yield to easy alternatives (I know that 'alter' means 'one of two'), but to explore your opportunities to the uttermost. You have made the name of Montgomery well known in artistic circles. I beg you to confer immortality on it.

I write this letter out of my love for you. Understand that and you'll know why I have taken it on myself to advise you in this way. We, neither of us, are men who speak our affection easily. Forgive the rambling nature of this letter, or blame it on my recent illness. Much awaits you. Be worthy of the challenge. It is your duty.

I am, my dear Frank,

Your loving father,

Herbert Montgomery

Frank leaned back in his chair and rattled the two sheets of paper in front of him. The handwriting had remained neat and perfectly formed right to the end of the letter. His father had not hurried, had written steadily until he had had said his say. The effect was immaculate, not a single alteration or crossing out. Perhaps, he thought, the old man had made a rough pencilled draft, before taking to his fountain pen. The finished effort was worth framing, hanging on the wall. He read it through again; Herbert had tried to give, in spite of the pomposity of some of the phrasing, an effect of the extemporaneous. 'It is your duty' . . .

Gillian and Rosemary entered the room.

'Here, read this,' he said to his wife.

She obeyed his instruction, standing, creasing her brow. When she had finished she held it out for him to take back.

'Give it to Rosie to read,' he said.

She handed the document over to her sister, who perused it with the same slightly professional care, determined to miss nothing. 'That's very good,' she pronounced at length.

'What's good about it?' Gillian asked, saving her husband the trouble.

Rosemary frowned as if searching for an answer. Her face, grave with no relief, made them uncomfortable. 'There is your father,' she began, 'thinking that he hasn't long to live. He's just had a stroke and expects at his time of life it won't be long before he's terminally ill.'

'He was wrong there,' Frank said. He'd keep this lawyer to truth.

'True he had two or three years left, and he became less and less active. But he did not see fit to alter or rewrite this letter.'

'He'd probably forgotten all about it,' Frank answered.

'I doubt it. He seems to have tried to come to terms with a serious problem he faced.'

'Problem?' Gillian, vaguely.

'He felt that his son spent too much time at his desk in the college at the expense of his painting. He said so often to you, Frank, to Gill and, heaven knows why, to me. I guess from what you've told me that he would have been delighted in the first place by his son's appointment as the head of one of the most prestigious art colleges in England. That would have been his ambition for you from the start. You seemed not to be falling in with that wish. Instead of attending university you studied art. I don't know how he expected you to end. In an attic, drugged to the eyes, wasting your life, or at best sitting in some half-hippy commune painting seascapes for visitors in the summer and scouring the shore in winter for chance finds. Instead, you find a teaching job and prosper. I guess he's surprised, slightly miffed to be found wrong in his prognostications, but in the end pleased. Then his mind is changed for him again. His son makes a reputation as a portraitist. He reads about him in the Sunday papers and the broadsheets. Frank Montgomery has become news. He's convinced and feels it's his duty to see that this son of his makes the most of his outstanding gifts. He perhaps suspects that you, like the rest of the world, prefer a life of ease. That you would choose to sit behind a desk making trivial decisions that will be gone and forgotten within five years, if not five minutes.'

'If you were arguing from the other point of view,' Frank said, 'you could say that putting dabs of colour on canvas was just as trivial.'

'Except that the efforts of the best dabbers give pleasure for hundreds of years and are reproduced thousands of times,' Gillian intervened.

'That's right.' Rosemary's face was serious again. 'What I've said is the truth, but the underlying foundation of his care for you is his love. He loved you, Frank.'

'He never said so. Except in this document.'

'Never the less.' Gillian, mocking both, split the word.

'What my father admired most of all was success. He was a competitive man, encouraging his pupils to compete against each other. That's why they did so well. That's why the school had such a good name. And what applied from the first year onwards in his school applied everywhere else. To become famous and make money. One or the other, or preferably both.'

They sat silent again.

'One good thing about your father', Gillian began, 'is that he didn't become more aggressive as he grew older. Some old people are so frustrated by their pain, and clumsiness, and their increasing inability to do things they've done well for the whole of their lives that it makes them angry and they take it out, or try to, on the people who are looking after them.'

'He always liked to be right,' Frank said.

'Don't we all?'

Again they sat, wordless, though not for long.

'Are you going to do anything about his letter?' Rosemary asked.

'I shouldn't think so. I shall read it again a few times and think about it. If you mean shall I give up my place at the university immediately, the answer is "no".' He drew in a deep breath and let it out slowly. 'Art is a complicated affair. My father has read articles about me for the past few years. And he believes them. What he doesn't believe, if he's thought about it all, which I doubt, is that in ten years' time those same newspapers, and for all I know these same critics, will be writing me off as old-fashioned, a painter with nothing to say about modern society, who has no relevance to contemporary humanity, whose methods are out of date, who never developed but painted the same old boring clichés in the same old boring way.'

'Do you think they will say this about you?' Gillian asked.

'I expect so. That's the way these Young Turks make their name.'

'They deliberately set out to undermine your reputation?'

'Yes. I'm not saying they don't believe what they're saying.

235

They shout it with such élan and force that I'm afraid some of their elders join the throng of unbelievers. Who'll be interested in what I'm painting when I'm seventy?'

'But galleries and museums are already buying your pictures. They won't want out-of-date pictures hanging round their walls.' Gillian sat upright, red in the face.

'Galleries and museums have cellars which are jam-packed with stuff no one wants to look at and they don't want to show. I'm pleased that my father was convinced that I was an outstanding painter. That's what he wanted to hear. I'd won the race. I'd received the prize, the praise, the applause. I doubt if he could say why he liked one picture rather than another. It served his purpose. It made him feel that there was some justice in the universe. His son had outshone them all.'

That quietened the women.

Rosemary roused herself. 'You are working on the assumption that in a few years' time experts will be speaking unfavourably of your work?'

'Yes. I am. And, moreover, the very things that I am most highly praised for now will bear the brunt of their attack.'

'That's pessimistic, isn't it?'

Before he could answer Gillian had butted in. 'You're not going to give up painting, are you?'

'No. I think what I am doing now is worth doing. I shall try to do both to the best of my ability. I hope I shall be learning, improving, trying new things all the time. There is one matter I'd like you to remember. When I stand in front of a canvas with a paintbrush in my hand, I don't consciously think in this way.'

'Do some?' Rosemary.

'Oh, yes. I could name them. They set out to paint what the critics say they should. Not everybody. Some artists are genuine experimentalists. They want to attempt something new to them- selves every time they paint. That's their temperament. We're all at the mercy of what we are, or are brought up to be. I'm a conser- vative. My paintings are realistic. I paint what I see. Not that that's true, but you know what I mean. In a few hundred years the faces in my paintings will seem as unusual as those of Cimabue or Van Eyck. They all have eyes and noses and mouths in the right places, and yet they look different from those I paint. I don't mean the clothes or the background; the faces are what I'm talking about.'

He stopped. Suddenly he threw back his head and laughed.

'What's so funny,' Gillian enquired.

'I've just thought of Father's letter. Every time he makes what he considers an important point, he backs away, knows I shan't believe him. That's just what I've been doing now.'

'You've inherited it from him?' Rosemary asked.

'Or imitated it. Copied the habit.'

'I was interested to see in this letter', Gill said, 'how uncertain he seemed when he was laying down the law about what you're to do. I'd always considered him as a man who knew his own mind and wasn't afraid to let other people know.'

'Yes, he did know his mind about matters which are fixed. *Fero, ferre, tuli, latum.* Principal parts of the verb to carry in Latin. He became so used to knocking such odd bits of Latin grammar into the thick heads of his pupils that he used the same tone for statements about life when he was outside the classroom where he was not so sure of his facts.'

'I think it sad that he'll never sit in this room again and be able to look at that picture of you and your mother or the tea caddy where he kept letters which needed answering.'

'Yes,' Frank said. 'It comes to us all.'

'Spoken like Father,' Gillian mocked.

They made a quick tour of the house, decided that they would hold the post-funeral wake there and that Rosemary would contact her caterers.

'And as soon as that's over,' Frank ordered, 'I'll go over the house with you two and you can decide what you want.'

'Hasn't he stipulated any legacies?' Gillian asked. 'Left it lock stock and barrel to you?'

'I'm afraid so.' He shook his head. 'I'll see that Gervase and the cleaning lady have something to remember him by.'

They held such conversations, in twos, sometimes all three, over the two weeks before Mrs Housley's burial. It seemed to comfort them. The sisters told Frank that the clearing of his father's house would be his responsibility, but that they would help him any time he needed it. He thanked them politely. He asked his father's housekeeper if she would come in and keep the house tidy until after the funeral. She volunteered to clear the wardrobes, said honestly that some of the clothes would do for her husband; the rest would go to charity shops. Next time she saw him she gave him two five-pound notes, three pound coins, some silver and two packets of indigestion tablets. 'These were in the pockets,' she said. 'I was surprised; Mr Montgomery was usually so careful with money.'

He thanked her. Gervase Lunn was invited over and walked the dead man's house with him. 'No, thank you, no. There is nothing. I was pleased to help him out and he always saw I was never out of pocket on that account.'

In the end Frank persuaded him to take a highly carved wooden French clock, early twentieth century.

'Oh, no. I couldn't. That is valuable.'

Frank, who thought it hideous, said in a low voice, 'You can look at it from time to time and it will remind you of my father.' A tear graced, disgraced, Lunn's cheek.

Mrs Housley's funeral service was well attended. The family looked prosperous, with the wives and grown-up children of four solicitors and two barristers, a medical man, and all seemed well used to these affairs. They had sent well-phrased letters of regret and sympathy to the sisters. At the buffet meal they were quietly humorous, except to Frank and the daughters. None of this appeared specially assumed; they knew their place in the world and how to conduct themselves.

'They all have such well-polished shoes,' Rosemary whispered to her brother-in-law.

'Would your mother have enjoyed their company? he asked.

'Not she. She said they were all stuffed shirts, but that they always knew how and when to behave. They'd never let the family down in public.'

'Do you meet them ever?'

'No. Not now. We did when we were small. I can remember sitting in a chair at Aunt Hetty's listening to the adults. I was bored to death. One aunt gave me a book of child's verse and I was allowed to bring it home.' She smiled. 'I learnt one or two, of my own volition. "The cow, the cow all red and white / I love with all my heart." '

The caterers made swift work of clearing the room and the visitors seemed in no hurry to stay.

'A rehearsal for Thursday,' Rosemary suddenly announced. 'We all know now what to do.'

Frank, slightly shocked at this irreverence, bit his lip. The girls looked at him with suspicion, but he made no comment.

Thursday, the day of Herbert Montgomery's funeral, proved sunny. At the church there sat behind the few family mourners a row of uniformed boys representing Herbert's old school. This surprised Frank, as did the presence of the Vice-Chancellor and the Professor of Architecture from Sheffield and some half-dozen senior members of the art college staff. He knew that his own secretary would be there. He failed to count accurately a good turnout of casual acquaintances which, again, Frank did not expect. His father had constantly complained that all his old friends were dead and that he knew no one he met. The rector announced himself as one of Herbert's old pupils, but Frank after a long talk already knew this. The clergyman compared Herbert's teaching very favourably with that he received a year or two later at Cambridge University, considered by *The Times* as the world's finest educational institution, he said. He laid great stress on the fields of business, politics, academia, high finance and, without saying so in so many words, attributed their triumphs in the wide world to the solid foundations laid in the early classrooms by Herbert Montgomery and his like. The deceased thus seemed an important influence on the present state of the country's recent affluence.

Her clergyman had made no such claims for Frances Housley. She had occupied a domestic role, caring for her husband, bringing up her daughters, supporting charitable efforts. The vicar there had spoken with a lugubrious voice and face, whereas the rector at Herbert's funeral was rubicund, smiled, cheered his congregation. Both men were, Frank guessed, only a year or two younger than he was, but they differed from each other in every possible way. One left Frances's funeral remembering her as a good woman, grey, unpretentious, kind with never a word nor a hair out of place. Herbert appeared dynamic, pointing higher for hundreds of the country's best young men. By Frances's choice they sang 'The Lord's my Shepherd'; at Herbert's behest they belted into some words to 'See the Conquering Hero' from *Judas Maccabaeus*, and even the scrubbed scholars behind him seemed to Frank to throw their shoulders back to sing this. It sounded loudly appropriate. Frank judged that some of the praise heaped on his dead father owed its power to the enthusiasm of the rector and organist, and he hoped that Gillian and her sister were not unduly put out if they made comparisons of the two parents. If they were, they said nothing.

The meeting afterwards at Herbert's house was a cheerful affair. The rector, even more huge than in the pulpit, talked to all. The sisters went like cheerleaders round the room, making sure everyone was at ease. The schoolboys were not to be seen, though the headmaster appeared, stroking his moustache.

The Vice-Chancellor shot back to Sheffield to an important meeting. 'I don't know to whom it's important. Not to me certainly. But they demand my presence. I'd much rather pay my last regards to a teacher who has left his mark,' he explained to Frank. 'They're the lifeblood of education.' He was represented by one of the professors in the divinity department, a Hebrew scholar, who ate and smiled with large teeth.

Frank shook hand after hand, bewildered. One thing he was certain about: his father would have been delighted by the talk and greetings, praise, reminiscences and judgements. When the caterers, the same efficient, pale manager and his half-dozen women, had cleared up, packed up and gone, and the mourners had made their way out, Frank stared about the room, now quiet, which an hour before had been crowded with noisy people, most of them with an air of importance. He felt low, as he'd felt when he'd won his first boyish prize for painting and found next day that the world was in no way altered.

'Isn't it quiet?' Rosemary asked, wide-eyed.

'Thank God,' Gillian answered.

'It was good, though,' Rosie ventured.

The other two scanned their shoes.

'Come and stay a few days with us,' Gillian invited her sister. She had discussed this with Frank.

'I can't really. I want to get the house cleared and put on the market. Then I'll come. I shan't be lonely, Gillian. Reassure yourself on that score.'

Three weeks later Frank stood in the same room on the exact spot by the hearth. The room was now cleared. He had spent a whole day taking what he wanted: not much. Gillian had been instructed to help herself and to choose some pieces for Rosie.

'She won't take anything.'

'Then you must choose for her.'

'She'll think I'm trying to clutter her house.'

'She won't. She'd a genuine affection for the old man.'

'For the old man's son.'

'Same thing,' he said.

In the end Gillian had presented her sister with some vases, dating from the time of Frank's mother, and a small silver bowl. Rosemary had wept.

Now Frank stood in his father's sitting room. Curtains and carpets remained to be included in the price of the house, so the appearance of the room seemed not quite empty. There was nothing of his father about the place. The garden outside stood tidy, ready for spring; this room, like the rest, had been dealt with by the cleaning lady. Both she and the gardener had been instructed to put in a day's and a morning's work each week until the house was sold.

Today, Frank had been thoroughly through the place. He had found nothing. The firm Rosie had suggested had done their work properly. He stalked across the room to examine the marks on the wall where Herbert's pictures had hung. Two of his mother's watercolours the son had kept, surprised that there were so few. His father must have sold them, or given them away. It had appeared that Herbert had been filling his dustbin for years with the detritus of his life. At one time there had been boxes full of paper, which had been disposed of.

Oddly, three old pipes lurked in the corner of a drawer; Herbert had not smoked for forty years. 'I believed Sir Richard Doll's research,' he used to pronounce, 'and though he went easy on cigars and pipes as opposed to cigarettes, I stopped.' He had clicked his fingers.

'Was it difficult?'

'Hellish. I couldn't have been easy to live with. But Edina put up with it and Frank was only a small boy. I was glad, though. I regained my sense of smell and though I was over fifty I found in the end I could run for buses.'

The man who had made these pronouncements – and Frank

241

could imagine him sitting in a high wooden chair, long since found redundant, laying down the law – knew right from wrong. It had to be imagination, for there had been few mementos. Of his mother he had found no trace. When she had died Herbert had passed her sketchbooks over to her son, with a gruff, 'These will be of more interest to you than me.' Frank treasured them, but they all came from the last years of her life. Of her earlier work he found nothing. Perhaps he had, or even she had, given them away to Edina's relatives. Since his first stroke – Frank gathered this at the funeral from the cleaning woman who expressed surprise that he knew nothing about it – his father had been burning piles of papers. Weather permitting they had had a bonfire every week.

'It will be easy for those left behind,' Herbert had said to her. 'I don't want Frank wasting his time sorting out unimportant rubbish.'

'He might like to be reminded of things,' she had said.

'He might not.'

Again Frank walked over the house. He stood in his parents' bedroom overlooking the street. He was not conceived here; that was in a house not half a mile away. He stared through the window at the trees in the avenue, a white car rushed by; an old man raised his walking stick in greeting to someone out of Frank's sight. The weather was unseasonable for summer, dull, the sky leaden. He switched on the light; it instituted a new sort of darkness. He switched off and walked to the back of the house, to his old bedroom, where he once did his homework. There had been no central heating then. In winter he had used a small paraffin stove, stronger on smell than heat. He saw the mark on the wall made by the table he had used, under the oddly placed light. Gillian had claimed the table, saying it was beautiful and useful. He thought it plain and rickety, but she'd soon have that set right. He kicked the faded carpet. His mother used to bring him hot drinks. It was a queerly shaped room, north-facing, utterly unattractive, better without its furniture in the pale light. He shrugged and listened for the sound of Gillian's car. She had expressed a wish to look over the house once more before it was sold.

'Why?' he demanded.

'It's where you used to live and I wondered if it would be any different now it's empty.'

She was late. He tried the other two bedrooms. There was nowhere to sit. With relief he heard a car draw up outside. Quickly he went down and opened the front door. Gillian stood, as if hesitating, at the front gate. When he called out to her she winced, stared at him unsmilingly guilty. By the time she reached the door she had recovered. 'Sorry I'm a bit late,' she began.

'Not at all. What's the programme?'

'I'd like to walk quietly round. It's completely cleared now, isn't it?'

'Yes.'

He ushered her into the drawing room. She moved in a few feet from the door, looked about her, strode suddenly over to the bow window, looked out, and then, turning back to the light, eyed the room again. She nodded to him and, receiving no acknowledgement, marched out to the passage and into the living room. This seemed darker, more forbidding, but Gillian, in the middle of the room, turned about.

'I've had it cleaned,' he said. 'Mrs What's-her-name and the gardener come in once a week.'

'The carpets and the curtains are shabby,' she said.

'Faded.'

'They won't add much to the selling price.'

'Probably not.'

There seemed some sort of restriction, constriction, between them, as if they could not allow themselves to talk easily.

She led the way into the kitchen. Shelves stood empty; gaps marked the position of the absent washing machine and the freezer and refrigerator.

'Nice size,' he said.

'Within reason,' she answered. 'Nowadays people like kitchens large enough to feed the whole family in. It saves time and effort, and gives another room over to leisure. This would be for the servants.'

'My parents rarely used the drawing room during my childhood. It seemed rather a place conferring status than being useful. They'd not much time for sitting about.'

'Nowadays,' she began, again after an awkward pause, 'they

243

always say that it's the kitchen and the bathroom that finally sell a house. Once the area's right and the house is in good order, it's these two which settle the final price.' She stared out of the kitchen window, back to him.

'Next?' he enquired. He realised that this empty, echoing house jangled her nerves. 'Upstairs?'

'Upstairs, please.'

In the front bedroom she looked silently down at the street, before suddenly turning towards him, sharply, fiercely. 'You know this house much better than I do.' Again a pause while he waited for her to continue. 'There seems nothing of your father about this place.'

'He took great trouble to clear it out. Bonfires for weeks on end. And the furniture makes the character of the room. These are bare boards and faded carpets. You didn't, or I didn't, notice them when he was about. Even recently, when he was ill and housebound.'

'I always thought', she said, 'that the furniture matched the man. Big, old-fashioned, well made, highly polished. Really filled the spaces.'

'I think it was my mother's parents' stuff. It was quite typical of her that once they had died and their house was cleared, she took their furniture and got rid of most of her own. She would judge it artistically, or according to its suitability. It's certainly somewhere near the age of the house.'

'When was that built?'

'Late nineteenth century. I hadn't looked at the deeds for years. They were in the safe.'

'I always connected it with your father and not your mother.'

'She died before you had the chance to know her well. When I applied for the job in Sheffield, I came up for the interview and then dashed over to Beechnall to see her in hospital.'

'Did she know she was going to die?'

'She knew how ill she was. I came up the next weekend when I'd been appointed. My father was delighted I'd managed to get the job. She smiled and congratulated me, said I'd do well. But she was so thin; there was nothing of her. Then she said that Charles Hughes, one of the best watercolourists in the world, had been trained there. She kept dropping in and out of sleep. It was weakness, I suppose. She recovered from that bout, lasted three years or more, but she was never the same again.'

They slowly made their way through the other bedrooms, then downstairs, out through the back door and into the garden. This had begun to reveal signs of autumn and the air chilled.

'That was my father's favourite. Rosa gallica. Complicata.' He spoke the words slowly, separating. 'It's like a big pink hedge rose.'

'I thought your mother did the garden?'

'She did. After she died Father had a gardener in to keep it tidy. The old man walked round it often enough and knew the name of a few flowers, which he'd bring out to impress. That is, till his memory began to go.'

They sat in a small wooden arbour over which roses climbed almost desperately.

'Did your father build this?'

'No fear. He was hopeless with his hands. Except with his bits of wood on the lathe. My mother would sketch it and then get a carpenter in to make it.'

'And they sat here together?'

'I can't remember one single time when I saw them together in here.'

Gillian looked startled. She sat on the seat and swung her legs like a child. 'I can't help thinking about your father's letter to you. Are you going to pay any attention to it?'

'Not really. Should I?'

'We've just been round this house, and there's nothing of your father left in it.'

'He saw to that. He burnt all his papers and letters. He considered them too private for strangers, even relatives, to be poking their noses into, or too worthless to keep.' He looked at his wife, sitting now on her hands in this damp place. 'You think I should pay some attention, do you?'

'He wanted you to concentrate on painting.'

'Yes. But he was a late convert. At one time he thought a painter was a kind of superior artisan and that the subject was barely worth studying in schools of any academic standing. If you did Latin and Greek you didn't waste your time in the art room.'

'He liked looking at pictures.'

'Yes. But he knew nothing about it, really. He knew all the classical legends or biblical anecdotes artists painted. But he'd sooner expound a line of Milton or Virgil than say anything about the way an artist had tackled his subject. It was the publicity I attracted that changed his mind. You'd have thought that someone educated in the old, cramped, élitist ways would have recognised and condemned modern hype, the cult of celebrity.'

'But it was you they praised. His son.'

'That's an even worse reason for rating something highly.'

'Well, you gave him pleasure. I think he would have liked grandchildren.'

'I expect he would. But we've tried often enough and failed.' She sighed loudly. 'Does it trouble you?' he asked.

'Not now. I'm used to it. As long as you don't mind.'

'No. We're career-orientated.' He laughed at this expression. 'I shall go on painting, fear you not. I was well taught and I've practised long enough. It may seem important to you, as it is to me. But it wouldn't be the end of the world if I stopped tomorrow. I've been thinking since your mother and my father died. It's not the end of the world. Your mother was really incapacitated and the old man not far from it.'

'Do you mean you've been thinking about death?'

'Yes. The week after the funerals, and everybody was being particularly nice to me at work, a woman who comes in two days a week to teach sculpture suffered a personal tragedy that made mine seem as nothing. She was a single parent; her husband had left her and never came near her. I'm not so sure he's not abroad somewhere. She had a daughter. When she came into the college, her mother looked after the child, who had just started school. The child died. She was a lovely girl, they all said, long curly hair, all smiles, talked like a grown-up, always fit. She suddenly died. She was staying overnight with her grandma and had bad headaches and was sick. She had a rash. The grandmother had been a nurse, knew what to do. Tested the rash with a drinking glass. She called an ambulance and they had her in in no time. The mother hadn't any means of contacting her daughter who was out lecturing somewhere and by the time she came home next day the child was dead. Just think. A five-year-old full of life one morning and by afternoon next day she was dead. It doesn't bear thinking of.'

'And the woman? What's she doing now?'

'She's back at college. Seems steady as a rock. The funeral was a small private affair.'

'Have you spoken to her?'

'Yes. I did my best. She thanked me, very politely. But they say she's devastated.'

'Who are they?'

'My secretary for one. She lost a near relative recently. She says both the mother and daughter are distraught. The girl feels she absented herself when she was most needed. She doesn't blame her mother, who did everything she could. But she thinks of the girl with a violent fever and headache, and no mother there to comfort her. And yet in my office she was quiet, in control. Subdued, but answered my questions, said she didn't need time off. She would manage.'

'What's her name?'

'Emma Walkyier. She's a good sculptor, as well as teacher.'

'You never mentioned any of this to me?'

'I thought', Frank said, 'you'd enough on your plate. It wouldn't, I judged, do me or you any good to know that someone else is in worse trouble.'

'It's obviously affected you,' Gillian said.

'Yes. It did. At the same time I was thinking hard about my father's letter. And I compared my lot with Ms Walkyier's.'

'And?'

'I was lucky. I have two careers. I have you. And she has a mother who let her daughter die.'

'And what conclusion do you draw?'

'None. As usual, I shall go on as I was. I'm as comfortable as I can be. I know what I'm about. If the Vice-Chancellor does propose making me one of his deputies I shall refuse, I think. That would only mean more form filling and attendance at useless meetings or ceremonies. But that poor woman haunts me. I said to her, "Emma, you're a brave woman" and she just raised her eyebrows. When she was about to go, she'd finished her cup of coffee and her biscuits, she stood up and I asked her, "Have you got any work in hand?" Sculpture, I meant. She'd been so calm, I thought I could ask her that; it might have encouraged her. It was like my father's letter. She answered in a very steady voice, "It hardly seems worth it," but then as she opened the door, she turned towards me, smiled and asked, "Don't you ever feel like that?" '

'What did you say?'

'Nothing. I was speechless. She gave me a little smile and closed the door, quiet as a mouse. I didn't hear her footsteps outside. Nothing.'

Gillian laid her hand on his arm. 'Come on,' she said. 'These seats are damp. Let's get the keys back to the estate agent and go home.'

As they passed for the last time through the house, she asked him, 'Do you ever feel like that?'

'Not with her sort of despair. I'm one of nature's optimists.'

The sky was brighter overhead, the clouds broken.

'I hope we don't have more rain tonight,' she said.

'No.'

The estate agent said he'd found a buyer, willing to pay the full price. They'd soon have the contracts drawn up.

'It's not surprising. The house is in excellent order and in a good district. An ideal house for a young family. Roomy, ceilings high but not ridiculously so. I wouldn't mind a son of mine choosing to live there.'

Gillian drove her husband home. Both spoke little, as the early afternoon grew brighter.

'I'd like to meet this Emma Walkyier of yours.'

'It can be arranged.' He spoke like himself.

'Are you hungry?' she asked.

'Now you mention it, yes.'

A ray of low sunshine lit them with shadows into the drive. A pile of letters lay on the mat, one from Buckingham Palace.

'You go and put your legs up,' Gillian commanded.

He bundled himself towards her, kissed her on the mouth. 'Good boy,' she said. 'Good boy.'

'If I'd a tail to wag, I'd wag it.'

She pointed at his chair. 'Sit, Fido, sit.'

He obeyed.